JACK LONDON
STORIES

THE GREAT WRITERS COLLECTION

JACK LONDON STORIES

Twenty-one exciting stories by the Master of Adventure

Jack London

Platt & Munk, Publishers/New York
A Division of Grosset & Dunlap

Library of Congress Catalog Card No. 60—12427

ISBN 0-448-41103-2 (Trade Edition)
ISBN 0-448-13044-0 (Library Edition)

Contents

PART ONE

The Call of the Wild

CONTENTS

CHAPTER 1

Into the Primitive

Buck did not read the newspapers or he would have known that trouble was brewing, not alone for himself but for every tide-water dog, strong of muscle and with warm, long hair, from Puget Sound to San Diego. Because men, groping in the Arctic darkness, had found a yellow metal, and because steamship and transportation companies were booming the find, thousands of men were rushing into the Northland. These men wanted dogs, and the dogs they wanted were heavy dogs, with strong muscles by which to toil, and furry coats to protect them from the frost.

Buck lived at a big house in the sun-kissed Santa Clara Valley. Judge Miller's place, it was called. It stood back from the road, half hidden among the trees, through which glimpses could be caught of the wide cool veranda that ran around its four sides. The house was approached by gravelled driveways which wound about through wide-spreading lawns and under the interlacing boughs of tall poplars. At the rear things were on even a more spacious scale than at the front. There were great stables, where a dozen grooms and boys held forth, rows of vineclad servants' cottages, an endless and orderly array of outhouses, long grape arbors, green pastures, orchards, and berry patches. Then there was the pumping plant for the artesian well, and the big cement tank where Judge Miller's boys took their morning plunge and kept cool in the hot afternoon.

And over this great demesne Buck ruled. Here he was born, and here he had lived the four years of his life. It was true, there were other dogs. There could not but be other dogs on so vast a place, but they did not count. They came and went, resided in the populous kennels, or lived obscurely in the recesses of the house after the fashion of Toots, the Japanese pug, or Ysabel, the Mexican hairless,—strange creatures that rarely put nose out of doors or set foot to ground. On the other hand, there were the fox terriers, a score of them at least, who yelped fearful promises at Toots and Ysabel looking out of the windows at them and protected by a legion of housemaids armed with brooms and mops.

But Buck was neither house-dog nor kennel dog. The whole realm was his. He plunged into the swimming tank or went hunting with the Judge's sons; he escorted Mollie and Alice, the Judge's daughters, on long twilight or early morning rambles; on wintry nights he lay at the Judge's feet before the roaring library fire; he carried the Judge's grandsons on his back, or rolled them in the grass, and guarded their footsteps through wild adventures down to the fountain in the stable yard, and even beyond, where the paddocks were, and the berry patches. Among the terriers he stalked imperiously, and Toots and Ysabel he utterly ignored, for he was king,—king over all creeping, crawling, flying things of Judge Miller's place, humans included.

His father, Elmo, a huge St. Bernard, had been the Judge's inseparable companion, and Buck bid fair to follow in the way of his father. He was not so large,—he weighed only one hundred and forty pounds,—for his mother, Shep, had been a Scotch shepherd dog. Nevertheless, one hundred and forty pounds, to which was added the dignity that comes of good living and universal respect, enabled him to carry himself in right royal fashion. During the four years since his puppyhood he had lived the life of a sated aristocrat; he had a fine pride in himself, was ever a trifle egotistical, as country gentlemen sometimes become because of their insular situation. But he had saved himself by not becoming a mere pampered house-dog. Hunting and kindred outdoor delights had kept down the fat and hardened his muscles; and to him, as to the cold-tubbing races, the love of water had been a tonic and a health preserver.

And this was the manner of dog Buck was in the fall of 1897, when the Klondike strike dragged men from all the world into the frozen North. But Buck did not read the newspapers, and he did not know that Manuel, one of the gardener's helpers, was an undesirable acquaintance. Manuel had one besetting sin. He loved to play Chinese lottery. Also, in his gambling, he had one besetting weakness—faith in a system; and this made his damnation certain. For to play a system requires money, while the wages of a gardener's helper do not lap over the needs of a wife and numerous progeny.

The Judge was at a meeting of the Raisin Growers' Association, and the boys were busy organizing an athletic club, on the memorable night of Manuel's treachery. No one saw him and Buck go off through the orchard on what Buck imagined was merely a stroll. And with the exception of a solitary man, no one saw them arrive at the little flag station known as College Park. This man talked with Manuel, and money chinked between them.

"You might wrap up the goods before you deliver 'em," the stranger said gruffly, and Manuel doubled a piece of stout rope around Buck's neck under the collar.

"Twist it, an' you'll choke 'em plentee," said Manuel, and the stranger grunted a ready affirmative.

Buck had accepted the rope with quiet dignity. To be sure, it was an unwonted performance: but he had learned to trust in men he knew, and to give them credit for a wisdom that outreached his own. But when the ends of the rope were placed in the stranger's hands, he growled menacingly. He had merely intimated his displeasure, in his pride believing that to intimate was to command. But to his surprise the rope tightened around his neck, shutting off his breath. In quick rage he sprang at the man, who met him halfway, grappled him close by the throat, and with a deft twist threw him over on his back. Then the rope tightened mercilessly, while Buck struggled in a fury, his tongue lolling out of his mouth and his great chest panting futilely. Never in all his life had he been so vilely treated, and never in all his life had he been so angry. But his strength ebbed, his eyes glazed, and he knew nothing when the train was flagged and the two men threw him into the baggage car.

The next he knew, he was dimly aware that his tongue was hurting and that he was being jolted along in some kind of a conveyance. The hoarse shriek of a locomotive whistling a crossing told him where he was. He had travelled too often with the Judge not to know the sensation of riding in a baggage car. He opened his eyes, and into them came the unbridled anger of a kidnapped king. The man sprang for his throat, but Buck was too quick for him. His jaws closed on the hand, nor did they relax till his senses were choked out of him once more.

"Yep, has fits," the man said, hiding his mangled hand from the baggageman, who had been attracted by the sounds of struggle. "I'm takin' 'm up for the boss to 'Frisco. A crack dog-doctor there thinks that he can cure 'm."

Concerning that night's ride, the man spoke most eloquently for himself, in a little shed back of a saloon on the San Francisco water front.

"All I get is fifty for it," he grumbled; "an' I wouldn't do it over for a thousand, cold cash."

His hand was wrapped in a bloody handkerchief, and the right trouser leg was ripped from knee to ankle.

"How much did the other mug get?" the saloon-keeper demanded.

"A hundred," was the reply. "Wouldn't take a sou less, so help me."

"That makes a hundred and fifty," the saloon-keeper calculated; "and he's worth it, or I'm a squarehead."

The kidnapper undid the bloody wrappings and looked at his lacerated hand. "If I don't get the hydrophoby—"

"It'll be because you was born to hang," laughed the saloon-keeper. "Here, lend me a hand before you pull your freight," he added.

Dazed, suffering intolerable pain from throat and tongue, with the life half throttled out of him, Buck attempted to face his tormentors. But he was thrown down and choked repeatedly, till they succeeded in filing the heavy brass collar from off his neck. Then the rope was removed, and he was flung into a cagelike crate.

There he lay for the remainder of the weary night, nursing his wrath and wounded pride. He could not understand what it all meant. What did they want with him, these strange men? Why were they keeping him pent up in this narrow crate? He did not know why, but he felt oppressed by the vague sense of impending calamity. Several times during the night he sprang to his feet when the shed door rattled open, expecting to see the Judge, or the boys at least. But each time it was the bulging face of the saloon-keeper that peered in at him by the sickly light of a tallow candle. And each time the joyful bark that trembled in Buck's throat was twisted into a savage growl.

But the saloon-keeper let him alone, and in the morning four men entered and picked up the crate. More tormentors, Buck decided, for they were evil-looking creatures, ragged and unkempt; and he stormed and raged at them through the bars. They only laughed and poked sticks at him, which he promptly assailed with his teeth till he realized that that was what they wanted. Whereupon he lay down sullenly and allowed the crate to be lifted into a wagon. Then he, and the crate in which he was imprisoned, began a passage through many hands.

Clerks in the express office took charge of him; he was carted about in another wagon; a truck carried him, with an assortment of boxes and parcels, upon a ferry steamer; he was trucked off the steamer into a great railway depot, and finally he was deposited in an express car.

For two days and nights this express car was dragged along at the tail of shrieking locomotives; and for two days and nights Buck neither ate nor drank. In his anger he had met the first advances of the express messengers with growls, and they had retaliated by teasing him. When he flung himself against the bars, quivering and frothing, they laughed at him and taunted him. They growled and barked like detestable dogs, mewed, and flapped their arms and crowed. It was all very silly, he knew; but therefore the more outrage to his dignity, and his anger waxed and waxed. He did not mind the hunger so much, but the lack of water caused him severe suffering and fanned his wrath to fever-pitch. For that matter, high-strung and finely sensitive, the ill treatment had flung him into a fever, which was fed by the inflammation of his parched and swollen throat and tongue.

He was glad for one thing: the rope was off his neck. That had given them an unfair advantage; but now that it was off, he would show them. They would never get another rope around his neck. Upon that he was resolved. For two days and nights he neither ate nor drank, and during those two days and nights of torment, he accumulated a fund of wrath that boded ill for whoever first fell foul of him. His eyes turned blood-shot, and he was metamorphosed into a raging fiend. So changed was he that the Judge himself would not have recognized him; and the express messengers breathed with relief when they bundled him off the train at Seattle.

Four men gingerly carried the crate from the wagon into a small, high-walled back yard. A stout man, with a red sweater that sagged generously at the neck, came out and signed the book for the driver. That was the man, Buck divined, the next tormentor, and he hurled himself savagely against the bars. The man smiled grimly, and brought a hatchet and a club.

"You ain't going to take him out now?" the driver asked.

"Sure," the man replied, driving the hatchet into the crate for a pry.

There was an instantaneous scattering of the four men who had carried it in, and from safe perches on top the wall they prepared to watch the performance.

Buck rushed at the splintering wood, sinking his teeth into it, surging and wrestling with it. Wherever the hatchet fell on the outside, he was there on the inside, snarling and growling, as furiously anxious to get out as the man in the red sweater was calmly intent on getting him out.

"Now, you red-eyed devil," he said, when he had made an opening sufficient for the passage of Buck's body. At the same time he dropped the hatchet and shifted the club to his right hand.

And Buck was truly a red-eyed devil, as he drew himself together for the spring, hair bristling, mouth foaming, a mad glitter in his blood-shot eyes. Straight at the man he launched his one hundred and forty pounds of fury, surcharged with the pent passion of two days and nights. In mid air, just as his jaws were about to close on the man, he received a shock that checked his body and brought his teeth together with an agonizing clip. He whirled over, fetching the ground on his back and side. He had never been struck by a club in his life, and did not understand. With a snarl that was part bark and more scream he was again on his feet and launched into the air. And again the shock came and he was brought crushingly to the ground. This time he was aware that it was the club, but his madness knew no caution. A dozen times he charged, and as often the club broke the charge and smashed him down.

After a particularly fierce blow he crawled to his feet, too dazed to rush. He staggered limply about, the blood flowing from nose and mouth and ears, his beautiful coat sprayed and flecked with bloody slaver. Then the man advanced and deliberately dealt him a frightful blow on the nose. All the pain he had endured was as nothing compared with the exquisite agony of this. With a roar that was almost lionlike in its ferocity, he again hurled himself at the man. But the man, shifting the club from right to left, coolly caught him by the under jaw, at the same time wrenching downward and backward. Buck described a complete circle in the air, and half of another, then crashed to the ground on his head and chest.

For the last time he rushed. The man struck the shrewd blow he had purposely withheld for so long, and Buck crumpled up and went down, knocked utterly senseless.

"He's no slouch at dog-breakin', that's wot I say," one of the men on the wall cried enthusiastically.

"Druther break cayuses any day, and twice on Sundays," was the reply of the driver, as he climbed on the wagon and started the horses.

Buck's senses came back to him, but not his strength. He lay where he had fallen, and from there he watched the man in the red sweater.

" 'Answers to the name of Buck,' " the man soliloquized, quoting from the saloon-keeper's letter which had announced the consignment of the crate and contents. "Well, Buck, my boy," he went on in a genial voice, "we've had our little ruction, and the best thing we can do is to let it go at that. You've learned your place, and I know mine. Be a good dog and all 'll go well and the goose hang high. Be a bad dog, and I'll whale the stuffin' outa you. Understand?"

As he spoke he fearlessly patted the head he had so mercilessly pounded, and though Buck's hair involuntarily bristled at touch of the hand, he endured it without protest. When the man brought him water he drank eagerly, and later bolted a generous meal of raw meat, chunk by chunk, from the man's hand.

He was beaten (he knew that); but he was not broken. He saw, once for all, that he stood no chance against a man with a club. He had learned a lesson, and in all his after life he never forgot it. That club was a revelation. It was his introduction to the reign of primitive law, and he met the introduction halfway. The facts of life took on a fiercer aspect; and while he faced that aspect uncowed, he faced it with all the latent cunning of his nature aroused. As the days went by, other dogs came, in crates and at the ends of ropes, some docilely, and some raging and roaring as he had come; and, one and all, he watched them pass under the dominion of the man in the red sweater. Again and again, as he looked at each brutal performance, the lesson was driven home to Buck: a man with a club was a lawgiver, a master to be obeyed, though not necessarily conciliated. Of this last Buck was never guilty, though he did see beaten dogs that fawned upon the man, and wagged their tails, and licked his hand. Also he saw one dog, that would neither conciliate nor obey, finally killed in the struggle for mastery.

Now and again men came, strangers, who talked excitedly, wheedlingly, and in all kinds of fashions to the man in the red sweater. And at such times that money passed between them the strangers took one or more of the dogs away with them. Buck wondered where they went, for they never came back; but the fear of the future was strong upon him, and he was glad each time when he was not selected.

Yet his time came, in the end, in the form of a little weazened man who spat broken English and many strange and uncouth exclamations which Buck could not understand.

"*Sacredam!*" he cried, when his eyes lit upon Buck. "Dat one dam bully dog! Eh? How moch?"

"Three hundred, and a present at that," was the prompt reply of the man in the red sweater. "And seein' it's government money, you ain't got no kick coming, eh, Perrault?"

Perrault grinned. Considering that the price of dogs had been boomed skyward by the unwonted demand, it was not an unfair sum for so fine an animal. The

Canadian Government would be no loser, nor would its despatches travel the slower. Perrault knew dogs, and when he looked at Buck he knew that he was one in a thousand— "One in ten t'ousand," he commented mentally.

Buck saw money pass between them, and was not surprised when Curly, a good-natured Newfoundland, and he were led away by the little weazened man. That was the last he saw of the man in the red sweater, and as Curly and he looked at receding Seattle from the deck of the *Narwhal,* it was the last he saw of the warm Southland. Curly and he were taken below by Perrault and turned over to a black-faced giant called François. Perrault was a French-Canadian, and swarthy; but François was a French-Canadian half-breed, and twice as swarthy. They were a new kind of men to Buck (of which he was destined to see many more), and while he developed no affection for them, he none the less grew honestly to respect them. He speedily learned that Perrault and François were fair men, calm and impartial in administering justice, and too wise in the way of dogs to be fooled by dogs.

In the 'tween-decks of the *Norwhal,* Buck and Curly joined two other dogs. One of them was a big, snow-white fellow from Spitzbergen who had been brought away by a whaling captain, and who had later accompanied a Geological Survey into the Barrens.

He was friendly, in a treacherous sort of way, smiling into one's face the while he meditated some underhand trick, as, for instance, when he stole from Buck's food at the first meal. As Buck sprang to punish him, the lash of François's whip sang through the air, reaching the culprit first; and nothing remained to Buck but to recover the bone. That was fair of François, he decided, and the half-breed began his rise in Buck's estimation.

The other dog made no advances, nor received any; also, he did not attempt to steal from the newcomers. He was a gloomy, morose fellow, and he showed Curly plainly that all he desired was to be left alone, and further, that there would be trouble if he were not left alone. "Dave" he was called, and he ate and slept, or yawned between times, and took interest in nothing, not even when the *Narwhal* crossed Queen Charlotte Sound and rolled and pitched and bucked like a thing possessed. When Buck and Curly grew excited, half wild with fear, he raised his head as though annoyed, favored them with an incurious glance, yawned, and went to sleep again.

Day and night the ship throbbed to the tireless pulse of the propeller, and though one day was very like another, it was apparent to Buck that the weather was steadily growing colder. At last, one morning, the propeller was quiet, and the *Narwhal* was pervaded with an atmosphere of excitement. He felt it, as did the other dogs, and knew that a change was at hand. François leashed them and brought them on deck. At the first step upon the cold surface, Buck's feet sank into a white mushy something very like mud. He sprang back with a snort. More of this white stuff was falling through the air. He shook himself, but more of it fell upon him. He sniffed it curiously, then licked some up on his tongue. It bit like fire, and the next instant was gone. This puzzled him. He tried it again, with the same result. The onlookers laughed uproariously, and he felt ashamed, he knew not why, for it was his first snow.

CHAPTER 2

The Law of Club and Fang

BUCK'S FIRST DAY on the Dyea beach was like a nightmare. Every hour was filled with shock and surprise. He had been suddenly jerked from the heart of civilization and flung into the heart of things primordial. No lazy, sun-kissed life was this, with nothing to do but loaf and be bored. Here was neither peace, nor rest, nor a moment's safety. All was confusion and action, and every moment life and limb were in peril. There was imperative need to be constantly alert; for these dogs and men were not town dogs and men. They were savages, all of them, who knew no law but the law of club and fang.

He had never seen dogs fight as these wolfish creatures fought, and his first experience taught him an unforgettable lesson. It is true, it was a vicarious experience, else he would not have lived to profit by it. Curly was the victim. They were camped near the log store, where she, in her friendly way, made advances to a husky dog the size of a full-grown wolf, though not half so large as she. There was no warning, only a leap in like a flash, a metallic clip of teeth, a leap out equally swift, and Curly's face was ripped open from eye to jaw.

It was the wolf manner of fighting, to strike and leap away; but there was more to it than this. Thirty or forty huskies ran to the spot and surrounded the combatants in an intent and silent circle. Buck did not comprehend that silent intentness, nor the eager way with which they were licking their chops. Curly rushed her antagonist, who struck again and leaped aside. He met her next rush with his chest, in a peculiar fashion that tumbled her off her feet. She never regained them. This was what the onlooking huskies had waited for. They closed in upon her, snarling and yelping, and she was buried, screaming with agony, beneath the bristling mass of bodies.

So sudden was it, and so unexpected, that Buck was taken aback. He saw Spitz run out his scarlet tongue in a way he had of laughing; and he saw François, swinging an axe, spring into the mess of dogs. Three men with clubs were helping him to scatter them. It did not take long. Two minutes from the time Curly went down, the last of her assailants were clubbed off. But she lay there limp and lifeless in the bloody, trampled snow, almost literally torn to pieces, the swart half-breed standing over her and cursing horribly. The scene often came back to Buck to trouble him in his sleep. So that was the way. No fairplay. Once down, that was the end of you. Well, he would see to it that he never went down. Spitz ran out his tongue and laughed again, and from that moment Buck hated him with a bitter and deathless hatred.

Before he had recovered from the shock caused by the tragic passing of Curly, he received another shock. François fastened upon him an arrangement of straps and buckles. It was a harness, such as he had seen the grooms put on the horses at home. And as he had seen horses work, so he was set to work, hauling François on a sled to the forest that fringed the valley, and returning with a load of firewood. Though his dignity was sorely hurt by thus being made a draught animal, he was too wise to rebel. He buckled down with a will and did his best, though it was all new and strange. François was stern, demanding instant obedience, and by virtue of his whip receiving instant obedience; while Dave, who was an experienced wheeler, nipped Buck's hind quarters whenever he was in error. Spitz was the leader, likewise experienced, and while he could not always get at Buck, he growled sharp reproof now and again, or cunningly threw his weight in the traces to jerk Buck into the way he should go. Buck learned easily, and under the combined tuition of his two mates and François made remarkable progress. Ere they returned to camp he knew enough to stop at "ho," to go ahead at "mush," to swing wide on the bends, and to keep clear of the wheeler when the loaded sled shot downhill at their heels.

"T'ree vair' good dogs," François told Perrault. "Dat Buck, heem pool lak hell. I tich heem queek as anyt'ing."

By afternoon, Perrault, who was in a hurry to be on the trail with his despatches, returned with two more dogs. "Billee" and "Joe" he called them, two brothers, and true huskies both. Sons of the one mother though they were, they were as different as day and night. Billee's one fault was his excessive good nature, while Joe was the very opposite, sour and introspective, with a perpetual snarl and a malignant eye. Buck received them in comradely fashion, Dave ignored them, while Spitz proceeded to thrash first one and then the other. Billee wagged his tail appeasingly, turned to run when he saw that appeasement was of no avail, and cried (still appeasingly) when Spitz's sharp teeth scored his flank. But no matter how Spitz circled, Joe whirled around on his heels to face him, mane bristling, ears laid back, lips writhing and snarling, jaws clipping together as fast as he could snap, and eyes diabolically gleaming—the incarnation of belligerent fear. So terrible was his appearance that Spitz was forced to forego disciplining him; but to cover his own discomfiture he turned upon the inoffensive and wailing Billee and drove him to the confines of the camp.

By evening Perrault secured another dog, an old husky, long and lean and gaunt, with a battle-scarred face and a single eye which flashed a warning of prowess that commanded respect. He was called Sol-leks, which means the Angry One. Like Dave, he asked nothing, gave nothing, expected nothing; and when he marched slowly and deliberately into their midst, even Spitz left him alone. He had one peculiarity which Buck was unlucky enough to discover. He did not like to be approached on his blind side. Of this offence Buck was unwittingly guilty, and the first knowledge he had of his indiscretion was when Sol-leks whirled upon him and slashed his shoulder to the bone for three inches up and down. Forever after Buck avoided his blind side, and to the last of their comradeship had no more trouble. His only apparent ambition, like Dave's, was to be left alone; though, as Buck was afterward to learn, each of them possessed one other and even more vital ambition.

That night Buck faced the great problem of sleeping. The tent, illumined by a candle, glowed warmly in the midst of the white plain; and when he, as a matter of course, entered it, both Perrault and François bombarded him with curses and cooking utensils, till he recovered from his consternation and fled ignominiously into the outer cold. A chill wind was blowing that nipped him sharply and bit with especial venom into his wounded shoulder. He lay down on the snow and attempted to sleep, but the frost soon drove him shivering to his feet. Miserable and disconsolate, he wandered about among the many tents, only to find that one place was as cold as another. Here and there savage dogs rushed upon him, but he bristled his neck-hair and snarled (for he was learning fast), and they let him go his way unmolested.

Finally an idea came to him. He would return and see how his own team mates were making out. To his astonishment, they had disappeared. Again he wandered about through the great camp, looking for them, and again he returned. Were they in the tent? No, that could not be, else he would not have been driven out. Then where could they possibly be? With drooping tail and shivering body, very forlorn indeed, he aimlessly circled the tent. Suddenly the snow gave way beneath his fore legs and he sank down. Something wriggled under his feet. He sprang back, bristling and snarling, fearful of the unseen and unknown. But a friendly little yelp reassured him, and he went back to investigate. A whiff of warm air ascended to his nostrils, and there, curled up under the snow in a snug ball, lay Billee. He whined placatingly, squirmed and wriggled to show his good will and intentions, and even ventured, as a bribe for peace, to lick Buck's face with his warm wet tongue.

Another lesson. So that was the way they did it, eh? Buck confidently selected a spot, and with much fuss and waste effort proceeded to dig a hole for himself. In a trice the heat from his body filled the confined space and he was asleep. The day had been long and arduous, and he slept soundly and comfortably, though he growled and barked and wrestled with bad dreams.

Nor did he open his eyes till roused by the noises of the waking camp. At first he did not know where he was. It had snowed during the night and he was completely buried. The snow walls pressed him on every side, and a great surge of fear swept through him—the fear of the wild thing for the trap. It was a token that he was harking back through his own life to the lives of his forbears; for he was a civilized dog, an unduly civilized dog, and of his own experience knew no trap and so could not of himself fear it. The muscles of his whole body contracted spasmodically and instinctively, the hair on his neck and shoulders stood on end, and with a ferocious snarl he bounded straight up into the blinding day, the snow flying about him in a flashing cloud. Ere he landed on his feet, he saw the white camp spread out before him and knew where he was and remembered all that had passed from the time he went for a stroll with Manuel to the hole he had dug for himself the night before.

A shout from François hailed his appearance. "Wot I say?" the dog driver cried to Perrault. "Dat Buck for sure learn queek as anyt'ing."

Perrault nodded gravely. As courier for the Canadian Government, bearing important despatches, he was anxious to secure the best dogs, and he was particularly gladdened by the possession of Buck.

Three more huskies were added to the team inside an hour, making a total of nine, and before another quarter of an hour had passed they were in harness and swinging up the trail toward the Dyea Cañon. Buck was glad to be gone, and though the work was hard he found he did not particularly despise it. He was surprised at the eagerness which animated the whole team and which was communicated to him; but still more surprising was the change wrought in Dave and Sol-leks. They were new dogs, utterly transformed by the harness. All passiveness and unconcern had dropped from them. They were alert and active, anxious that the work should go well, and fiercely irritable with whatever, by delay or confusion, retarded that work. The toil of the traces seemed the supreme expression of their being, and all that they lived for and the only thing in which they took delight.

Dave was wheeler or sled dog, pulling in front of him was Buck, then came Sol-leks; the rest of the team was strung out ahead, single file, to the leader, which position was filled by Spitz.

Buck had been purposely placed between Dave and Sol-leks so that he might receive instruction. Apt scholar that he was, they were equally apt teachers, never allowing him to linger long in error, and enforcing their teaching with their sharp teeth. Dave was fair and very wise. He never nipped Buck without cause, and he never failed to nip him when he stood in need of it. As François's whip backed him up, Buck found it to be cheaper to mend his ways than to retaliate. Once, during a brief halt, when he got tangled in the traces and delayed the start, both Dave and Sol-leks flew at him and administered a sound trouncing. The resulting tangle was even worse, but Buck took good care to keep the traces clear thereafter; and ere the day was done, so well had he mastered his work, his mates about ceased nagging him. François's whip snapped less frequently, and Perrault even honored Buck by lifting up his feet and carefully examining them.

It was a hard day's run, up the Cañon, through Sheep Camp, past the Scales and the timber line, across glaciers and snowdrifts hundreds of feet deep, and over the great Chilcoot Divide, which stands between the salt water and the fresh and guards forbiddingly the sad and lonely North. They made good time down the chain of lakes which fills the craters of extinct volcanoes, and late that night pulled into the huge camp at the head of Lake Bennett, where thousands of gold-seekers were building boats against the breakup of the ice in the spring. Buck made his hole in the snow and slept the sleep of the exhausted just, but all too early was routed out in the cold darkness and harnessed with his mates to the sled.

That day they made forty miles, the trail being packed; but the next day, and for many days to follow, they broke their own trail, worked harder, and made poorer time. As a rule, Perrault travelled ahead of the team, packing the snow with webbed shoes to make it easier for them. François, guiding the sled at the gee-pole, sometimes exchanged places with him, but not often. Perrault was in a hurry, and he prided himself on his knowledge of ice, which knowledge was indispensable, for the fall ice was very thin, and where there was swift water, there was no ice at all.

Day after day, for days unending, Buck toiled in the traces. Always, they broke camp in the dark, and the first gray of dawn found them hitting the trail with fresh miles reeled off behind them. And always they pitched camp after dark, eating their bit of fish, and crawling to sleep into the snow. Buck was ravenous. The pound and a half of sun-dried salmon, which was his ration for each day, seemed to go nowhere. He never had enough, and suffered from perpetual hunger pangs. Yet the other dogs, because they weighed less and were born to the life, received a pound only of the fish and managed to keep in good condition.

He swiftly lost the fastidiousness which had characterized his old life. A dainty eater, he found that his mates, finishing first, robbed him of his unfinished ration. There was no defending it. While he was fighting off two or three, it was disappearing down the throats of the others. To remedy this, he ate as fast as they; and, so greatly did hunger compel him, he was not above taking what did not belong to him. He watched and learned. When he saw Pike, one of the new dogs, a clever malingerer and thief, slyly steal a slice of bacon when Perrault's back was turned, he duplicated the performance the following day, getting away with the whole chunk. A great uproar was raised, but he was unsuspected, while Dub, an awkward blunderer who was always getting caught, was punished for Buck's misdeed.

This first theft marked Buck as fit to survive in the hostile Northland environment. It marked his adaptability, his capacity to adjust himself to changing conditions, the lack of which would have meant swift and terrible death. It marked, further, the decay or going to pieces of his moral nature, a vain thing and a handicap in the ruthless struggle for existence. It was all well enough in the Southland, under the law of love and fellowship, to respect private property and personal feelings; but in the Northland, under the law of club and fang, whoso took such things into account was a fool, and in so far as he observed them he would fail to prosper.

Not that Buck reasoned it out. He was fit, that was all, and unconsciously he accommodated himself to the new mode of life. All his days, no matter what the odds, he had never run from a fight. But the club of the man in the red sweater had beaten into him a more fundamental and primitive code. Civilized, he could have died for a moral consideration, say the defence of Judge Miller's riding-whip; but the completeness of his decivilization was now evidenced by his ability to flee from the defence of a moral consideration and so save his hide. He did not steal for joy of it, but because of the clamor of his stomach. He did not rob openly, but stole secretly and cunningly, out of respect for club and fang. In short, the things he did were done because it was easier to do them than not to do them.

His development (or retrogression) was rapid. His

muscles became hard as iron and he grew callous to all ordinary pain. He achieved an internal as well as external economy. He could eat anything, no matter how loathsome or indigestible; and, once eaten, the juices of his stomach extracted the last least particle of nutriment; and his blood carried it to the farthest reaches of his body, building it into the toughest and stoutest of tissues. Sight and scent became remarkably keen, while his hearing developed such acuteness that in his sleep he heard the faintest sound and knew whether it heralded peace or peril. He learned to bite the ice out with his teeth when it collected between his toes; and when he was thirsty and there was a thick scum of ice over the water hole, he would break it by rearing and striking it with stiff fore legs. His most conspicuous trait was an ability to scent the wind and forecast it a night in advance. No matter how breathless the air when he dug his nest by tree or bank, the wind that later blew inevitably found him to leeward, sheltered and snug.

And not only did he learn by experience, but instincts long dead became alive again. The domesticated generations fell from him. In vague ways he remembered back to the youth of the breed, to the time the wild dogs ranged in packs through the primeval forest and killed their meat as they ran it down. It was no task for him to learn to fight with cut and slash and the quick wolf snap. In this manner had fought forgotten ancestors. They quickened the old life within him, and the old tricks which they had stamped into the heredity of the breed were his tricks. They came to him without effort or discovery, as though they had been his always. And when, on the still cold nights, he pointed his nose at a star and howled long and wolflike, it was his ancestors, dead and dust, pointing nose at star and howling down through the centuries and through him. And his cadences were their cadences, the cadences which voiced their woe and what to them was the meaning of the stillness, and the cold, and dark.

Thus, as token of what a puppet thing life is, the ancient song surged through him and he came into his own again; and he came because men had found a yellow metal in the North, and because Manuel was a gardener's helper whose wages did not lap over the needs of his wife and divers small copies of himself.

CHAPTER 3

The Dominant Primordial Beast

THE DOMINANT PRIMORDIAL beast was strong in Buck, and under the fierce conditions of trail life it grew and grew. Yet it was a secret growth. His new-born cunning gave him poise and control. He was too busy adjusting himself to the new life to feel at ease, and not only did he not pick fights, but he avoided them whenever possible. A certain deliberateness characterized his attitude. He was not prone to rashness and precipitate action; and in the bitter hatred between him and Spitz he betrayed no impatience, shunned all offensive acts.

On the other hand, possibly because he divined in Buck a dangerous rival, Spitz never lost an opportunity of showing his teeth. He even went out of his way to bully Buck, striving constantly to start the fight which could end only in the death of one or the other.

Early in the trip this might have taken place had it not been for an unwonted accident. At the end of this day they made a bleak and miserable camp on the shore of

Lake Le Barge. Driving snow, a wind that cut like a white-hot knife, and darkness, had forced them to grope for a camping place. They could hardly have fared worse. At their backs rose a perpendicular wall of rock, and Perrault and François were compelled to make their fire and spread their sleeping robes on the ice of the lake itself. The tent they had discarded at Dyea in order to travel light. A few sticks of driftwood furnished them with a fire that thawed down through the ice and left them to eat supper in the dark.

Close in under the sheltering rock Buck made his nest. So snug and warm was it, that he was loath to leave it when François distributed the fish which he had first thawed over the fire. But when Buck finished his ration and returned, he found his nest occupied. A warning snarl told him that the trespasser was Spitz. Till now Buck had avoided trouble with his enemy, but this was too much. The beast in him roared. He sprang upon Spitz with a fury which surprised them both, and Spitz particularly, for his whole experience with Buck had gone to teach him that his rival was an unusually timid dog, who managed to hold his own only because of his great weight and size.

François was surprised, too, when they shot out in a tangle from the disrupted nest and he divined the cause of the trouble. "A-a-ah!" he cried to Buck. "Gif it to heem, by Gar! Gif it to heem, the dirty t'eef!"

Spitz was equally willing. He was crying with sheer rage and eagerness as he circled back and forth for a chance to spring in. Buck was no less eager, and no less cautious, as he likewise circled back and forth for the advantage. But it was then that the unexpected happened, the thing which projected their struggle for supremacy far into the future, past many a weary mile of trail and toil.

An oath from Perrault, the resounding impact of a club upon a bony frame, and a shrill yelp of pain, heralded the breaking forth of pandemonium. The camp was suddenly discovered to be alive with skulking furry forms, —starving huskies, four or five score of them, who had scented the camp from some Indian village. They had crept in while Buck and Spitz were fighting, and when the two men sprang among them with stout clubs they showed their teeth and fought back. They were crazed by the smell of the food. Perrault found one with head buried in the grub-box. His club landed heavily on the gaunt ribs, and the grub-box was capsized on the ground. On the instant a score of the famished brutes were scrambling for the bread and bacon. The clubs fell upon them unheeded. They yelped and howled under the rain of blows, but struggled none the less madly till the last crumb had been devoured.

In the meantime the astonished team-dogs had burst out of their nests only to be set upon by the fierce invaders. Never had Buck seen such dogs. It seemed as though their bones would burst through their skins. They were mere skeletons, draped loosely in draggled hides, with blazing eyes and slavered fangs. But the hunger-madness made them terrifying, irresistible. There was no opposing them. The team-dogs were swept back against the cliff at the first onset. Buck was beset by three huskies, and in a trice his head and shoulders were ripped and slashed.

The din was frightful. Billee was crying as usual. Dave and Sol-leks, dripping blood from a score of wounds, were fighting bravely side by side. Joe was snapping like a demon. Once, his teeth closed on the fore leg of a husky, and he crunched down through the bone. Pike, the malingerer, leaped upon the crippled animal, breaking its neck with a quick flash of teeth and a jerk. Buck got a frothing adversary by the throat, and was sprayed with blood when his teeth sank through the jugular. The warm taste of it in his mouth goaded him to greater fierceness. He flung himself upon another, and at the same time felt teeth sink into his own throat. It was Spitz, treacherously attacking from the side.

Perrault and François, having cleaned out their part of the camp, hurried to save their sled-dogs. The wild wave of famished beasts rolled back before them, and Buck shook himself free. But it was only for a moment. The two men were compelled to run back to save the grub, upon which the huskies returned to the attack on the team. Billee, terrified into bravery, sprang through the savage circle and fled away over the ice. Pike and Dub followed on his heels, with the rest of the team behind. As Buck drew himself together to spring after them, out of the tail of his eye he saw Spitz rush upon him, with the evident intention of overthrowing him. Once off his feet and under that mass of huskies, there was no hope for him. But he braced himself to the shock of Spitz's charge, then joined the flight out on the lake.

Later, the nine team-dogs gathered together and sought shelter in the forest. Though unpursued, they were in a sorry plight. There was not one who was not wounded in four or five places, while some were wounded grievously. Dub was badly injured in a hind leg; Dolly, the last husky added to the team at Dyea, had a badly torn throat; Joe had lost an eye; while Billee, the good-natured, with an ear chewed and rent to ribbons, cried and whimpered throughout the night. At daybreak they limped warily back to camp, to find the marauders gone and the two men in bad tempers. Fully half their grub supply was gone. The huskies had chewed through the sled lashings and canvas coverings. In fact, nothing, no matter how remotely eatable, had escaped them. They had eaten a pair of Perrault's moose-hide moccasins, chunks out of the leather traces, and even two feet of lash from the end of François's whip. He broke from a mournful contemplation of it to look over his wounded dogs.

"Ah, my frien's," he said softly, "mebbe it mek you mad dog, dose many bites. Mebbe all mad dog, sacredam! Wot you t'ink, eh, Perrault?"

The courier shook his head dubiously. With four hundred miles of trail still between him and Dawson, he could ill afford to have madness break out among his dogs. Two hours of cursing and exertion got the harnesses into shape, and the wound-stiffened team was under way, struggling painfully over the hardest part of the trail they had yet encountered, and for that matter, the hardest between them and Dawson.

The Thirty Mile River was wide open. Its wild water defied the frost, and it was in the eddies only and in the quiet places that the ice held at all. Six days of exhausting toil were required to cover those thirty terrible miles. And terrible they were, for every foot of them was accomplished at the risk of life to dog and man. A dozen times, Perrault, nosing the way, broke through the ice bridges, being saved by the long pole he carried, which he so held that it fell each time across the hole made by his body. But a cold snap was on, the thermometer registering fifty below zero, and each time he broke through he was compelled for very life to build a fire and dry his garments.

Nothing daunted him. It was because nothing daunted him that he had been chosen for government courier. He took all manner of risks, resolutely thrusting his little weazened face into the frost and struggling on from dim dawn to dark. He skirted the frowning shores on rim ice that bent and crackled under foot and upon which they dared not halt. Once, the sled broke through, with Dave and Buck, and they were half-frozen and all but drowned by the time they were dragged out. The usual fire was necessary to save them. They were coated solidly with ice, and the two men kept them on the run around the fire, sweating and thawing, so close that they were singed by the flames.

At another time Spitz went through, dragging the whole team after him up to Buck, who strained backward with all his strength, his fore paws on the slippery edge and the ice quivering and snapping all around. But behind him was Dave, likewise straining backward, and behind the sled was François, pulling till his tendons cracked.

Again, the rim ice broke away before and behind, and there was no escape except up the cliff. Perrault scaled it by a miracle, while François prayed for just that miracle; and with every thong and sled lashing and the last bit of harness rove into a long rope, the dogs were hoisted, one by one, to the cliff crest. François came up last, after the sled and load. Then came the search for a place to descend, which descent was ultimately made by the aid of the rope, and night found them back on the river with a quarter of a mile to the day's credit.

By the time they made the Hootalinqua and good ice, Buck was played out. The rest of the dogs were in like condition; but Perrault, to make up lost time, pushed them late and early. The first day they covered thirty-five miles to the Big Salmon; the next day thirty-five more to the Little Salmon; the third day forty miles, which brought them well up toward the Five Fingers.

Buck's feet were not so compact and hard as the feet of the huskies. His had softened during the many generations since the day his last wild ancestor was tamed by a cave-dweller or river man. All day long he limped in agony, and camp once made, lay down like a dead dog. Hungry as he was, he would not move to receive his ration of fish, which François had to bring to him. Also, the dog-driver rubbed Buck's feet for half an hour each night after supper, and sacrificed the tops of his own moccasins to make four moccasins for Buck. This was a great relief, and Buck caused even the weazened face of Perrault to twist itself into a grin one morning, when François forgot the moccasins and Buck lay on his back, his four feet waving appealingly in the air, and refused to budge without them. Later his feet grew hard to the trail, and the worn-out foot-gear was thrown away.

At the Pelly one morning, as they were harnessing up,

Dolly, who had never been conspicuous for anything, went suddenly mad. She announced her condition by a long, heart-breaking wolf howl that sent every dog bristling with fear, then sprang straight for Buck. He had never seen a dog go mad, nor did he have any reason to fear madness; yet he knew that here was horror, and fled away from it in a panic. Straight away he raced, with Dolly, panting and frothing, one leap behind; nor could she gain on him, so great was his terror, nor could he leave her, so great was her madness. He plunged through the wooded breast of the island, fled down to the lower end, crossed a back channel filled with rough ice to another island, gained a third island, curved back to the main river, and in desperation started to cross it. And all the time, though he did not look, he could hear her snarling just one leap behind. François called to him a quarter of a mile away and he doubled back, still one leap ahead, gasping painfully for air and putting all his faith in that François would save him. The dog-driver held the axe poised in his hand, and as Buck shot past him the axe crashed down upon mad Dolly's head.

Buck staggered over against the sled, exhausted, sobbing for breath, helpless. This was Spitz's opportunity. He sprang upon Buck, and twice his teeth sank into his unresisting foe and ripped and tore the flesh to the bone. Then François's lash descended, and Buck had the satisfaction of watching Spitz receive the worst whipping as yet administered to any of the team.

"One devil, dat Spitz," remarked Perrault. "Some dam day heem keel dat Buck."

"Dat Buck two devils," was François's rejoinder. "All

de tam I watch dat Buck I know for sure. Lissen: some dam fine day heem get mad lak hell an' den heem chew dat Spitz all up an' spit heem out on de snow. Sure. I know."

From then on it was war between them. Spitz, as lead-dog and acknowledged master of the team, felt his supremacy threatened by this strange Southland dog. And strange Buck was to him, for of the many Southland dogs he had known, not one had shown up worthily in camp and on trail. They were all too soft, dying under the toil, the frost, and starvation. Buck was the exception. He alone endured and prospered, matching the husky in strength, savagery, and cunning. Then he was a masterful dog, and what made him dangerous was the fact that the club of the man in the red sweater had knocked all blind pluck and rashness out of his desire for mastery. He was preëminently cunning, and could bide his time with a patience that was nothing less than primitive.

It was inevitable that the clash for leadership should come. Buck wanted it. He wanted it because it was his nature, because he had been gripped tight by that nameless, incomprehensible pride of the trail and trace—that pride which holds dogs in the toil to the last gasp, which lures them to die joyfully in the harness, and breaks their hearts if they are cut out of the harness. This was the pride of Dave as wheel-dog, of Sol-leks as he pulled with all his strength; the pride that laid hold of them at break of camp, transforming them from sour and sullen brutes into straining, eager, ambitious creatures; the pride that spurred them on all day and dropped them at pitch of camp at night, letting them fall back into gloomy unrest and uncontent. This was the pride that bore up Spitz and made him thrash the sled-dogs who blundered and shirked in the traces or hid away at harness-up time in the morning. Likewise it was this pride that made him fear Buck as a possible lead-dog. And this was Buck's pride, too.

He openly threatened the other's leadership. He came between him and the shirks he should have punished. And he did it deliberately. One night there was a heavy snowfall, and in the morning Pike, the malingerer, did not appear. He was securely hidden in his nest under a foot of snow. François called him and sought him in vain. Spitz was wild with wrath. He raged through the camp, smelling and digging in every likely place, snarling so frightfully that Pike heard and shivered in his hiding-place.

But when he was at last unearthed, and Spitz flew at him to punish him, Buck flew, with equal rage, in between. So unexpected was it, and so shrewdly managed, that Spitz was hurled backward and off his feet. Pike, who had been trembling abjectly, took heart at this open mutiny, and sprang upon his overthrown leader. Buck, to whom fair-play was a forgotten code, likewise sprang upon Spitz. But François, chuckling at the incident while unswerving in the administration of justice, brought his lash down upon Buck with all his might. This failed to drive Buck from his prostrate rival, and the butt of the whip was brought into play. Half-stunned by the blow, Buck was knocked backward and the lash laid upon him again and again, while Spitz soundly punished the many times offending Pike.

In the days that followed, as Dawson grew closer and

closer, Buck still continued to interfere between Spitz and the culprits; but he did it craftily, when François was not around. With the covert mutiny of Buck, a general insubordination sprang up and increased. Dave and Sol-leks were unaffected, but the rest of the team went from bad to worse. Things no longer went right. There was continual bickering and jangling. Trouble was always afoot, and at the bottom of it was Buck. He kept François busy, for the dog-driver was in constant apprehension of the life-and-death struggle between the two which he knew must take place sooner or later; and on more than one night the sounds of quarrelling and strife among the other dogs turned him out of his sleeping robe, fearful that Buck and Spitz were at it.

But the opportunity did not present itself, and they pulled into Dawson one dreary afternoon with the great fight still to come. Here were many men, and countless dogs, and Buck found them all at work. It seemed the ordained order of things that dogs should work. All day they swung up and down the main street in long teams, and in the night their jingling bells still went by. They hauled cabin logs and firewood, freighted up to the mines, and did all manner of work that horses did in the Santa Clara Valley. Here and there Buck met Southland dogs, but in the main they were the wild wolf husky breed. Every night, regularly, at nine, at twelve, at three, they lifted a nocturnal song, a weird and eerie chant, in which it was Buck's delight to join.

With the aurora borealis flaming coldly overhead, or the stars leaping in the frost dance, and the land numb and frozen under its pall of snow, this song of the huskies might have been the defiance of life, only it was pitched in minor key, with long-drawn wailings and half-sobs, and was more the pleading of life, the articulate travail of existence. It was an old song, old as the breed itself — one of the first songs of the younger world in a day when songs were sad. It was invested with the woe of unnumbered generations, this plaint by which Buck was so strangely stirred. When he moaned and sobbed, it was with the pain of living that was of old the pain of his wild fathers, and the fear and mystery of the cold and dark that was to them fear and mystery. And that he should be stirred by it marked the completeness with which he harked back through the ages of fire and roof to the raw beginnings of life in the howling ages.

Seven days from the time they pulled into Dawson, they dropped down the steep bank by the Barracks to the Yukon Trail, and pulled for Dyea and Salt Water. Perrault was carrying despatches if anything more urgent than those he had brought in; also, the travel pride had gripped him, and he purposed to make the record trip of the year. Several things favored him in this. The week's rest had recuperated the dogs and put them in thorough trim. The trail they had broken into the country was packed hard by later journeyers. And further, the police had arranged in two or three places deposits of grub for dog and man, and he was travelling light.

They made Sixty Mile, which is a fifty-mile run, on the first day; and the second day saw them booming up the Yukon well on their way to Pelly. But such splendid running was achieved not without great trouble and vexation on the part of François. The insidious revolt led by Buck had destroyed the solidarity of the team. It no longer was as one dog leaping in the traces. The encouragement Buck gave the rebels led them into all kinds of petty misdemeanors. No more was Spitz a leader greatly to be feared. The old awe departed, and they grew equal to challenging his authority. Pike robbed him of half a fish one night, and gulped it down under the protection of Buck. Another night Dub and Joe fought Spitz and made him forego the punishment they deserved. And even Billee, the good-natured, was less good-natured, and whined not half so placatingly as in former days. Buck never came near Spitz without snarling and bristling menacingly. In fact, his conduct approached that of a bully, and he was given to swaggering up and down before Spitz's very nose.

The breaking down of discipline likewise affected the dogs in their relations with one another. They quarrelled and bickered more than ever among themselves, till at times the camp was a howling bedlam. Dave and Sol-leks alone were unaltered, though they were made irritable by the unending squabbling. François swore strange barbarous oaths, and stamped the snow in futile rage, and tore his hair. His lash was always singing among the dogs, but it was of small avail. Directly his back was turned they were at it again. He backed up Spitz with his whip, while Buck backed up the remainder of the team. François knew he was behind all the trouble, and Buck knew he knew; but Buck was too clever ever again to be caught red-handed. He worked faithfully in the harness, for the toil had become a delight to him; yet it was a greater delight slyly to precipitate a fight amongst his mates and tangle the traces.

At the mouth of the Tahkeena, one night after supper,

Dub turned up a snowshoe rabbit, blundered it, and missed. In a second the whole team was in full cry. A hundred yards away was a camp of the Northwest Police, with fifty dogs, huskies all, who joined the chase. The rabbit sped down the river, turned off into a small creek, up the frozen bed of which it held steadily. It ran lightly on the surface of the snow, while the dogs ploughed through by main strength. Buck led the pack, sixty strong, around bend after bend, but he could not gain. He lay down low to the race, whining eagerly, his splendid body flashing forward, leap by leap, in the wan white moonlight. And leap by leap, like some pale frost wraith, the snowshoe rabbit flashed on ahead.

All that stirring of old instincts which at stated periods drives men out from the sounding cities to forest and plain to kill things by chemically propelled leaden pellets, the blood lust, the joy to kill — all this was Buck's, only it was infinitely more intimate. He was ranging at the head of the pack, running the wild thing down, the living meat, to kill with his own teeth and wash his muzzle to the eyes in warm blood.

There is an ecstasy that marks the summit of life, and beyond which life cannot rise. And such is the paradox of living, this ecstasy comes when one is most alive, and it comes as a complete forgetfulness that one is alive. This ecstasy, this forgetfulness of living, comes to the artist, caught up and out of himself in a sheet of flame; it comes to the soldier, war-mad on a stricken field and refusing quarter; and it came to Buck, leading the pack, sounding the old wolf-cry, straining after the food that was alive and that fled swiftly before him through the moonlight.

He was sounding the deeps of his nature, and of the parts of his nature that were deeper than he, going back into the womb of Time. He was mastered by the sheer surging of life, the tidal wave of being, the perfect joy of each separate muscle, joint, and sinew in that it was everything that was not death, that it was aglow and rampant, expressing itself in movement, flying exultantly under the stars and over the face of dead matter that did not move.

But Spitz, cold and calculating even in his supreme moods, left the pack and cut across a narrow neck of land where the creek made a long bend around. Buck did not know of this, and as he rounded the bend, the frost wraith of a rabbit still flitting before him, he saw another and larger frost wraith leap from the overhanging bank into the immediate path of the rabbit. It was Spitz. The rabbit could not turn, and as the white teeth broke its back in mid air it shrieked as loudly as a stricken man may shriek. At sound of this, the cry of Life plunging down from Life's apex in the grip of Death, the full pack at Buck's heels raised a hell's chorus of delight.

Buck did not cry out. He did not check himself, but drove in upon Spitz, shoulder to shoulder, so hard that he missed the throat. They rolled over and over in the powdery snow. Spitz gained his feet almost as though he had not been overthrown, slashing Buck down the shoulder and leaping clear. Twice his teeth clipped together, like the steel jaws of a trap, as he backed away for better footing, with lean and lifting lips that writhed and snarled.

In a flash Buck knew it. The time had come. It was to the death. As they circled about, snarling, ears laid back, keenly watchful for the advantage, the scene came to Buck with a sense of familiarity. He seemed to remember it all, — the white woods, and earth, and moonlight, and the thrill of battle. Over the whiteness and silence brooded a ghostly calm. There was not the faintest whisper of air — nothing moved, not a leaf quivered, the visible breaths of the dogs rising slowly and lingering in the frosty air. They had made short work of the snowshoe rabbit, these dogs that were ill-tamed wolves; and they were now drawn up in an expectant circle. They, too, were silent, their eyes only gleaming and their breaths drifting slowly upward. To Buck it was nothing new or strange, this scene of old time. It was as though it had always been, the wonted way of things.

Spitz was a practised fighter. From Spitzbergen through the Arctic, and across Canada and the Barrens, he had held his own with all manner of dogs and achieved to mastery over them. Bitter rage was his, but never blind rage. In passion to rend and destroy, he never forgot that his enemy was in like passion to rend and destroy. He never rushed till he was prepared to receive a rush; never attacked till he had first defended that attack.

In vain Buck strove to sink his teeth in the neck of the big white dog. Wherever his fangs struck for the softer flesh, they were countered by the fangs of Spitz. Fang clashed fang, and lips were cut and bleeding, but Buck could not penetrate his enemy's guard. Then he warmed up and enveloped Spitz in a whirlwind of rushes. Time and time again he tried for the snow-white throat, where life bubbled near to the surface, and each time and every time Spitz slashed him and got away. Then Buck took to rushing, as though for the throat, when, suddenly drawing back his head and curving in from the side, he would drive his shoulder at the shoulder of Spitz, as a ram by which to overthrow him. But instead, Buck's shoulder was slashed down each time as Spitz leaped lightly away.

Spitz was untouched, while Buck was streaming with blood and panting hard. The fight was growing desperate. And all the while the silent and wolfish circle waited to finish off whichever dog went down. As Buck grew winded, Spitz took to rushing, and he kept him staggering for footing. Once Buck went over, and the whole circle of sixty dogs started up; but he recovered himself, almost in mid air, and the circle sank down again and waited.

But Buck possessed a quality that made for greatness — imagination. He fought by instinct, but he could fight by head as well. He rushed, as though attempting the old shoulder trick, but at the last instant swept low to the snow and in. His teeth closed on Spitz's left fore leg. There was a crunch of breaking bone, and the white dog faced him on three legs. Thrice he tried to knock him over, then repeated the trick and broke the right fore leg. Despite the pain and helplessness, Spitz struggled madly to keep up. He saw the silent circle, with gleaming eyes, lolling tongues, and silvery breaths drifting upward, closing in upon him as he had seen similar circles close in upon beaten antagonists in the past. Only this time he was the one who was beaten.

There was no hope for him. Buck was inexorable. Mercy was a thing reserved for gentler climes. He manœuvred for the final rush. The circle had tightened till he could feel the breaths of the huskies on his flanks. He could see them, beyond Spitz and to either side, half crouching for the spring, their eyes fixed upon him. A pause seemed to fall. Every animal was motionless as though turned to stone. Only Spitz quivered and bristled as he staggered back and forth, snarling with horrible menace, as though to frighten off impending death. Then Buck sprang in and out; but while he was in, shoulder had at last squarely met shoulder. The dark circle became a dot on the moon-flooded snow as Spitz disappeared from view. Buck stood and looked on, the successful champion, the dominant primordial beast who had made his kill and found it good.

CHAPTER 4

Who Has Won to Mastership

"EH? WOT I SAY? I spik true w'en I say dat Buck two devils."

This was François's speech next morning when he discovered Spitz missing and Buck covered with wounds. He drew him to the fire and by its light pointed them out.

"Dat Spitz fight lak hell," said Perrault, as he surveyed the gaping rips and cuts.

"An' dat Buck fight lak two hells," was François's answer. "An' now we make good time. No more Spitz, no more trouble, sure."

While Perrault packed the camp outfit and loaded the sled, the dog-driver proceeded to harness the dogs. Buck trotted up to the place Spitz would have occupied as leader; but François, not noticing him, brought Sol-leks to the coveted position. In his judgment, Sol-leks was the best lead-dog left. Buck sprang upon Sol-leks in a fury, driving him back and standing in his place.

"Eh? eh?" François cried, slapping his thighs gleefully.

"Look at dat Buck. Heem keel dat Spitz, heem t'ink to take de job."

"Go 'way, Chook!" he cried, but Buck refused to budge.

He took Buck by the scruff of the neck, and though the dog growled threateningly, dragged him to one side and replaced Sol-leks. The old dog did not like it, and showed plainly that he was afraid of Buck. François was obdurate, but when he turned his back Buck again displaced Sol-leks, who was not at all unwilling to go.

François was angry. "Now, by Gar, I feex you!" he cried, coming back with a heavy club in his hand.

Buck remembered the man in the red sweater, and retreated slowly; nor did he attempt to charge in when Sol-leks was once more brought forward. But he circled just beyond the range of the club, snarling with bitterness and rage; and while he circled he watched the club so as to dodge it if thrown by François, for he was become wise in the way of clubs.

The driver went about his work, and he called to Buck when he was ready to put him in his old place in front of Dave. Buck retreated two or three steps. François followed him up, whereupon he again retreated. After some time of this, François threw down the club, thinking that Buck feared a thrashing. But Buck was in open revolt. He wanted, not to escape a clubbing, but to have the leadership. It was his by right. He had earned it, and he would not be content with less.

Perrault took a hand. Between them they ran him about for the better part of an hour. They threw clubs at him. He dodged. They cursed him, and his fathers and mothers before him, and all his seed to come after him down to the remotest generation, and every hair on his body and drop of blood in his veins; and he answered curse with snarl and kept out of their reach. He did not try to run away, but retreated around and around the camp advertising plainly that when his desire was met, he would come in and be good.

François sat down and scratched his head. Perrault looked at his watch and swore. Time was flying, and they should have been on the trail an hour gone. François scratched his head again. He shook it and grinned sheepishly at the courier, who shrugged his shoulders in sign that they were beaten. Then François went up to where Sol-leks stood and called to Buck. Buck laughed, as dogs laugh, yet kept his distance. François unfastened Sol-leks's traces and put him back in his old place. The team stood harnessed to the sled in an unbroken line, ready for the trail. There was no plack for Buck save at the front. Once more François called, and once more Buck laughed and kept away.

"T'row down de club," Perrault commanded.

François complied, whereupon Buck trotted in, laughing triumphantly, and swung around into position at the head of the team. His traces were fastened, the sled broken out, and with both men running they dashed out on to the river trail.

Highly as the dog-driver had forevalued Buck, with his two devils, he found, while the day was yet young, that he had undervalued. At a bound Buck took up the duties of leadership; and where judgment was required, and quick thinking and quick acting, he showed himself the superior even of Spitz, of whom François had never seen an equal.

But it was in giving the law and making his mates live up to it, that Buck excelled. Dave and Sol-leks did not mind the change in leadership. It was none of their business. Their business was to toil, and toil mightily, in the traces. So long as that were not interfered with, they did not care what happened. Billee, the good-natured, could lead for all they cared so long as he kept order. The rest of the team, however, had grown unruly during the last days of Spitz, and their surprise was great now that Buck proceeded to lick them into shape.

Pike, who pulled at Buck's heels, and who never put an ounce more of his weight against the breast-band than he was compelled to do, was swiftly and repeatedly shaken for loafing; and ere the first day was done he was pulling more than ever before in his life. The first night in camp, Joe, the sour one, was punished roundly — a thing that Spitz had never succeeded in doing. Buck simply smothered him by virtue of superior weight, and cut him up till he ceased snapping and began to whine for mercy.

The general tone of the team picked up immediately. It recovered its old-time solidarity, and once more the dogs leaped as one dog in the traces. At the Rink Rapids two native huskies, Teek and Koona, were added; and the celerity with which Buck broke them in took away François's breath.

"Nevaire such a dog as dat Buck!" he cried. "No, nevaire! Heem worth one t'ousan' dollair, by Gar! Eh? Wot you say, Perrault?"

And Perrault nodded. He was ahead of the record then, and gaining day by day. The trail was in excellent condition, well packed and hard, and there was no new-fallen snow with which to contend. It was not too cold. The temperature dropped to fifty below zero and remained there the whole trip. The men rode and ran by turn, and the dogs were kept on the jump, with but infrequent stoppages.

The Thirty Mile River was comparatively coated with ice, and they covered in one day going out what had taken them ten days coming in. In one run they made a sixty-mile dash from the foot of Lake Le Barge to the White Horse Rapids. Across Marsh, Tagish, and Bennett (seventy miles of lakes), they flew so fast that the man whose turn it was to run towed behind the sled at the end of a rope. And on the last night of the second week they topped White Pass and dropped down the sea slope with the lights of Skaguay and of the shipping at their feet.

It was a record run. Each day for fourteen days they had averaged forty miles. For three days Perrault and François threw chests up and down the main street of Skaguay and were deluged with invitations to drink, while the team was the constant centre of a worshipful crowd of dog-busters and mushers. Then three or four western bad men aspired to clean out the town, were riddled like pepperboxes for their pains, and public interest turned to other idols. Next came official orders. François called Buck to him, threw his arms around him, wept over him. And that was the last of François and Perrault. Like other men, they passed out of Buck's life for good.

A Scotch half-breed took charge of him and his mates, and in company with a dozen other dog-teams he started back over the weary trail to Dawson. It was no light running now, nor record time, but heavy toil each day, with a heavy load behind; for this was the mail train, carrying word from the world to the men who sought gold under the shadow of the Pole.

Buck did not like it, but he bore up well to the work, taking pride in it after the manner of Dave and Sol-leks, and seeing that his mates, whether they prided in it or not, did their fair share. It was a monotonous life, operating with machine-like regularity. One day was very like another. At a certain time each morning the cooks turned out, fires were built, and breakfast was eaten. Then, while some broke camp, others harnessed the dogs, and they were under way an hour or so before the darkness fell which gave warning of dawn. At night, camp was made. Some pitched the flies, others cut firewood and pine boughs for the beds, and still others carried water or ice for the cooks. Also, the dogs were fed. To them, this was the one feature of the day, though it was good to loaf around, after the fish was eaten, for an hour or so with the other dogs, of which there were fivescore and odd. There were fierce fighters among them, but three battles with the fiercest brought Buck to mastery, so that when he bristled and showed his teeth they got out of his way.

Best of all, perhaps, he loved to lie near the fire, hind legs crouched under him, fore legs stretched out in front, head raised, and eyes blinking dreamily at the flames. Sometimes he thought of Judge Miller's big house in the sun-kissed Santa Clara Valley, and of the cement swimming-tank, and Ysabel, the Mexican hairless, and Toots, the Japanese pug; but oftener he remembered the man in the red sweater, the death of Curly, the great fight with Spitz, and the good things he had eaten or would like to eat. He was not homesick. The Sunland was very dim and distant, and such memories had no power over him. Far more potent were the memories of his heredity that gave things he had never seen before a seeming familiarity; the instincts (which were but the memories of his ancestors become habits) which had lapsed in later days, and still later in him, quickened and became alive again.

Sometimes as he crouched there, blinking dreamily at the flames, it seemed that the flames were of another fire, and that as he crouched by this other fire he saw another and different man from the half-breed cook before him. This other man was shorter of leg and longer of arm, with muscles that were stringy and knotty rather than rounded and swelling. The hair of this man was long and matted, and his head slanted back under it from the eyes. He uttered strange sounds, and seemed very much afraid of the darkness, into which he peered continually, clutching in his hand, which hung midway between knee and foot, a stick with a heavy stone made fast to the end. He was all but naked, a ragged and fire-scorched skin hanging part way down his back, but on his body there was much hair. In some places, across the chest and shoulders and down the outside of the arms and thighs, it was matted into almost a thick fur. He did not stand erect, but with trunk inclined forward from the hips, on legs that bent at the knees. About his body there was a peculiar springiness, or resiliency, almost catlike, and a quick alertness as of one who lived in perpetual fear of things seen and unseen.

At other times this hairy man squatted by the fire with head between his legs and slept. On such occasions his elbows were on his knees, his hands clasped above his head as though to shed rain by the hairy arms. And beyond that fire, in the circling darkness, Buck could see many gleaming coals, two by two, always two by two, which he knew to be the eyes of great beasts of prey. And he could hear the crashing of their bodies through the undergrowth, and the noises they made in the night. And dreaming there by the Yukon bank, with lazy eyes blinking at the fire, these sounds and sights of another world would make the hair to rise along his back and stand on end across his shoulders and up his neck, till he whimpered low and suppressedly, or growled softly, and the half-breed cook shouted at him, "Hey, you Buck, wake up!" Whereupon the other world would vanish and the real world come into his eyes, and he would get up and yawn and stretch as though he had been asleep.

It was a hard trip, with the mail behind them, and the heavy work wore them down. They were short of weight and in poor condition when they made Dawson, and should have had a ten days' or a week's rest at least. But in two days' time they dropped down the Yukon bank from the Barracks, loaded with letters for the outside. The dogs were tired, the drivers grumbling, and to make matters worse, it snowed every day. This meant a soft trail, greater friction on the runners, and heavier pulling for the dogs; yet the drivers were fair through it all, and did their best for the animals.

Each night the dogs were attended to first. They ate before the drivers ate, and no man sought his sleeping-robe till he had seen to the feet of the dogs he drove. Still, their strength went down. Since the beginning of the winter they had travelled eighteen hundred miles, dragging sleds the whole weary distance; and eighteen hundred miles will tell upon life of the toughest. Buck stood it, keeping his mates up to their work and maintaining discipline, though he too was very tired. Billee cried and whimpered regularly in his sleep each night. Joe was sourer than ever, and Sol-leks was unapproachable, blind side or other side.

But it was Dave who suffered most of all. Something had gone wrong with him. He became more morose and irritable, and when camp was pitched at once made his nest, where his driver fed him. Once out of the harness and down, he did not get on his feet again till harness-up time in the morning. Sometimes, in the traces, when jerked by a sudden stoppage of the sled, or by straining to start it, he would cry out with pain. The driver examined him, but could find nothing. All the drivers became interested in his case. They talked it over at meal-time, and over their last pipes before going to bed, and one night they held a consultation. He was brought from his nest to the fire and was pressed and prodded till he cried out many times. Something was wrong inside, but they could locate no broken bones, could not make it out.

By the time Cassiar Bar was reached, he was so weak that he was falling repeatedly in the traces. The Scotch half-breed called a halt and took him out of the team, making the next dog, Sol-leks, fast to the sled. His intention was to rest Dave, letting him run free behind the sled. Sick as he was, Dave resented being taken out, grunting and growling while the traces were unfastened, and whimpering broken-heartedly when he saw Sol-leks in the position he had held and served so long. For the pride of trace and trail was his, and sick unto death, he could not bear that another dog should do his work.

When the sled started, he floundered in the soft snow alongside the beaten trail, attacking Sol-leks with his teeth, rushing against him and trying to thrust him off into the soft snow on the other side, striving to leap inside his traces and get between him and the sled, and all the while whining and yelping and crying with grief and pain. The half-breed tried to drive him away with the whip; but he paid no heed to the stinging lash, and the man had not the heart to strike harder. Dave refused to run quietly on the trail behind the sled, where the going was easy, but continued to flounder alongside in the soft snow, where the going was most difficult, till exhausted. Then he fell, and lay where he fell, howling lugubriously as the long train of sleds churned by.

With the last remnant of his strength he managed to stagger along behind till the train made another stop, when he floundered past the sleds to his own, where he stood alongside Sol-leks. His driver lingered a moment to get a light for his pipe from the man behind. Then he returned and started his dogs. They swung out on the trail with remarkable lack of exertion, turned their heads uneasily, and stopped in surprise. The driver was surprised, too; the sled had not moved. He called his comrades to witness the sight. Dave had bitten through both of Sol-leks's traces, and was standing directly in front of the sled in his proper place.

He pleaded with his eyes to remain there. The driver was perplexed. His comrades talked of how a dog could break its heart through being denied the work that killed it, and recalled instances they had known, where dogs, too old for the toil, or injured, had died because they were cut out of the traces. Also they held it a mercy, since Dave was to die anyway, that he should die in the traces, heart-easy and content. So he was harnessed in again, and proudly he pulled as of old, though more than once he cried out involuntarily from the bite of his inward hurt. Several times he fell down and was dragged in the traces, and once the sled ran upon him so that he limped thereafter in one of his hind legs.

But he held out till camp was reached, when his driver made a place for him by the fire. Morning found him too weak to travel. At harness-up time he tried to crawl to his driver. By convulsive efforts he got on his feet, staggered, and fell. Then he wormed his way forward slowly toward where the harnesses were being put on his mates. He would advance his fore legs and drag up his body with a sort of hitching movement, when he would advance his fore legs and hitch ahead again for a few more inches. His strength left him, and the last his mates saw of him he lay gasping in the snow and yearning toward them. But they could hear him mournfully howling till they passed out of sight behind a belt of river timber.

Here the train was halted. The Scotch half-breed slowly retraced his steps to the camp they had left. The men ceased talking. A revolver-shot rang out. The man came back hurriedly. The whips snapped, the bells tinkled merrily, the sleds churned along the trail; but Buck knew, and every dog knew, what had taken place behind the belt of river trees.

CHAPTER 5

The Toil of Trace and Trail

THIRTY DAYS FROM THE TIME it left Dawson, the Salt Water Mail, with Buck and his mates at the fore, arrived at Skaguay. They were in a wretched state, worn out and worn down. Buck's one hundred and forty pounds had dwindled to one hundred and fifteen. The rest of his mates, though lighter dogs, had relatively lost more weight than he. Pike, the malingerer, who, in his lifetime of deceit, had often successfully feigned a hurt leg, was now limping in earnest. Sol-leks was limping, and Dub was suffering from a wrenched shoulder-blade.

They were all terribly footsore. No spring or rebound was left in them. Their feet fell heavily on the trail, jarring their bodies and doubling the fatigue of a day's travel. There was nothing the matter with them except that they were dead tired. It was not the dead tiredness that comes through brief and excessive effort, from which recovery is a matter of hours; but it was the dead tiredness that comes through the slow and prolonged strength drainage of months of toil. There was no power of recuperation left, no reserve strength to call upon. It had been all used, the last least bit of it. Every muscle, every fibre, every cell, was tired, dead tired. And there was reason for it. In less than five months they had travelled twenty-five hundred miles, during the last eighteen hundred of which they had had but five days' rest. When they arrived at Skaguay they were apparently on their last legs. They could barely keep the traces taut, and on the down grades just managed to keep out of the way of the sled.

"Mush on, poor sore feets," the driver encouraged them as they tottered down the main street of Skaguay. "Dis is de las'. Den we get one long res'. Eh? For sure. One bully long res'."

The drivers confidently expected a long stopover. Themselves, they had covered twelve hundred miles with two days' rest, and in the nature of reason and common justice they deserved an interval of loafing. But so many were the men who had rushed into the Klondike, and so many were the sweethearts, wives, and kin that had not rushed in, that the congested mail was taking on Alpine proportions; also, there were official orders. Fresh batches of Hudson Bay dogs were to take the places of those worthless for the trail. The worthless ones were to be got rid of, and, since dogs count for little against dollars, they were to be sold.

Three days passed, by which time Buck and his mates found how really tired and weak they were. Then, on the morning of the fourth day, two men from the States came along and bought them, harness and all, for a song. The men addressed each other as "Hal" and "Charles." Charles was a middle-aged, lightish-colored man, with weak and watery eyes and a mustache that twisted fiercely and vigorously up, giving the lie to the limply drooping lip it concealed. Hal was a youngster of nineteen or twenty, with a big Colt's revolver and a hunting-knife strapped about him on a belt that fairly bristled with cartridges. This belt was the most salient thing about him. It advertised his callowness—a callowness sheer and unutterable. Both men were manifestly out of place, and why such as they should adventure the North is part of the mystery of things that passes understanding.

Buck heard the chaffering, saw the money pass between the man and the Government agent, and knew that the Scotch half-breed and the mail-train drivers were passing out of his life on the heels of Perrault and François and the others who had gone before. When driven with his mates to the new owners' camp, Buck saw a slipshod and slovenly affair, tent half stretched, dishes unwashed, everything in disorder; also, he saw a woman. "Mercedes" the men called her. She was Charles's wife and Hal's sister—a nice family party.

Buck watched them apprehensively as they proceeded to take down the tent and load the sled. There was a great deal of effort about their manner, but no businesslike method. The tent was rolled into an awkward bundle three times as large as it should have been. The tin dishes were packed away unwashed. Mercedes continually fluttered in the way of her men and kept up an unbroken chattering of remonstrance and advice. When they put a clothes-sack on the front of the sled, she suggested it should go on the back; and when they had it put on the back, and covered it over with a couple of other bundles, she discovered overlooked articles which could abide nowhere else but in that very sack, and they unloaded again.

Three men from a neighboring tent came out and looked on, grinning and winking at one another.

"You've got a right smart load as it is," said one of them; "and it's not me should tell you your business, but I wouldn't tote that tent along if I was you."

"Undreamed of!" cried Mercedes, throwing up her hands in dainty dismay. "However in the world could I manage without a tent?"

"It's springtime, and you won't get any more cold weather," the man replied.

She shook her head decidedly, and Charles and Hal put the last odds and ends on top the mountainous load.

"Think it'll ride?" one of the men asked.

"Why shouldn't it?" Charles demanded rather shortly.

"Oh, that's all right, that's all right," the man hastened meekly to say. "I was just a-wonderin', that is all. It seemed a mite top-heavy."

Charles turned his back and drew the lashings down as well as he could, which was not in the least well.

"An' of course the dogs can hike along all day with that contraption behind them," affirmed a second of the men.

"Certainly," said Hal, with freezing politeness, taking

hold of the gee-pole with one hand and swinging his whip from the other. "Mush!" he shouted. "Mush on there!"

The dogs sprang against the breast-bands, strained hard for a few moments, then relaxed. They were unable to move the sled.

"The lazy brutes, I'll show them," he cried, preparing to lash out at them with the whip.

But Mercedes interfered, crying, "Oh, Hal, you mustn't," as she caught hold of the whip and wrenched it from him. "The poor dears! Now you must promise you won't be harsh with them for the rest of the trip, or I won't go a step."

"Precious lot you know about dogs," her brother sneered; "and I wish you'd leave me alone. They're lazy, I tell you, and you've got to whip them to get anything out of them. That's their way. You ask any one. Ask one of those men."

Mercedes looked at them imploringly, untold repugnance at sight of pain written in her pretty face.

"They're weak as water, if you want to know," came the reply from one of the men. "Plum tuckered out, that's what's the matter. They need a rest."

"Rest be blanked," said Hal, with his beardless lips; and Mercedes said, "Oh!" in pain and sorrow at the oath.

But she was a clannish creature, and rushed at once to the defence of her brother. "Never mind that man," she said pointedly. "You're driving our dogs, and you do what you think best with them."

Again Hal's whip fell upon the dogs. They threw themselves against the breast-bands, dug their feet into the packed snow, got down low to it, and put forth all their strength. The sled held as though it were an anchor. After two efforts, they stood still, panting. The whip was whistling savagely, when once more Mercedes interfered. She dropped on her knees before Buck, with tears in her eyes, and put her arms around his neck.

"You poor, poor dears," she cried sympathetically, "why don't you pull hard?—then you wouldn't be whipped." Buck did not like her, but he was feeling too miserable to resist her, taking it as part of the day's miserable work.

One of the onlookers, who had been clenching his teeth to suppress hot speech, now spoke up:—

"It's not that I care a whoop what becomes of you, but for the dogs' sakes I just want to tell you, you can help them a mighty lot by breaking out that sled. The runners are froze fast. Throw your weight against the gee-pole, right and left, and break it out."

A third time the attempt was made, but this time, following the advice, Hal broke out the runners which had been frozen to the snow. The overloaded and unwieldy sled forged ahead, Buck and his mates struggling frantically under the rain of blows. A hundred yards ahead the path turned and sloped steeply in the main street. It would have required an experienced man to keep the top-heavy sled upright, and Hal was not such a man. As they swung on the turn the sled went over, spilling half its load through the loose lashings. The dogs never stopped. The lightened sled bounded on its side behind them. They were angry because of the ill treatment they had received and the unjust load. Buck was raging. He broke into a run, the team following his lead. Hal cried "Whoa! whoa!" but they gave no heed. He tripped and was pulled off his feet. The capsized sled ground over him, and the dogs dashed on up the street, adding to the gayety of Skaguay as they scattered the remainder of the outfit along its chief thoroughfare.

Kind-hearted citizens caught the dogs and gathered up the scattered belongings. Also, they gave advice. Half the load and twice the dogs, if they ever expected to reach Dawson, was what was said. Hal and his sister and brother-in-law listened unwillingly, pitched tent, and overhauled the outfit. Canned goods were turned out that made men laugh, for canned goods on the Long Trail was a thing to dream about. "Blankets for a hotel," quoth one of the men who laughed and helped. "Half as many is too much; get rid of them. Throw away that tent, and all those dishes—who's going to wash them, anyway? Good Lord, do you think you're travelling on a Pullman?"

And so it went, the inexorable elimination of the superfluous. Mercedes cried when her clothes-bags were dumped on the ground and article after article was thrown out. She cried in general, and she cried in particular over each discarded thing. She clasped hands about knees, rocking back and forth broken-heartedly. She averred she would not go an inch, not for a dozen Charleses. She appealed to everybody and to everything, finally wiping her eyes and proceeding to cast out even articles of apparel that were imperative necessaries. And in her zeal, when she had finished with her own, she attacked the belongings of her men and went through them like a tornado.

This accomplished, the outfit, though cut in half, was still a formidable bulk. Charles and Hal went out in the evening and bought six Outside dogs. These, added to the six of the original team, and Teek and Koona, the huskies obtained at the Rink Rapids on the record trip, brought the team up to fourteen. But the Outside dogs, though practically broken in since their landing, did not amount to much. Three were short-haired pointers, one was a Newfoundland, and the other two were mongrels of indeterminate breed. They did not seem to know anything, these newcomers. Buck and his comrades looked upon them with disgust, and though he speedily taught them their places and what not to do, he could not teach them what to do. They did not take kindly to trace and trail. With the exception of the two mongrels, they were bewildered and spirit-broken by the strange savage environment in which they found themselves and by the ill treatment they had received. The two mongrels were without spirit at all; bones were the only things breakable about them.

With the newcomers hopeless and forlorn, and the old team worn out by twenty-five hundred miles of continuous trail, the outlook was anything but bright. The two men, however, were quite cheerful. And they were proud, too. They were doing the thing in style, with fourteen dogs. They had seen other sleds depart over the Pass for Dawson, or come in from Dawson, but never had they seen a sled with so many as fourteen dogs. In the nature of Arctic travel there was a reason why fourteen dogs should not drag one sled, and that was that one sled could not carry the food for fourteen dogs. But Charles and Hal did not know this. They had worked the trip out with a pencil, so much to a dog, so many dogs, so many days, Q. E. D. Mercedes looked over their shoulders and nodded comprehensively, it was all so very simple.

Late next morning Buck led the long team up the street. There was nothing lively about it, no snap or go in him and his fellows. They were starting dead weary. Four times he had covered the distance between Salt Water and Dawson, and the knowledge that, jaded and tired, he was facing the same trail once more, made him bitter. His heart was not in the work, nor was the heart of any dog. The Outsides were timid and frightened, the Insides without confidence in their masters.

Buck felt vaguely that there was no depending upon these two men and the woman. They did not know how to do anything, and as the days went by it became apparent that they could not learn. They were slack in all things, without order or discipline. It took them half the night to pitch a slovenly camp, and half the morning to break that camp and get the sled loaded in fashion so slovenly that for the rest of the day they were occupied in stopping and rearranging the load. Some days they did not make ten miles. On other days they were unable to get started at all. And on no day did they succeed in making more than half the distance used by the men as a basis in their dog-food computation.

It was inevitable that they should go short on dog-food.

But they hastened it by overfeeding, bringing the day nearer when underfeeding would commence. The Outside dogs, whose digestions had not been trained by chronic famine to make the most of little, had voracious appetites. And when, in addition to this, the worn-out huskies pulled weakly, Hal decided that the orthodox ration was too small. He doubled it. And to cap it all, when Mercedes, with tears in her pretty eyes and a quaver in her throat, could not cajole him into giving the dogs still more, she stole from the fish-sacks and fed them slyly. But it was not food that Buck and the huskies needed, but rest. And though they were making poor time, the heavy load they dragged sapped their strength severely.

Then came the underfeeding. Hal awoke one day to the fact that his dog-food was half gone and the distance only quarter covered; further, that for love or money no additional dog-food was to be obtained. So he cut down even the orthodox ration and tried to increase the day's travel. His sister and brother-in-law seconded him; but they were frustrated by their heavy outfit and their own incompetence. It was a simple matter to give the dogs less food; but it was impossible to make the dogs travel faster, while their own inability to get under way earlier in the morning prevented them from travelling longer hours. Not only did they not know how to work dogs, but they did not know how to work themselves.

The first to go was Dub. Poor blundering thief that he was, always getting caught and punished, he had none the less been a faithful worker. His wrenched shoulder-blade, untreated and unrested, went from bad to worse, till finally Hal shot him with the big Colt's revolver. It is a saying of the country that an Outside dog starves to death on the ration of the husky, so the six Outside dogs under Buck could do no less than die on half the ration of the husky. The Newfoundland went first, followed by the three short-haired pointers, the two mongrels hanging more grittily on to life, but going in the end.

By this time all the amenities and gentlenesses of the Southland had fallen away from the three people. Shorn of its glamour and romance, Arctic travel became to them a reality too harsh for their manhood and womanhood. Mercedes ceased weeping over the dogs, being too occupied with weeping over herself and with quarrelling with her husband and brother. To quarrel was the one thing they were never too weary to do. Their irritability arose out of their misery, increased with it, doubled upon it, outdistanced it. The wonderful patience of the trail which comes to men who toil hard and suffer sore, and remain sweet of speech and kindly, did not come to these two men and the woman. They had no inkling of such a patience. They were stiff and in pain; their muscles ached, their bones ached, their very hearts ached; and because of this they became sharp of speech, and hard words were first on their lips in the morning and last at night.

Charles and Hal wrangled whenever Mercedes gave them a chance. It was the cherished belief of each that he did more than his share of the work, and neither forbore to speak this belief at every opportunity. Sometimes Mercedes sided with her husband, sometimes with her brother. The result was a beautiful and unending family quarrel. Starting from a dispute as to which should chop a few sticks for the fire (a dispute which concerned only Charles and Hal), presently would be lugged in the rest of the family, fathers, mothers, uncles, cousins, people thousands of miles away, and some of them dead. That Hal's views on art, or the sort of society plays his mother's brother wrote, should have anything to do with the chopping of a few sticks of firewood, passes comprehension; nevertheless the quarrel was as likely to tend in that direction as in the direction of Charles's political prejudices. And that Charles's sister's tale-bearing tongue should be relevant to the building of a Yukon fire, was apparent only to Mercedes, who disburdened herself of copious opinions upon that topic, and incidentally upon a few other traits unpleasantly peculiar to her husband's family. In the meantime the fire remained unbuilt, the camp half pitched, and the dogs unfed.

Mercedes nursed a special grievance—the grievance of sex. She was pretty and soft, and had been chivalrously treated all her days. But the present treatment by her husband and brother was everything save chivalrous. It was her custom to be helpless. They complained. Upon which impeachment of what to her was her most essential sex-prerogative, she made their lives unendurable. She no longer considered the dogs, and because she was sore and tired, she persisted in riding on the sled. She was pretty and soft, but she weighed one hundred and twenty pounds — a lusty last straw to the load dragged by the weak and starving animals. She rode for days, till they fell in the traces and the sled stood still. Charles and Hal begged her to get off and walk, pleaded with her, entreated the while she wept and importuned Heaven with a recital of their brutality.

On one occasion they took her off the sled by main strength. They never did it again. She let her legs go limp like a spoiled child, and sat down on the trail. They went on their way, but she did not move. After they had travelled three miles they unloaded the sled, came back for her, and by main strength put her on the sled again.

In the excess of their own misery they were callous to the suffering of their animals. Hal's theory, which he practised on others, was that one must get hardened. He had started out preaching it to his sister and brother-in-law. Failing there, he hammered it into the dogs with a club. At the Five Fingers the dog-food gave out, and a toothless old squaw offered to trade them a few pounds of frozen horse-hide for the Colt's revolver that kept the big hunting-knife company at Hal's hip. A poor substitute for food was this hide, just as it had been stripped from the starved horses of the cattlemen six months back. In its frozen state it was more like strips of galvanized iron, and when a dog wrestled it into his stomach it thawed into thin and innutritious leathery strings and into a mass of short hair, irritating and indigestible.

And through it all Buck staggered along at the head of the team as in a nightmare. He pulled when he could; when he could no longer pull, he fell down and remained down till blows from whip or club drove him to his feet again. All the stiffness and gloss had gone out of his beautiful furry coat. The hair hung down, limp and draggled, or matted with dried blood where Hal's club had bruised him. His muscles had wasted away to knotty strings, and the flesh pads had disappeared, so that each rib and every bone in his frame were outlined cleanly through the loose hide that was wrinkled in folds of emptiness. It was heartbreaking, only Buck's heart was unbreakable. The man in the red sweater had proved that.

As it was with Buck, so was it with his mates. They were perambulating skeletons. There were seven all together, including him. In their very great misery they had become insensible to the bite of the lash or the bruise of the club. The pain of the beating was dull and distant, just as the things their eyes saw and their ears heard seemed dull and distant. They were not half living, or quarter living. They were simply so many bags of bones in which sparks of life fluttered faintly. When a halt was made, they dropped down in the traces like dead dogs, and the spark dimmed and paled and seemed to go out. And when the club or whip fell upon them, the spark fluttered feebly up, and they tottered to their feet and staggered on.

There came a day when Billee, the good-natured, fell and could not rise. Hal had traded off his revolver, so he took the axe and knocked Billee on the head as he lay in the traces, then cut the carcass out of the harness and dragged it to one side. Buck saw, and his mates saw, and they knew that this thing was very close to them. On the next day Koona went, and but five of them remained: Joe, too far gone to be malignant; Pike, crippled and limping, only half conscious and not conscious enough longer to malinger; Sol-leks, the one-eyed, still faithful to the toil of trace and trail, and mournful in that he had so little strength with which to pull; Teek, who had not travelled so far that winter and who was now beaten more than the others because he was fresher; and Buck, still at the head of the team, but no longer enforcing discipline or striving to enforce it, blind with weakness half the time and keeping the trail by the loom of it and by the dim feel of his feet.

It was beautiful spring weather, but neither dogs nor humans were aware of it. Each day the sun rose earlier and set later. It was dawn by three in the morning, and twilight lingered till nine at night. The whole long day was a blaze of sunshine. The ghostly winter silence had given way to the great spring murmur of awakening life. This murmur arose from all the land, fraught with the joy of living. It came from the things that lived and moved again, things which had been as dead and which had not moved during the long months of frost. The sap was rising in the pines. The willows and aspens were bursting out in young buds. Shrubs and vines were putting on fresh garbs of green. Crickets sang in the nights, and in the days all manner of creeping, crawling things rustled forth into the sun. Partridges and woodpeckers were booming and knocking in the forest. Squirrels were chattering, birds singing, and overhead honked the wild-fowl driving up from the south in cunning wedges that split the air.

From every hill slope came the trickle of running water, the music of unseen fountains. All things were thawing, bending, snapping. The Yukon was straining to break loose the ice that bound it down. It ate away from beneath; the sun ate from above. Air-holes formed, fissures sprang and spread apart, while thin sections of ice fell through bodily into the river. And amid all this bursting, rending, throbbing of awakening life, under the blazing sun and through the soft-sighing breezes, like wayfarers to death, staggered the two men, the woman, and the huskies.

With the dogs falling, Mercedes weeping and riding, Hal swearing innocuously, and Charles's eyes wistfully watering, they staggered into John Thornton's camp at the mouth of White River. When they halted, the dogs dropped down as though they had all been struck dead. Mercedes dried her eyes and looked at John Thornton. Charles sat down on a log to rest. He sat down very slowly and painstakingly, what of his great stiffness. Hal did the talking. John Thornton was whittling the last touches on an axe-handle he had made from a stick of birch. He whittled and listened, gave monosyllabic replies, and, when it was asked, terse advice. He knew the breed, and he gave his advice in the certainty that it would not be followed.

"They told us up above that the bottom was dropping out of the trail and that the best thing for us to do was to lay over," Hal said, in response to Thornton's warning to take no more chances on the rotten ice. "They told us we couldn't make White River, and here we are." This last with a sneering ring of triumph in it.

"And they told you true," John Thornton answered. "The bottom's likely to drop out at any moment. Only fools, with the blind luck of fools, could have made it. I tell you straight, I wouldn't risk my carcass on that ice for all the gold in Alaska."

"That's because you're not a fool, I suppose," said Hal. "All the same, we'll go on to Dawson." He uncoiled his whip. "Get up there, Buck! Hi! Get up there! Mush on!"

Thornton went on whittling. It was idle, he knew, to get between a fool and his folly; while two or three fools more or less would not alter the scheme of things.

But the team did not get up at the command. It had long since passed into the stage where blows were required to rouse it. The whip flashed out, here and there, on its merciless errands. John Thornton compressed his lips. Sol-leks was the first to crawl to his feet. Teek followed. Joe came next, yelping with pain. Pike made painful efforts. Twice he fell over, when half up, and on the third attempt managed to rise. Buck made no effort. He lay quietly where he had fallen. The lash bit into him again and again, but he neither whined nor struggled. Several times Thornton started, as though to speak, but changed his mind. A moisture came into his eyes, and, as the whipping continued, he arose and walked irresolutely up and down.

This was the first time Buck had failed, in itself a sufficient reason to drive Hal into a rage. He exchanged the whip for the customary club. Buck refused to move under the rain of heavier blows which now fell upon him. Like his mates, he was barely able to get up, but, unlike them, he had made up his mind not to get up. He had a vague feeling of impending doom. This had been strong upon him when he pulled in to the bank, and it had not departed from him. What of the thin and rotten ice he had felt under his feet all day, it seemed that he sensed disaster close at hand, out there ahead on the ice where his master was trying to drive him. He refused to stir. So greatly had he suffered, and so far gone was he, that the blows did not hurt much. And as they continued to fall upon him, the spark of life within flickered and went down. It was nearly out. He felt strangely numb. As though from a great distance, he was aware that he was being beaten. The last sensations of pain left him. He no longer felt anything, though very faintly he could hear the impact of the club upon his body. But it was no longer his body, it seemed so far away.

And then, suddenly, without warning, uttering a cry that was inarticulate and more like the cry of an animal, John Thornton sprang upon the man who wielded the club. Hal was hurled backward, as though struck by a falling tree. Mercedes screamed. Charles looked on wistfully, wiped his watery eyes, but did not get up because of his stiffness.

John Thornton stood over Buck, struggling to control himself, too convulsed with rage to speak.

"If you strike that dog again, I'll kill you," he at last managed to say in a choking voice.

"It's my dog," Hal replied, wiping the blood from his mouth as he came back. "Get out of my way, or I'll fix you. I'm going to Dawson."

Thornton stood between him and Buck, and evinced no intention of getting out of the way. Hal drew his long hunting-knife. Mercedes screamed, cried, laughed, and manifested the chaotic abandonment of hysteria. Thornton rapped Hal's knuckles with the axe-handle, knocking the knife to the ground. He rapped his knuckles again as he tried to pick it up. Then he stooped, picked it up himself, and with two strokes cut Buck's traces.

Hal had no fight left in him. Besides, his hands were full with his sister, or his arms, rather; while Buck was too near dead to be of further use in hauling the sled. A few minutes later they pulled out from the bank and down the river. Buck heard them go and raised his head to see. Pike was leading, Sol-leks was at the wheel, and between were Joe and Teek. They were limping and staggering. Mercedes was riding the loaded sled. Hal guided at the gee-pole, and Charles stumbled along in the rear.

As Buck watched them, Thornton knelt beside him and with rough, kindly hands searched for broken bones. By the time his search had disclosed nothing more than many bruises and a state of terrible starvation, the sled was a quarter of a mile away. Dog and man watched it crawling along over the ice. Suddenly, they saw its back end drop down, as into a rut, and the gee-pole, with Hal clinging to it, jerk into the air. Mercedes's scream came to their ears. They saw Charles turn and make one step to run back, and then a whole section of ice give way and dogs and humans disappear. A yawning hole was all that was to be seen. The bottom had dropped out of the trail.

John Thornton and Buck looked at each other.

"You poor devil," said John Thornton, and Buck licked his hand.

CHAPTER 6

For the Love of a Man

When John Thornton froze his feet in the previous December, his partners had made him comfortable and left him to get well, going on themselves up the river to get out a raft of saw-logs for Dawson. He was still limping slightly at the time he rescued Buck, but with the continued warm weather even the slight limp left him. And here, lying by the river bank through the long spring days, watching the running water, listening lazily to the songs of birds and the hum of nature, Buck slowly won back his strength.

A rest comes very good after one has travelled three thousand miles, and it must be confessed that Buck waxed lazy as his wounds healed, his muscles swelled out, and the flesh came back to cover his bones. For that matter, they were all loafing — Buck, John Thornton, and Skeet and Nig—waiting for the raft to come that was to carry them down to Dawson. Skeet was a little Irish setter who early made friends with Buck, who, in a dying condition, was unable to resent her first advances. She had the doctor trait which some dogs possess, and as a mother cat washes her kittens, so she washed and cleansed Buck's wounds. Regularly, each morning after he had finished his breakfast, she performed her self-appointed task, till he came to look for her ministrations as much as he did for Thornton's. Nig, equally friendly, though less demonstrative, was a huge black dog, half bloodhound and half deerhound, with eyes that laughed and a boundless good nature.

To Buck's surprise these dogs manifested no jealousy toward him. They seemed to share the kindliness and largeness of John Thornton. As Buck grew stronger they enticed him into all sorts of ridiculous games, in which Thornton himself could not forbear to join, and in this fashion Buck romped through his convalescence and into a new existence. Love, genuine passionate love, was his for the first time. This he had never experienced at Judge Miller's down in the sun-kissed Santa Clara Valley. With the Judge's sons, hunting and tramping, it had been a working partnership; with the Judge's grandsons, a sort of pompous guardianship; and with the Judge himself, a stately and dignified friendship. But love that was feverish and burning, that was adoration, that was madness, it had taken John Thornton to arouse.

This man had saved his life, which was something; but, further, he was the ideal master. Other men saw to the welfare of their dogs from a sense of duty and business expediency; he saw to the welfare of his as if they were his own children, because he could not help it. And he saw further. He never forgot a kindly greeting or a cheering word, and to sit down for a long talk with them ("gas" he called it) was as much his delight as theirs. He had a way of taking Buck's head roughly between his hands, and resting his own head upon Buck's, of shaking him back and forth, the while calling him ill names that to Buck were love names. Buck knew no greater joy than that rough embrace and the sound of murmured oaths, and at each jerk back and forth it seemed that his heart would be shaken out of his body so great was its ecstasy. And when, released, he sprang to his feet, his mouth laughing, his eyes eloquent, his throat vibrant with unuttered sound, and in that fashion remained without movement, John Thornton would reverently exclaim, "God! you can all but speak!"

Buck had a trick of love expression that was akin to hurt. He would often seize Thornton's hand in his mouth and close so fiercely that the flesh bore the impress of his teeth for some time afterward. And as Buck understood the oaths to be love words, so the man understood this feigned bite for a caress.

For the most part, however, Buck's love was expressed in adoration. While he went wild with happiness when Thornton touched him or spoke to him, he did not seek these tokens. Unlike Skeet, who was wont to shove her nose under Thornton's hand and nudge and nudge till petted, or Nig, who would stalk up and rest his great head on Thornton's knee, Buck was content to adore at a distance. He would lie by the hour, eager, alert, at Thornton's feet, looking up into his face, dwelling upon it, studying it, following with keenest interest each fleeting expression, every movement or change of feature. Or, as chance might have it, he would lie farther away, to the side or rear, watching the outlines of the man and the occasional movements of his body. And often, such was the communion in which they lived, the strength of Buck's gaze would draw John Thornton's head around, and he would return the gaze, without speech, his heart shining out of his eyes as Buck's heart shone out.

For a long time after his rescue, Buck did not like Thornton to get out of his sight. From the moment he left the tent to when he entered it again, Buck would follow at his heels. His transient masters since he had come into the Northland had bred in him a fear that no master could be permanent. He was afraid that Thornton would pass out of his life as Perrault and François and the Scotch half-breed had passed out. Even in the night, in his dreams, he was haunted by this fear. At such times he would shake off sleep and creep through the chill to the flap of the tent, where he would stand and listen to the sound of his master's breathing.

But in spite of this great love he bore John Thornton, which seemed to bespeak the soft civilizing influence, the strain of the primitive, which the Northland had aroused in him, remained alive and active. Faithfulness and devotion, things born of fire and roof, were his; yet he retained his wildness and wiliness. He was a thing of the wild, come in from the wild to sit by John Thornton's fire, rather than a dog of the soft Southland stamped with the marks of generations of civilization. Because of his very great love, he could not steal from this man but from any other man, in any other camp, he did not hesitate an instant; while the cunning with which he stole enabled him to escape detection.

His face and body were scored by the teeth of many dogs, and he fought as fiercely as ever and more shrewdly. Skeet and Nig were too good-natured for quarrelling — besides, they belonged to John Thornton; but the strange dog, no matter what the breed or valor, swiftly acknowledged Buck's supremacy or found himself struggling for life with a terrible antagonist. And Buck was merciless. He had learned well the law of club and fang, and he never forewent an advantage or drew back from a foe he had started on the way to Death. He had lessoned from Spitz, and from the chief fighting dogs of the police and mail, and knew there was no middle course. He must master or be mastered; while to show mercy was a weakness. Mercy did not exist in the primordial life. It was misunderstood for fear, and such misunderstandings made for death. Kill or be killed, eat or be eaten, was the law; and this mandate, down out of the depths of Time, he obeyed.

He was older than the days he had seen and the breaths he had drawn. He linked the past with the present, and the eternity behind him throbbed through him in a mighty rhythm to which he swayed as the tides and seasons swayed. He sat by John Thornton's fire, a broad-breasted dog, white-fanged and long-furred; but behind him were the shades of all manner of dogs, half-wolves and wild wolves, urgent and prompting, tasting the savor of the meat he ate, thirsting for the water he drank, scenting the wind with him, listening with him and telling him the sounds made by the wild life in the forest, dictating his moods, directing his actions, lying down to sleep with him when he lay down, and dreaming with him and beyond him and becoming themselves the stuff of his dreams.

So peremptorily did these shades beckon him, that each day mankind and the claims of mankind slipped farther from him. Deep in the forest a call was sounding, and as often as he heard this call, mysteriously thrilling and luring, he felt compelled to turn his back upon the fire and the beaten earth around it, and to plunge into the forest, and on and on, he knew not where or why; nor did he wonder where or why, the call sounding imperiously, deep in the forest. But as often as he gained the soft unbroken earth and the green shade, the love for John Thornton drew him back to the fire again.

Thornton alone held him. The rest of mankind was as nothing. Chance travellers might praise or pet him; but he was cold under it all, and from a too demonstrative man he would get up and walk away. When Thornton's partners, Hans and Pete, arrived on the long-expected raft, Buck refused to notice them till he learned they were close to Thornton; after that he tolerated them in a passive sort of way, accepting favors from them as though he favored them by accepting. They were of the same large type as Thornton, living close to the earth, thinking simply and seeing clearly; and ere they swung the raft into the big eddy by the saw-mill at Dawson, they understood Buck and his ways, and did not insist upon an intimacy such as obtained with Skeet and Nig.

For Thornton, however, his love seemed to grow and

grow. He, alone among men, could put a pack upon Buck's back in the summer travelling. Nothing was too great for Buck to do, when Thornton commanded. One day (they had grub-staked themselves from the proceeds of the raft and left Dawson for the head-waters of the Tanana) the men and dogs were sitting on the crest of a cliff which fell away, straight down, to naked bed-rock three hundred feet below. John Thornton was sitting near the edge, Buck at his shoulder. A thoughtless whim seized Thornton, and he drew the attention of Hans and Pete to the experiment he had in mind. "Jump, Buck!" he commanded, sweeping his arm out and over the chasm. The next instant he was grappling with Buck on the extreme edge, while Hans and Pete were dragging them back into safety.

"It's uncanny," Pete said, after it was over and they had caught their speech.

Thornton shook his head. "No, it is splendid, and it is terrible, too. Do you know, it sometimes makes me afraid."

"I'm not hankering to be the man that lays hands on you while he's around," Pete announced conclusively, nodding his head toward Buck.

"Py Jingo!" was Hans's contribution. "Not mineself either."

It was at Circle City, ere the year was out, that Pete's apprehensions were realized. "Black" Burton, a man evil-tempered and malicious, had been picking a quarrel with a tenderfoot at the bar, when Thornton stepped good-naturedly between. Buck, as was his custom, was lying in a corner, head on paws, watching his master's every action. Burton struck out, without warning, straight from the shoulder. Thornton was sent spinning, and saved himself from falling only by clutching the rail of the bar.

Those who were looking on heard what was neither bark nor yelp, but a something which is best described as a roar, and they saw Buck's body rise up in the air as he left the floor for Burton's throat. The man saved his life by instinctively throwing out his arm, but was hurled backward to the floor with Buck on top of him. Buck loosed his teeth from the flesh of the arm and drove in again for the throat. This time the man succeeded only in partly blocking, and his throat was torn open. Then the crowd was upon Buck, and he was driven off; but while a surgeon checked the bleeding, he prowled up and down, growling furiously, attempting to rush in, and being forced back by an array of hostile clubs. A "miners' meeting," called on the spot, decided that the dog had sufficient provocation, and Buck was discharged. But his reputation was made, and from that day his name spread through every camp in Alaska.

Later on, in the fall of the year, he saved John Thornton's life in quite another fashion. The three partners were lining a long and narrow poling-boat down a bad stretch of rapids on the Forty-Mile Creek. Hans and Pete moved along the bank, snubbing with a thin Manila rope from tree to tree, while Thornton remained in the boat, helping its descent by means of a pole, and shouting directions to the shore. Buck, on the bank, worried and anxious, kept abreast of the boat, his eyes never off his master.

At a particularly bad spot, where a ledge of barely submerged rocks jutted out into the river, Hans cast off the rope, and, while Thornton poled the boat out into the stream, ran down the bank with the end in his hand to snub the boat when it had cleared the ledge. This it did, and was flying down-stream in a current as swift as a mill-race, when Hans checked it with the rope and checked too suddenly. The boat flirted over and snubbed in to the bank, bottom up, while Thornton, flung sheer out of it, was carried down-stream toward the worst part of the rapids, a stretch of wild water in which no swimmer could live.

Buck had sprung in on the instant, and at the end of three hundred yards, amid a mad swirl of water, he overhauled Thornton. When he felt him grasp his tail, Buck headed for the bank, swimming with all his splendid strength. But the progress shoreward was slow; the progress down-stream amazingly rapid. From below came the fatal roaring where the wild current went wilder and was rent in shreds and spray by the rocks which thrust through like the teeth of an enormous comb. The suck of the water as it took the beginning of the last steep pitch was frightful, and Thornton knew that the shore was impossible. He scraped furiously over a rock, bruised across a second, and struck a third with crushing force. He clutched its slippery top with both hands, releasing Buck, and above the roar of the churning water shouted: "Go, Buck! Go!"

Buck could not hold his own, and swept on down-stream, struggling desperately, but unable to win back. When he heard Thornton's command repeated, he partly reared out of the water, throwing his head high, as though for a last look, then turned obediently toward the bank. He swam powerfully and was dragged ashore by Pete and Hans at the very point where swimming ceased to be possible and destruction began.

They knew that the time a man could cling to a slippery rock in the face of that driving current was a matter of minutes, and they ran as fast as they could up the bank to a point far above where Thornton was hanging on. They attached the line with which they had been snubbing the boat to Buck's neck and shoulders, being careful that it should neither strangle him nor impede his swimming, and launched him into the stream. He struck out boldly, but not straight enough into the stream. He discovered the mistake too late, when Thornton was abreast of him and a bare half-dozen strokes away while he was being carried helplessly past.

Hans promptly snubbed with the rope, as though Buck were a boat. The rope thus tightening on him in the sweep of the current, he was jerked under the surface, and under the surface he remained till his body struck against the bank and he was hauled out. He was half drowned, and Hans and Pete threw themselves upon him, pounding the breath into him and the water out of him. He staggered to his feet and fell down. The faint sound of Thornton's voice came to them, and though they could not make out the words of it, they knew that he was in his extremity. His master's voice acted on Buck like an electric shock. He sprang to his feet and ran up the bank ahead of the men to the point of his previous departure.

Again the rope was attached and he was launched, and again he struck out, but this time straight into the stream. He had miscalculated once, but he would not be guilty of it a second time. Hans paid out the rope, permitting no slack, while Pete kept it clear of coils. Buck held on till he was on a line straight above Thornton; then he turned, and with the speed of an express train headed down upon him. Thornton saw him coming, and, as Buck struck him like a battering ram, with the whole force of the current behind him, he reached up and closed with both arms around the shaggy neck. Hans snubbed the rope around the tree, and Buck and Thornton were jerked under the water. Strangling, suffocating, sometimes one uppermost and sometimes the other, dragging over the jagged bottom, smashing against rocks and snags, they veered in to the bank.

Thornton came to, belly downward and being violently propelled back and forth across a drift log by Hans and Pete. His first glance was for Buck, over whose limp and apparently lifeless body Nig was setting up a howl, while Skeet was licking the wet face and closed eyes. Thornton was himself bruised and battered, and he went carefully over Buck's body, when he had been brought around, finding three broken ribs.

"That settles it," he announced. "We camp right here." And camp they did, till Buck's ribs knitted and he was able to travel.

That winter, at Dawson, Buck performed another exploit, not so heroic, perhaps, but one that put his name many notches higher on the totem-pole of Alaskan fame. This exploit was particularly gratifying to the three men; for they stood in need of the outfit which it furnished, and were enabled to make a long-desired trip into the virgin East, where miners had not yet appeared. It was brought about by a conversation in the Eldorado Saloon, in which men waxed boastful of their favorite dogs. Buck, because of his record, was the target for these men, and Thornton was driven stoutly to defend him. At the end of half an hour one man stated that his dog could start a sled with five hundred pounds and walk off with it; a second bragged six hundred for his dog; and a third seven hundred.

"Pooh! pooh!" said John Thornton. "Buck can start a thousand pounds."

"And break it out? and walk off with it for a hundred yards?" demanded Matthewson, a Bonanza King, he of the seven hundred vaunt.

"And break it out, and walk off with it for a hundred yards," John Thornton said coolly.

"Well," Matthewson said, slowly and deliberately, so that all could hear, "I've got a thousand dollars that says he can't. And there it is." So saying, he slammed a sack of gold dust of the size of a bologna sausage down upon the bar.

Nobody spoke. Thornton's bluff, if bluff it was, had been called. He could feel a flush of warm blood creeping up his face. His tongue had tricked him. He did not know whether Buck could start a thousand pounds. Half a ton! The enormousness of it appalled him. He had great faith in Buck's strength and had often thought him capable of starting such a load; but never, as now, had he faced the possibility of it, the eyes of a dozen men fixed upon him, silent and waiting. Further, he had no thousand dollars; nor had Hans or Pete.

"I've got a sled standing outside now, with twenty

fifty-pound sacks of flour on it," Matthewson went on with brutal directness, "so don't let that hinder you."

Thornton did not reply. He did not know what to say. He glanced from face to face in the absent way of a man who has lost the power of thought and is seeking somewhere to find the thing that will start it going again. The face of Jim O'Brien, a Mastodon King and old-time comrade, caught his eyes. It was as a cue to him, seeming to rouse him to do what he would never have dreamed of doing.

"Can you lend me a thousand?" he asked, almost in a whisper.

"Sure," answered O'Brien, thumping down a plethoric sack by the side of Matthewson's. "Though it's little faith I'm having, John, that the beast can do the trick."

The Eldorado emptied its occupants into the street to see the test. The tables were deserted, and the dealers and gamekeepers came forth to see the outcome of the wager and to lay odds. Several hundred men, furred and mittened, banked around the sled within easy distance. Matthewson's sled, loaded with a thousand pounds of flour, had been standing for a couple of hours, and in the intense cold (it was sixty below zero) the runners had frozen fast to the hard-packed snow. Men offered odds of two to one that Buck could not budge the sled. A quibble arose concerning the phrase "break out." O'Brien contended it was Thornton's privilege to knock the runners loose, leaving Buck to "break it out" from a dead standstill. Matthewson insisted that the phrase included breaking the runners from the frozen grip of the snow. A majority of the men who had witnessed the making of the bet decided in his favor, whereat the odds went up to three to one against Buck.

There were no takers. Not a man believed him capable of the feat. Thornton had been hurried into the wager, heavy with doubt; and now that he looked at the sled itself, the concrete fact, with the regular team of ten dogs curled up in the snow before it, the more impossible the task appeared. Matthewson waxed jubilant.

"Three to one!" he proclaimed. "I'll lay you another thousand at that figure, Thornton. What d'ye say?"

Thornton's doubt was strong in his face but his fighting spirit was aroused — the fighting spirit that soars above odds, fails to recognize the impossible, and is deaf to all save the clamor for battle. He called Hans and Pete to him. Their sacks were slim, and with his own the three partners could rake together only two hundred dollars. In the ebb of their fortunes, this sum was their total capital; yet they laid it unhesitatingly against Matthewson's six hundred.

The team of ten dogs was unhitched, and Buck, with his own harness, was put into the sled. He had caught the contagion of the excitement, and he felt that in some way he must do a great thing for John Thornton. Murmurs of admiration at his splendid appearance went up. He was in perfect condition, without an ounce of superfluous flesh, and the one hundred and fifty pounds that he weighed were so many pounds of grit and virility. His furry coat shone with the sheen of silk. Down the neck and across the shoulders, his mane, in repose as it was, half bristled and seemed to lift with every movement, as though excess of vigor made each particular hair alive and active. The great breast and heavy fore legs were no more than in proportion with the rest of the body, where the muscles showed in tight rolls underneath the skin. Men felt these muscles and proclaimed them hard as iron, and the odds went down to two to one.

"Gad, sir! Gad, sir!" stuttered a member of the latest dynasty, a king of the Skookum Benches. "I offer you eight hundred for him, sir, before the test, sir; eight hundred just as he stands."

Thornton shook his head and stepped to Buck's side.

"You must stand off from him," Matthewson protested. "Free play and plenty of room."

The crowd fell silent; only could be heard the voices of the gamblers vainly offering two to one. Everybody acknowledged Buck a magnificent animal, but twenty fifty-pound sacks of flour bulked too large in their eyes for them to loosen their pouch-strings.

Thornton knelt down by Buck's side. He took his head in his two hands and rested cheek on cheek. He did not playfully shake him, as was his wont, or murmur soft love curses; but he whispered in his ear. "As you love me, Buck. As you love me," was what he whispered. Buck whined with suppressed eagerness.

The crowd was watching curiously. The affair was growing mysterious. It seemed like a conjuration. As Thornton got to his feet, Buck seized his mittened hand between his jaws, pressing in with his teeth and releasing slowly, half-reluctantly. It was the answer, in terms, not of speech, but of love. Thornton stepped well back.

"Now, Buck," he said.

Buck tightened the traces, then slacked them for a

matter of several inches. It was the way he had learned.

"Gee!" Thornton's voice rang out, sharp in the tense silence.

Buck swung to the right, ending the movement in a plunge that took up the slack and with a sudden jerk arrested his one hundred and fifty pounds. The load quivered, and from under the runners arose a crisp crackling.

"Haw!" Thornton commanded.

Buck duplicated the manœuvre, this time to the left. The crackling turned into a snapping, the sled pivoting and the runners slipping and grating several inches to the side. The sled was broken out. Men were holding their breaths, intensely unconscious of the fact.

"Now, MUSH!"

Thornton's command cracked out like a pistol-shot. Buck threw himself forward, tightening the traces with a jarring lunge. His whole body was gathered compactly together in the tremendous effort, the muscles writhing and knotting like live things under the silky fur. His great chest was low to the ground, his head forward and down, while his feet were flying like mad, the claws scarring the hard-packed snow in parallel grooves. The sled swayed and trembled, half-started forward. One of his feet slipped, and one man groaned aloud. Then the sled lurched ahead in what appeared a rapid succession of jerks, though it never really came to a dead stop again . . . half an inch . . . an inch . . . two inches. . . . The jerks perceptibly diminished; as the sled gained momentum, he caught them up, till it was moving steadily along.

Men gasped and began to breathe again, unaware that for a moment they had ceased to breathe. Thornton was running behind, encouraging Buck with short, cheery words. The distance had been measured off, and as he neared the pile of firewood which marked the end of the hundred yards, a cheer began to grow and grow, which burst into a roar as he passed the firewood and halted at command. Every man was tearing himself loose, even Matthewson. Hats and mittens were flying in the air. Men were shaking hands, it did not matter with whom, and bubbling over in a general incoherent babel.

But Thornton fell on his knees beside Buck. Head was against head, and he was shaking him back and forth. Those who hurried up heard him cursing Buck, and he cursed him long and fervently, and softly and lovingly.

"Gad, sir! Gad, sir!" spluttered the Skookum Bench king. "I'll give you a thousand for him, sir, a thousand, sir — twelve hundred, sir."

Thornton rose to his feet. His eyes were wet. The tears were streaming frankly down his cheeks. "Sir," he said to the Skookum Bench king, "no, sir. You can go to hell, sir. It's the best I can do for you, sir."

Buck seized Thornton's hand in his teeth. Thornton shook him back and forth. As though animated by a common impulse, the onlookers drew back to a respectful distance; nor were they again indiscreet enough to interrupt.

CHAPTER 7

The Sounding of the Call

WHEN BUCK EARNED sixteen hundred dollars in five minutes for John Thornton, he made it possible for his master to pay off certain debts and to journey with his partners into the East after a fabled lost mine, the history of which was as old as the history of the country. Many men had sought it; few had found it; and more than a few there were who had never returned from the quest. This lost mine was steeped in tragedy and shrouded in mystery. No one knew of the first man. The oldest tradition stopped before it got back to him. From the beginning there had been an ancient and ramshackle cabin. Dying men had sworn to it, and to the mine the site of which it marked, clinching their testimony with nuggets that were unlike any known grade of gold in the Northland.

But no living man had looted this treasure house, and the dead were dead; wherefore John Thornton and Pete and Hans, with Buck and half a dozen other dogs, faced into the East on an unknown trail to achieve where men and dogs as good as themselves had failed. They sledded seventy miles up the Yukon, swung to the left into the Stewart River, passed the Mayo and the McQuestion, and held on until the Stewart itself became a streamlet, threading the upstanding peaks which marked the backbone of the continent.

John Thornton asked little of man or nature. He was unafraid of the wild. With a handful of salt and a rifle he could plunge into the wilderness and fare wherever he pleased and as long as he pleased. Being in no haste, Indian fashion, he hunted his dinner in the course of the day's travel; and if he failed to find it, like the Indian, he kept on traveling, secure in the knowledge that sooner or later he would come to it. So, on this great journey into the East, straight meat was the bill of fare, ammunition and tools principally made up the load on the sled, and the time card was drawn upon the limitless future.

To Buck it was boundless delight, this hunting, fishing, and indefinite wandering through strange places. For weeks at a time they would hold on steadily, day after day, and for weeks upon end they would camp, here and there, the dogs loafing and the men burning holes through frozen muck and gravel and washing countless pans of dirt by the heat of the fire. Sometimes they went hungry, sometimes they feasted riotously, all according to the abundance of game and the fortune of hunting. Summer arrived, and dogs and men packed on their backs, rafted across blue mountain lakes, and descended or ascended unknown rivers in slender boats whipsawed from the standing forest.

The months came and went, and back and forth they

twisted through the uncharted vastness, where no men were and yet where men had been if the Lost Cabin were true. They went across divides in summer blizzards, shivered under the midnight sun on naked mountains between the timber line and the eternal snows, dropped into summer valleys amid swarming gnats and flies, and in the shadows of glaciers picked strawberries and flowers as ripe and fair as any the Southland could boast. In the fall of the year they penetrated a weird lake country, sad and silent, where wild fowl had been, but where then there was no life nor sign of life — only the blowing of chill winds, the forming of ice in sheltered places, and the melancholy rippling of waves on lonely beaches.

And through another winter they wandered on the obliterated trails of men who had gone before. Once, they came upon a path blazed through the forest, an ancient path, and the Lost Cabin seemed very near. But the path began nowhere and ended nowhere, and it remained mystery, as the man who made it and the reason he made it remained mystery. Another time they chanced upon the time-graven wreckage of a hunting lodge, and amid the shreds of rotted blankets John Thornton found a long-barreled flintlock. He knew it for a Hudson's Bay Company gun of the young days in the Northwest, when such a gun was worth its height in beaver skins packed flat. And that was all — no hint as to the man who in an early day had reared the lodge and left the gun among the blankets.

Spring came on once more, and at the end of all their wandering they found, not the Lost Cabin, but a shallow placer in a broad valley where the gold showed like yellow butter across the bottom of the washing pan. They sought no farther. Each day they worked earned them thousands of dollars in clean dust and nuggets, and they worked every day. The gold was sacked in moose-hide bags, fifty pounds to the bag, and piled like so much firewood outside the spruce-bough lodge. Like giants they toiled, days flashing on the heels of days like dreams as they heaped the treasure up.

There was nothing for the dogs to do, save the hauling in of meat now and again that Thornton killed, and Buck spent long hours musing by the fire. The vision of the short-legged hairy man came to him more frequently, now that there was little work to be done; and often, blinking by the fire, Buck wandered with him in that other world which he remembered.

The salient thing of this other world seemed fear. When he watched the hairy man sleeping by the fire, head between his knees and hands clasped above, Buck saw that he slept restlessly, with many starts and awakenings, at which times he would peer fearfully into the darkness and fling more wood upon the fire. Did they walk by the beach of a sea, where the hairy man gathered shellfish and ate them as he gathered, it was with eyes that roved everywhere for hidden danger and with legs prepared to run like the wind at its first appearance. Through the forest they crept noiselessly, Buck at the hairy man's heels; and they were alert and vigilant, the pair of them, ears twitching and moving and nostrils quivering, for the man heard and smelled as keenly as Buck. The hairy man could spring up into the trees and travel ahead as fast as on the ground, swinging by the arms from limb to limb, sometimes a dozen feet apart, letting go and catching, never falling, never missing his grip. In fact, he seemed as much at home among the trees as on the ground; and Buck had memories of nights of vigil spent beneath trees wherein the hairy man roosted, holding on tightly as he slept.

And closely akin to the visions of the hairy man was the call still sounding in the depths of the forest. It filled him with a great unrest and strange desires. It caused him to feel a vague, sweet gladness, and he was aware of wild yearnings and stirrings for he knew not what. Sometimes he pursued the call into the forest, looking for it as though it were a tangible thing, barking softly or defiantly, as the mood might dictate. He would thrust his nose into the cool wood moss, or into the black soil where long grasses grew, and snort with joy at the fat earth smells; or he would crouch for hours, as if in concealment, behind fungus-covered trunks of fallen trees, wide-eyed and wide-eared to all that moved and sounded about him. It might be, lying thus, that he hoped to surprise this call he could not understand. But he did not know why he did these various things. He was impelled to do them, and did not reason about them at all.

Irresistible impulses seized him. He would be lying in camp, dozing lazily in the heat of the day, when suddenly his head would lift and his ears cock up, intent and listening, and he would spring to his feet and dash away, and on and on, for hours, through the forest aisles and across the open spaces where the niggerheads bunched. He loved to run down dry watercourses, and to creep and spy upon the bird life in the woods. For a day at a time he would lie in the underbrush where he could watch the partridges drumming and strutting up and down. But especially he loved to run in the dim twilight of the summer midnights, listening to the subdued and sleepy murmurs of the forest, reading signs and sounds as man may read a book, and seeking for the mysterious something that called — called, waking or sleeping, at all times, for him to come.

One night he sprang from sleep with a start, eager-eyed, nostrils quivering and scenting, his mane bristling in recurrent waves. From the forest came the call (or one note of it, for the call was many noted), distinct and definite as never before — a long-drawn howl, like, yet unlike, any noise made by husky dog. And he knew it, in the old familiar way, as a sound heard before. He sprang through the sleeping camp and in swift silence dashed through the woods. As he drew closer to the cry he went more slowly, with caution in every movement, till he came to an open place among the trees, and looking out saw, erect on haunches, with nose pointed to the sky, a long, lean, timber wolf.

He had made no noise, yet it ceased from its howling and tried to sense his presence. Buck stalked into the open, half crouching, body gathered compactly together, tail straight and stiff, feet falling with unwonted care. Every movement advertised commingled threatening and overture of friendliness. It was the menacing truce that marks the meeting of wild beasts that prey. But the wolf fled at sight of him. He followed, with wild leapings, in a frenzy to overtake. He ran him into a blind channel, in the bed of the creek, where a timber jam barred the way.

The wolf whirled about, pivoting on his hind legs after the fashion of Joe and of all cornered husky dogs, snarling and bristling, clipping his teeth together in a continuous and rapid succession of snaps.

Buck did not attack, but circled him about and hedged him in with friendly advances. The wolf was suspicious and afraid; for Buck made three of him in weight, while his head barely reached Buck's shoulder. Watching his chance, he darted away, and the chase was resumed. Time and again he was cornered and the thing repeated, though he was in poor condition or Buck could not so easily have overtaken him. He would run till Buck's head was even with his flank, when he would whirl around at bay, only to dash away again at the first opportunity.

But in the end Buck's pertinacity was rewarded; for the wolf, finding that no harm was intended, finally sniffed noses with him. Then they became friendly, and played about in the nervous, half-coy way with which fierce beasts belie their fierceness. After some time of this the wolf started off at an easy lope in a manner that plainly showed he was going somewhere. He made it clear to Buck that he was to come, and they ran side by side through the sombre twilight, straight up the creek bed, into the gorge from which it issued, and across the bleak divide where it took its rise.

On the opposite slope of the watershed they came down into a level country where were great stretches of forest and many streams, and through these great stretches they ran steadily, hour after hour, the sun rising higher and the day growing warmer. Buck was wildly glad. He knew he was at last answering the call, running by the side of his wood brother toward the place from where the call surely came. Old memories were coming upon him fast, and he was stirring to them as of old he stirred to the realities of which they were the shadows. He had done this thing before, somewhere in that other and dimly remembered world, and he was doing it again, now, running free in the open, the unpacked earth underfoot, the wide sky overhead.

They stopped by a running stream to drink, and, stopping, Buck remembered John Thornton. He sat down. The wolf started on toward the place from where the call surely came, then returned to him, sniffing noses and making actions as though to encourage him. But Buck turned about and started slowly on the back track. For the better part of an hour the wild brother ran by his side, whining softly. Then he sat down, pointed his nose upward, and howled. It was a mournful howl, and as Buck held steadily on his way he heard it grow faint and fainter until it was lost in the distance.

John Thornton was eating dinner when Buck dashed into camp and sprang upon him in a frenzy of affection, overturning him, scrambling upon him, licking his face, biting his hand—"playing the general tomfool," as John Thornton characterized it, the while he shook Buck back and forth and cursed him lovingly.

For two days and nights Buck never left camp, never let Thornton out of his sight. He followed him about at his work, watched him while he ate, saw him into his blankets at night and out of them in the morning. But after two days the call in the forest began to sound more imperiously than ever. Buck's restlessness came back on him, and he was haunted by recollections of the wild brother, and of the smiling land beyond the divide and the run side by side through the wide forest stretches. Once again he took to wandering in the woods, but the wild brother came no more; and though he listened through long vigils, the mournful howl was never raised.

He began to sleep out at night, staying away from camp for days at a time; and once he crossed the divide at the head of the creek and went down into the land of timber and streams. There he wandered for a week, seeking vainly for fresh sign of the wild brother, killing his meat as he traveled and traveling with the long, easy lope that seems never to tire. He fished for salmon in a broad stream that emptied somewhere into the sea, and by this stream he killed a large black bear, blinded by the mosquitoes while likewise fishing, and raging through the forest helpless and terrible. Even so, it was a hard fight, and it aroused the last latent remnants of Buck's ferocity. And two days later, when he returned to his kill and found a dozen wolverines quarreling over the spoil, he scattered them like chaff; and those that fled left two behind who would quarrel no more.

The blood-longing became stronger than ever before. He was a killer, a thing that preyed, living on the things that lived, unaided, alone, by virtue of his own strength and prowess, surviving triumphantly in a hostile environment where only the strong survived. Because of all this he became possessed of a great pride in himself, which communicated itself like a contagion to his physical being. It advertised itself in all his movements, was apparent in the play of every muscle, spoke plainly as speech in the way he carried himself, and made his glorious furry coat if anything more glorious. But for the stray brown on his muzzle and above his eyes, and for the splash of white hair that ran midmost down his chest, he might well have been mistaken for a gigantic wolf, larger than the largest of the breed. From his St. Bernard father he had inherited size and weight, but it was his shepherd mother who had given shape to that size and weight. His muzzle was the long wolf muzzle, save that it was larger than the muzzle of any wolf; and his head, somewhat broader, was the wolf head on a massive scale.

His cunning was wolf cunning, and wild cunning; his intelligence, shepherd intelligence and St. Bernard intelligence; and all this, plus an experience gained in the fiercest of schools, made him as formidable a creature as any that roamed the wild. A carnivorous animal, living on a straight meat diet, he was in full flower, at the high tide of his life, overspilling with vigor and virility. When Thornton passed a caressing hand along his back, a snapping and crackling followed the hand, each hair discharging its pent magnetism at the contact. Every part, brain and body, nerve tissue and fiber, was keyed to the most exquisite pitch; and between all the parts there was a perfect equilibrium or adjustment. To sights and sounds and events which required action, he responded with lightninglike rapidity. Quickly as a husky dog could leap to defend from attack or to attack, he could leap twice as quickly. He saw the movement, or heard sound, and responded in less time than another dog required to compass the mere seeing or hearing. He perceived and determined and responded in the same instant. In point of fact the three actions of perceiving, determining, and responding were sequential; but so infinitesmal were the intervals of time between them that they appeared simultaneous. His muscles were surcharged with vitality, and snapped into play sharply, like steel springs. Life streamed through him in splendid flood, glad and rampant, until it seemed that it would burst him asunder in sheer ecstasy and pour forth generously over the world.

"Never was there such a dog," said John Thornton one day, as the partners watched Buck marching out of camp.

"When he was made, the mold was broke," said Pete.

"Py jingo! I t'ink so mineself," Hans affirmed.

They saw him marching out of camp, but they did not see the instant and terrible transformation which took place as soon as he was within the secrecy of the forest. He no longer marched. At once he became a thing of the wild, stealing along softly, catfooted, a passing shadow that appeared and disappeared among the shadows. He knew how to take advantage of every cover, to crawl on his belly like a snake, and like a snake to leap and strike. He could take a ptarmigan from its nest, kill a rabbit as it slept, and snap in mid-air the little chipmunks fleeing a second too late for the trees. Fish, in open pools, were not too quick for him; nor were beaver, mending their dams, too wary. He killed to eat, not from wantonness; but he preferred to eat what he killed himself. So a lurking humor ran through his deeds, and it was his delight to steal upon the squirrels, and, when he all but had them, to let them go, chattering in mortal fear to the treetops.

As the fall of the year came on, the moose appeared in greater abundance, moving slowly down to meet the winter in the lower and less rigorous valleys. Buck had already dragged down a stray part-grown calf; but he wished strongly for larger and more formidable quarry, and he came upon it one day on the divide at the head of the creek. A band of twenty moose had crossed over from the land of streams and timber, and chief among them was a great bull. He was in a savage temper, and, standing over six feet from the ground, was as formidable an antagonist as ever Buck could desire. Back and forth the bull tossed his great palmated antlers, branching to fourteen points and embracing seven feet within the tips. His small eyes burned with a vicious and bitter light, while he roared with fury at sight of Buck.

From the bull's side, just forward of the flank, protruded a feathered arrow end, which accounted for his savageness. Guided by that instinct which came from the old hunting days of the primordial world, Buck proceeded to cut the bull out from the herd. It was no slight task. He would bark and dance about in front of the bull, just out of reach of the great antlers and of the terrible splay hoofs which could have stamped his life out with a single blow. Unable to turn his back on the fanged danger and go on, the bull would be driven into paroxysms of rage. At such moments he charged Buck, who retreated craftily, luring him on by a simulated inability to escape. But when he was thus separated from his fellows, two or three of the younger bulls would charge back upon Buck and enable the wounded bull to rejoin the herd.

There is a patience of the wild — dogged, tireless, persistent as life itself — that holds motionless for endless hours the spider in its web, the snake in its coils, the panther in its ambuscade; this patience belongs peculiarly to life when it hunts its living food; and it belonged to Buck as he clung to the flank of the herd, retarding its march, irritating the young bulls, worrying the cows with their half-grown calves, and driving the wounded bull mad with helpless rage. For half a day this continued. Buck multiplied himself, attacking from all sides, enveloping the herd in a whirlwind of menace, cutting out his victim as fast as it could rejoin its mates, wearing out the patience of creatures preyed upon, which is a lesser patience than that of creatures preying.

As the day wore along and the sun dropped to its bed in the northwest (the darkness had come back and the fall nights were six hours long), the young bulls retraced their steps more and more reluctantly to the aid of their beset leader. The down-coming winter was harrying them on to the lower levels, and it seemed they could never shake off this tireless creature that held them back. Besides, it was not the life of the herd, or of the young bulls, that was threatened. The life of only one member was demanded, which was a remoter interest than their lives, and in the end they were content to pay the toll.

As twilight fell the old bull stood with lowered head, watching his mates — the cows he had known, the calves he had fathered, the bulls he had mastered — as they shambled on at a rapid pace through the fading light. He could not follow, for before his nose leaped the merciless fanged terror that would not let him go. Three hundredweight more than half a ton he weighed; he had lived a long, strong life, full of fight and struggle, and at the end he faced death at the teeth of a creature whose head did not reach beyond his great knuckled knees.

From then on, night and day, Buck never left his prey, never gave it a moment's rest, never permitted it to browse the leaves of trees or the shoots of young birch and willow. Nor did he give the wounded bull opportunity to slake his burning thirst in the slender trickling streams they crossed. Often, in desperation, he burst into long stretches of flight. At such times Buck did not attempt to stay him, but loped easily at his heels, satisfied with the way the game was played, lying down when the moose stood still, attacking him fiercely when he strove to eat or drink.

The great head drooped more and more under its trees of horns, and the shambling trot grew weaker and weaker. He took to standing for long periods, with nose to the ground and dejected ears dropped limply; and Buck found more time in which to get water for himself and in which to rest. At such moments, panting with red lolling tongue and with eyes fixed upon the big bull, it appeared to Buck that a change was coming over the face of things. He could feel a new stir in the land. As the moose were coming into the land, other kinds of life were coming in. Forest and stream and air seemed palpitant with their presence. The news of it was borne in upon him, not by sight or sound, or smell, but by some other and subtler sense. He heard nothing, saw nothing, yet knew that the land was somehow different; that through it strange things were afoot and ranging; and he resolved to investigate after he had finished the business in hand.

At last, at the end of the fourth day, he pulled the great

moose down. For a day and a night he remained by the kill, eating and sleeping, turn and turn about. Then, rested, refreshed and strong, he turned his face toward camp and John Thornton. He broke into the long easy lope, and went on, hour after hour, never at loss for the tangled way, heading straight home through strange country with a certitude of direction that put man and his magnetic needle to shame.

As he held on he became more and more conscious of the new stir in the land. There was life abroad in it different from the life which had been there throughout the summer. No longer was this fact borne in upon him in some subtle, mysterious way. The birds talked of it, the squirrels chattered about it, the very breeze whispered of it. Several times he stopped and drew in the fresh morning air in great sniffs, reading a message which made him leap on with greater speed. He was oppressed with a sense of calamity happening if it were not calamity already happened; and as he crossed the last watershed and dropped down into the valley toward camp, he proceeded with greater caution.

Three miles away he came upon a fresh trail that sent his neck hair rippling and bristling. It led straight toward camp and John Thornton. Buck hurried on, swiftly and stealthily, every nerve straining and tense, alert to the multitudinous details which told a story — all but the end. His nose gave him a varying description of the passage of the life on the heels of which he was travelling. He remarked the pregnant silence of the forest. The bird life had flitted. The squirrels were in hiding. One only he saw – a sleek gray fellow, flattened against a gray dead limb so that he seemed a part of it, a woody excrescence upon the wood itself.

As Buck slid along with the obscureness of a gliding shadow, his nose was jerked suddenly to the side as though a positive force had gripped and pulled it. He followed the new scent into a thicket and found Nig. He was lying on his side, dead where he had dragged himself, an arrow protruding, head and feathers, from either side of his body.

A hundred yards farther on, Buck came upon one of the sled dogs Thornton had bought in Dawson. This dog was thrashing about in a death struggle, directly on the trail, and Buck passed around him without stopping. From the camp came the faint sound of many voices, rising and falling in a singsong chant. Bellying forward to the edge of the clearing, he found Hans, lying on his face, feathered with arrows like a porcupine. At the same instant Buck peered out where the spruce-bough lodge had been and saw what made his hair leap straight up on his neck and shoulders. A gust of overpowering rage swept over him. He did not know that he growled, but he growled aloud with a terrible ferocity. For the last time in his life he allowed passion to usurp cunning and reason, and it was because of his great love for John Thornton that he lost his head.

The Yeehats were dancing about the wreckage of the spruce-bough lodge when they heard a fearful roaring and saw rushing upon them an animal the like of which they had never seen before. It was Buck, a live hurricane of fury, hurling himself upon them in a frenzy to destroy. He sprang at the foremost man (it was the chief of the

Yeehats), ripping the throat wide open till the rent jugular spouted a fountain of blood. He did not pause to worry the victim, but ripped in passing, with the next bound tearing wide the throat of a second man. There was no withstanding him. He plunged about in their very midst, tearing, rending, destroying, in constant and terrific motion which defied the arrows they discharged at him. In fact, so inconceivably rapid were his movements, and so closely were the Indians tangled together, that they shot one another with the arrows; and one young hunter, hurling a spear at Buck in mid-air, drove it through the chest of another hunter with such force that the point broke through the skin of the back and stood out beyond. Then a panic seized the Yeehats, and they fled in terror to the woods, proclaiming as they fled the advent of the Evil Spirit.

And truly Buck was the Fiend incarnate raging at their heels and dragging them down like deer as they raced through the trees. It was a fateful day for the Yeehats. They scattered far and wide over the country, and it was not till a week later that the last of the survivors gathered together in a lower valley and counted their losses. As for Buck, wearying of the pursuit, he returned to the desolated camp. He found Pete where he had been killed in his blankets in the first moment of surprise. Thornton's desperate struggle was fresh-written on the earth, and Buck scented every detail of it down to the edge of a deep pool. By the edge, head and fore feet in the water, lay Skeet, faithful to the last. The pool itself, muddy and discolored from the sluice boxes, effectually hid what it contained, and it contained John Thornton; for Buck followed his trace into the water, from which no trace led away.

All day Buck brooded by the pool or roamed restlessly about the camp. Death, as a cessation of movement, as a passing out and away from the lives of the living, he knew, and he knew John Thornton was dead. It left a great void in him, somewhat akin to hunger, but a void which ached and ached, and which food could not fill. At times, when he paused to contemplate the carcasses of the Yeehats, he forgot the pain of it; and at such times he was aware of a great pride in himself — a pride greater than any he had yet experienced. He had killed man, the noblest game of all, and he had killed in the face of the law of club and fang. He sniffed the bodies curiously. They had died so easily. It was harder to kill a husky dog than them. They were no match at all, were it not for their arrows and spears and clubs. Thenceforward he would be unafraid of them except when they bore in their hands their arrows, spears, and clubs.

Night came on and a full moon rose high over the trees into the sky, lighting the land till it lay bathed in ghostly day. And with the coming of the night, brooding and mourning by the pool, Buck became alive to a stirring of the new life in the forest other than that which the Yeehats had made. He stood up, listening and scenting. From far away drifted a faint, sharp yelp, followed by a chorus of similar sharp yelps. As the moments passed the yelps grew closer and louder. Again Buck knew them as things heard in that other world which persisted in his memory. He walked to the center of the open space and listened. It was the call, the many noted call, sounding more luringly and compelling than ever before. And as never before, he was ready to obey. John Thornton was dead. The last tie was broken. Man and the claims of man no longer bound him.

Hunting their living meat, as the Yeehats were hunting it, on the flanks of the migrating moose, the wolf pack had at last crossed over from the land of streams and timber and invaded Buck's valley. Into the clearing where the moonlight streamed, they poured in a silvery flood; and in the center of the clearing stood Buck, motionless as a statue, waiting their coming. They were awed, so still and large he stood, and a moment's pause fell, till the boldest one leaped straight for him. Like a flash Buck struck, breaking the neck. Then he stood, without movement as before, the stricken wolf rolling in agony behind him. Three others tried it in sharp succession; and one after the other they drew back, streaming blood from slashed throats or shoulders.

This was sufficient to fling the whole pack forward, pell-mell, crowded together, blocked and confused by its eagerness to pull down the prey. Buck's marvelous quickness and agility stood him in good stead. Pivoting on his hind legs, and snapping and gashing, he was everywhere at once, presenting a front which was apparently unbroken, so swiftly did he whirl and guard from side to side. But to prevent them from getting behind him, he was forced back, down past the pool and into the creek bed, till he brought up against a high gravel bank. He worked along to a right angle in the bank which the men had made in the course of mining, and in this angle he came to bay, protected on three sides and with nothing to do but face the front.

And so well did he face it, that at the end of half an hour the wolves drew back discomfited. The tongues of all were out and lolling, the white fangs showing cruelly white in the moonlight. Some were lying down with heads raised and ears pricked forward; others stood on their feet, watching him; and still others were lapping water from the pool. One wolf, long and lean and gray, advanced cautiously, in a friendly manner, and Buck recognized the wild brother with whom he had run for a night and a day. He was whining softly, and, as Buck whined, they touched noses.

Then an old wolf, gaunt and battle-scarred, came forward. Buck writhed his lips into the preliminary of a snarl, but sniffed noses with him. Whereupon the old wolf sat down, pointed nose at the moon, and broke out the long wolf howl. The others sat down and howled. And now the call came to Buck in unmistakable accents. He, too, sat down and howled. This over, he came out of his angle and the pack crowded around him, sniffing in half-friendly, half-savage manner. The leaders lifted the yelp of the pack and sprang away into the woods. The wolves swung in behind, yelping in chorus. And Buck ran with them, side by side with the wild brother, yelping as he ran.

And here may well end the story of Buck. The years were not many when the Yeehats noted a change in the breed of timber wolves; for some were seen with splashes of brown on head and muzzle, and with a rift of white centering down the chest. But more remarkable than this, the Yeehats tell of a Ghost Dog that runs at the head of the pack. They are afraid of this Ghost Dog, for it has cunning greater than they, stealing from their camps in fierce winters, robbing their traps, slaying their dogs, and defying the bravest hunters.

Nay, the tale grows worse. Hunters there are who fail to return to the camp, and hunters there have been whom their tribesmen found with throats slashed cruelly open and with wolf prints about them in the snow greater than the prints of any wolf. Each fall, when the Yeehats follow the movement of the moose, there is a certain valley which they never enter. And women there are who become sad when the word goes over the fire of how the Evil Spirit came to select that valley for an abiding place.

In the summers there is one visitor, however, to that valley, of which the Yeehats do not know. It is a great, gloriously coated wolf, like, and yet unlike, all other wolves. He crosses alone from the smiling timber land and comes down into an open space among the trees. Here a yellow stream flows from rotted moose-hide sacks and sinks into the ground, with long grasses growing through it and vegetable mould overrunning it and hiding its yellow from the sun; and here he muses for a time, howling once, long and mournfully, ere he departs.

But he is not always alone. When the long winter nights come on and the wolves follow their meat into the lower valleys, he may be seen running at the head of the pack through the pale moonlight or glimmering borealis, leaping gigantic above his fellows, his great throat a-bellow as he sings a song of the younger world, which is the song of the pack.

PART TWO

The Cruise of the Dazzler

CONTENTS

CHAPTER 1

Brother and Sister

THEY RAN ACROSS the shining sand, the Pacific thundering its long surge at their backs, and when they gained the roadway leaped upon bicycles and dived at faster pace into the green avenues of the park. There were three of them, three boys, in as many bright-colored sweaters, and they "scorched" along the cycle path as dangerously near the speed limit as is the custom of boys in bright-colored sweaters to go. They may have exceeded the speed limit. A mounted park policeman thought so, but was not sure, and contented himself with cautioning them as they flashed by. They acknowledged the warning promptly, and on the next turn of the path as promptly forgot it, which is also a custom of boys in bright-colored sweaters.

Shooting out through the entrance to Golden Gate Park, they turned into San Francisco, and took the long sweep of the descending hills at a rate that caused pedestrians to turn and watch them anxiously. Through the city streets the bright sweaters flew, turning and twisting to escape climbing the steeper hills, and, when the steep hills were unavoidable, doing stunts to see which would first gain the top.

The boy who more often hit up the pace, led the scorching, and instituted the stunts was called Joe by his companions. It was "follow the leader," and he led, the merriest and boldest in the bunch. But as they pedaled into the Western Addition, among the large and comfortable residences, his laughter became less loud and frequent, and he unconsciously lagged in the rear. At Laguna and Vallejo streets his companions turned off to the right.

"So long, Fred," he called as he turned his wheel to the left. "So long, Charley."

"See you tonight!" they called back.

"No — I can't come," he answered.

"Aw, come on," they begged.

"No, I've got to dig. So long!"

As he went on alone, his face grew grave and a vague worry came into his eyes. He began resolutely to whistle, but this dwindled away till it was a thin and very subdued little sound, which ceased altogether as he rode up the driveway to a large two-storied house.

"Oh, Joe!"

He hesitated before the door to the library. Bessie was there, he knew, studiously working up her lessons. She must be nearly through with them, too, for she was always done before dinner, and dinner could not be many minutes away. As for his lessons, they were as yet untouched. The thought made him angry. It was bad enough to have one's sister — and two years younger at that — in the same grade, but to have her continually head and shoulders above him in scholarship was a most intolerable thing. Not that he was dull. No one knew better than himself that he was not dull. But somehow — he did not quite know how — his mind was on other things and he was usually unprepared.

"Joe—please come here." There was the slightest possible plaintive note in her voice this time.

"Well?" he said, thrusting aside the portière with an impetuous movement.

He said it gruffly, but he was half sorry for it the next instant when he saw a slender little girl regarding him with wistful eyes across the big reading table heaped with books. She was curled up, with pencil and pad, in an easy chair of such generous dimensions that it made her seem more delicate and fragile than she really was.

"What is it, Sis?" he asked more gently, crossing over to her side.

She took his hand in hers and pressed it against her cheek, and as he stood beside her came closer to him with a nestling movement.

"What is the matter, Joe dear?" she asked softly. "Won't you tell me?"

He remained silent. It struck him as ridiculous to confess his troubles to a little sister, even if her reports *were* higher than his. And the little sister struck him as ridiculous to demand his troubles of him. "What a soft cheek she has!" he thought as she pressed her face gently against his hand. If he could but tear himself away—it was all so foolish! Only he might hurt her feelings, and, in his experience, girls' feelings were very easily hurt.

She opened his fingers and kissed the palm of his hand. It was like a rose leaf falling; it was also her way of asking her question over again.

"Nothing's the matter," he said decisively. And then, quite inconsistently, he blurted out, "Father!"

His worry was now in her eyes. "But father is so good and kind, Joe," she began. "Why don't you try to please him? He doesn't ask much of you, and it's all for your own good. It's not as though you were a fool, like some boys. If you would only study a little bit—"

"That's it! Lecturing!" he exploded, tearing his hand roughly away. "Even you are beginning to lecture me now. I suppose the cook and the stableboy will be at it next."

He shoved his hands into his pockets and looked forward into a melancholy and desolate future filled with interminable lectures and lecturers innumerable.

"Was that what you wanted me for?" he demanded, turning to go.

She caught at his hand again. "No, it wasn't; only you looked so worried that I thought—I—" Her voice broke, and she began again freshly. "What I wanted to tell you was that we're planning a trip across the bay to Oakland, next Saturday, for a tramp in the hills."

"Who's going?"

"Myrtle Hayes—"

"What! That little softy?" he interrupted.

"I don't think she is a softy," Bessie answered with spirit. "She's one of the sweetest girls I know."

"Which isn't saying much, considering the girls you know. But go on. Who are the others?"

"Pearl Sayther, and her sister Alice, and Jessie Hilborn, and Sadie French, and Edna Crothers. That's all the girls."

Joe sniffed disdainfully. "Who are the fellows, then?"

"Maurice and Felix Clement, Dick Schofield, Burt Layton, and—"

"That's enough. Milk-and-water chaps, all of them."

"I—I wanted to ask you and Fred and Charley," she said in a quavering voice. "That's what I called you in for—to ask you to come."

"And what are you going to do?" he asked.

"Walk, gather wild flowers — the poppies are all out now — eat luncheon at some nice place, and — and —"

"Come home," he finished for her.

Bessie nodded her head. Joe put his hands in his pockets again, and walked up and down.

"A sissy outfit, that's what it is," he said abruptly; "and a sissy program. None of it for me, please."

She tightened her trembling lips and struggled on bravely. "What would you rather do?" she asked.

"I'd sooner take Fred and Charley and go off somewhere and do something—well, anything."

He paused and looked at her. She was waiting patiently for him to proceed. He was aware of his inability to express in words what he felt and wanted, and all his trouble and general dissatisfaction rose up and gripped hold of him.

"Oh, you can't understand!" he burst out. "You can't understand. You're a girl. You like to be prim and neat, and to be good in deportment and ahead in your studies. You don't care for danger and adventure and such things, and you don't care for boys who are rough, and have life and go in them, and all that. You like good little boys in white collars, with collars always clean and hair always combed, who like to stay in at recess and be petted by the teacher and told how they're always up in their studies; nice little boys who never get into scrapes—who are too busy walking around and picking flowers and eating lunches with girls, to get into scrapes. Oh, I know the kind—afraid of their own shadows, and no more spunk in them than in so many sheep. That's what they are—sheep. Well, I'm not a sheep, and there's no more to be said. And I don't want to go on your picnic, and, what's more, I'm not going."

The tears welled up in Bessie's brown eyes, and her lips were trembling. This angered him unreasonably. What were girls good for, anyway?—always blubbering, and interfering, and carrying on. There was no sense in them.

"A fellow can't say anything without making you cry," he began, trying to appease her. "Why, I didn't mean anything, Sis. I didn't, sure. I—"

He paused helplessly and looked down at her. She was sobbing, and at the same time shaking with the effort to control her sobs, while big tears were rolling down her cheeks.

"Oh, you—you girls!" he cried, and strode wrathfully out of the room.

CHAPTER 2

"The Draconian Reforms"

A FEW MINUTES LATER, and still wrathful, Joe went in to dinner. He ate silently, though his father and mother and Bessie kept up a genial flow of conversation. There she was, he communed savagely with his plate, crying one minute, and the next all smiles and laughter. Now that wasn't his way. If *he* had anything sufficiently important to cry about, rest assured he wouldn't get over it for days. Girls were hypocrites, that was all there was to it. They didn't feel one hundredth part of all that they said when they cried. It stood to reason that they didn't. It must be that they just carried on because they enjoyed it. It made them feel good to make other people miserable, especially boys. That was why they were always interfering.

Thus reflecting sagely, he kept his eyes on his plate and did justice to the fare; for one cannot scorch from the Cliff House to the Western Addition via the park without being guilty of a healthy appetite.

Now and then his father directed a glance at him in a certain mildly anxious way. Joe did not see these glances, but Bessie saw them, every one. Mr. Bronson was a middle-aged man, well developed and of heavy build, though not fat. His was a rugged face, square-jawed and stern-featured, though his eyes were kindly and there were lines about the mouth that betokened laughter rather than severity. A close examination was not required to discover the resemblance between him and Joe. The same broad forehead and strong jaw characterized them both, and the eyes, taking into consideration the difference of age, were as like as peas from one pod.

"How are you getting on, Joe?" Mr. Bronson asked finally. Dinner was over and they were about to leave the table.

"Oh, I don't know," Joe answered carelessly, and then added: "We have examinations tomorrow. I'll know then."

"Whither bound?" his mother questioned, as he turned to leave the room. She was a slender, willowy woman, whose brown eyes Bessie's were, and likewise her tender ways.

"To my room," Joe answered. "To work," he supplemented.

She rumpled his hair affectionately, and bent and kissed him. Mr. Bronson smiled approval at him as he went out, and he hurried up the stairs, resolved to dig hard and pass the examinations of the coming day.

Entering his room, he locked the door and sat down at a desk most comfortably arranged for a boy's study. He ran his eye over his textbooks. The history examination came the first thing in the morning, so he would begin on that. He opened the book where a page was turned down, and began to read:

> Shortly after the Draconian reforms, a war broke out between Athens and Megara respecting the island of Salamis, to which both cities laid claim.

That was easy; but what were the Draconian reforms? He must look them up. He felt quite studious as he ran over the back pages, till he chanced to raise his eyes above the top of the book and saw on a chair a baseball mask and a catcher's glove. They shouldn't have lost that game last Saturday, he thought, and they wouldn't have, either, if it hadn't been for Fred. He wished Fred wouldn't fumble so. He could hold a hundred difficult balls in succession, but when a critical point came, he'd let go of even a dewdrop. He'd have to send him out in the field and bring in Jones to first base. Only Jones was so excitable. He could hold any kind of a ball, no matter how critical the play was, but there was no telling what he would do with the ball after he got it.

Joe came to himself with a start. A pretty way of studying history! He buried his head in his book and began:

> Shortly after the Draconian reforms —

He read the sentence through three times, and then recollected that he had not looked up the Draconian reforms.

A knock came at the door. He turned the pages over with a noisy flutter, but made no answer.

The knock was repeated, and Bessie's "Joe, dear" came to his ears.

"What do you want?" he demanded. But before she could answer he hurried on: "No admittance. I'm busy."

"I came to see if I could help you," she pleaded. "I'm all done, and I thought—"

"Of course you're all done!" he shouted. "You always are!"

He held his head in both his hands to keep his eyes on the book. But the baseball mask bothered him. The more he attempted to keep his mind on the history the more in his mind's eye he saw the mask resting on the chair and all the games in which it had ever played its part.

This would never do. He deliberately placed the book face downward on the desk and walked over to the chair. With a swift sweep he sent both mask and glove hurtling under the bed, and so violently that he heard the mask rebound from the wall.

> Shortly after the Draconian reforms, a war broke out between Athens and Megara —

The mask had rolled back from the wall. He wondered if it had rolled back far enough for him to see it. No, he wouldn't look. What did it matter if it had rolled out? That wasn't history. He wondered—

He peered over the top of the book, and there was the mask peeping out at him from under the edge of the bed. This was not to be borne. There was no use attempting to study while that mask was around. He went over and fished it out, crossed the room to the closet, and tossed it inside, then locked the door. That was settled, thank goodness! Now he could do some work.

He sat down again.

> Shortly after the Draconian reforms, a war broke out between Athens and Megara respecting the island of Salamis, to which both cities laid claim.

Which was all very well, if he had only found out what the Draconian reforms were. A soft glow pervaded the room, and he suddenly became aware of it. What could cause it? He looked out of the window. The setting sun was slanting its long rays against low-hanging masses of summer clouds, turning them to warm scarlet and rosy red; and it was from them that the red light, mellow and glowing, was flung earthward.

His gaze dropped from the clouds to the bay beneath. The sea breeze was dying down with the day, and off Fort Point a fishing boat was creeping into port before the last light breeze. A little beyond, a tug was sending up a twisted pillar of smoke as it towed a three-masted schooner to sea. His eyes wandered over toward the Marin County shore. The line where land and water met was already in darkness, and long shadows were creeping up the hills toward Mount Tamalpais, which was sharply silhouetted against the western sky.

Oh, if he, Joe Bronson, were only on that fishing boat and sailing in with a deep-sea catch! Or if he were on that schooner, heading out into the sunset, into the world! That was life, that was living, doing something and being something in the world. And, instead, here he was, pent up in a close room, racking his brains about people dead and gone thousands of years before he was born. He jerked himself away from the window as though held there by some physical force, and resolutely carried his chair and history into the farthest corner of the room, where he sat down with his back to the window.

An instant later, so it seemed to him, he found himself again staring out of the window and dreaming. How he had got there he did not know. His last recollection was the finding of a subheading in a page on the right-hand side of the book which read: "The Laws and Constitution of Draco." And then, evidently like walking in one's sleep, he had come to the window. How long had he been there? he wondered. The fishing boat which he had seen off Fort Point was now crawling into Meiggs's Wharf. This denoted nearly an hour's lapse of time. The sun had long since set; a solemn grayness was brooding over the water, and the first faint stars were beginning to twinkle over the crest of Mount Tamalpais.

He turned, with a sigh, to go back into his corner, when a long whistle, shrill and piercing, came to his ears. That was Fred. He sighed again. The whistle repeated itself. Then another whistle joined it. They were waiting on the corner—lucky fellows!

Well, they wouldn't see him this night. Both whistles arose in duet. He writhed in his chair and groaned. No, they wouldn't see him this night, he reiterated, at the same time rising to his feet. It was certainly impossible for him to join them when he had not yet learned about the Draconian reforms. The same force which had held him to the window now seemed drawing him across the room to the desk. It made him put the history on top of his schoolbooks, and he had the door unlocked and was halfway into the hall before he realized it. He started to return, but the thought came to him that he could go out for a little while and then come back and do his work.

A very little while, he promised himself, as he went downstairs. He went down faster and faster, till at the bottom he was going three steps at a time. He popped his cap on his head and went out of the side entrance in a rush; and ere he reached the corner the reforms of Draco were as far away in the past as Draco himself, while the examinations on the morrow were equally far away in the future.

CHAPTER 3

"Brick," "Sorrel-Top" and "Reddy"

"WHAT'S UP?" Joe asked, as he joined Fred and Charley.

"Kites," Charley answered. "Come on. We're tired out waiting for you."

The three set off down the street to the brow of the hill, where they looked down upon Union Street, far below and almost under their feet. This they called the Pit, and it was well named. Themselves they called the Hill-dwellers, and a descent into the Pit by the Hill-dwellers was looked upon by them as a great adventure.

Scientific kiteflying was one of the keenest pleasures of these three particular Hill-dwellers, and six or eight kites strung out on a mile of twine and soaring into the clouds was an ordinary achievement for them. They were compelled to replenish their kite supply often; for whenever an accident occurred, and the string broke, or a ducking kite dragged down the rest, or the wind suddenly died out, their kites fell into the Pit, from which place they were unrecoverable. The reason for this was the young people of the Pit were a piratical and robber race with peculiar ideas of ownership and property rights.

On a day following an accident to a kite of one of the Hill-dwellers, the selfsame kite could be seen riding the air attached to a string which led down into the Pit to the lairs of the Pit People. So it came about that the Pit People, who were a poor folk and unable to afford scientific kiteflying, developed great proficiency in the art when their neighbors the Hill-dwellers took it up.

There was also an old sailorman who profited by this recreation of the Hill-dwellers; for he was learned in sails and air currents, and being deft of hand and cunning, he fashioned the best-flying kites that could be obtained. He lived in a rattletrap shanty close to the water, where he could still watch with dim eyes the ebb and flow of the tide, and the ships pass out and in, and where he could revive old memories of the days when he, too, went down to the sea in ships.

To reach his shanty from the Hill one had to pass through the Pit, and thither the three boys were bound. They had often gone for kites in the daytime, but this was their first trip after dark, and they felt it to be, as it indeed was, a hazardous adventure.

In simple words, the Pit was merely the cramped and narrow quarters of the poor, where many nationalities crowded together in cosmopolitan confusion, and lived as best they could, amid much dirt and squalor. It was still early evening when the boys passed through on their way to the sailorman's shanty, and no mishap befell them, though some of the Pit boys stared at them savagely and hurled a taunting remark after them, now and then.

The sailorman made kites which were not only splendid fliers but which folded up and were very convenient to carry. Each of the boys bought a few, and, with them wrapped in compact bundles and under their arms, started back on the return journey.

"Keep a sharp lookout for the b'ys," the kitemaker cautioned them. "They're like to be cruisin' round after dark."

"We're not afraid," Charley assured him; "and we know how to take care of ourselves."

Used to the broad and quiet streets of the Hill, the boys were shocked and stunned by the life that teemed in the close-packed quarter. It seemed some thick and monstrous growth of vegetation, and that they were wading through it. They shrank closely together in the tangle of narrow streets as though for protection, conscious of the strangeness of it all, and how unrelated they were to it.

Children and babies sprawled on the sidewalk and under their feet. Bareheaded and unkempt women gossiped in the doorways or passed back and forth with scant marketings in their arms. There was a general odor of decaying fruit and fish, a smell of staleness and putridity. Big hulking men slouched by, and ragged little girls walked gingerly through the confusion with foaming buckets of beer in their hands. There was a clatter and garble of foreign tongues and brogues, shrill cries, quarrels and wrangles, and the Pit pulsed with a great and steady murmur, like the hum of the human hive that it was.

"Phew! I'll be glad when we're out of it," Fred said. He spoke in a whisper, and Joe and Charley nodded grimly that they agreed with him. They were not inclined to speech, and they walked as rapidly as the crowd permitted, with much the same feelings as those of travelers in a dangerous and hostile jungle.

And danger and hostility stalked in the Pit. The inhabitants seemed to resent the presence of these strangers from the Hill. Dirty little urchins abused them as they passed, snarling with assumed bravery, and prepared to run away at the first sign of attack. And still other little urchins formed a noisy parade at the heels of the boys, and grew bolder with increasing numbers.

"Don't mind them," Joe cautioned. "Take no notice, but keep right on. We'll soon be out of it."

"No, we're in for it," said Fred, in an undertone. "Look there!"

On the corner they were approaching, four or five boys of about their own age were standing. The light from a street lamp fell upon them and disclosed one with vivid red hair. It could be no other than "Brick" Simpson, the redoubtable leader of a redoubtable gang. Twice within their memory he had led his gang up the Hill and spread panic and terror among the Hill-dwelling young folk, who fled wildly to their homes, while their fathers and mothers hurriedly telephoned for the police.

At sight of the group on the corner, the rabble at the heels of the three boys melted away on the instant with like manifestations of fear. This but increased the anxiety of the boys, though they held boldly on their way.

The red-haired boy detached himself from the group,

and stepped before them, blocking their path. They essayed to go around him, but he stretched out his arm.

"Wot yer doin' here?" he snarled. "Why don't yer stay where yer b'long?"

"We're just going home," Fred said mildly.

Brick looked at Joe. "Wot yer got under yer arm?" he demanded.

Joe contained himself and took no heed of him. "Come on," he said to Fred and Charley, at the same time starting to brush past the gang leader.

But with a quick blow Brick Simpson struck him in the face, and with equal quickness snatched the bundle of kites from under his arm.

Joe uttered an inarticulate cry of rage, and, all caution flung to the winds, sprang at his assailant.

This was evidently a surprise to the gang leader, who expected least of all to be attacked in his own territory. He retreated backward, still clutching the kites, and divided between desire to fight and desire to retain his capture.

The latter desire dominated him, and he turned and fled swiftly down the narrow side street into a labyrinth of streets and alleys. Joe knew that he was plunging into the wilderness of the enemy's country, but his sense of both property and pride had been offended, and he took up the pursuit hotfooted.

Fred and Charley followed after, though he outdistanced them, and behind came the three other members of the gang, emitting a whistling call while they ran which was evidently intended for the assembling of the rest of the band. As the chase proceeded, these whistles were answered from many different directions, and soon a score of dark figures were tagging at the heels of Fred and Charley, who, in turn, were straining every muscle to keep the swifter-footed Joe in sight.

Brick Simpson darted into a vacant lot, aiming for a "slip," as such things are called which are prearranged passages through fences and over sheds and houses and around dark holes and corners, where the unfamiliar pursuer must go more carefully and where the chances are many that he will soon lose the track.

But Joe caught Brick before he could attain his end, and together they rolled over and over in the dirt, locked in each other's arms. By the time Fred and Charley and the gang had come up, they were on their feet, facing each other. "Wot d' ye want, eh?" the redheaded gang-leader was saying in a bullying tone. "Wot d' ye want? That's wot I wanter know."

"I want my kites," Joe answered.

Brick Simpson's eyes sparkled at the intelligence. Kites were something he stood in need of himself.

"Then you've got to fight fer 'em," he announced.

"Why should I fight for them?" Joe demanded indignantly. "They're mine." Which went to show how ignorant he was of the ideas of ownership and property rights which obtained among the People of the Pit.

A chorus of jeers and catcalls went up from the gang, which clustered behind its leader like a pack of wolves.

"Why should I fight for them?" Joe reiterated.

" 'Cos I say so," Simpson replied. "An' wot I say goes. Understand?"

But Joe did not understand. He refused to understand

that Brick Simpson's word was law in San Francisco, or any part of San Francisco. His love of honesty and right dealing was offended, and all his fighting blood was up.

"You give those kites to me, right here and now," he threatened, reaching out his hand for them.

But Simpson jerked them away. "D' ye know who I am?" he demanded. "I'm Brick Simpson, an' I don't 'low no one to talk to me in that tone of voice."

"Better leave him alone," Charley whispered in Joe's ear. "What are a few kites? Leave him alone and let's get out of this."

"They're my kites," Joe said slowly in a dogged manner. "They're my kites, and I'm going to have them."

"You can't fight the crowd," Fred interfered; "and if you do get the best of him they'll all pile on you."

The gang, observing this whispered colloquy, and mistaking it for hesitancy on the part of Joe, set up its wolflike howling again.

"Afraid! afraid!" the young roughs jeered and taunted. "He's too high-toned, he is! Mebbe he'll spoil his nice clean shirt, and then what 'll mama say?"

"Shut up!" their leader snapped authoritatively, and the noise obediently died away.

"Will you give me those kites?" Joe demanded, advancing determinedly.

"Will you fight for 'em?" was Simpson's counterdemand.

"Yes," Joe answered.

"Fight! fight!" the gang began to howl again.

"And it's me that'll see fair play," said a man's heavy voice.

All eyes were instantly turned upon the man who had

approached unseen and made this announcement. By the electric light, shining brightly on them from the corner, they made him out to be a big, muscular fellow, clad in a working-man's garments. His feet were incased in heavy brogans, a narrow strap of black leather held his overalls about his waist, and a black and greasy cap was on his head. His face was grimed with coal dust, and a coarse blue shirt, open at the neck, revealed a wide throat and massive chest.

"An' who're you?" Simpson snarled, angry at the interruption.

"None of yer business," the newcomer retorted tartly. "But, if it'll do you any good, I'm a fireman on the China steamers, and, as I said, I'm goin' to see fair play: That's my business. Your business is to give fair play. So pitch in, and don't be all night about it."

The three boys were as pleased by the appearance of the fireman as Simpson and his followers were displeased. They conferred together for several minutes when Simpson deposited the bundle of kites in the arms of one of his gang and stepped forward.

"Come on, then," he said, at the same time pulling off his coat.

Joe handed his to Fred, and sprang toward Brick. They put up their fists and faced each other. Almost instantly Simpson drove in a fierce blow and ducked cleverly away and out of reach of the blow which Joe returned. Joe felt a sudden respect for the abilities of his antagonist, but the only effect upon him was to arouse all the doggedness of his nature and make him utterly determined to win.

Awed by the presence of the fireman, Simpson's followers confined themselves to cheering Brick and jeering Joe. The two boys circled round and round, attacking, feinting, and guarding, and now one and then the other getting in a telling blow. Their positions were in marked contrast. Joe stood erect, planted solidly on his feet, with legs wide apart and head up. On the other hand, Simpson crouched till his head was nearly lost between his shoulders, and all the while he was in constant motion, leaping and springing and manœuvering in the execution of a score or more of tricks quite new and strange to Joe.

At the end of a quarter of an hour, both were very tired, though Joe was much fresher. Tobacco, ill food, and unhealthy living were telling on the gang leader, who was panting and sobbing for breath. Though at first (and because of superior skill) he had severely punished Joe, he was now weak and his blows were without force. Growing desperate, he adopted what might be called not an unfair but a mean method of attack: he would manœuver, leap in and strike swiftly, and then, ducking forward, fall to the ground at Joe's feet. Joe could not strike him while he was down, and so would step back until he could get on his feet again, when the thing would be repeated.

But Joe grew tired of this, and prepared for him. Timing his blow with Simpson's attack, he delivered it just as Simpson was ducking forward to fall. Simpson fell, but he fell over on one side, whither he had been driven by the impact of Joe's fist upon his head. He rolled over and got halfway to his feet, where he remained, crying and gasping. His followers called upon him to get up, and he tried once or twice, but was too exhausted and stunned.

"I give in," he said. "I'm licked."

The gang had become silent and depressed at its leader's defeat.

Joe stepped forward.

"I'll trouble you for those kites," he said to the boy who was holding them.

"Oh, I dunno," said another member of the gang, shoving in between Joe and his property. His hair was also a vivid red. "You've got to lick me before you kin have 'em."

"I don't see that," Joe said bluntly. "I've fought and I've won, and there's nothing more to it."

"Oh, yes, there is," said the other. "I'm 'Sorrel-top' Simpson. Brick's my brother. See?"

And so, in this fashion, Joe learned another custom of the Pit People of which he had been ignorant.

"All right," he said, his fighting blood more fully aroused than ever by the unjustness of the proceeding. "Come on."

Sorrel-top Simpson, a year younger than his brother, proved to be a most unfair fighter, and the good-natured fireman was compelled to interfere several times before the second of the Simpson clan lay on the ground and acknowledged defeat.

This time Joe reached for his kites without the slightest doubt that he was to get them. But still another lad stepped in between him and his property. The telltale hair, vividly red, sprouted likewise on this lad's head, and Joe knew him at once for what he was, another member of the Simpson clan. He was a younger edition of his brothers, somewhat less heavily built, with a face covered with a vast quantity of freckles, which showed plainly under the electric light.

"You don't git them there kites till you git me," he

challenged in a piping little voice. "I'm 'Reddy' Simpson, an' you ain't licked the fambly till you've licked me."

The gang cheered admiringly, and Reddy stripped a tattered jacket preparatory for the fray.

"Git ready," he said to Joe.

Joe's knuckles were torn, his nose was bleeding, his lip was cut and swollen, while his shirt had been ripped down from throat to waist. Further, he was tired, and breathing hard.

"How many more are there of you Simpsons?" he asked. "I've got to get home, and if your family's much larger this thing is liable to keep on all night."

"I'm the last an' the best," Reddy replied. "You gits me an' you gits the kites. Sure."

"All right," Joe sighed. "Come on."

While the youngest of the clan lacked the strength and skill of his elders, he made up for it by a wildcat manner of fighting that taxed Joe severely. Time and again it seemed to him that he must give in to the little whirlwind; but each time he pulled himself together and went doggedly on. For he felt that he was fighting for principle, as his forefathers had fought for principle; also, it seemed to him that the honor of the Hill was at stake, and that he, as its representative, could do nothing less than his very best.

So he held on and managed to endure his opponent's swift and continuous rushes till that young and less experienced person at last wore himself out with his own exertions, and from the ground confessed that, for the first time in its history, the "Simpson fambly was beat."

CHAPTER 4

The Biter Bitten

BUT LIFE IN THE PIT at best was a precarious affair, as the three Hill-dwellers were quickly to learn. Before Joe could even possess himself of his kites, his astonished eyes were greeted with the spectacle of all his enemies, the fireman included, taking to their heels in wild flight. As the little girls and urchins had melted away before the Simpson gang, so was melting away the Simpson gang before some new and correspondingly awe-inspiring group of predatory creatures.

Joe heard terrified cries of "Fish gang!" "Fish gang!" from those who fled, and he would have fled himself from this new danger, only he was breathless from his last encounter, and knew the impossibility of escaping whatever threatened. Fred and Charley felt mighty longings to run away from a danger great enough to frighten the redoubtable Simpson gang and the valorous fireman, but they could not desert their comrade.

Dark forms broke into the vacant lot, some surrounding

the boys and others dashing after the fugitives. That the laggards were overtaken was evidenced by the cries of distress that went up, and when later the pursuers returned, they brought with them the luckless and snarling Brick, still clinging fast to the bundle of kites.

Joe looked curiously at this latest band of marauders. They were young men of from seventeen and eighteen to twenty-three and -four years of age, and bore the unmistakable stamp of the hoodlum class. There were vicious faces among them — faces so vicious as to make Joe's flesh creep as he looked at them. A couple grasped him tightly by the arms, and Fred and Charley were similarly held captive.

"Look here, you," said one who spoke with the authority of leader, "we've got to inquire into this. Wot's be'n goin' on here? Wot're you up to, Redhead? Wot you be'n doin'?"

"Ain't be'n doin' nothin'," Simpson whined.

"Looks like it." The leader turned up Brick's face to the electric light. "Who's been paintin' you up like that?" he demanded.

Brick pointed at Joe, who was forthwith dragged to the front.

"Wot was you scrappin' about?"

"Kites — my kites," Joe spoke up boldly. "That fellow tried to take them away from me. He's got them under his arm now."

"Oh, he has, has he? Look here, you Brick, we don't put up with stealin' in this territory. See? You never rightly owned nothin'. Come, fork over the kites. Last call."

The leader tightened his grasp threateningly, and Simpson, weeping tears of rage, surrendered the plunder.

"Wot yer got under yer arm?" the leader demanded abruptly of Fred, at the same time jerking out the bundle. "More kites, eh? Reg'lar kite factory gone and got itself lost," he remarked finally, when he had appropriated Charley's bundle. "Now, wot I wants to know is wot we 're goin' to do to you t'ree chaps?" he continued in a judicial tone.

"What for?" Joe demanded hotly. "For being robbed of our kites?"

"Not at all, not at all," the leader responded politely; "but for luggin' kites round these quarters an' causin' all this unseemly disturbance. It's disgraceful; that's wot it is — disgraceful."

At this juncture, when the Hill-dwellers were the center of attraction, Brick suddenly wormed out of his jacket, squirmed away from his captors, and dashed across the lot to the slip for which he had been originally headed when overtaken by Joe. Two or three of the gang shot over the fence after him in noisy pursuit. There was much barking and howling of back-yard dogs and clattering of shoes over sheds and boxes. Then there came a splashing of water, as though a barrel of it had been precipitated to the ground. Several minutes later the pursuers returned, very sheepish and very wet from the deluge presented them by the wily Brick, whose voice, high up in the air from some friendly housetop, could be heard defiantly jeering them.

This event apparently disconcerted the leader of the

gang, and just as he turned to Joe and Fred and Charley, a long and peculiar whistle came to their ears from the street — the warning signal, evidently, of a scout posted to keep a lookout. The next moment the scout himself came flying back to the main body, which was already beginning to retreat.

"Cops!" he panted.

Joe looked, and he saw two helmeted policemen approaching, with bright stars shining on their breasts.

"Let's get out of this," he whispered to Fred and Charley.

The gang had already taken to flight, and they blocked the boys' retreat in one quarter, and in another they saw the policemen advancing. So they took to their heels in the direction of Brick Simpson's slip, the policemen hot after them and yelling bravely for them to halt.

But young feet are nimble, and young feet when frightened become something more than nimble, and the boys were first over the fence and plunging wildly through a maze of back yards. They soon found that the policemen were discreet. Evidently they had had experiences in slips, and they were satisfied to give over the chase at the first fence.

No street lamps shed their light here, and the boys blundered along through the blackness with their hearts in their mouths. In one yard, filled with mountains of crates and fruit boxes, they were lost for a quarter of an hour. Feel and quest about as they would, they encountered nothing but endless heaps of boxes. From this wilderness they finally emerged by way of a shed roof, only to fall into another yard, cumbered with countless empty chicken coops.

Farther on they came upon the contrivance which had soaked Brick Simpson's pursuers with water. It was a cunning arrangement. Where the slip led through a fence with a board missing, a long slat was so arranged that the ignorant wayfarer could not fail to strike against it. This slat was the spring of the trap. A light touch upon it was sufficient to disconnect a heavy stone from a barrel perched overhead and nicely balanced. The disconnecting of the stone permitted the barrel to turn over and spill its contents on the one beneath who touched the slat.

The boys examined the arrangement with keen appreciation. Luckily for them, the barrel was overturned, or they too would have received a ducking, for Joe, who was in advance, had blundered against the slat.

"I wonder if this is Simpson's back yard?" he queried softly.

"It must be," Fred concluded, "or else the back yard of some member of his gang."

Charley put his hands warningly on both their arms.

"Hist! What's that?" he whispered.

They crouched down on the ground. Not far away was the sound of someone moving about. Then they heard a noise of falling water, as from a faucet into a bucket. This was followed by steps boldly approaching. They crouched lower, breathless with apprehension.

A dark form passed by within arm's reach and mounted on a box to the fence. It was Brick himself, resetting the trap. They heard him arrange the slat and stone, then right the barrel and empty into it a couple of buckets of water. As he came down from the box to go after more water, Joe sprang upon him, tripped him up, and held him to the ground.

"Don't make any noise," he said. "I want you to listen to me."

"Oh, it's you, is it?" Simpson replied, with such obvious relief in his voice as to make them feel relieved also. "Wot d' ye want here?"

"We want to get out of here," Joe said, "and the shortest way's the best. There's three of us, and you're only one—"

"That's all right, that's all right," the gang leader interrupted. "I'd just as soon show you the way out as not. I ain't got nothin' 'gainst you. Come on an' follow me, an' don't step to the side, an' I'll have you out in no time."

Several minutes later they dropped from the top of a high fence into a dark alley.

"Follow this to the street," Simpson directed; "turn to the right two blocks, turn to the right again for three, an' yer on Union. Tra-la-loo."

They said good-by, and as they started down the alley received the following advice:

"Nex' time you bring kites along, you'd best leave 'em to home."

CHAPTER 5

Home Again

FOLLOWING Brick Simpson's directions, they came into Union Street, and without further mishap gained the Hill. From the brow they looked down into the Pit, whence arose that steady, indefinable hum which comes from crowded human places.

"I'll never go down there again, not as long as I live," Fred said with a great deal of savagery in his voice. "I wonder what became of the fireman."

"We're lucky to get back with whole skins," Joe cheered them philosophically.

"I guess we left our share, and you more than yours," laughed Charley.

"Yes," Joe answered. "And I've got more trouble to face when I get home. Good night, fellows."

As he expected, the door on the side porch was locked, and he went around to the dining room and entered like a burglar through a window. As he crossed the wide hall, walking softly toward the stairs, his father came out of the library. The surprise was mutual, and each halted aghast.

Joe felt a hysterical desire to laugh, for he thought that he knew precisely how he looked. In reality he looked far worse than he imagined. What Mr. Bronson saw was a boy with hat and coat covered with dirt, his whole face smeared with the stains of conflict, and, in particular, a badly swollen nose, a bruised eyebrow, a cut and swollen lip, a scratched cheek, knuckles still bleeding, and a shirt torn open from throat to waist.

"What does this mean, sir?" Mr. Bronson finally managed to articulate.

Joe stood speechless. How could he tell, in one brief sentence, all the whole night's happenings? — for all that must be included in his explanation of what his luckless disarray meant.

"Have you lost your tongue?" Mr. Bronson demanded with an appearance of impatience.

"I've—I've—"

"Yes, yes," his father encouraged.

"I've—well, I've been down in the Pit," Joe succeeded in blurting out.

"I must confess that you look like it — very much like it indeed." Mr. Bronson spoke severely, but if ever by great effort he conquered a smile, that was the time. "I presume," he went on, "that you do not refer to the abiding place of sinners, but rather to some definite locality in San Francisco. Am I right?"

Joe swept his arm in a descending gesture toward Union Street, and said: "Down there, sir."

"And who gave it that name?"

"I did," Joe answered, as though confessing to a specified crime.

"It's most appropriate, I'm sure, and denotes imagination. It couldn't really be bettered. You must do well at school, sir, with your English."

This did not increase Joe's happiness, for English was the only study of which he did not have to feel ashamed.

And, while he stood thus a silent picture of misery and disgrace, Mr. Bronson looked upon him through the eyes of his own boyhood with an understanding which Joe could not have believed possible.

"However, what you need just now is not a discourse, but a bath and court plaster and witch hazel and cold water bandages," Mr. Bronson said, "so to bed with you. You'll need all the sleep you can get, and you'll feel stiff and sore tomorrow morning, I promise you."

The clock struck one as Joe pulled the bedclothes around him; and the next he knew he was being worried by a soft, insistent rapping, which seemed to continue through several centuries, until at last, unable to endure it longer, he opened his eyes and sat up.

The day was streaming in through the window — bright and sunshiny day. He stretched his arms to yawn; but a shooting pain darted through all the muscles, and his arms came down more rapidly than they had gone up. He looked at them with a bewildered stare, till suddenly the events of the night rushed in upon him, and he groaned.

The rapping still persisted, and he cried: "Yes, I hear. What time is it?"

"Eight o'clock," Bessie 's voice came to him through the

door. "Eight o'clock, and you'll have to hurry if you don't want to be late for school."

"Goodness!" He sprang out of bed precipitately, groaned with the pain from all his stiff muscles, and collapsed slowly and carefully on a chair. "Why didn't you call me sooner?" he growled.

"Father said to let you sleep."

Joe groaned again, in another fashion. Then his history book caught his eye, and he groaned yet again and in still another fashion.

"All right," he called. "Go on. I'll be down in a jiffy."

He did come down in fairly brief order; but if Bessie had watched him descend the stairs she would have been astounded at the remarkable caution he observed and at the twinges of pain that every now and then contorted his face. As it was, when she came upon him in the dining room she uttered a frightened cry and ran over to him.

"What's the matter, Joe?" she asked tremulously. "What has happened?"

"Nothing," he grunted, putting sugar on his porridge.

"But surely —" she began.

"Please don't bother me," he interrupted. "I'm late, and I want to eat my breakfast."

And just then Mrs. Bronson caught Bessie's eye, and that young lady, still mystified, made haste to withdraw herself.

Joe was thankful to his mother for that, and thankful that she refrained from remarking upon his appearance. Father had told her; that was one thing sure. He could trust her not to worry him; it was never her way.

And, meditating in his way, he hurried through with

his solitary breakfast, vaguely conscious in an uncomfortable way that his mother was fluttering anxiously about him. Tender as she always was, he noticed that she kissed him with unusual tenderness as he started out with his books swinging at the end of a strap; and he also noticed, as he turned the corner, that she was still looking after him through the window.

But of more vital importance than that, to him, was his stiffness and soreness. As he walked along, each step was an effort and a torment. Severely as the reflected sunlight from the cement sidewalk hurt his bruised eye, and severely as his various wounds pained him, still more severely did he suffer from his muscles and joints. He had never imagined such stiffness. Each individual muscle in his whole body protested when called upon to move. His fingers were badly swollen, and it was agony to clasp and unclasp them; while his arms were sore from wrist to elbow. This, he said to himself, was caused by the many blows which he had warded off from his face and body. He wondered if Brick Simpson was in similar plight, and the thought of their mutual misery made him feel a certain kinship for that redoubtable young ruffian.

When he entered the school yard he quickly became aware that he was the center of attraction for all eyes. The boys crowded around in an awe-stricken way, and even his classmates and those with whom he was well acquainted looked at him with a certain respect he had never seen before.

CHAPTER 6

Examination Day

IT WAS PLAIN that Fred and Charley had spread the news of their descent into the Pit, and of their battle with the Simpson clan and the Fishes. He heard the nine-o'clock bell with feelings of relief, and passed into the school, a mark for admiring glances from all the boys. The girls, too, looked at him in a timid and fearful way — as they might have looked at Daniel when he came out of the lions' den, Joe thought, or at David after his battle with Goliath. It made him uncomfortable and painfully self-conscious, this hero-worshiping, and he wished heartily that they would look in some other direction for a change.

Soon they did look in another direction. While big sheets of foolscap were being distributed to every desk, Miss Wilson, the teacher (an austere-looking young woman who went through the world as though it were a refrigerator, and who, even on the warmest days in the classroom. was to be found with a shawl or cape about her shoulders), arose, and on the blackboard where all could see wrote the Roman numeral "I." Every eye, and there were fifty pairs of them, hung with expectancy upon her hand, and in the pause that followed the room was quiet as the grave.

Underneath the Roman numeral "I" she wrote: "*(a) What were the laws of Draco? (b) Why did an Athenian orator say that they were written 'not in ink, but in blood'?*"

Forty-nine heads bent down and forty-nine pens scratched lustily across as many sheets of foolscap. Joe's head alone remained up, and he regarded the blackboard with so blank a stare that Miss Wilson, glancing over her shoulder after having written "II," stopped to look at him. Then she wrote:

"*(a) How did the war between Athens and Megara, respecting the island of Salamis, bring about the reforms of Solon? (b) In what way did they differ from the laws of Draco?*"

She turned to look at Joe again. He was staring as blankly as ever.

"What is the matter, Joe?" she asked. "Have you no paper?"

"Yes, I have, thank you," he answered, and began moodily to sharpen a lead pencil.

He made a fine point to it. Then he made a very fine point. Then, and with infinite patience, he proceeded to make it very much finer. Several of his classmates raised their heads inquiringly at the noise. But he did not notice. He was too absorbed in his pencil-sharpening and in thinking thoughts far away from both pencil-sharpening and Greek history.

"Of course you all understand that the examination papers are to be written with ink."

Miss Wilson addressed the class in general, but her eyes rested on Joe.

Just as it was about as fine as it could possibly be the point broke, and Joe began over again.

"I am afraid, Joe, that you annoy the class," Miss Wilson said in final desperation.

He put the pencil down, closed the knife with a snap, and returned to his blank staring at the blackboard. What did he know about Draco? or Solon? or the rest of the Greeks? It was a flunk, and that was all there was to it. No need for him to look at the rest of the questions, and even if he did know the answers to two or three, there was no use in writing them down. It would not prevent the flunk. Besides, his arm hurt him too much to write. It hurt his eyes to look at the blackboard, and his eyes hurt even when they were closed; and it seemed positively to hurt him to think.

So the forty-nine pens scratched on in a race after Miss Wilson, who was covering the blackboard with question after question; and he listened to the scratching, and watched the questions growing under her chalk, and was very miserable indeed. His head seemed whirling around. It ached inside and was sore outside, and he did not seem to have any control of it at all.

He was beset with memories of the Pit, like scenes from some monstrous nightmare, and, try as he would, he could not dispel them. He would fix his mind and eyes on Miss Wilson. She was now sitting at her desk, and even as he looked at her the face of Brick Simpson, impudent and pugnacious, would arise before him. It was of no use. He felt sick and sore and tired and worthless. There was nothing to be done but flunk. And when, after an age of waiting, the papers were collected, his went in a blank, save for his name, the name of the examination, and the date, which were written across the top.

After a brief interval, more papers were given out, and the examination in arithmetic began. He did not trouble himself to look at the questions. Ordinarily he might have pulled through such an examination, but in his present state of mind and body he knew it was impossible. He contented himself with burying his face in his hands and hoping for the noon hour. Once, lifting his eyes to the clock, he caught Bessie looking anxiously at him across the room from the girls' side. This but added to his discomfort. Why was she bothering him? No need for her to trouble. She was bound to pass. Then why couldn't she leave him alone? So he gave her a particularly glowering look and buried his face in his hands again. Nor did he lift it till the twelve-o'clock gong rang, when he handed in a second blank paper and passed out with the boys.

Fred and Charley and he usually ate lunch in a corner of the yard which they had arrogated to themselves; but this day, by some remarkable coincidence, a score of other boys had elected to eat their lunches on the same spot. Joe surveyed them with disgust. In his present condition he did not feel inclined to receive hero worship. His head ached too much, and he was troubled over his failure in the examinations; and there were more to come in the afternoon.

He was angry with Fred and Charley. They were chattering like magpies over the adventures of the night (in which, however, they did not fail to give him chief credit), and they conducted themselves in quite a patronizing fashion toward their awed and admiring schoolmates. But every attempt to make Joe talk was a failure. He grunted and gave short answers, and said "yes" and "no" to questions asked with the intention of drawing him out.

He was longing to get away somewhere by himself, to throw himself down some place on the green grass and forget his aches and pains and troubles. He got up to go and find such a place, and found half a dozen of his following tagging after him. He wanted to turn around and scream at them to leave him alone, but his pride restrained him. A great wave of disgust and despair swept over him, and then an idea flashed through his mind. Since he was sure to flunk in his examinations, why endure the afternoon's torture, which could not but be worse than the morning's? And on the impulse of the moment he made up his mind.

He walked straight on to the school yard gate and passed out. Here his worshipers halted in wonderment, but he kept on to the corner and out of sight. For some time he wandered along aimlessly, till he came to the tracks of a cable road. A downtown car happening to stop to let off passengers, he stepped aboard and ensconced himself in an outside corner seat. The next thing he was aware of, the car was swinging around on its turntable and he was hastily scrambling off. The big ferry building stood before him. Seeing and hearing nothing, he had been carried through the heart of the business section of San Francisco.

He glanced up at the tower clock on top of the ferry

building. It was ten minutes after one — time enough to catch the quarter-past-one boat. That decided him, and without the least idea in the world as to where he was going, he paid ten cents for a ticket, passed through the gate, and was soon speeding across the bay to the pretty city of Oakland.

In the same aimless and unwitting fashion, he found himself, an hour later, sitting on the stringpiece of the Oakland city wharf and leaning his aching head against a friendly timber. From where he sat he could look down upon the decks of a number of small sailing craft. Quite a crowd of curious idlers had collected to look at them, and Joe found himself growing interested.

There were four boats, and from where he sat he could make out their names. The one directly beneath him had the name *Ghost* painted in large green letters on its stern. The other three, which lay beyond, were called respectively *La Caprice,* the *Oyster Queen,* and the *Flying Dutchman.*

Each of these boats had cabins built amidships, with short stovepipes projecting through the roofs, and from the pipe of the *Ghost* smoke was ascending. The cabin doors were open and the roof slide pulled back, so that Joe could look inside and observe the inmate, a young fellow of nineteen or twenty who was engaged just then in cooking. He was clad in long sea boots which reached the hips, blue overalls, and dark woolen shirt. The sleeves, rolled back to the elbows, disclosed sturdy, sun-bronzed arms, and when the young fellow looked up his face proved to be equally bronzed and tanned.

The aroma of coffee arose to Joe's nose, and from a

light iron pot came the unmistakable smell of beans nearly done. The cook placed a frying pan on the stove, wiped it around with a piece of suet when it had heated, and tossed in a thick chunk of beefsteak. While he worked he talked with a companion on deck, who was busily engaged in filling a bucket overside and flinging the salt water over heaps of oysters that lay on the deck. This completed, he covered the oysters with wet sacks, and went into the cabin, where a place was set for him on a tiny table, and where the cook served the dinner and joined him in eating it.

All the romance of Joe's nature stirred at the sight. That was life. They were living, and gaining their living, out in the free open, under the sun and sky, with the sea rocking beneath them, and the wind blowing on them, or the rain falling on them, as the chance might be. Each day and every day he sat in a room, pent up with fifty more of his kind, racking his brains and cramming dry husks of knowledge, while they were doing all this, living glad and careless and happy, rowing boats and sailing, and cooking their own food, and certainly meeting with adventures such as one only dreams of in the crowded schoolroom.

Joe sighed. He felt that he was made for this sort of life and not for the life of a scholar. As a scholar he was undeniably a failure. He had flunked in his examinations, while at that very moment, he knew, Bessie was going triumphantly home, her last examination over and done, and with credit. Oh, it was not to be borne! His father was wrong in sending him to school. That might be well enough for boys who were inclined to study, but it was manifest that he was not so inclined. There were more careers in life than that of the schools. Men had gone down to the sea in the lowest capacity, and risen in greatness, and owned great fleets, and done great deeds, and left their names on the pages of time. And why not he, Joe Bronson?

He closed his eyes and felt immensely sorry for himself; and when he opened his eyes again he found that he had been asleep, and that the sun was sinking fast.

It was after dark when he arrived home, and he went straight to his room and to bed without meeting any one. He sank down between the cool sheets with a sigh of satisfaction at the thought that, come what would, he need no longer worry about his history. Then another and unwelcome thought obtruded itself, and he knew that the next school term would come, and that six months thereafter, another examination in the same history awaited him.

CHAPTER 7

Father and Son

ON THE FOLLOWING MORNING, after breakfast, Joe was summoned to the library by his father, and he went in almost with a feeling of gladness that the suspense of waiting was over. Mr. Bronson was standing by the window. A great chattering of sparrows outside seemed to have attracted his attention. Joe joined him in looking out, and saw a fledgeling sparrow on the grass, tumbling ridiculously about in its efforts to stand on its feeble baby legs. It had fallen from the nest in the rosebush that climbed over the window, and the two parent sparrows were wild with anxiety over its plight.

"It 's a way young birds have," Mr. Bronson remarked, turning to Joe with a serious smile, "and I dare say you are on the verge of a somewhat similar predicament, my boy," he went on. "I am afraid things have reached a crisis, Joe. I have watched it coming on for a year now — your poor scholarship, your carelessness and inattention, your constant desire to be out of the house and away in search of adventures of one sort or another."

He paused, as though expecting a reply; but Joe remained silent.

"I have given you plenty of liberty. I believe in liberty. The finest souls grow in such soil. So I have not hedged you in with endless rules and irksome restrictions. I have asked little of you, and you have come and gone pretty much as you pleased. In a way, I have put you on your honor, made you largely your own master, trusting to your sense of right to restrain you from going wrong and at least to keep you up in your studies. And you have failed me. What do you want me to do? Set you certain bounds and time limits? Keep a watch over you? Compel you by main strength to go through your books?

"I have here a note," Mr. Bronson said after another pause, in which he picked up an envelope from the table and drew forth a written sheet.

Joe recognized the stiff and uncompromising scrawl of Miss Wilson, and his heart sank.

His father began to read:

> Listlessness and carelessness have characterized his term's work, so that when the examinations came he was wholly unprepared. In neither history nor arithmetic did he attempt to answer a question, passing in his papers perfectly blank. These examinations took place in the morning. In the afternoon he did not take the trouble even to appear for the remainder.

Mr. Bronson ceased reading and looked up.

"Where were you in the afternoon?" he asked.

"I went across on the ferry to Oakland," Joe answered, not caring to offer his aching head and body in extenuation.

"That is what is called 'playing hooky,' is it not?"

"Yes, sir," Joe answered.

"The night before the examinations, instead of studying, you saw fit to wander away and involve yourself in a disgraceful fight with hoodlums. I did not say anything at the time. In my heart I think I might almost have forgiven you that, if you had done well in your schoolwork."

Joe had nothing to say. He knew that there was his side to the story, but he felt that his father did not understand, and that there was little use of telling him.

"The trouble with you, Joe, is carelessness and lack of concentration. What you need is what I have not given you, and that is rigid discipline. I have been debating for some time upon the advisability of sending you to some military school, where your tasks will be set for you, and what you do every moment in the twenty-four hours will be determined for you —"

"Oh, father, you don't understand, you can't understand!" Joe broke forth at last. "I try to study — I honestly try to study; but somehow — I don't know how — I can't study. Perhaps I am a failure. Perhaps I am not made for study. I want to go out into the world. I want to see life — to live. I don't want any military academy; I 'd sooner go to sea — anywhere I can do something and be something."

Mr. Bronson looked at him kindly. "It is only through study that you can hope to do something and be something in the world," he said.

Joe threw up his hand with a gesture of despair.

"I know how you feel about it," Mr. Bronson went on; "but you are only a boy, very much like that young sparrow we were watching. If at home you have not sufficient control over yourself to study, then away from home, out in the world which you think is calling to you, you will likewise not have sufficient control over yourself to do the work of that world.

"But I am willing, Joe, I am willing, after you have finished high school and before you go into the university, to let you out into the world for a time."

"Let me go now?" Joe asked impulsively.

"No; it is too early. You haven't your wings yet. You are too unformed, and your ideals and standards are not yet thoroughly fixed."

"But I shall not be able to study," Joe threatened. "I know I shall not be able to study."

Mr. Bronson consulted his watch and arose to go. "I have not made up my mind yet," he said. "I do not know what I shall do — whether I shall give you another trial at the public school or send you to a military academy."

He stopped a moment at the door and looked back. "But remember this, Joe," he said. "I am not angry with you; I am more grieved and hurt. Think it over, and tell me this evening what you intend to do."

His father passed out, and Joe heard the front door close after him. He leaned back in the big easy chair and closed his eyes. A military school! He feared such an institution as the animal fears a trap. No, he would certainly never go to such a place. And as for public school — He sighed deeply at the thought of it. He was given till evening to make up his mind as to what he intended to do. Well, he knew what he would do, and he did not have to wait till evening to find it out.

He got up with a determined look on his face, put on his hat, and went out the front door. He would show his father that he could do his share of the world's work, he thought as he walked along — he would show him.

By the time he reached the school he had his whole plan worked out definitely. Nothing remained but to put it through. It was the noon hour, and he passed in to his room and packed up his books unnoticed. Coming out through the yard, he encountered Fred and Charley.

"What's up?" Charley asked.

"Nothing," Joe grunted.

"What are you doing there?"

"Taking my books home, of course. What did you suppose I was doing?"

"Come, come," Fred interposed. "Don't be so mysterious. I don't see why you can't tell us what has happened."

"You'll find out soon enough," Joe said significantly—more significantly that he had intended.

And, for fear that he might say more, he turned his back on his astonished chums and hurried away. He went straight home and to his room, where he busied himself at once with putting everything in order. His clothes he hung carefully away, changing the suit he had on for an older one. From his bureau he selected a couple of changes of underclothing, a couple of cotton shirts, and half a dozen pairs of socks. To these he added as many handkerchiefs, a comb, and a toothbrush.

When he had bound the bundle in stout wrapping paper he contemplated it with satisfaction. Then he went over to his desk and took from a small inner compartment his savings for some months, which amounted to several dollars. This sum he had been keeping for the Fourth of July, but he thrust it into his pocket with hardly a regret. Then he pulled a writing pad over to him, sat down and wrote:

Don't look for me. I am a failure and I am going away to sea. Don't worry about me. I am all right and able to take care of myself. I shall come back some day, and then you will all be proud of me. Good-by, papa, and mama, and Bessie.

JOE.

This he left lying on his desk where it could easily be seen. He tucked the bundle under his arm, and, with a last farewell look at the room, stole out.

CHAPTER 8

'Frisco Kid and the New Boy

'FRISCO KID was discontented — discontented and disgusted; though this would have seemed impossible to the boys who fished from the dock above and envied him mightily. He frowned, got up from where he had been sunning himself on top of the *Dazzler's* cabin, and kicked off his heavy rubber boots. Then he stretched himself on the narrow side deck and dangled his feet in the cool salt water.

"Now, that's freedom," thought the boys who watched him. Besides, those long sea boots, reaching the hips and buckled to the leather strap about the waist, held a strange and wonderful fascination for them. They did not know that 'Frisco Kid did not possess such things as shoes; that the boots were an old pair of Pete Le Maire's and were three sizes too large for him; nor could they guess how uncomfortable they were to wear on a hot summer day.

The cause of 'Frisco Kid's discontent was those very boys who sat on the stringpiece and admired him; but his disgust was the result of quite another event. Further, the *Dazzler* was short one in its crew, and he had to do more work than was justly his share. He did not mind the cooking, nor the washing down of the decks and the pumping; but when it came to the paint scrubbing and dishwashing, he rebelled. He felt that he had earned the right to be exempt from such scullion work. That was all the green boys were fit for; while he could make or take in sail, lift anchor, steer, and make landings.

"Stan' from un'er!" Pete Le Maire, captain of the *Dazzler* and lord and master of 'Frisco Kid, threw a bundle into the cockpit and came aboard by the starboard rigging.

"Come! Queeck!" he shouted to the boy who owned the bundle, and who now hesitated on the dock. It was a good fifteen feet to the deck of the sloop, and he could not reach the steel stay by which he must descend.

"Now! One, two, three!" the Frenchman counted good-naturedly, after the manner of all captains when their crews are shorthanded.

The boy swung his body into space and gripped the rigging. A moment later he struck the deck, his hands tingling warmly from the friction.

"Kid, dis is ze new sailor. I make your acquaintance." Pete smirked and bowed, and stood aside. "Mistaire Sho Bronson," he added as an afterthought.

The two boys regarded each other silently for a moment. They were evidently about the same age, though the stranger looked the heartier and the stronger of the two. 'Frisco Kid put out his hand, and they shook.

"So you're thinking of tackling the water, eh?" he asked.

Joe Bronson nodded, and glanced curiously about him before answering. "Yes; I think the Bay life will suit me for a while, and then, when I've got used to it, I'm going to sea in the forecastle."

"In the what? In the *what,* did you say?"

"In the forecastle—the place where the sailors live," he explained, flushing and feeling doubtful of his pronunciation.

"Oh, the fo'c'sle. Know anything about going to sea?"

"Yes—no; that is, except what I've read."

'Frisco Kid whistled, turned on his heel in a lordly manner, and went into the cabin.

"Going to sea!" he remarked to himself as he built the fire and set about cooking supper. "In the 'forecastle,' too—and thinks he'll like it!"

In the meantime Pete Le Maire was showing the newcomer about the sloop as though he were a guest. Such affability and charm did he display that 'Frisco Kid, popping his head up through the scuttle to call them to supper, nearly choked in his effort to suppress a grin.

Joe Bronson enjoyed that supper. The food was rough but good, and the smack of the salt air and the sea fittings around him gave zest to his appetite. The cabin was clean and snug, and, though not large, the accomodations surprised him. Every bit of space was utilized. The table swung to the centerboard case on hinges, so that when not in use it actually occupied almost no room at all. On either side, and partly under the deck, were two bunks. The blankets were rolled back, and they sat on the well-scrubbed bunk boards while they ate. A swinging sea lamp of brightly polished brass gave them light, which in the daytime could be obtained through the four deadeyes, or small round panes of heavy glass which were fitted into the walls of the cabin. On the side of the door were the stove and wood box, on the other the cupboard. The front end of the cabin was ornamented with a couple of rifles and a shotgun, while exposed by the rolled-back blankets of Pete's bunk was a cartridge-lined belt carrying a brace of revolvers.

It all seemed like a dream to Joe. Countless times he had imagined scenes somewhat similar to this; but here he was, right in the midst of it, and already it seemed as though he had known his two companions for years. Pete was smiling genially at him across the board. His was really a villainous countenance, but to Joe it seemed only "weather-beaten." 'Frisco Kid was describing to him, between mouthfuls, the last sou'easter the *Dazzler* had weathered, and Joe experienced an increasing awe for this boy who had lived so long upon the water and knew so much about it.

The captain, however, drank a glass of wine, and topped it off with a second and a third, and then, a vicious flush lighting his swarthy face, stretched out on top of his blankets, where he soon was snoring loudly.

"Better turn in and get a couple of hours' sleep," 'Frisco Kid said kindly, pointing Joe's bunk out to him. "We'll most likely be up the rest of the night."

Joe obeyed, but he could not fall asleep so readily as the others. He lay with his eyes wide open, watching the hands of the alarm clock that hung in the cabin, and thinking how quickly event had followed event in the last twelve hours. Only that very morning he had been a schoolboy, and now he was a sailor, shipped on the *Dazzler*, and bound he knew not whither. His fifteen years increased to twenty at the thought of it, and he felt every inch a man — a sailorman at that. He wished Charley and Fred could see him now. Well, they would hear of it quick enough. He could see them talking it over, and the other boys crowding around. "Who?" "What!—Joe Bronson?" "Yes, he's run away to sea. Used to chum with us, you know."

Joe pictured the scene proudly. Then he softened at the thought of his mother worrying, but hardened again at the recollection of his father. Not that his father was not good and kind; but he did not understand boys, Joe thought. That was where the trouble lay. Only that morning he had said that the world wasn't a playground, and that the boys who thought it was were liable to make sore mistakes and be glad to get home again. Well, *he* knew that there was plenty of hard work and rough experience in the world; but *he* also thought boys had some rights and should be allowed to do a lot of things without being questioned. He'd show him he could take care of himself; and anyway, he could write home after he got settled down to his new life.

A skiff grazed the side of the *Dazzler* softly and interrupted his reveries. He wondered why he had not heard the sound of the rowlocks. Then two men jumped over the cockpit rail and came into the cabin.

"Bli' me, if 'ere they ain't snoozin'," said the first of the newcomers, deftly rolling 'Frisco Kid out of his blankets with one hand and reaching for the wine bottle with the other.

Pete put his head up on the other side of the centerboard, his eyes heavy with sleep, and made them welcome.

" 'Oo's this?" asked "the Cockney," as 'Frisco Kid called him, smacking his lips over the wine and rolling Joe out upon the floor. "Passenger?"

"No, no," Pete made haste to answer. "Ze new sailorman. Vaire good boy."

"Good boy or not, he's got to keep his tongue a-tween his teeth," growled the second newcomer, who had not yet spoken, glaring fiercely at Joe.

"I say," queried the other man, " 'ow does 'e whack up on the loot? I 'ope as me an' Bill 'ave a square deal."

"Ze *Dazzler* she take one share — what you call — one third; den we split ze rest in five shares. Five men, five shares. Vaire good."

It was all Greek to Joe, except he knew that he was in some way the cause of the quarrel. In the end Pete had his way, and the newcomers gave in after much grumbling. After they had drunk their coffee all hands went on deck.

"Just stay in the cockpit an' keep out of their way," 'Frisco Kid whispered to Joe. "I'll teach you the ropes an' everything when we ain't in a hurry."

Joe's heart went out to him in sudden gratitude, for the strange feeling came to him that, of those on board, to 'Frisco Kid, and to 'Frisco Kid only, could he look for help in time of need. Already a dislike for Pete was growing up within him. Why, he could not say—he just simply felt it. A creaking of blocks for'ard, and the huge mainsail loomed above him in the night. Bill cast off the bowline. The Cockney followed with the stern. 'Frisco Kid gave her the jib as Pete jammed up the tiller, and the *Dazzler* caught the breeze, heeling over for mid-channel. Joe heard some talking in low tones of not putting up the side lights, and of keeping a sharp lookout, but all he could comprehend was that some law of navigation was being violated.

The water-front lights of Oakland began to slip past. Soon the stretches of docks and the shadowy ships began to be broken by dim sweeps of marshland, and Joe knew that they were heading out for San Francisco Bay. The wind was blowing from the north in mild squalls, and the *Dazzler* cut noiselessly through the landlocked water.

"Where are we going?" Joe asked the Cockney, in an endeavor to be friendly and at the same time satisfy his curiosity.

"Oh, my pardner 'ere, Bill—we're goin' to take a cargo from 'is factory," that worthy airily replied.

Joe thought he was rather a funny-looking individual to own a factory; but conscious that stranger things yet might be found in this new world he was entering, he said nothing. He had already exposed himself to 'Frisco Kid in the matter of his pronunciation of "fo'c'sle," and he had no desire further to show his ignorance.

A little after that he was sent in to blow out the cabin lamp. The *Dazzler* tacked about and began to work in toward the north shore. Everybody kept silent, save for occasional whispered questions and answers which passed between Bill and the Captain. Finally the sloop was run into the wind and the jib and mainsail lowered cautiously.

"Short hawse, you know," Pete whispered to 'Frisco Kid, who went for'ard and dropped the anchor, paying out the slightest quantity of slack.

The *Dazzler's* skiff was brought alongside, as was also the small boat the two strangers had come aboard in.

"See that that cub don't make a fuss," Bill commanded in an undertone, as he joined his partner in his own boat.

"Can you row?" 'Frisco Kid asked as they got into the other boat. Joe nodded his head. "Then take these oars, and don't make a racket."

'Frisco Kid took the second pair, while Pete steered. Joe noticed that the oars were muffled with sennit, and that even the row-lock sockets were protected by leather. It was impossible to make a noise except by a mis-stroke, and Joe had learned to row on Lake Merrit well enough to avoid that. They followed in the wake of the first boat, and glancing aside, he saw they were running along the length of a pier which jutted out from the land. A couple of ships, with riding lanterns burning brightly, were moored to it, but they kept just beyond the edge of the light. He stopped rowing at the whispered command of 'Frisco Kid. Then the boats grounded like ghosts on a tiny beach, and they clambered out.

Joe followed the men, who picked their way carefully up a twenty-foot bank. At the top he found himself on a narrow railway track which ran between huge piles of rusty scrap iron. These piles, separated by tracks, extended in every direction, he could not tell how far, though in the distance he could see the vague outlines of some great factorylike building. The men began to carry loads of the iron down to the beach, and Pete, gripping him by the arm and again warning him to not make any noise, told him to do likewise. At the beach they turned their loads over to 'Frisco Kid, who loaded them, first in one skiff and then in the other. As the boats settled under the weight, he kept pushing them farther and farther out, in order that they should keep clear of the bottom.

Joe worked away steadily, though he could not help marveling at the queerness of the whole business. Why should there be such a mystery about it, and why such care taken to maintain silence? He had just begun to ask himself these questions, and a horrible suspicion was forming itself in his mind, when he heard the hoot of an owl from the direction of the beach. Wondering at an owl being in so unlikely a place, he stooped to gather a fresh load of iron. But suddenly a man sprang out of the gloom, flashing a dark lantern full upon him. Blinded by the light, he staggered back. Then a revolver in the man's hand went off. All Joe realized was that he was being shot at, while his legs manifested an overwhelming desire to get away. Even if he had so wished, he could not very well have stayed to explain to the excited man with the smoking revolver. So he took to his heels for the beach, colliding with another man with a dark lantern who came running around the end of one of the piles of iron. This second man quickly regained his feet, and peppered away at Joe as he flew down the bank.

He dashed out into the water for the boat. Pete at the bow oars and 'Frisco Kid at the stroke had the skiff's nose pointed seaward and were calmly awaiting his arrival. They had their oars all ready for the start, but they held them quietly at rest, notwithstanding that both men on the bank had begun to fire at them. The other skiff lay closer inshore, partially aground. Bill was trying to shove it off, and was calling on the Cockney to lend a hand; but that gentleman had lost his head completely, and came floundering through the water hard after Joe. No sooner had Joe climbed in over the stern than he followed him. This extra weight on the stern of the heavily loaded craft nearly swamped them; as it was, a dangerous quantity of water was shipped. In the meantime the men on the bank had reloaded their pistols and opened fire again, this time with better aim. The alarm had spread. Voices and cries could be heard from the ships on the pier, along which men were running. In the distance a police whistle was being frantically blown.

"Get out!" 'Frisco Kid shouted. "You ain't a-going to sink us if I know it. Go and help your pardner!"

But the Cockney's teeth were chattering with fright, and he was too unnerved to move or speak.

"T'row ze crazy man out!" Pete ordered from the bow. At this moment a bullet shattered an oar in his hand, and he coolly proceeded to ship a spare one.

"Give us a hand, Joe," 'Frisco Kid commanded.

Joe understood, and together they seized the terror-stricken creature and flung him overboard. Two or three bullets splashed about him as he came to the surface just in time to be picked up by Bill, who had at last succeeded in getting clear.

"Now," Pete called, and a few strokes into the darkness quickly took them out of the zone of fire.

So much water had been shipped that the light skiff was

in danger of sinking at any moment. While the other two rowed, and by the Frenchman's orders, Joe began to throw out the iron. This saved them for the time being; but just as they swept alongside the *Dazzler* the skiff lurched, shoved a side under, and turned turtle, sending the remainder of the iron to the bottom. Joe and 'Frisco Kid came up side by side, and together they clambered aboard with the skiff's painter in tow. Pete had already arrived, and now helped them out.

By the time they had canted the water out of the swamped boat, Bill and his partner appeared on the scene. All hands worked rapidly, and almost before Joe could realize, the mainsail and jib had been hoisted, the anchor broken out, and the *Dazzler* was leaping down the channel. Off a bleak piece of marshland, Bill and the Cockney said good-by and cast loose in their skiff. Pete, in the cabin, bewailed their bad luck in various languages, and sought consolation in the wine bottle.

The wind freshened as they got clear of the land, and soon the *Dazzler* was heeling it with her lee deck buried and the water churning by halfway up the cockpit rail. Side lights had been hung out. 'Frisco Kid was steering, and by his side sat Joe, pondering over the events of the night.

He could no longer blind himself to the facts. His mind was in a whirl of apprehension. If he had done wrong, he reasoned, he had done it through ignorance; and he did not feel shame for the past so much as he did fear of the future. His companions were thieves and robbers — the Bay pirates, of whose unlawful deeds he had heard vague tales. And here he was, right in the midst of them, already possessing information which could send them to state's prison. This very fact, he knew, would force them to keep a sharp watch upon him and so lessen his chances of escape. But escape he would, at the very first opportunity.

At this point his thoughts were interrupted by a sharp squall, which hurled the *Dazzler* over till the sea rushed inboard. 'Frisco Kid luffed quickly, at the same time slacking off the mainsheet. Then, singlehanded — for Pete remained below, and Joe sat still looking idly on — he proceeded to reef down.

CHAPTER 9

Joe Tries Taking French Leave

THE SQUALL which had so nearly capsized the *Dazzler* was of short duration, but it marked the rising of the wind, and soon puff after puff was shrieking down upon them out of the north. The mainsail was spilling the wind, and slapping and thrashing about till it seemed it would tear itself to pieces. The sloop was rolling wildly in the quick sea which had come up. Everything was in confusion; but even Joe's untrained eye showed him that it was an orderly confusion. He could see that 'Frisco Kid knew just what to do, and just how to do it. As he watched him he learned a lesson, the lack of which has made failures of the lives of many men — *knowledge of one's own capacities.* 'Frisco Kid knew what he was able to do, and because of this he had confidence in himself. He was cool and self-possessed, working hurriedly but not carelessly. There was no bungling. Every reef point was drawn down to stay. Other accidents might occur, but the next squall, or the next forty squalls, would not carry one of these reef knots away.

He called Joe for'ard to help stretch the mainsail by means of swinging on the peak and throat halyards. To lie out on the long bowsprit and put a single reef in the jib was a slight task compared with what had been already accomplished; so a few moments later they were again in the cockpit. Under the other lad's directions, Joe flattened down the jib sheet, and, going into the cabin, let down a foot or so of centerboard. The excitement of the struggle had chased all unpleasant thoughts from his mind. Patterning after the other boy, he had retained his coolness. He had executed his orders without fumbling, and at the same time without undue slowness. Together they had exerted their puny strength in the face of violent nature, and together they had outwitted her.

He came back to where his companion stood at the tiller steering, and he felt proud of him and of himself. And when he read the unspoken praise in 'Frisco Kid's eyes he blushed like a girl at her first compliment. But the next instant the thought flashed across him that this boy was a thief, a common thief, and he instinctively recoiled. His whole life had been sheltered from the harsher things of the world. His reading, which had been of the best, had laid a premium upon honesty and uprightness, and he had learned to look with abhorrence upon the criminal classes. So he drew a little away from 'Frisco Kid and remained silent. But 'Frisco Kid, devoting all his energies to the handling of the sloop, had no time in which to remark this sudden change of feeling on the part of his companion.

Yet there was one thing Joe found in himself that surprised him. While the thought of 'Frisco Kid being a thief was repulsive to him, 'Frisco Kid himself was not. Instead of feeling an honest desire to shun him, he felt drawn toward him. He could not help liking him, though he knew not why. Had he been a little older he would have understood that it was the lad's good qualities which appealed to him — his coolness and self-reliance, his manliness and bravery, and a certain kindliness and sympathy in his nature. As it was, he thought it his own natural badness which prevented him from disliking 'Frisco Kid, and while he felt shame at his own weakness, he could not smother the sort of regard which he felt growing up for this common thief, this Bay pirate.

"Take in two or three feet on the skiff's painter," commanded 'Frisco Kid, who had an eye for everything.

The skiff was towing with too long a painter, and was behaving very badly. Every once in a while it would hold back till the towrope tautened, then come leaping ahead and sheering and dropping slack till it threatened to shove its nose under the huge whitecaps which roared hungrily on every hand. Joe climbed over the cockpit rail upon the slippery afterdeck, and made his way to the bitt to which the skiff was fastened.

"Be careful," 'Frisco Kid warned, as a heavy puff struck the *Dazzler* and careened her dangerously over on her side. "Keep one turn round the bitt, and heave in on it when the painter slacks."

It was ticklish work for a greenhorn. Joe threw off all the turns save the last, which he held with one hand, while with the other he attempted to bring in on the painter. But at that instant it tightened with a tremendous jerk, the boat sheering sharply into the crest of a heavy sea. The rope slipped from his hands and began to fly out over the stern. He clutched it frantically, and was dragged after it over the sloping deck.

"Let her go! Let her go!" 'Frisco Kid roared.

Joe let go just as he was on the verge of going overboard, and the skiff dropped rapidly astern. He glanced in a shamefaced way at his companion, expecting to be sharply reprimanded for his awkwardness. But 'Frisco Kid smiled good-naturedly.

"That 's all right," he said. "No bones broke, and nobody overboard. Better to lose a boat than a man any day. That's what I say. Besides, I shouldn't have sent you out there. And there 's no harm done. We can pick it up all right. Go in and drop some more centerboard — a couple of feet — and then come out and do what I tell you. But don't be in a hurry. Take it easy and sure."

Joe dropped the centerboard, and returned, to be stationed at the jib sheet.

"Hard a-lee!" 'Frisco Kid cried, throwing the tiller down and following it with his body. "Cast off! That 's right! Now lend a hand on the mainsheet!"

Together, hand over hand, they came in on the reefed mainsail. Joe began to warm up with the work. The *Dazzler* turned on her heel like a race horse and swept into the wind, her canvas snarling and her sheets slatting like hail.

"Draw down the jib sheet!"

Joe obeyed, and the headsail, filling, forced her off on the other tack. This manœuver had turned Pete's bunk from the lee to the weather side, and rolled him out on the cabin floor, where he lay in a drunken stupor.

'Frisco Kid, with his back against the tiller, and holding

the sloop off that it might cover their previous course, looked at him with an expression of disgust, and muttered: "The dog! We could well go to the bottom, for all he'd care or do!"

Twice they tacked, trying to go over the same ground, and then Joe discovered the skiff bobbing to windward in the starlit darkness.

"Plenty of time," 'Frisco Kid cautioned, shooting the *Dazzler* into the wind toward it and gradually losing headway.

"Now!"

Joe leaned over the side, grasped the trailing painter, and made it fast to the bitt. Then they tacked ship again and started on their way. Joe still felt sore over the trouble he had caused, but 'Frisco Kid quickly put him at ease.

"Oh, that's nothing," he said. "Everybody does that when they're beginning. Now, some men forget all about the trouble they had in learning, and get mad when a greeny makes a mistake. I never do. Why, I remember —"

And here he told Joe of many of the mishaps which fell to him when, as a little lad, he first went on the water, and of some of the severe punishments for the same which were measured out to him. He had passed the running end of a lanyard over the tiller neck, and, as they talked, they sat side by side and close against each other, in the shelter of the cockpit.

"What place is that?" Joe asked as they flew by a lighthouse perched on a rocky headland.

"Goat Island. They've got a naval training station for boys over on the other side, and a torpedo magazine. There's jolly good fishing, too — rock cod. We'll pass to the lee of it and make across and anchor in the shelter of Angel Island. There's a quarantine station there. Then, when Pete gets sober, we'll know where he wants to go. You can turn in now and get some sleep. I can manage all right."

Joe shook his head. There had been too much excitement for him to feel in the least like sleeping. He could not bear to think of it, with the *Dazzler* leaping and surging along, and shattering the seas into clouds of spray on her weather bow. His clothes had half dried already, and he preferred to stay on deck and enjoy it. The lights of Oakland had dwindled till they made only a hazy flare against the sky; but to the south the San Francisco lights, topping hills and sinking into valleys, stretched miles upon miles. Starting from the great ferry building and passing on to Telegraph Hill, Joe was soon able to locate the principal places of the city. Somewhere over in that maze of light and shadow was the home of his father, and perhaps even now they were thinking and worrying about him; and over there his sister Bessie was sleeping cozily, to wake up in the morning and wonder why her brother Joe did not come down to breakfast. Joe shivered. It was almost morning. Then, slowly, his head drooped over on 'Frisco Kid's shoulder, and soon he was fast asleep.

"Come! Wake up! We're going into anchor."

Joe roused with a start, bewildered at the unusual scene; for sleep had banished his troubles for the time being, and he knew not where he was. Then he remembered. The wind had dropped with the night. Beyond, the heavy aftersea was still rolling, but the *Dazzler* was creeping up in the shelter of a rocky island. The sky was clear, and the air had the snap and vigor of early morning about it. The rippling water was laughing in the rays of the sun, just shouldering above the eastern sky line. To the south lay Alcatraz Island, and from its gun-crowned heights a flourish of trumpets saluted the day. In the west the Golden Gate yawned between the Pacific Ocean and San Francisco Bay. A full-rigged ship, with her lightest canvas, even to the skysails, set, was coming slowly in on the flood tide.

It was a pretty sight. Joe rubbed the sleep from his eyes and remained gazing till 'Frisco Kid told him to go for'ard and make ready for dropping the anchor.

"Overhaul about fifty fathoms of chain," he ordered, "and then stand by." He eased the sloop gently into the wind, at the same time casting off the jib sheet. "Let go the jib halyards and come in on the downhaul!"

Joe had seen the manœuver performed the previous night, and so was able to carry it out with fair success.

"Now! Over with the mud hook! Watch out for turns! Lively, now!"

The chain flew out with startling rapidity, and brought the *Dazzler* to rest. 'Frisco Kid went for'ard to help, and together they lowered the mainsail, furled it in shipshape manner, made all fast with the gaskets, and put the crutches under the main boom.

"Here's a bucket." 'Frisco Kid passed him the article in question. "Wash down the decks, and don't be afraid of the water, nor of the dirt, neither. Here's a broom. Give it what for, and have everything shining. When you get that done, bail out the skiff; she opened her seams a little last night. I'm going below to cook breakfast."

The water was soon sloshing merrily over the deck,

while the smoke pouring from the cabin stove carried a promise of good things to come. Time and again Joe lifted his head from his task to take in the scene. It was one to appeal to any healthy boy, and he was no exception. The romance of it stirred him strangely, and his happiness would have been complete could he have escaped remembering who and what his companions were. But the thought of this, and of Pete in his bleary, drunken sleep below, marred the beauty of the day. He had been unused to such things, and was shocked at the harsh reality of life. But instead of hurting him, as it might a lad of weaker nature, it had the opposite effect. It strengthened his desire to be clean and strong, and to not be ashamed of himself in his own eyes. He glanced about him and sighed. Why could not men be honest and true? It seemed too bad that he must go away and leave all this; but the events of the night were strong upon him, and he knew that in order to be true to himself he must escape.

At this juncture he was called to breakfast. He discovered that 'Frisco Kid was as good a cook as he was sailor, and made haste to do justice to the fare. There were mush and condensed milk, beefsteak and fried potatoes, and all topped off with good French bread, butter, and coffee. Pete did not join them, though 'Frisco Kid attempted a couple of times to rouse him. He mumbled and grunted, half opened his bleared eyes, then went to snoring again.

"Can't tell when he's going to get those spells," 'Frisco Kid explained, when Joe, having finished washing the dishes, came on deck. "Sometimes he won't get that way for a month, and others he won't be decent for a week at a stretch. Sometimes he's good-natured, and sometimes he's dangerous. So the best thing to do is to let him alone and keep out of his way. And don't cross him, for if you do there's liable to be trouble."

"Come on, let's take a swim," he added, abruptly changing the subject to one more agreeable. "Can you swim?"

Joe nodded. "What's that place?" he asked as he poised before diving, pointing toward a sheltered beach on the island, where there were several buildings and a large number of tents.

"Quarantine station. Lots of smallpox coming in now on the China steamers, and they make them go there till the doctors say they're safe to land. I tell you, they're strict about it, too. Why —"

Splash! Had 'Frisco Kid finished his sentence just then, instead of diving overboard, much trouble might have been saved to Joe. But he did not finish it, and Joe dived after him.

"I'll tell you what," 'Frisco Kid suggested half an hour later, while they clung to the bobstay preparatory to climbing out. "Let's catch a mess of fish for dinner, and then turn in and make up for the sleep we lost last night. What d' you say?"

They made a race to clamber aboard, but Joe was shoved over the side again. When he finally did arrive, the other lad had brought to light a pair of heavily leaded, large-hooked lines, and a mackerel keg of salt sardines.

"Bait," he said. "Just shove a whole one on. They're not a bit partic'lar. Swallow the bait, hook and all, and go — that's their caper. The fellow that don't catch first fish has to clean 'em."

Both sinkers started on their long descent together, and

seventy feet of line whizzed out before they came to rest. But at the instant his sinker touched the bottom Joe felt the struggling jerks of a hooked fish. As he began to haul in he glanced at 'Frisco Kid, and saw that he, too, had evidently captured a finny prize. The race between them was exciting. Hand over hand the wet lines flashed inboard; but 'Frisco Kid was more expert, and his fish tumbled into the cockpit first. Joe's followed an instant later – a three-pound rock cod. He was wild with joy. It was magnificent, the largest fish he had ever landed or ever seen landed. Over went the lines again, and up they came with two mates of the ones already captured. It was sport royal. Joe would have certainly continued till he had fished the Bay empty had not 'Frisco Kid persuaded him to stop.

"We've got enough for three meals now," he said, "so there's no use in having them spoil. Besides, the more you catch, the more you clean, and you'd better start in right away. I'm going to bed."

Joe did not mind. In fact, he was glad he had not caught the first fish, for it helped out a little plan which had come to him while in swimming. He threw the last cleaned fish into a bucket of water, and glanced about him. The quarantine station was a bare half mile away, and he could make out a soldier pacing up and down at sentry duty on the beach. Going into the cabin, he listened to the heavy breathing of the sleepers. He had to pass so close to 'Frisco Kid to get his bundle of clothes that he decided not to take them. Returning outside, he carefully pulled the skiff alongside, got aboard with a pair of oars, and cast off.

At first he rowed very gently in the direction of the station, fearing the chance of noise if he made undue haste. But gradually he increased the strength of his strokes till he had settled down to the regular stride. When he had covered half the distance he glanced about. Escape was sure now, for he knew, even if he were discovered, that it would be impossible for the *Dazzler* to get under way and head him off before he made the land and the protection of that man who wore the uniform of Uncle Sam.

The report of a gun came to him from the shore, but his back was in that direction and he did not bother to turn around. A second report followed, and a bullet cut the water within a couple of feet of his oar blade. This time he did turn around. The soldier on the beach was leveling his rifle at him for a third shot.

CHAPTER 10

Joe Loses Liberty and Finds a Friend

JOE WAS IN a predicament, and a very tantalizing one at that. A few minutes of hard rowing would bring him to the beach and to safety; but on that beach, for some unaccountable reason, stood a United States soldier who persisted in firing at him.

When Joe saw the gun aimed at him for the third time, he backed water hastily. As a result the skiff came to a standstill, and the soldier, lowering his rifle, regarded him intently.

"I want to come ashore! Important!" Joe shouted out to him.

The man in uniform shook his head.

"But it's important, I tell you! Won't you let me come ashore?"

He took a hurried look in the direction of the *Dazzler*. The shots had evidently awakened Pete; for the mainsail had been hoisted, and as he looked he saw the anchor broken out and the jib flung to the breeze.

"Can't land here!" the soldier shouted back. "Smallpox!"

"But I must!" he cried, choking down a half sob and preparing to row.

"Then I'll shoot," was the cheering response, and the rifle came to shoulder again.

Joe thought rapidly. The island was large. Perhaps there were no soldiers farther on, and if he only once got ashore he did not care how quickly they captured him. He might catch the smallpox, but even that was better than going back to the Bay pirates. He whirled the skiff half about to the right, and threw all his strength against the oars. The cove was quite wide, and the nearest point which he must go around a good distance away. Had he been more of a sailor he would have gone in the other direction for the opposite point, and thus had the wind on his pursuers. As it was, the *Dazzler* had a beam wind in which to overtake him.

It was nip and tuck for a while. The breeze was light and not very steady, so sometimes he gained and sometimes they. Once it freshened till the sloop was within a hundred yards of him, and then it dropped suddenly flat, the *Dazzler's* big mainsail flapping idly from side to side.

"Ah! you steal ze skiff, eh?" Pete howled at him, running into the cabin for his rifle. "I fix you! You come back queeck, or I kill you!" But he knew the soldier was watching them from the shore, and did not dare to fire, even over the lad's head.

Joe did not think of this, for he, who had never been shot at in all his previous life, had been under fire twice in the last twenty-four hours. Once more or less couldn't amount to much. So he pulled steadily away, while Pete raved like a wild man, threatening him with all manner of punishments once he laid hands upon him again. To complicate matters, 'Frisco Kid waxed mutinous.

"Just you shoot him and I 'll see you hung for it, see if I don't," he threatened. "You'd better let him go. He's a good boy and all right, and not raised for the life you and I are leading."

"You too, eh!" the Frenchman shrieked, beside himself with rage. "Den I fix you, you rat!"

He made a rush for the boy, but 'Frisco Kid led him a lively chase from cockpit to bowsprit and back again. A sharp capful of wind arriving just then, Pete abandoned the one chase for the other. Springing to the tiller and slacking away on the mainsheet — for the wind favored — he headed the sloop down upon Joe. The latter made one tremendous spurt, then gave up in despair and hauled in his oars. Pete let go the mainsheet, lost steerage way as he rounded up alongside the motionless skiff, and dragged Joe out.

"Keep mum," 'Frisco Kid whispered to him while the irate Frenchman was busy fastening the painter. "Don't talk back. Let him say all he wants to, and keep quiet. It'll be better for you."

But Joe's Anglo-Saxon blood was up and he did not heed.

"Look here, Mr. Pete, or whatever your name is," he commenced, "I give you to understand that I want to quit, and that I'm going to quit. So you'd better put me ashore at once. If you don't, I'll put you in prison, or my name's not Joe Bronson."

'Frisco Kid waited the outcome fearfully. Pete was aghast. He was being defied aboard his own vessel, and by a boy. Never had such a thing been heard of. He knew he was committing an unlawful act in detaining him, while at the same time he was afraid to let him go with the information he had gathered concerning the sloop and its occupation. The boy had spoken the unpleasant truth when he said he could send him to prison. The only thing for him to do was to bully him.

"You will, eh?" His shrill voice rose wrathfully. "Den you come too. You row ze boat last-a night — answer me dat! You steal ze iron — answer me dat! You run away — answer me dat! And den you say you put me in jail? Bah!"

"But I didn't know," Joe protested.

"Ha, ha! Dat is funny. You tell dat to ze judge; mebbe him laugh, eh?"

"I say I didn't," Joe reiterated manfully. "I didn't know I'd shipped along with a lot of pirates and thieves."

'Frisco Kid winced at this epithet, and had Joe been looking at him he would have seen him flush.

"And now that I do know," he continued, "I wish to be put ashore. I don't know anything about the law, but I do know right and wrong, and I'm willing to take my chance with any judge for whatever wrong I have done — with all the judges in the United States, for that matter. And that's more than you can say, Mr. Pete."

"You say dat, eh? Vaire good. But you are one big t'ief —"

"I'm not! Don't you dare call me that again!" Joe's face was pale, and he was trembling — but not with fear.

"T'ief!" the Frenchman taunted back.

"You lie!"

Joe had not been a boy among boys for nothing. He knew the penalty which attached itself to the words he had just spoken, and he expected to receive it. So he was not overmuch surprised when he picked himself up from the floor of the cockpit an instant later, his head still ringing from a stiff blow between the eyes.

"Say dat one time more," Pete bullied, his fist raised and prepared to strike.

Tears of anger stood in Joe's eyes, but he was calm and in dead earnest. "When you say I am a thief, Pete, you lie. You can kill me, but still I will say you lie."

"No, you don't!" 'Frisco Kid had darted in like a wildcat, preventing a second blow and shoving the Frenchman back across the cockpit.

"You leave the boy alone," he continued, suddenly unshipping and arming himself with the heavy iron tiller, and standing between them. "This thing's gone just about as far as it's going to go. You big fool, can't you see the stuff the boy's made out of? He speaks true. He's right, and he knows it, and you could kill him and he wouldn't give in. There's my hand on it, Joe." He turned and extended his hand to Joe, who returned the grip. "You've got spunk, and you're not afraid to show it."

Pete's mouth twisted itself in a sickly smile, but the evil gleam in his eyes gave it the lie. He shrugged his shoulders and said: "Ah! So? He does not dee-sire dat I him call pet names. Ha, ha! It is only ze sailorman play. Let us — what you call — forgive and forget, eh? Vaire good; forgive and forget."

He reached out his hand, but Joe refused to take it.

'Frisco Kid nodded approval, while Pete, still shrugging his shoulders and smiling, passed into the cabin.

"Slack off ze mainsheet," he called out, "and run down for Hunter's Point. For one time I will cook ze dinner, and den you will say dat is ze vaire good dinner. Ah! Pete is ze great cook!"

"That's the way he always does — gets real good and cooks when he wants to make up," 'Frisco Kid hazarded, slipping the tiller into the rudderhead and obeying the order. "But even then you can't trust him."

Joe nodded his head, but did not speak. He was in no mood for conversation. He was still trembling from the excitement of the last few moments, while deep down he questioned himself on how he had behaved, and found naught to be ashamed of.

The afternoon sea breeze had sprung up and was now rioting in from the Pacific. Angel Island was fast dropping astern, and the water front of San Francisco showing up, as the *Dazzler* plowed along before it. Soon they were in the midst of the shipping, passing in and out among the vessels which had come from the uttermost ends of the earth. Later they crossed the fairway, where the ferry steamers, crowded with passengers, passed backward and forward between San Francisco and Oakland. One came so close that the passengers crowded to the side to see the gallant little sloop and the two boys in the cockpit. Joe gazed almost enviously at the row of down-turned faces. They all were going to their homes, while he — he was going he knew not whither, at the will of Pete Le Maire. He was half tempted to cry out for help; but the foolishness of such an act struck him, and he held his tongue. Turning his head, his eyes wandered along the smoky heights of the city, and he fell to musing on the strange ways of men and ships on the sea.

'Frisco Kid watched him from the corner of his eye, following his thoughts as accurately as though he spoke them aloud.

"Got a home over there somewhere?" he queried suddenly, waving his hand in the direction of the city.

Joe started, so correctly had his thought been anticipated. "Yes," he said simply.

"Tell us about it."

Joe rapidly described his home, though forced to go into greater detail because of the curious questions of his companion. 'Frisco Kid was interested in everything, especially in Mrs. Bronson and Bessie. Of the latter he could not seem to tire, and poured forth question after question concerning her. So peculiar and artless were some of them that Joe could hardly forbear to smile.

"Now tell me about your home," he said, when he at last had finished.

'Frisco Kid seemed suddenly to harden, and his face took on a stern look which the other had never seen there before. He swung his foot idly to and fro, and lifted a dull eye to the main-peak blocks, with which, by the way, there was nothing the matter.

"Go ahead," the other encouraged.

"I haven't no home."

The four words left his mouth as though they had been forcibly ejected, and his lips came together after them almost with a snap.

Joe saw he had touched a tender spot, and strove to

ease the way out of it again. "Then the home you did have." He did not dream that there were lads in the world who never had known homes, or that he had only succeeded in probing deeper.

"Never had none."

"Oh!" His interest was aroused, and he now threw solicitude to the winds. "Any sisters?"

"Nope."

"Mother?"

"I was so young when she died that I don't remember her."

"Father?"

"I never saw much of him. He went to sea — anyhow, he disappeared."

"Oh!" Joe did not know what to say, and an oppressive silence, broken only by the churn of the *Dazzler's* forefoot, fell upon them.

Just then Pete came out to relieve at the tiller, while they went in to eat. Both lads hailed his advent with feelings of relief, and the awkwardness vanished over the dinner, which was all their skipper had claimed it to be. Afterward 'Frisco Kid relieved Pete, and while he was eating, Joe washed up the dishes and put the cabin shipshape. Then they all gathered in the stern, where the captain strove to increase the general cordiality by entertaining them with descriptions of life among the pearl divers of the South Seas.

In this fashion the afternoon wore away. They had long since left San Francisco behind, rounded Hunter's Point, and were now skirting the San Mateo shore. Joe caught a glimpse, once, of a party of cyclists rounding a cliff on the San Bruno Road, and remembered the time when he had gone over the same ground on his own wheel. That was only a month or two before, but it seemed an age to him now, so much had there been to come between.

By the time supper had been eaten and the things cleared away, they were well down the Bay, off the marshes behind which Redwood City clustered. The wind had gone down with the sun, and the *Dazzler* was making but little headway, when they sighted a sloop bearing down upon them on the dying wind. 'Frisco Kid instantly named it as the *Reindeer*, to which Pete, after a deep scrutiny, agreed. He seemed greatly pleased at the meeting.

"Epont Nelson runs her," 'Frisco Kid informed Joe. "They've got something big down here, and they're always after Pete to tackle it with them. He knows more about it, whatever it is."

Joe nodded and looked at the approaching craft curiously. Though somewhat larger, it was built on about the same lines as the *Dazzler* — which meant, above everything else, that it was built for speed. The mainsail was so large that it was like that of a racing yacht, and it carried the points for no less than three reefs in case of rough weather. Aloft and on deck everything was in place; nothing was untidy or useless. From running gear to standing rigging, everything bore evidence of thorough order and smart seamanship.

The *Reindeer* came up slowly in the gathering twilight, and went to anchor not a biscuit toss away. Pete followed suit with the *Dazzler*, and then went in the skiff to pay them a visit. The two lads stretched themselves out on top of the cabin and awaited his return.

"Do you like the life?" Joe broke silence.

The other turned on his elbow. "Well — I do, and then again I don't. The fresh air and the salt water, and all that, and the freedom — that's all right; but I don't like the — the —" he paused a moment, as though his tongue had failed in its duty, and then blurted out, "the stealing."

"Then why don't you quit it?" Joe liked the lad more than he dared confess, and he felt a sudden missionary zeal come upon him.

"I will, just as soon as I can turn my hand to something else."

"But why not now?"

Now is the accepted time, was ringing in Joe's ears, and if the other wished to leave, it seemed a pity that he did not, and at once.

"Where can I go? What can I do? There 's nobody in all the world to lend me a hand, just as there never has been. I tried it once, and learned my lesson too well to do it again in a hurry."

"Well, when I get out of this I'm going home. Guess my father was right, after all. And I don't see — maybe — what's the matter with you going with me?" He said this last impulsively, without thinking, and 'Frisco Kid knew it.

"You don't know what you're talking about," he answered. "Fancy me going off with you! What'd your father say? And — and the rest? How would he think of me? And what'd he do?"

Joe felt sick at heart. He realized that in the spirit of the moment he had given an invitation which, on sober thought, he knew would be impossible to carry out. He tried to imagine his father receiving in his own house a stranger like 'Frisco Kid. No, that was not to be thought of. Then, forgetting his own plight, he fell to racking his brains for some other method by which 'Frisco Kid could get away from his present surroundings.

"He might turn me over to the police," the other went on, "and send me to a refuge. I'd die first, before I'd let that happen to me. And besides, Joe, I'm not of your kind, and you know it. Why, I'd be like a fish out of water, what with all the things I don't know. Nope; I guess I'll have to wait a little before I strike out. But there 's only one thing for you to do, and that's to go straight home. First chance I get, I'll land you, and then deal with Pete —"

"No, you don't" Joe interrupted hotly. "When I leave I'm not going to leave you in trouble on my account. So don't you try anything like that. I'll get away, never fear; and if I can figure it out, I want you to come along too — come along, anyway, and figure it out afterwards. What d' you say?"

'Frisco Kid shook his head, and, gazing up at the starlit heavens, wandered off into daydreams of the life he would like to lead, but from which he seemed inexorably shut out. The seriousness of life was striking deeper than ever into Joe's heart, and he lay silent, thinking hard. A mumble of heavy voices came to them from the *Reindeer;* from the land the solemn notes of a church bell floated across the water; while the summer night wrapped them slowly in its warm darkness.

CHAPTER 11

'Frisco Kid Tells His Story

AFTER THE CONVERSATION died away, the two lads lay upon the cabin for perhaps an hour.

Then, without saying a word, 'Frisco Kid went below and struck a light. Joe could hear him fumbling about, and a little later heard his own name called softly. On going into the cabin, he saw 'Frisco Kid sitting on the edge of the bunk, a sailor's ditty box on his knees, and in his hand a carefully folded page from a magazine.

"Does she look like this?" he asked, smoothing it out and turning it that the other might see.

It was a half-page illustration of two girls and a boy, grouped in an old-fashioned, roomy attic, and evidently holding a council of some sort. The girl who was talking faced the onlooker, while the backs of the two others were turned.

"Who?" Joe queried, glancing in perplexity from the picture to 'Frisco Kid's face.

"Like — like your sister — Bessie." The name seemed reluctant to come from his lips.

Joe was nonplused for the moment. He could see no bearing between the two in point, and, anyway, girls were rather silly creatures to waste one's time over. "He's actually blushing," he thought, regarding the soft glow on the other's cheeks. He felt an irresistible desire to laugh, but tried to smother it down.

"No, no, don't!" 'Frisco Kid cried, snatching the paper away and putting it back in the ditty box with shaking fingers. Then he added more slowly: "I thought I — I kind of thought you would understand, and — and —"

His lips trembled and his eyes glistened with unwonted moistness as he turned hastily away.

The next instant Joe was by his side on the bunk, his arm around him. Prompted by some instinctive monitor, he had done it before he thought. A week before he could not have imagined himself in such an absurd situation — his arm around a boy! but now it seemed the most natural thing in the world. He did not comprehend, but he knew that, whatever it was, it was something that seemed of deep importance to his companion.

"Go ahead and tell us," he urged. "I'll understand."

"No, you won't; you can't."

"Yes — sure. Go ahead."

'Frisco Kid choked and shook his head. "I don't think I could, anyway. It's more the things I feel, and I don't know how to put them in words." Joe's arm wrapped about him reassuringly, and he went on: "Well, it's this way. You see, I don't know much about the land, and people, and homes, and I never had no brothers, or sisters, or playmates. All the time I didn't know it, but I was lonely — sort of missed them down in here somewheres." He placed a hand over his breast to locate the seat of loss. "Did you ever feel downright hungry? Well, that's just the way I used to feel, only a different kind of hunger, and me not knowing what it was. But one day, oh, a long time back, I got a-hold of a magazine, and saw a picture — that picture, with the two girls and the boy talking together. I thought it must be fine to be like them, and I got to thinking about the things they said and did, till it came to me all of a sudden like, and I knew that it was just loneliness was the matter with me.

"But, more than anything else, I got to wondering about the girl who looks out of the picture right at you. I was thinking about her all the time, and by and by she became real to me. You see, it was making believe, and I knew it all the time; and then again I didn't. Whenever I'd think of the men, and the work, and the hard life, I'd know it was make-believe; but when I'd think of her, it wasn't. I don't know; I can't explain it."

Joe remembered all his own adventures which he had imagined on land and sea, and nodded. He at least understood that much.

"Of course it was all foolishness, but to have a girl like that for a friend seemed more like heaven to me than anything else I knew of. As I said, it was a long while back, and I was only a little kid. That's when Nelson gave me my name, and I've never been anything but 'Frisco Kid ever since. But the girl in the picture; I was always getting that picture out to look at her, and before long, if I wasn't square, why, I felt ashamed to look at her. Afterwards, when I was older, I came to look at it in another way. I thought, 'Suppose, Kid, some day you were to meet a girl like that, what would she think of you? Could she like you? Could she be even the least bit of a friend to you?' And then I'd make up my mind to be better, to try and do something with myself so that she or any of her kind of people would not be ashamed to know me.

"That's why I learned to read. That's why I ran away. Nicky Perrata, a Greek boy, taught me my letters, and it wasn't till after I learned to read that I found out there was anything really wrong in Bay pirating. I'd been used to it ever since I could remember, and several people I knew made their living that way. But when I did find out, I ran away, thinking to quit it for good. I'll tell you about it sometime, and how I'm back at it again.

"Of course she seemed a real girl when I was a youngster, and even now she sometimes seems that way, I've thought so much about her. But while I'm talking to you it all clears up and she comes to me in this light; she stands just for——well, for a better, cleaner life than this, and one I'd like to live; and if I could live it, why, I'd come to know that kind of girls, and their kind of people—your kind, that's what I mean. So I was wondering about your sister and you, and that's why—I don't know; I guess I was just wondering. But I suppose you know lots of girls like that, don't you?"

Joe nodded his head in token that he did.

"Then tell me about them; something — anything," he added, as he noted the fleeting expression of doubt in the other's eyes.

"Oh, that's easy," Joe began valiantly. To a certain extent he did understand the lad's hunger, and it seemed a simple enough task to satisfy him. "To begin with, they're like—hem!—why, they're like—girls, just girls." He broke off with a miserable sense of failure.

'Frisco Kid waited patiently, his face a study in expectancy.

Joe struggled vainly to marshal his ideas. To his mind, in quick succession, came the girls with whom he had gone to school, the sisters of the boys he knew, and those who were his sister's friends—slim girls and plump girls, tall girls and short girls, blue-eyed and brown-eyed, curly-haired, black-haired, golden-haired; in short, a regular procession of girls of all sorts and descriptions. But, to save himself, he could say nothing about them. Anyway, he'd never been a "sissy," and why should he be expected to know anything about them? "All girls are alike," he concluded desperately. "They're just the same as the ones you know, Kid. Sure they are."

"But I don't know any."

Joe whistled. "And never did?"

"Yes, one—Carlotta Gispardi. But she couldn't speak English; and she died. I don't care; though I never knew any, I seem to know as much about them as you do."

"And I guess I know more about adventures all over the world than you do," Joe retorted.

Both boys laughed. But a moment later Joe fell into deep thought. It had come upon him quite swiftly that he had not been duly grateful for the good things of life he did possess. Already home, father, and mother had assumed a greater significance to him; but he now found himself placing a higher personal value upon his sister, his chums and friends. He never had appreciated them properly, he thought, but henceforth—well, there would be a different tale to tell.

The voice of Pete hailing them put a finish to the conversation, for they both ran on deck.

"Get up ze mainsail, and break out ze hook!" he shouted. "And den tail on to ze *Reindeer!* No side lights!"

"Come! Cast off those gaskets! Lively!" 'Frisco Kid ordered. "Now lay onto the peak halyards — there, that rope; cast it off the pin. And don't hoist ahead of me. There! Make fast! We'll stretch it afterwards. Run aft and come in on the mainsheet! Shove the helm up!"

Under the sudden driving power of the mainsail, the *Dazzler* strained and tugged at her anchor like an impatient horse, till the muddy iron left the bottom with a rush, and she was free.

"Let go the sheet! Come for'ard again, and lend a hand on the chain! Stand by to give her the jib!" 'Frisco Kid, the boy who mooned over a picture of a girl in a magazine, had vanished, and 'Frisco Kid the sailor, strong and dominant, was on deck. He ran aft and tacked about as the jib rattled aloft in the hands of Joe, who quickly joined him. Just then the *Reindeer,* like a monstrous bat, passed to leeward of them in the gloom.

"Ah! dose boys! Dey take all-a night!" they heard Pete exclaim; and then the gruff voice of Nelson, who said: "Never you mind, Frenchy. I learned the Kid his sailorizing, and I ain't never been ashamed of him yet."

The *Reindeer* was the faster boat, but by spilling the

wind from her sails they managed so that the boys could keep them in sight. The breeze came steadily in from the west, with a promise of early increase. The stars were being blotted out by driving masses of clouds, which indicated a greater velocity in the upper strata. 'Frisco Kid surveyed the sky. "Going to have it good and stiff before morning," he prophesied, and Joe guessed so, too.

A couple of hours later both boats stood in for the land, and dropped anchor not more than a cable's length from the shore. A little wharf ran out, the bare end of which was perceptible to them, though they could discern a small yacht lying to a buoy a short distance away.

As on the previous night, everything was in readiness for hasty departure. The anchors could be tripped and the sails flung out on a moment's notice. Both skiffs came over noiselessly from the *Reindeer*. Nelson had given one of his two men to Pete, so that each skiff was doubly manned. They were not a very prepossessing bunch of men—at least, Joe though so, for their faces bore a savage seriousness which almost made him shiver. The captain of the *Dazzler* buckled on his pistol belt and placed a rifle and a small double-block tackle in the boat. Nelson was also armed, while his men wore at their hips the customary sailor's sheath knife. They were very slow and careful to avoid noise in getting into the boats, Pete pausing long enough to warn the boys to remain quietly aboard and not try any tricks.

"Now'd be your chance, Joe, if they hadn't taken the skiffs," 'Frisco Kid whispered, when the boats had vanished into the loom of the land.

"What's the matter with the *Dazzler*?" was the unexpected answer. "We could up sail and away before you could say Jack Robinson."

They crawled for'ard and began to hoist the mainsail. The anchor they could slip, if necessary, and save the time of pulling it up. But at the first rattle of the halyards on the sheaves a warning "Hist!" came to them through the darkness, followed by a loudly whispered "Drop that!"

Glancing in the direction from which these sounds proceeded, they made out a white face peering at them from over the rail of the other sloop.

"Aw, it's only the *Reindeer's* boy," 'Frisco Kid said. "Come on."

Again they were interrupted at the first rattling of the blocks.

"I say, you fellers, you'd better let go them halyards pretty quick, I'm a-tellin' you, or I'll give you what for!"

This threat being dramatically capped by the click of a cocking pistol, 'Frisco Kid obeyed and went grumbling back to the cockpit. "Oh, there's plenty more chances to come," he whispered consolingly to Joe. "Pete was cute, wasn't he? Kind of thought you'd be trying to make a break, and fixed it so you couldn't."

Nothing came from the shore to indicate how the pirates were faring. Not a dog barked, not a light flared; yet the air seemed quivering with an alarm about to burst forth. The night had taken on a strained feeling of intensity, as though it held in store all kinds of terrible things. The boys felt this keenly as they huddled against each other in the cockpit and waited.

"You were going to tell me about your running away,"

Joe ventured finally, "and why you came back again."

'Frisco Kid took up the tale at once, speaking in a muffled undertone close to the other's ear.

"You see, when I made up my mind to quit the life, there wasn't a soul to lend me a hand; but I knew that the only thing for me to do was to get ashore and find some kind of work, so I could study. Then I figured there'd be more chance in the country than in the city; so I gave Nelson the slip. I was on the *Reindeer* then — one night on the Alameda oyster beds, and headed back from the Bay. But they were all Portuguese farmers thereabouts, and none of them had work for me. Besides, it was in the wrong time of the year—winter. That shows how much I knew about the land.

"I'd saved up a couple of dollars, and I kept traveling back, deeper and deeper into the country, looking for work and buying bread and cheese, and such things, from the storekeepers. I tell you it was cold, nights, sleeping out without blankets, and I was always glad when morning came. But worse than that was the way everybody looked on me. They were all suspicious, and not a bit afraid to show it, and sometimes they'd sick their dogs on me and tell me to get along. Seemed as though there wasn't no place for me on the land. Then my money gave out, and just about the time I was good and hungry I got captured."

"Captured! What for?"

"Nothing. Living, I suppose. I crawled into a haystack to sleep one night, because it was warmer, and along comes a village constable and arrests me for being a tramp. At first they thought I was a runaway, and telegraphed my description all over. I told them I didn't have no people, but they wouldn't believe me for a long while. And then, when nobody claimed me, the judge sent me to a boys' 'refuge' in San Francisco."

He stopped and peered intently in the direction of the shore. The darkness and the silence in which the men had been swallowed up were profound. Nothing was stirring save the rising wind.

"I thought I'd die in that 'refuge.' Just like being in jail. You were locked up and guarded like any prisoner. Even then, if I could have liked the other boys it wouldn't have been so bad. But they were mostly street boys of the worst sort, without one spark of manhood or one idea of square dealing and fair play. There was only one thing I did like, and that was the books. Oh, I did lots of reading, I tell you. But that couldn't make up for the rest. I wanted the freedom, and the sunlight, and the salt water. And what had I done to be kept in prison and herded with such a gang? Instead of doing wrong, I had tried to do good, to make myself better, and that's what I got for it. I wasn't old enough, you see.

"Sometimes I'd see the sunshine dancing on the water and showing white on the sails, and the *Reindeer* cutting through it just as you please, and I'd get that sick I wouldn't know hardly what I did. And then the boys would come against me with some of their meannesses, and I'd start in to lick the whole kit of them. Then the men in charge'd lock me up and punish me. After I couldn't stand it no longer, I watched my chance, and cut and run for it. Seemed as though there wasn't no place on the land for me, so I picked up with Pete and went back on the Bay. That's about all there is to it, though I'm going to try it again when I get a little older — old enough to get a square deal for myself."

"You're going to go back on the land with me," Joe said authoritatively, laying a hand on his shoulder; "that's what you're going to do. As for —"

Bang! A revolver shot rang out from the shore. Bang! Bang! More guns were speaking sharply and hurriedly. A man's voice rose wildly on the air and died away. Somebody began to cry for help. Both boys were to their feet on the instant, hoisting the mainsail and getting everything ready to run. The *Reindeer* boy was doing likewise. A man, roused from his sleep on the yacht, thrust an excited head through the skylight, but withdrew it hastily at sight of the two stranger sloops. The intensity of waiting was broken, the time for action come.

CHAPTER 12

Perilous Hours

HEAVING IN ON the anchor chain till it was up and down, 'Frisco Kid and Joe ceased from their exertions. Everything was in readiness to give the *Dazzler* the jib and go. They strained their eyes in the direction of the shore. The clamor had died away, but here and there lights were beginning to flash. The creaking of a block and tackle came to their ears, and they heard Nelson's voice singing out "Lower away!" and "Cast off!"

"Pete forgot to oil it," 'Frisco Kid commented, referring to the tackle.

"Takin' their time about it, ain't they?" the boy on the *Reindeer* called over to them, sitting down on the cabin and mopping his face after the exertion of hoisting the mainsail singlehanded.

"Guess they're all right," 'Frisco Kid rejoined.

"Say, you," the man on the yacht cried through the skylight, not venturing to show his head. "You'd better go away."

"And you'd better stay below and keep quiet," was the response.

"We'll take care of ourselves. See you do the same," replied the boy on the *Reindeer.*

"If I was only out of this, I'd show you," the man threatened.

"Lucky for you you're not," was the response.

"Here they come!"

The two skiffs shot out of the darkness and came alongside. Some kind of an altercation was going on, as Pete's shrill voice attested.

"No, no!" he cried. "Put it on ze *Dazzler.* Ze *Reindeer* she sail too fast-a, and run away, oh, so queeck, and never more I see it. Put it on ze *Dazzler*. Eh? W'at you say?"

"All right," Nelson agreed. "We'll whack up afterwards. But hurry up. Out with you, lads, and heave her up. My arm's broke."

The men tumbled out, ropes were cast inboard, and all hands, with the exception of Joe, tailed on. The shouting of men, the sound of oars, and the rattling and slapping of blocks and sails, told that the men on shore were getting under way for the pursuit.

"Now!" Nelson commanded. "All together! Don't let her come back or you 'll smash the skiff. There she takes it! A long pull and a strong pull! Once again! And yet again! Get a turn there, somebody, and take a spell."

Though the task was but half accomplished, they were exhausted by the strenuous effort, and hailed the rest eagerly. Joe glanced over the side to discover what the heavy object might be, and saw the vague outlines of a very small office safe.

"Now, all together! Take her on the run, and don't let her stop! Yo, ho! Heave, ho! Once again! And another! Over with her!"

Straining and gasping, with tense muscles and heaving chests, they brought the cumbersome weight over the side, rolled it on top of the rail, and lowered it into the cockpit on the run. The cabin doors were thrown apart, and it was moved along, end for end, till it lay on the cabin floor, snug against the end of the centerboard case. Nelson had followed it aboard to superintend. His left arm hung helpless at his side, and from the fingertips blood dripped with monotonous regularity. He did not seem to mind it, however; nor even the mutterings of the human storm he had raised ashore, and which, to judge by the sounds, was even now threatening to break upon them.

"Lay your course for the Golden Gate," he said to Pete, as he turned to go. "I'll try to stand by you; but if you get lost in the dark, I'll meet you outside, off the Farralones, in the morning." He sprang into the skiff after the men, and, with a wave of his uninjured arm, cried heartily: "And then it 's Mexico, my jolly rovers — Mexico and summer weather!"

Just as the *Dazzler*, freed from her anchor, paid off under the jib and filled away, a dark sail loomed under her stern, barely missing the skiff in tow. The cockpit of the stranger was crowded with men, who raised their voices angrily at sight of the pirates. Joe had half a mind to run for'ard and cut the halyards so that they might be captured. As he had told Pete the day before, he had done nothing to be ashamed of, and was not afraid to go before a court of justice. But the thought of 'Frisco Kid restrained him. He wished to take him ashore with him, but in so doing he did not wish to take him to jail. So he began to experience a keen interest in the escape of the *Dazzler,* after all.

The pursuing sloop rounded up hurriedly to come about after them, and in the darkness fouled the yacht which lay at anchor. The man aboard of her, thinking that at last his time had come, let out one wild yell, and ran on deck, screaming for help. In the confusion of the collision Pete and the boys slipped away into the night.

The *Reindeer* had already disappeared, and by the time Joe and 'Frisco Kid had the running gear coiled down and everything in shape, they were standing out in open water. The wind was freshening constantly, and the *Dazzler* heeling a lively clip through the comparatively smooth water. Before an hour had passed, the lights of Hunter's Point were well on her starboard beam. 'Frisco Kid went below to make coffee, but Joe remained on deck, watching the lights of south San Francisco grow, and speculating on his destination. Mexico! They were going to sea in such a frail craft! Impossible! At least, it seemed so to him, for his conceptions of ocean travel were limited to steamers and full-rigged ships, and he did not know how the tiny fishing boats ventured the open sea. He was beginning to feel half sorry that he had not cut the halyards, and longed to ask Pete a thousand questions; but just as the first was on his lips, that worthy ordered him to go below and get some coffee, and then to turn in. He was followed shortly afterward by 'Frisco Kid, Pete remaining at his lonely task of beating down the Bay and out to sea. Twice Pete heard the waves buffeted back from some flying forefoot, and once he saw a sail to leeward on the opposite tack, which luffed sharply and came about at sight of him. But the darkness favored, and he heard no more of it — perhaps because he worked into the wind closer by a point, and held on his way with a rebellious shaking after leech.

Shortly after dawn the boys were called and came sleepily on deck. The day had broken cold and gray, while the wind had attained half a gale. Joe noted with astonishment the white tents of the quarantine station on Angel Island. San Francisco lay a smoky blur on the southern horizon, while the night, still lingering on the western edge of the world, slowly withdrew before their eyes. Pete was just finishing a long reach into the Raccoon Strait, and, at the same time, studiously regarding a plunging sloop yacht half a mile astern.

"Dey t'ink to catch ze *Dazzler*, eh? Bah!" And he brought the craft in question about, laying a course straight for the Golden Gate.

The pursuing yacht followed suit. Joe watched her a few moments. She held an apparently parallel course to them, and forged ahead much faster.

"Why, at this rate they'll have us in no time!" he cried.

Pete laughed. "You t'ink so? Bah! Dey outfoot; we outpoint. Dey are scared of ze wind; we wipe ze eye of ze wind. Ah! you wait — you see."

"They're traveling ahead faster," 'Frisco Kid explained, "but we're sailing closer to the wind. In the end we'll beat them, even if they have the nerve to cross the bar, which I don't think they have. Look! See!"

Ahead could be seen the great ocean surges, flinging themselves skyward and bursting into roaring caps of smother. In the midst of it, now rolling her dripping bottom clear, now sousing her deck load of lumber far above the guards, a coasting steam schooner was lumbering heavily into port. It was magnificent, this battle between man and the elements. Whatever timidity he had entertained fled away, and Joe's nostrils began to dilate and his eyes to flash at the nearness of the impending struggle.

Pete called for his oilskins and sou'wester, and Joe also was equipped with a spare suit. Then he and 'Frisco Kid were sent below to lash and cleat the safe in place. In the midst of this task Joe glanced at the firm name gilt-lettered on the face of it, and read, *Bronson & Tate*. Why, that was his father and his father's partner. That was their safe, their money! 'Frisco Kid, nailing the last retaining cleat on the floor of the cabin, looked up and followed his fascinated gaze.

"That's rough, isn't it?" he whispered. "Your father?"

Joe nodded. He could see it all now. They had run in to San Andreas, where his father worked the big quarries, and most probably the safe contained the wages of the thousand men or so whom his firm employed. "Don't say anything," he cautioned.

'Frisco Kid agreed knowingly. "Pete can't read, anyway," he added, "and the chances are that Nelson won't know what your name is. But, just the same, it's pretty rough. They'll break it open and divide up as soon as they can, so I don't see what you're going to do about it."

"Wait and see." Joe had made up his mind that he would do his best to stand by his father's property. At the worst, it could only be lost; and that would surely be the case were he not along; while, being along, he at least held a fighting chance to save or to be in position to recover it. Responsibilities were showering upon him thick and fast. Three days before he had had but himself to consider. Then, in some subtle way, he had felt a certain accountability for 'Frisco Kid's future welfare; and after that, and still more subtly, he had become aware of duties which he owed to his position, to his sister, to his chums, and to friends. And now, by a most unexpected chain of circumstances, came the pressing need of service for his father's sake. It was a call upon his deepest strength, and he responded bravely. While the future might be doubtful, he had no doubt of himself; and this very state of mind, this self-confidence, by a generous alchemy, gave him added strength. Nor did he fail to be vaguely aware of it, and to grasp dimly at the truth that confidence breeds confidence — strength, strength.

"Now she takes it!" Pete cried.

Both lads ran into the cockpit. They were on the edge of the breaking bar. A huge forty-footer reared a foam-crested head far above them, stealing their wind for the moment and threatening to crush the tiny craft like an eggshell. Joe held his breath. It was the supreme moment. Pete luffed straight into it, and the *Dazzler* mounted the steep slope with a rush, poised a moment on the giddy summit, and fell into the yawning valley beyond. Keeping off in the intervals to fill the mainsail, and luffing into the combers, they worked their way across the dangerous stretch. Once they caught the tail end of a whitecap and were well-nigh smothered in the froth; but otherwise the sloop bobbed and ducked with the happy facility of a cork.

To Joe it seemed as though he had been lifted out of himself, out of the world. Ah, this was life! This was action! Surely it could not be the old, commonplace world he had lived in so long! The sailors, grouped on the streaming deck load of the steamer, waved their sou'-westers, nor, on the bridge, was the captain above expressing his admiration for the plucky craft.

"Ah! You see! You see!" Pete pointed astern.

The sloop yacht had been afraid to venture it, and was skirting back and forth on the inner edge of the bar. The chase was off. A pilot boat, running for shelter from the coming storm, flew by them like a frightened bird, passing the steamer as though the latter were standing still.

Half an hour later the *Dazzler* passed beyond the last smoking sea and was sliding up and down on the long Pacific swell. The wind had increased its velocity and necessitated a reefing down of jib and mainsail. Then she laid off again, full and free on the starboard tack, for the Farralones, thirty miles away. By the time breakfast was cooked and eaten they picked up the *Reindeer*, hove to and working offshore to the south and west. The wheel was lashed down, and there was not a soul on deck.

Pete complained bitterly against such recklessness. "Dat is ze one fault of Nelson. He no care. He is afraid of not'ing. Some day he will die, oh, so vaire queeck! I know, I know."

Three times they circled about the *Reindeer*, running under her weather quarter and shouting in chorus, before they brought anybody on deck. Sail was then made at once, and together the two cockleshells plunged away into the vastness of the Pacific. This was necessary, as 'Frisco Kid informed Joe, in order to have an offing before the whole fury of the storm broke upon them. Otherwise they would be driven on the lee shore of the California coast. "Grub and water," he said, could be obtained by running in to the land when fine weather came. He also congratulated Joe upon the fact that he was not seasick — which circumstance likewise brought praise from Pete, and put him in better humor with his mutinous sailor.

"I'll tell you what we'll do," 'Frisco Kid whispered, while cooking dinner. "Tonight we'll drag Pete down —"

"Drag Pete down?"

"Yes, and tie him up good and snug — as soon as it gets dark. Then put out the lights and make a run for it. Get to port anyway, anywhere, just so long as we shake loose from Nelson. You'll save your father's money, and I'll go away somewhere, over on the other side of the world, and begin all over again."

"Then we'll have to call it off, that's all."

"Call what off?"

"Tying Pete up and running for it."

"No, sir; that's decided upon."

"Now, listen here: I'll not have a thing to do with it — I'll go on to Mexico first — if you don't make me one promise."

"And what's the promise?"

"Just this: you place yourself in my hands from the moment we get ashore, and trust to me. You don't know anything about the land, anyway — you said so. And I'll fix it with my father — I know I can — so that you can get to study, and get an education, and be something else than a Bay pirate or a sailor. That's what you'd like, isn't it?"

Though he said nothing, 'Frisco Kid showed how well he liked it by the expression of his face.

"And it'll be no more than your due, either," Joe continued. "You've stood by me, and you'll have recovered my father's money. He'll owe it to you."

"But I don't do things that way. Think I do a man a favor just to be paid for it?"

"Now you keep quiet. How much do you think it'd cost my father to recover that safe? Give me your promise, that's all, and when I've got things arranged, if you don't like them you can back out. Come on; that's fair."

They shook hands on the bargain, and proceeded to map out their line of action for the night.

But the storm yelling down out of the northwest had something entirely different in store for the *Dazzler* and her crew. By the time dinner was over they were forced to put double reefs in mainsail and jib, and still the gale had not reached its height. The sea, also, had been kicked up till it was a continuous succession of water mountains, frightful and withal grand to look upon from the low deck of the sloop. It was only when the sloops were tossed up on the crests of the waves at the same time that they caught sight of each other. Occasional fragments of seas swashed into the cockpit or dashed aft clear over the cabin, and before long Joe was stationed at the small pump to keep the well dry.

At three o'clock, watching his chance, Pete motioned to the *Reindeer* that he was going to heave to and get out a sea anchor. This latter was of the nature of a large shallow canvas bag, with the mouth held open by triangularly lashed spars. To this the towing ropes were attached, on the kite principle, so that the greatest resisting surface was presented to the water. The sloop, drifting so much faster, would thus be held bow on to both wind and sea — the safest possible position in a storm. Nelson waved his hand in response that he understood, and to go ahead.

Pete went for'ard to launch the sea anchor himself, leaving it to 'Frisco Kid to put the helm down at the proper moment and run into the wind.

The Frenchman poised on the slippery foredeck, waiting an opportunity. But at this moment the *Dazzler* lifted into an unusually large sea, and, as she cleared the summit, caught a heavy snort of the gale at the very instant she was righting herself to an even keel.

Thus there was not the slightest yield to this sudden pressure coming on her sails and mast gear.

Snap! Crash! The steel weather rigging was carried away at the lanyards, and mast, jib, mainsail, blocks, stays, sea anchor, Pete — everything — went over the side. Almost by a miracle, the captain clutched at the bobstay and managed to get one hand up and over the bowsprit. The boys ran for'ard to drag him into safety, and Nelson, observing the disaster, put up his helm and instantly ran the *Reindeer* down to the rescue of the imperiled crew.

CHAPTER 13

The End of the Cruise

PETE WAS UNINJURED from the fall overboard with the *Dazzler's* mast, but the sea anchor which had gone with him had not escaped so easily. The gaff of the mainsail had been driven through it, and it refused to work. The wreckage, thumping alongside, held the sloop in a quartering slant to the seas — not so dangerous a position as it might be, nor as safe, either.

"Good-by, old-a *Dazzler*. Never no more you wipe ze eye of ze wind. Never no more you kick your heels at ze crack gentleman yachts."

So the captain lamented, standing in the cockpit and surveying the ruin with wet eyes. Even Joe, who bore him great dislike, felt sorry for him at this moment. As the horse is to the Arab, so the ship is to the sailor, and Pete suffered his loss keenly. A heavier blast of the wind caught the jagged crest of a wave and hurled it upon the helpless craft.

"Can't we save her?" Joe spluttered.

'Frisco Kid shook his head.

"Or the safe?"

"Impossible," he answered. "Couldn't lay another boat alongside for a United States mint. As it is, it'll keep us guessing to save ourselves."

Another sea swept over them, and the skiff, which had long since been swamped, dashed itself to pieces against the stern. Then the *Reindeer* towered above them on a mountain of water. Joe caught himself half shrinking back, for it seemed she would fall down squarely on top of them; but the next instant she dropped into the gaping trough, and they were looking down upon her far below. It was a striking picture — one Joe was destined never to forget. The *Reindeer* was wallowing in the snow-white smother, her rails flush with the sea, the water scudding across her deck in foaming cataracts. The air was filled with flying spray, which made the scene appear hazy and unreal. One of the men was clinging to the perilous after-deck and striving to cast off the waterlogged skiff. The boy, leaning far over the cockpit rail and holding on for dear life, was passing him a knife. The second man stood at the wheel, putting it up with flying hands, and forcing the sloop to pay off. By him, his injured arm in a sling, was Nelson, his sou'wester gone and his fair hair plastered in wet, wind-blown ringlets about his face. His whole attitude breathed indomitability, courage, strength. Joe looked upon him in sudden awe, and, realizing the enormous possibilities in the man, felt sorrow for the way in which they had been wasted. A pirate — a robber! In that flashing moment he caught a glimpse of truth, grasped at the mystery of success and failure. Of such stuff as

Nelson were heroes made; but they possessed wherein he lacked — the power of choice, the careful poise of mind, the sober control of soul.

These were the thoughts which came to Joe in the flight of a second. Then the *Reindeer* swept skyward and hurtled across their bow to leeward on the breast of a mighty billow.

"Ze wild man! Ze wild man!" Pete shrieked, watching her in amazement. "He t'inks he can jibe! He will die! We will all die! He must come about! Oh, ze fool! Ze fool!"

But time was precious, and Nelson ventured the chance. At the right moment he jibed the mainsail over and hauled back on the wind.

"Here she comes! Make ready to jump for it!" 'Frisco Kid cried to Joe.

The *Reindeer* dashed by their stern, heeling over till the cabin windows were buried, and so close that it appeared she must run them down. But a freak of the waters lurched the two crafts apart. Nelson, seeing that the manœuver had miscarried, instantly instituted another. Throwing the helm hard up, the *Reindeer* whirled on her heel, thus swinging her overhanging main boom closer to the *Dazzler*. Pete was the nearest, and the opportunity could last no longer than a second. Like a cat he sprang, catching the footrope with both hands. Then the *Reindeer* forged ahead, dipping him into the sea at every plunge. But he clung on, working inboard every time he emerged, till he dropped into the cockpit, as Nelson squared off to run down to leeward and repeat the manœuver.

"Your turn next," 'Frisco Kid said.

"No, yours," Joe replied.

"But I know more about the water," 'Frisco Kid insisted.

"I can swim as well as you," said the other.

It would have been hard to forecast the outcome of this dispute; but, as it was, the swift rush of events made any settlement useless. The *Reindeer* had jibed over and was plowing back at breakneck speed, careening at such an angle that it seemed she must surely capsize. It was a gallant sight.

The storm burst in fury, the shouting wind flattening the ragged crests till they boiled. The *Reindeer* dipped from view behind an immense wave. The wave rolled on, but where the sloop had been the boys noted with startled eyes only the angry waters. Doubting, they looked a second time. There was no *Reindeer*. They were alone on the ocean.

"God have mercy on their souls!"

Joe was too horrified at the suddenness of the catastrophe to utter a sound.

"Sailed her clean under, and, with the ballast she carried, went straight to bottom," 'Frisco Kid gasped when he could speak. "Pete always said Nelson would drown himself that way someday! And now they're all gone. It's dreadful — dreadful. But now we've got to look out for ourselves, I tell you! The back of the storm broke in that puff, but the sea'll kick up worse yet as the wind eases down. Lend a hand, and hang on with the other. We've got to get her head on."

Together, knives in hand, they crawled for'ard, where the pounding wreckage hampered the boat sorely. 'Frisco

Kid took the lead in the ticklish work, but Joe obeyed orders like a veteran. Every minute or so the bow was swept by the sea, and they were pounded and buffeted about like a pair of shuttlecocks. First the main portion of the wreckage was securely fastened to the for'ard bitts; then, breathless and gasping, more often under the water than out, it was cut and hack at the tangle of halyards, sheets, stays, and tackles. The cockpit was taking water rapidly, and it was a race between swamping and completing the task. At last, however, everything stood clear save the lee rigging. 'Frisco Kid slashed the lanyards. The storm did the rest. The *Dazzler* drifted swiftly to leeward of the wreckage, till the strain on the line fast to the for'ard bitts jerked her bow into place, and she ducked dead into the eye of the wind and sea.

Pausing but for a cheer at the success of their undertaking, the two lads raced aft, where the cockpit was half full and the dunnage of the cabin all afloat. With a couple of buckets procured from the stern lockers, they proceeded to fling the water overboard. It was heartbreaking work, for many a barrelful was flung back upon them again; but they persevered, and when night fell, the *Dazzler*, bobbing merrily at her sea anchor, could boast that her pumps sucked once more. As 'Frisco Kid had said, the backbone of the storm was broken, though the wind had veered to the west, where it still blew stiffly.

"If she holds," 'Frisco Kid said, referring to the breeze, "we'll drift to the California coast, somewhere long in, tomorrow. There's nothing to do now but wait."

They said little, oppressed by the loss of their comrades and overcome with exhaustion, preferring to huddle against each other for the sake of warmth and companionship. It was a miserable night, and they shivered constantly from the cold. Nothing dry was to be obtained aboard, food, blankets, everything being soaked with the salt water. Sometimes they dozed; but these intervals were short and harassing, for it seemed as if each of the two boys took turns in waking with such a sudden start as to rouse the other.

At last day broke, and they looked about. Wind and sea had dropped considerably, and there was no question as to the safety of the *Dazzler*. The coast was nearer than they had expected, its cliffs showing dark and forbidding in the gray of dawn. But with the rising of the sun they could see the yellow beaches, flanked by the white surf, and, beyond — it seemed too good to be true — the clustering houses and smoking chimneys of a town.

"It's Santa Cruz!" 'Frisco Kid cried. "And we'll run no risk of being wrecked in the surf!"

"Then you think we'll save the safe?" Joe queried.

"Yes, indeed we will! There isn't much of a sheltered harbor for large vessels, but with this breeze we'll run right up the mouth of the San Lorenzo River. Then there's a little lake like, and boathouses. Water smooth as glass. Come on. We'll be in in time for breakfast."

Bringing to light some spare coils of rope from the lockers, he put a clove hitch on the standing part of the sea-anchor hawser, and carried the new running line aft, making it fast to the stern bitts. Then he cast off from the for'ard bitts. Naturally the *Dazzler* swung off into the trough, completed the evolution, and pointed her nose toward shore. A couple of spare oars from below, and as many water-soaked blankets, sufficed to make a jury mast and sail. When this was in place Joe cast loose from the wreckage, which was now towing astern, while 'Frisco Kid took the tiller.

"How's that?" said 'Frisco Kid, as he finished making the *Dazzler* fast fore and aft, and stepped upon the string-piece of the tiny wharf. "What'll we do next, captain?"

Joe looked up in quick surprise. "Why — I — what's the matter?"

"Well, aren't you captain now? Haven't we reached land? I'm crew from now on, you know. What's your orders?"

Joe caught the spirit of it. "Pipe all hands for breakfast; that is — wait a minute."

Diving below, he possessed himself of the money he had stowed away in his bundle when he came aboard. Then he locked the cabin door, and they went uptown in search of restaurants. Over the breakfast Joe planned the next move, and, when they had done, communicated it to 'Frisco Kid.

In response to his inquiry the cashier told him when the morning train started for San Francisco. He glanced at the clock.

"I've just time to catch it," he said to 'Frisco Kid. "Here is the key to the cabin door. Keep it locked, and don't let anybody come aboard. Here's money. Eat at the restaurants. Dry your blankets and sleep in the cockpit. I'll be back tomorrow. And don't yet anybody into that cabin. Good-by."

With a hasty handgrip, he sped down the street to the depot. The conductor, when he punched his ticket, looked at him with surprise. And well he might, for it was not the custom of his passengers to travel in sea boots and sou'-westers. But Joe did not mind. He did not even notice. He had bought a paper and was absorbed in its contents. Before long his eyes caught an interesting paragraph:

SUPPOSED TO HAVE BEEN LOST.

The tug *Sea Queen,* chartered by Bronson & Tate, has returned from a fruitless cruise outside the heads. No news of value could be obtained concerning the pirates who so daringly carried off their safe at San Andreas last Tuesday night. The lighthouse keeper at the Farralones mentions having sighted the two sloops Wednesday morning, clawing offshore in the teeth of the gale. It is supposed by shipping men that they perished in the storm with their ill-gotten treasure. Rumor has it that, in addition to a large sum in gold, the safe contained papers of even greater importance.

When Joe had read this he felt a great relief. It was evident no one had been killed at San Andreas on the night of the robbery, else there would have been some comment on it in the paper. Nor, if they had had any clue to his own whereabouts, would they have omitted such a striking bit of information.

At the depot in San Francisco the curious onlookers were surprised to see a boy clad conspicuously in sea boots and sou'wester hail a cab and dash away in it. But Joe was in a hurry. He knew his father's hours, and was fearful lest he should not catch him before he went to luncheon.

The office boy scowled at him when he pushed open the door and asked to see Mr. Bronson; nor could the head clerk, when summoned by this strange-looking intruder, recognize him.

"Don't you know me, Mr. Willis?"

Mr. Willis looked a second time. "Why, it 's Joe Bronson! Of all things under the sun, where did you drop from? Go right in. Your father's in there."

Mr. Bronson stopped dictating to his stenographer, looked up, and said: "Hello! where have you been?"

"To sea," Joe answered demurely enough, not sure of just what kind of a reception he was to get, and fingering his sou'wester nervously.

"Short trip, eh? How did you make out?"

"Oh, so-so." He had caught the twinkle in his father's eye, and knew that it was all clear sailing. "Not so bad — er — that is, considering."

"Considering?"

"Well, not exactly that; rather, it might have been worse, and, well — I don't know that it could have been better."

"You interest me; sit down." Then, turning to the stenographer, "You may go, Mr. Brown, and — hum — I sha'n't need you any more today."

It was all Joe could do to keep from crying, so kindly and naturally had his father received him — making him feel at once as if not the slightest thing uncommon had occurred. It was if he had just returned from a vacation, or, man grown, had come back from some business trip.

"Now go ahead, Joe. You were speaking to me a moment ago in conundrums, and have aroused my curiosity to a most uncomfortable degree."

Thereat Joe sat down and told what had happened, all that had happened, from the previous Monday night to that moment. Each little incident he related, every detail, not forgetting his conversations with 'Frisco Kid nor his plans concerning him. His face flushed and he was carried away with the excitement of the narrative, while Mr. Bronson was almost as interested, urging him on whenever he slackened his pace, but otherwise remaining silent.

"So you see," Joe said at last, "it couldn't possibly have turned out any better."

"Ah, well," Mr. Bronson deliberated judiciously, "it may be so, and then again it may not."

"I don't see it." Joe felt sharp disappointment at his father's qualified approval. It seemed to him that the return of the safe merited something stronger.

That Mr. Bronson fully comprehended the way Joe felt about it was clearly in evidence, for he went on: "As to the matter of the safe, all hail to you, Joe. Credit, and plenty of it, is your due. Mr. Tate and I have already spent five hundred dollars in attempting to recover it. So important was it that we have also offered five thousand dollars reward, and this morning were even considering the advisability of increasing the amount. But, my son" — Mr. Bronson stood up, resting a hand affectionately on his boy's shoulder —"there be certain things in this world which are of still greater importance than gold or papers which represent that which gold may buy. How about *yourself?* There's the point. Will you sell the best possibilities of your life right now for a million dollars?"

Joe shook his head.

"As I said, that's the point. A human life the treasure of the world cannot buy; nor can it redeem one which is misspent; nor can it make full and complete and beautiful a life which is dwarfed and warped and ugly. How about yourself? What is to be the effect of all these strange adventures on your life — *your* life, Joe? Are you going to pick yourself up tomorrow and try it over again? Or the next day, or the day after? Do you understand? Why, Joe, do you think for one moment that I could place against the best value of my son's life the paltry value of a safe? And *can* I say, until time has told me, whether this trip of yours could not possibly have been better? Such an experience is as potent for evil as for good. One dollar is exactly like another — there are many in the world; but no Joe is like my Joe, nor can there be any others in the world to take his place. Don't you see, Joe? Don't you understand?"

Mr. Bronson's voice broke slightly, and the next instant Joe was sobbing as though his heart would break. He had never understood this father of his before, and he knew now the pain he must have caused him, to say nothing of his mother and sister. But the four stirring days he had spent had given him a clearer view of the world and humanity, and he had always possessed the power of putting his thoughts into speech; so he spoke of these things and the lessons he had learned, the conclusions he had drawn from his conversations with 'Frisco Kid, from his talks with Pete, from the graphic picture he retained of the *Reindeer* and Nelson as they wallowed in the trough beneath him. And Mr. Bronson listened and, in turn, understood.

"But what of 'Frisco Kid, father?" Joe asked when he had finished.

"Hum! There's a great deal of promise in the boy, from

what you say of him." Mr. Bronson hid the twinkle in his eye this time. "And, I must confess, he seems perfectly capable of shifting for himself."

"Sir?" Joe could not believe his ears.

"Let us see, then. He is at present entitled to the half of five thousand dollars, the other half of which belongs to you. It was you two who preserved the safe from the bottom of the Pacific, and if you only had waited a little longer, Mr. Tate and I might have increased the reward."

"Oh!" Joe caught a glimmering of the light. "Part of that is easily arranged, father. I simply refuse to take my half. As to the other — that isn't exactly what 'Frisco Kid desires. He wants friends — and — and — though you didn't say so, they are far higher than gold, nor càn gold buy them. He wants friends and a chance for an education — not twenty-five hundred dollars."

"Don't you think it would be better that he choose for himself?"

"Ah, no. That's all arranged."

"Arranged?"

"Yes, sir. He's captain on sea, and I'm captain on land. So he's under my charge now."

"Then you have the power of attorney for him in the present negotiations? Good. I'll make a proposition. The twenty-five hundred dollars shall be held in trust by me, on his demand at any time. We'll settle about yours afterward. Then he shall be put on probation for, say, a year — as messenger first, and then in the office. You can either coach him in his studies, or he can attend night school. And after that, if he comes through his period of probation with flying colors, I'll give him the same opportunities for an education that you possess. It all depends on himself. And now, Mr. Attorney, what have you to say to my offer in the interests of your client?"

"That I close with it at once — and thank you." Father and son shook hands.

"And what are you going to do now, Joe?"

"I'm going to send a telegram to 'Frisco Kid first, and then hurry home."

"Then wait a minute till I call up San Andreas and tell Mr. Tate the good news, and I'll go with you."

"Mr. Willis," Mr. Bronson said as they left the outer office, "do you remain in charge, and kindly tell the clerks that they are free for the rest of the day.

"And I say," he called back as they entered the elevator, "don't forget the office boy."

PART THREE

Other Stories of Adventure

CONTENTS

In Yeddo Bay

Somewhere along Theater Street he had lost it. He remembered being hustled somewhat roughly on the bridge over one of the canals that cross that busy thoroughfare. Possibly some slant-eyed, light-fingered pickpocket was even then enjoying the fifty-odd yen his purse had contained. And then again, he thought, he might have lost it himself, just lost it carelessly.

Hopelessly, and for the twentieth time, he searched in all his pockets for the missing purse. It was not there. His hand lingered in his empty hip pocket, and he woefully regarded the voluble and vociferous restaurant-keeper, who insanely clamored: "Twenty-five sen! You pay now! Twenty-five sen!"

"But my purse!" the boy said. "I tell you I've lost it somewhere."

Whereupon the restaurant keeper lifted his arms indignantly and shrieked: "Twenty-five sen! Twenty-five sen! You pay now!"

Quite a crowd had collected, and it was growing embarrassing for Alf Davis.

It was so ridiculous and petty, Alf thought. Such a disturbance about nothing! And, decidedly, he must be doing something. Thoughts of diving wildly through that forest of legs, and of striking out at whoever opposed him, flashed through his mind; but, as though divining his purpose, one of the waiters, a short and chunky chap with an evil-looking cast in one eye, seized him by the arm.

"You pay now! You pay now! Twenty-five sen!" yelled the proprietor, hoarse with rage.

Alf was red in the face, too, from mortification; but he resolutely set out on another exploration. He had given up the purse, pinning his last hope on stray coins. In the little change-pocket of his coat he found a ten-sen piece and five copper sen; and remembering having recently missed a ten-sen piece, he cut the seam of the pocket and resurrected the coin from the depths of the lining. Twenty-five sen he held in his hand, the sum required to pay for the supper he had eaten. He turned them over to the proprietor, who counted them, grew suddenly calm, and bowed obsequiously — in fact, the whole crowd bowed obsequiously and melted away.

Alf Davis was a young sailor, just turned sixteen, on board the *Annie Mine*, an American sealing schooner which had run into Yokohama to ship its season's catch of skins to London. And in this his second trip ashore he was beginning to catch his first puzzling glimpses of the Oriental mind. He laughed when the bowing and kowtowing was over, and turned on his heel to confront another problem. How was he to get aboard ship? It was eleven o'clock at night, and there would be no ship's boats ashore, while the outlook for hiring a native boatman, with nothing but empty pockets to draw upon, was not particularly inviting.

Keeping a sharp lookout for shipmates, he went down to the pier. At Yokohama there are no long lines of wharves. The shipping lies out at anchor, enabling a few hundred of the short-legged people to make a livelihood by carrying passengers to and from the shore.

A dozen sampan men and boys hailed Alf and offered their services. He selected the most favorable-looking one, an old and beneficent-appearing man with a withered leg. Alf stepped into his sampan and sat down. It was quite dark and he could not see what the old fellow was doing, though he evidently was doing nothing about shoving off and getting under way. At last he limped over and peered into Alf's face.

"Ten sen," he said.

"Yes, I know, ten sen," Alf answered carelessly. "But hurry up. American schooner."

"Ten sen. You pay now," the old fellow insisted.

Alf felt himself grow hot all over at the hateful words "pay now." "You take me to American schooner; then I pay," he said.

But the man stood up patiently before him, held out his hand, and said, "Ten sen. You pay now."

Alf tried to explain. He had no money. He had lost his purse. But he would pay. As soon as he got aboard the American schooner, then he would pay. No; he would not even go aboard the American schooner. He would call to his shipmates, and they would give the sampan man the ten sen first. After that he would go aboard. So it was all right, of course.

To all of which the beneficent-appearing old man replied: "You pay now. Ten sen." And, to make matters worse, the other sampan men squatted on the pier steps, listening.

Alf, chagrined and angry, stood up to step ashore. But the old fellow laid a detaining hand on his sleeve. "You give shirt now. I take you 'Merican schooner," he proposed.

Then it was that all of Alf's American independence flamed up in his breast. The Anglo-Saxon has a born dislike of being imposed upon, and to Alf this was sheer robbery! Ten sen was equivalent to six American cents, while his shirt, which was of good quality and was new, had cost him two dollars.

He turned his back on the man without a word, and went out to the end of the pier, the crowd, laughing with great gusto, following at his heels. The majority of them were heavy-set, muscular fellows, and the July night being one of sweltering heat, they were clad in the least possible raiment. The water people of any race are rough and turbulent, and it struck Alf that to be out at midnight on a pier end with such a crowd of wharfmen, in a big Japanese city, was not as safe as it might be.

One burly fellow, with a shock of black hair and ferocious eyes, came up. The rest shoved after him to take part in the discussion.

"Give me shoes," the man said. "Give me shoes now. I take you 'Merican schooner."

Alf shook his head; whereat the crowd clamored that he accept the proposal. Now the Anglo-Saxon is so constituted that to browbeat or bully him is the last way under the sun of getting him to do any certain thing. He will dare willingly, but he will not permit himself to be driven. So this attempt of the boatmen to force Alf only aroused all the dogged stubbornness of his race. The same qualities were in him that are in men who lead forlorn hopes; and there, under the stars, on the lonely pier, encircled by the jostling and shouldering gang, he resolved that he would die rather than submit to the indignity of being robbed of a single stitch of clothing. Not value, but principle, was at stake.

Then somebody thrust roughly against him from behind. He whirled about with flashing eyes, and the circle involuntarily gave ground. But the crowd was growing more boisterous. Each and every article of clothing he had on was demanded by one or another, and these demands were shouted simultaneously at the tops of very healthy lungs.

Alf had long since ceased to say anything, but he knew that the situation was getting dangerous, and that the only thing left to him was to get away. His face was set doggedly, his eyes glinted like points of steel, and his body was firmly and confidently poised. This air of determination sufficiently impressed the boatmen to make them give way before him when he started to walk toward the shore end of the pier. But they trooped along beside him and behind him, shouting and laughing more noisily than ever. One of the youngsters, about Alf's size and build, impudently snatched his cap from his head; but before he could put it on his own head, Alf struck out from the shoulder, and sent the fellow rolling on the stones.

The cap flew out of his hand and disappeared among

the many legs. Alf did some quick thinking; his sailor pride would not permit him to leave the cap in their hands. He followed in the direction it had sped, and soon found it under the bare foot of a stalwart fellow, who kept his weight stolidly upon it. Alf tried to get the cap out by a sudden jerk, but failed. He shoved against the man's leg, but the man only grunted. It was challenge direct, and Alf accepted it. Like a flash one leg was behind the man and Alf had thrust strongly with his shoulder against the fellow's chest. Nothing could save the man from the fierce vigorousness of the trick, and he was hurled over and backward.

Next, the cap was on Alf's head and his fists were up before him. Then Alf whirled about to prevent attack from behind, and all those in that quarter fled precipitately. This was what he wanted. None remained between him and the shore end. The pier was narrow. Facing them and threatening with his fist those who attempted to pass him on either side, he continued his retreat. It was exciting work, walking backward and at the same time checking that surging mass of men. It was the battles fought by many sailors, more than his own warlike front, that gave Alf the victory.

Where the pier adjoins the shore was the station of the harbor police, and Alf backed into the electric-lighted office, very much to the amusement of the dapper lieutenant in charge. The sampan men, grown quiet and orderly, clustered like flies by the open door, through which they could see and hear what passed.

Alf explained his difficulty in few words, and demanded,

as the privilege of a stranger in a strange land, that the lieutenant put him aboard in the police boat. The lieutenant, in turn, who knew all the "rules and regulations" by heart, explained that the harbor police were not ferrymen, and that the police boats had other functions to perform than that of transporting belated and penniless sailormen to their ships. He also said he knew the sampan men to be natural-born robbers, but that so long as they robbed within the law he was powerless. It was their right to collect fares in advance, and who was he to command them to take a passenger and collect fare at the journey's end? Alf acknowledged the justice of his remarks, but suggested that while he could not command he might persuade. The lieutenant was willing to oblige, and went to the door, from where he delivered a speech to the crowd. But they, too, knew their rights, and, when the officer had finished, shouted in chorus their abominable "Ten sen! You pay now! You pay now!"

"You see, I can do nothing," the lieutenant said, who, by the way, spoke perfect English. "But I have warned them not to harm or molest you, so you will be safe, at least. The night is warm and half over. Lie down somewhere and go to sleep. I would permit you to sleep here in the office, were it not against the rules and regulations."

Alf thanked him for his kindness and courtesy; but the sampan men had aroused all his pride of race and doggedness, and the problem could not be solved that way. To sleep out the night on the stones was an acknowledgment of defeat.

"The sampan men refuse to take me out?"

The lieutenant nodded.

"And you refuse to take me out?"

Again the lieutenant nodded.

"Well, then, it's not in the rules and regulations that you can prevent my taking myself out?"

The lieutenant was perplexed. "There is no boat," he said.

"That's not the question," Alf proclaimed hotly. "If I take myself out, everybody's satisfied and no harm done?"

"Yes; what you say is true," persisted the puzzled lieutenant. "But you cannot take yourself out."

"You just watch me," was the retort.

Down went Alf's cap on the office floor. Right and left he kicked off his low-cut shoes. Trousers and shirt followed.

"Remember," he said in ringing tones, "I, as a citizen of the United States, shall hold you, the city of Yokohama, and the government of Japan responsible for those clothes. Good night."

He plunged through the doorway, scattering the astounded boatmen to either side, and ran out on the pier. But they quickly recovered and ran after him, shouting with glee at the new phase the situation had taken on. It was a night long remembered among the water folk of Yokohama town. Straight to the end Alf ran, and, without pause, dived off cleanly and neatly into the water. He struck out with a lusty, single-overhand stroke till curiosity prompted him to halt for a moment. Out of the darkness, from where the pier should be, voices were calling to him.

He turned on his back, floated, and listened.

"All right! All right!" he could distinguish from the babel. "No pay now; pay bime by! Come back! Come back now; pay bime by!"

"No, thank you," he called back. "No pay at all. Good night."

Then he faced about in order to locate the *Annie Mine*. She was fully a mile away, and in the darkness it was no easy task to get her bearings. First, he settled upon a blaze of lights which he knew nothing but a man-of-war could make. That must be the United States warship *Lancaster*. Somewhere to the left and beyond should be the *Annie Mine*. But to the left he made out three lights close together. That could not be the schooner. For the moment he was confused. He rolled over on his back and shut his eyes, striving to construct a mental picture of the harbor as he had seen it in daytime. With a snort of satisfaction he rolled back again. The three lights evidently belonged to the big English tramp steamer. Therefore the schooner must lie somewhere between the three lights and the *Lancaster*. He gazed long and steadily, and there, very dim and low, but at the point he expected, burned a single light — the anchor light of the *Annie Mine*.

And it was a fine swim under the starshine. The air was warm as the water, and the water as warm as tepid milk. The good salt taste of it was in his mouth, the tingling of it along his limbs; and the steady beat of his heart, heavy and strong, made him glad for living.

But beyond being glorious the swim was uneventful. On the right hand he passed the many-lighted *Lancaster*, on the left hand the English tramp, and ere long the *Annie Mine* loomed large above him. He grasped the hanging rope ladder and drew himself noiselessly on deck. There was no one in sight. He saw a light in the galley, and knew that the captain's son, who kept the lonely anchor watch, was making coffee. Alf went forward to the forecastle. The men were snoring in their bunks, and in that confined space the heat seemed to him insufferable. So he put on a thin cotton shirt and a pair of dungaree trousers, tucked blanket and pillow under his arm, and went up on deck and out on the forecastlehead.

Hardly had he begun to doze when he was roused by a boat coming alongside and hailing the anchor watch. It was the police boat, and to Alf it was given to enjoy the excited conversation that ensued. Yes, the captain's son recognized the clothes. They belonged to Alf Davis, one of the seamen. What had happened? No; Alf Davis had not come aboard. He was ashore. He was not ashore? Then he must be drowned. Here both the lieutenant and the captain's son talked at the same time, and Alf could make out nothing. Then he heard them come forward and rouse out the crew. The crew grumbled sleepily and said that Alf Davis was not in the forecastle; whereupon the captain's son waxed indignant at the Yokohama police and their ways, and the lieutenant quoted rules and regulations in despairing accents.

Alf rose up from the forecastlehead and extended his hand, saying:

"I guess I'll take those clothes. Thank you for bringing them aboard so promptly."

"I don't see why he couldn't have brought you aboard inside of them," said the captain's son.

And the police lieutenant said nothing, though he

turned the clothes over somewhat sheepishly to their rightful owner.

The next day, when Alf started to go ashore, he found himself surrounded by shouting and gesticulating, though very respectful, sampan men, all extraordinarily anxious to have him for a passenger. Nor did the one he selected say, "You pay now," when he entered his boat. When Alf prepared to step out on to the pier, he offered the man the customary ten sen. But the man drew himself up and shook his head.

"You all right," he said. "You no pay. You never no pay. You bully boy and all right."

And for the rest of the *Annie Mine's* stay in port, the sampan men refused money at Alf Davis's hand. Out of admiration for his pluck and independence, they had given him the freedom of the harbor.

Chris Farrington, Able Seaman

"If you vas in der old country ships, a liddle shaver like you vood pe only der boy, und you vood wait on der able seamen. Und ven der able seaman sing out, 'Boy, der water jug!' You vood jump quick, like a shot, und bring der water jug. Und ven der able seaman sing out, 'Boy, my boots!' you vood get der boots. Und you vood pe politeful, und say 'Yes sir' und 'No sir.' But you pe in der American ship, und you t'ink you are so good as der able seamen. Chris, mine boy, I haf ben a sailorman for twenty-two years, und do you t'ink you are so good as me? I vas a sailorman pefore you vas borned, und I knot und reef und splice ven you play mit topstrings und fly kites."

"But you are unfair, Emil!" cried Chris Farrington, his sensitive face flushed and hurt. He was a slender though strongly built young fellow of seventeen, with Yankee ancestry writ large all over him.

"Dere you go vonce again!" the Swedish sailor exploded. "My name is Mister Johansen, und a kid of a boy like you call me 'Emil'! It vas insulting, und comes pecause of der American ship!"

"But you call me 'Chris'!" the boy expostulated, reproachfully.

"But you vas a boy."

"Who does a man's work," Chris retorted. "And because I do a man's work I have as much right to call you by your first name as you me. We are all equals in this fo'c'sle, and you know it. When we signed for the voyage in San Francisco, we signed as sailors on the *Sophie Sutherland*, and there was no difference made with any of us. Haven't I always done my work? Did I ever shirk? Did you or any other man ever have to take a wheel for me? Or a lookout? Or go aloft?"

"Chris is right," interrupted a young English sailor. "No man has had to do a tap of his work yet. He signed as good as any of us, and he's shown himself as good —"

"Better!" broke in a Nova Scotia man. "Better than some of us! When we struck the sealing grounds he turned out to be next to the best boat steerer aboard. Only French Louis, who'd been at it for years, could beat him. I'm only a boat puller, and you're only a boat puller, too, Emil Johansen, for all your twenty-two years at sea. Why don't you become a boat steerer?"

"Too clumsy," laughed the Englishman, "and too slow."

"Little that counts, one way or the other," joined in Dane Jurgensen, coming to the aid of his Scandinavian brother. "Emil is a man grown and an able seaman; the boy is neither."

And so the argument raged back and forth, the Swedes, Norwegians, and Danes, because of race kinship, taking the part of Johansen, and the English, Canadians, and Americans taking the part of Chris. From an unprejudiced point of view, the right was on the side of Chris. As he had truly said, he did a man's work, and the same work that any of them did. But they were prejudiced, and badly so, and out of the words which passed rose a standing quarrel which divided the forecastle into two parties.

The *Sophie Sutherland* was a seal hunter, registered out of San Francisco, and engaged in hunting the furry sea animals along the Japanese coast north to Bering Sea. The other vessels were two-masted schooners, but she was a three-master and the largest in the fleet. In fact, she was a full-rigged, three-topmast schooner, newly built.

Although Chris Farrington knew that justice was with him, and that he performed all his work faithfully and well, many a time, in secret thought, he longed for some pressing emergency to arise whereby he could demonstrate to the Scandinavian seamen that he also was an able seaman.

But one stormy night, by an accident for which he was in nowise accountable, in overhauling a spare anchor chain he had all the fingers of his left hand badly crushed And his hopes were likewise crushed, for it was impossible for him to continue hunting with the boats, and he was forced to stay idly aboard until his fingers should heal. Yet, although he little dreamed it, this very accident was to give him the long-looked-for opportunity.

One afternoon in the latter part of May the *Sophie Sutherland* rolled sluggishly in a breathless calm. The seals were abundant, the hunting good, and the boats were all away and out of sight. And with them was almost every man of the crew. Besides Chris, there remained only the captain, the sailing master, and the Chinese cook.

The captain was captain only by courtesy. He was an old man, past eighty, and blissfully ignorant of the sea and its ways; but he was the owner of the vessel, and hence the honorable title. Of course the sailing master, who was really captain, was a thoroughgoing seaman. The mate, whose post was aboard, was out with the boats, having temporarily taken Chris's place as boat steerer.

When good weather and good sport came together, the boats were accustomed to range far and wide, and often did not return to the schooner until long after dark. But for all that it was a perfect hunting day, Chris noted a growing anxiety on the part of the sailing master. He paced the deck nervously, and was constantly sweeping the horizon with his marine glasses. Not a boat was in sight. As sunset arrived, he even sent Chris aloft to the mizzentopmast-head, but with no better luck. The boats could not possibly be back before midnight.

Since noon the barometer had been falling with startling rapidity, and all the signs were ripe for a great storm — how great, not even the sailing master anticipated. He and Chris set to work to prepare for it. They put storm gaskets on the furled topsails, lowered and stowed the foresail and spanker and took in the two inner jibs. In the one remaining jib they put a single reef, and a single reef in the mainsail.

Night had fallen before they finished, and with the darkness came the storm. A low moan swept over the sea, and the wind struck the *Sophie Sutherland* flat. But she righted quickly, and with the sailing master at the wheel, sheered her bow into within five points of the wind. Working as well as he could with his bandaged hand, and with the feeble aid of the Chinese cook, Chris went forward and backed the jib over to the weather side. This, with the flat mainsail, left the schooner hove to.

"God help the boats! It's no gale! It's a typhoon!" the sailing master shouted to Chris at eleven o'clock. "Too much canvas! Got to get two more reefs into that mainsail, and got to do it right away!" He glanced at the old captain, shivering in oilskins at the binnacle and holding on for dear life. "There's only you and I, Chris — and the cook; but he's next to worthless!"

In order to make the reef, it was necessary to lower the mainsail, and the removal of this after pressure was bound to make the schooner fall off before the wind and sea because of the forward pressure of the jib.

"Take the wheel!" the sailing master directed. "And when I give the word, hard up with it! And when she's square before it, steady her! And keep her there! We'll heave to again as soon as I get the reefs in!"

Gripping the kicking spokes, Chris watched him and the reluctant cook go forward into the howling darkness. The *Sophie Sutherland* was plunging into the huge head seas and wallowing tremendously, the tense steel stays and taut rigging humming like harp strings to the wind. A buffeted cry came to his ears, and he felt the schooner's bow paying off of its own accord. The mainsail was down!

He ran the wheel hard over and kept anxious track of the changing direction of the wind on his face and of the heave of the vessel. This was the crucial moment. In performing the evolution she would have to pass broadside to the surge before she could get before it. The wind was blowing directly on his right cheek, when he felt the *Sophie Sutherland* lean over and begin to rise toward the sky — up — up — an infinite distance! Would she clear the crest of the gigantic wave?

Again by the feel of it, for he could see nothing, he knew that a wall of water was rearing and curving far above him along the whole weather side. There was an instant's calm as the liquid wall intervened and shut off the wind. The schooner righted, and for that instant seemed at perfect rest. Then she rolled to meet the descending rush.

Chris shouted to the captain to hold tight, and prepared himself for the shock. But the man did not live who could face it. An ocean of water smote Chris's back, and his clutch on the spokes was loosened as if it were a baby's. Stunned, powerless, like a straw on the face of a torrent, he was swept onward he knew not whither. Missing the corner of the cabin, he was dashed forward along the poop runway a hundred feet or more, striking violently against the foot of the foremast. A second wave, crushing inboard, hurled him back the way he had come, and left him half-drowned where the poop steps should have been.

Bruised and bleeding, dimly conscious, he felt for the rail and dragged himself to his feet. Unless something could be done, he knew the last moment had come. As he faced the poop the wind drove into his mouth with suffocating force. This fact brought him back to his senses with a start. The wind was blowing from dead aft! The schooner was out of the trough and before it! But the send of the sea was bound to broach her to again. Crawling up the runway, he managed to get to the wheel just in time to prevent this. The binnacle light was still burning. They were safe!

That is, he and the schooner were safe. As to the welfare of his three companions he could not say. Nor did he dare leave the wheel in order to find out, for it took every second of his undivided attention to keep the vessel to her course. The least fraction of carelessness and the heave of the sea under the quarter was liable to thrust her into the trough. So, a boy of one hundred and forty pounds, he clung to his herculean task of guiding the two hundred straining tons of fabric amid the chaos of the great storm forces.

Half an hour later, groaning and sobbing, the captain crawled to Chris's feet. All was lost, he whimpered. He was smitten unto death. The galley had gone by the board, the mainsail and running gear, the cook, everything!

"Where's the sailing master?" Chris demanded, when he had caught breath after steadying a wild lurch of the schooner. It was no child's play to steer a vessel under single-reefed jib before a typhoon.

"Clean up for'ard," the old man replied. "Jammed under the fo'c'sle-head, but still breathing. Both his arms are broken, he says, and he doesn't know how many ribs. He's hurt bad."

"Well, he'll drown there the way she's shipping water through the hawsepipes. Go for'ard!" Chris commanded, taking charge of things as a matter of course. "Tell him not to worry; that I'm at the wheel. Help him as much as you can, and make him help —" he stopped and ran the spokes to starboard as a tremendous billow rose under the stern and yawed the schooner to port—"and make him help himself for the rest. Unship the fo'c'sle hatch and get him down into a bunk. Then ship the hatch again."

The captain turned his aged face forward and wavered pitifully. The waist of the ship was full of water to the bulwarks. He had just come through it, and knew death lurked every inch of the way.

"Go!" Chris shouted, fiercely. And as the fear-stricken man started, "And take another look for the cook!"

Two hours later, almost dead from suffering, the captain returned. He had obeyed orders. The sailing master was helpless although safe in a bunk; the cook was gone. Chris sent the captain below to the cabin to change his clothes.

After interminable hours of toil, day broke cold and gray. Chris looked about him. The *Sophie Sutherland* was racing before the typhoon like a thing possessed. There was no rain, but the wind whipped the spray of the sea mast-high, obscuring everything except in the immediate neighborhood.

Two waves only could Chris see at a time—the one before and the one behind. So small and insignificant the schooner seemed on the long Pacific roll! Rushing up a maddening mountain, she would poise like a cockleshell on the giddy summit, breathless and rolling, leap outward and down into the yawning chasm beneath, and bury herself in the smother of foam at the bottom. Then the recovery, another mountain, another sickening upward rush, another poise, and the downward crash! Abreast of him, to starboard, like a ghost of the storm, Chris saw the cook dashing apace with the schooner. Evidently, when washed overboard, he had grasped and become entangled in a trailing halyard.

For three hours more, alone with this gruesome companion, Chris held the *Sophie Sutherland* before the wind and sea. He had long since forgotten his mangled fingers. The bandages had been torn away, and the cold, salt spray had eaten into the half-healed wounds until they were numb and no longer pained. But he was not cold. The terrific labor of steering forced the perspiration from every pore. Yet he was faint and weak with hunger and exhaustion, and hailed with delight the advent on deck of the captain, who fed him all of a pound of cake chocolate. It strengthened him at once.

He ordered the captain to cut the halyard by which the cook's body was towing, and also to go forward and cut loose the jib halyard and sheet. When he had done so, the jib fluttered a couple of moments like a handkerchief, then tore out of the boltropes and vanished. The *Sophie Sutherland* was running under bare poles.

By noon the storm had spent itself, and by six in the evening the waves had died down sufficiently to let Chris leave the helm. It was almost hopeless to dream of the small boats weathering the typhoon, but there is always the chance in saving human life, and Chris at once applied himself to going back over the course along which he had fled. He managed to get a reef in one of the inner jibs and two reefs in the spanker, and then, with the aid of the watch tackle, to hoist them to the stiff breeze that yet blew. And all through the night, tacking back and forth on the back track, he shook out canvas as fast as the wind would permit.

The injured sailing master had turned delirious, and between tending him and lending a hand with the ship, Chris kept the captain busy. "Taught me more seamanship," as he afterward said, "than I'd learned on the whole voyage." But by daybreak the old man's feeble frame succumbed, and he fell off into exhausted sleep on the weather poop.

Chris, who could now lash the wheel, covered the tired man with blankets from below, and went fishing in the lazaretto for something to eat. But by the day following he found himself forced to give in, drowsing fitfully by the wheel and waking ever and anon to take a look at things.

On the afternoon of the third day he picked up a schooner, dismasted and battered. As he approached, close-hauled on the wind, he saw her decks crowded by an unusually large crew, and on sailing in closer, made out among others the faces of his missing comrades. And he was just in the nick of time, for they were fighting a losing fight at the pumps. An hour later they, with the crew of the sinking craft, were aboard the *Sophie Sutherland.*

Having wandered so far from their own vessel, they had taken refuge on the strange schooner just before the storm broke. She was a Canadian sealer on her first voyage, and, as was now apparent, her last.

The captain of the *Sophie Sutherland* had a story to tell, also, and he told it well — so well, in fact, that when all hands were gathered together on deck during the dog-watch, Emil Johansen strode over to Chris and gripped him by the hand.

"Chris," he said, so loudly that all could hear, "Chris, I gif in. You vas yoost so good a sailorman as I. You vas a bully boy und able seaman, und I pe proud for you!

"Und Chris!" He turned as if he had forgotten something, and called back, "From dis time always you call me 'Emil' mitout der 'Mister'!"

The "Fuzziness" of Hoockla-Heen

HOOCKLA-HEEN half-crouched, half-knelt in the tall, dank grass. Not a motion passed over him, yet he had been there a long, long hour. In his hands he held a slender bow, with bone-barbed arrow strung in place; and he would have seemed turned to stone had it not been for the look of eagle alertness in his face. In fact, he was never more alive than at that very moment. His nostrils gave him full report of the green and growing things, of the budded willows and quaking aspens down by the edge of the low bank, of the great red raspberries thickly studding the bushes at his back, and over to the right, a dozen paces away and well hidden, he knew there must be a clump of the bright-colored but poisonous snake-flower.

His senses told him many things. He felt the moisture of the grass creeping and soaking through his moose-hide trousers and chilling his knees, and by its breath on his brow he knew the light breeze was hauling slowly around in the pale wake of the moon. And of the low hum of sound which rose from the land, his ears distinguished each component part — the rustling of the leaves and grasses, the calls of birds and squirrels and wild fowl, and the myriad noises of a vast insect life.

But chief of all was one sound which made his face grow tense with expectancy. Just before him a tangle of sticks and poles, laid together in rude order, dammed the swampy stream and formed a shallow pond. Through a break in the dam the water gurgled noisily. That, however, was not the sound which held him. From above he heard the faint, sharp slap of some object upon the earth, followed by the plump of a body into water. Then silence settled down again, and he stared steadily at the break through which the water slipped away.

But as he waited a new sound disturbed him. From far below came the low whine of a dog, and once the crackle of a broken twig. And although he felt vexation at this, his face gave no sign, while he centered his whole consciousness in his one sense of hearing. From above there came a low splashing, nearer than before, and from below the crackle of another breaking twig, likewise nearer.

It was as if these approaching sounds were running a race, and he wished the one from the water to win. And win it did, for a ripple broke the surface of the pond and a small log floated into the opening in the dam. Shoving it along, he could make out a large, ratlike head, with little, round ears laid back and nearly lost in hair.

Hoockla-Heen bent his bow noiselessly and waited. The animal pushed and shoved at the log, trying to block the opening. Failing in this, it crawled cautiously out on the dam, exposing three feet and more of body, covered with fur of heavy chestnut-brown. A crackle of twigs from below, and the animal rose suspiciously on its hind legs to listen. Then it was that Hoockla-Heen felt the thrill of achievement, the consciousness of having done and done well, as the arrow sped through the moonlight, singing its shrill song and transfixing the animal, which knew its end in the sound.

The boy, for Hoockla-Heen could boast but twelve years, sprang upright and called out joyously. A like call from below and a tremendous crashing of underbrush answered him; and as he stooped and lifted the beaver by its broad, flat tail, another boy broke out of the bushes and waded to him through the grass.

"And hast thou got old gray nose at last?" the newcomer questioned, excitedly.

"Aye," Hoockla-Heen made answer, coldly, hiding his exultation under an impassive mask. "Aye, old gray nose, and small thanks to thee, Klanik, who flounder over the ground like a blind bull moose and make much noise."

"I came softly," the other boy replied, a little hurt by the censure.

"Yes, with a whining dog."

"Broken Tooth would follow me, but I sent him back," said Klanik. "Did you know," he went on, eagerly, "that the tribe is to journey down to see these white men of the Yukon?"

Upon that, Hoockla-Heen danced gleefully up and down. Klanik joined hands with him, and they circled round and round till, in sheer excess of joy, the dance was turned into a wrestling bout, and they were panting and straining to the utmost. Klanik finally slipped on the beaver's tail, and Hoockla-Heen, profiting by the advantage, forced him suddenly backward and pressed his shoulders into the soggy ground. Then they sprang to their feet, laughing, and started down the trail to camp with the burden of the beaver shared between them.

On the way Klanik told of what had taken place at the council. Kootznaloo, one of their bravest hunters, had wandered off the previous fall, and after a long absence had returned with incredible tales of the white men. He had gone down the White River farther than the tribe had ever ventured; he had gone to the great Yukon, and the wonderful city of Dawson. At the council he had spoken of the many furs the tribe possessed, of how highly furs were esteemed by the white men, and of his plan for the tribe to go down to Dawson and trade these furs for immense wealth in guns and blankets and scarlet cloths.

But Ya-Koo, the maker of medicine, had opposed him. As they all knew, he, too, had been among the white men once upon a time, and he could tell them that the white men were very bad. This Kootznaloo denied; the white men were very good, he said, in token whereof had he not returned with a fine new gun?

So the discussion waged to and fro. Many who had never seen white men had agreed with Kootznaloo. Moreover, all of them were anxious to possess fine new guns like his. Hoockla-Heen's father, Kow-Whi, who was chief, had also declared in favor of Kootznaloo's project; and Ya-Koo, though he was medicine man to the tribe, had been forced to give in. In two days, it had been decided, now that summer was come and the rivers running free, the whole tribe, men, women and children, would load their canoes and depart for the wonder city.

For some time after Klanik had finished telling of what

occurred at the council the boys walked on in silence. Then Klanik spoke again, gravely: "It is not to be believed that these white men are white, all over white — face, hands, everything."

"Aye," Hoockla-Heen answered, absently, "and their eyes are of the color of summer skies when there are no clouds."

Klanik looked at him curiously, for Klanik knew many strange things concerning Hoockla-Heen of which Hoockla-Heen himself was ignorant — things which Kow-Whi and Ya-Koo had commanded should never be spoken.

But Hoockla-Heen went on: "And their womenkind are fair and soft, and their hair is yellow, quite yellow, and often I remember —"

He stopped suddenly and looked into the curious eyes of his chum.

"What dost thou remember?" Klanik queried, gently. "Thou hast never seen the white men and their womenkind."

"I remember —"

"Truly art thou Hoockla-Heen, the dreamer."

"Aye, I dream." Hoockla-Heen shook his head sadly. "Surely, I dream."

He put his hand before him as if to dispel some vision, and after that, till camp was reached, there was silence between them. But when Hoockla-Heen crept into his furs and pulled the bearskin over him, he could not close his eyes, and sleep was far from him. It was the old sickness, *com-ta-nitch-i-wyan*, come back to him again — the dreamsickness which he had thought outgrown. It was the sickness which, when a little boy, had made the chil dren draw away from him in fear, and the tears come into the eyes of the squaws when they looked upon him. The dream-sickness — how it had made his childhood miserable!

Of course all men dreamed, and even the wolf dogs; but they dreamed with their eyes shut, when they slept, and he had dreamed with eyes wide open, broad awake. And the men dreamed about things they knew, about hunting and fishing; but he had dreamed about things he did not know, and which nobody else knew. Haunting memories of things he could not express had come to him; and it seemed, if only he could think back, that all would be clear, only, try as he would, he could not think back.

At such times he felt very much as he did when he was sick of the river fever, and his head was dizzy, his eyes trembling and watery, and his fingers felt twice their natural size, strangely large and fuzzy. Ah, that was it, the very word — fuzzy! That was the way his head felt when he tried to think back.

Then, as he gradually outgrew and forgot it, the dream-sickness had left him. The medicine man, Ya-Koo, had made public incantation over him, and besought the bad spirits to depart from him, and privately he had told him to think back no more, lest misfortune should fall upon him. And he had obeyed, and the thing had gone from him. But now it had come back again. Was there ever such an unhappy boy? He clenched his hands passionately, and for hours stared blindly into the blackness above him.

Chief Kow-Whi's canoe led the procession of the tribe, and with him were Hoockla-Heen and Klanik. All day they had been sweeping down the Yukon, rounding one great bend after another, but they had not landed. They passed one place early in the day where men, white men, were firing off their guns excitedly. Kootznaloo paddled alongside Kow-Whi's canoe and explained that he thought it must be a custom of the white men, although he had never seen the like during the time he spent among them. But after a brief deliberation, not being sure that it was merely a custom, they had decided not to venture in, but to run on to Dawson.

And all day Hoockla-Heen had had attacks of the dream-sickness; and when he had looked a long way off at the white men discharging their guns, he had suffered from an especially severe attack. The fuzziness had been almost overpowering. He was also worried by a feeling that something was going to happen — what he did not know.

He tried to tell Klanik about it, but Klanik had retorted, "Don't be a baby; nothing'll eat you." After that he kept quiet, although he was sure that he was not afraid. Instead, he was very anxious that the thing should happen, whatever it was.

At midday the flotilla swung along a series of mighty bluffs and rounded an abrupt turn. Here the Klondike emptied its swollen flood into the Yukon, and here, suddenly, without warning, Dawson burst upon their astonished eye.

As far as they could see, from river rim to mountainside, was a sea of tents and cabins. And this sea of dwellings spilled over the river rim and down into the water, where the bank was lined for a mile and a half with boats — boats, three and four deep, and scows, dories, canoes and huge rafts, all heaped high with provisions and the possessions of men. The suddenness and the vastness of it took away the breath of the old chief, Kow-Whi, and he could only gaze in speechless wonder.

Hoockla-Heen was almost suffocating with fuzziness. He reached up hurriedy and held his head with both hands. Oh, if he could only understand! What did it all mean?

Klanik cried out sharply to him for missing stroke with his paddle, and with an effort of will he controlled himself. They drove in close to the shore and by the barracks, where were the Northwest mounted police and where the British banner floated.

Hoockla-Heen pointed to it and said, "That is a *flag.*"

"How dost thou know, dreamer?" Klanik demanded.

But Hoockla-Heen did not hear. They were drifting past a great barge loaded with huge animals, as large as a large moose. The sight frightened the women, and several of the canoes sheered out into the stream to give it a wide berth.

"And what manner of animal is that?" Klanik asked, mischievously.

"That is —" Hoockla-Heen hesitated a moment, and then went on confidently, "that is a *horse.*"

"Truly," agreed Kootznaloo, whose canoe was alongside, "those be horses. I have seen them before, and they are harmless. But how dost thou know, O Hoockla-Heen?"

Hoockla-Heen shook his head and bent to his paddle as the canoes whirled in to a landing. When all had been made fast, they climbed the steep bank and came out upon an open space among the houses. Flags were flying everywhere, but flags different from the one which floated over the barracks; and everywhere were men, firing guns and revolvers into the air and shouting like mad.

A great crowd filled the open space, and as the wide-eyed Indians took up their position on the outskirts the noise died away, and in the center, on a heap of lumber, a man rose and began to speak. Very often he pointed to a flag which flew above his head, and every little while he was interrupted by clappings of hands and great rolling shouts and volleys of gunshots. At such times he would pause and drink water from a glass which stood on a box beside him.

"Oh! Oh!" Hoockla-Heen cried, striving to clutch at the phantoms which were fluttering through his mind.

"Strange-looking boy, that, for an Indian," remarked a man in a draggled mackinaw jacket, who now and then pulled out a writing pad and took down notes.

Hoockla-Heen glanced quickly at him, although he did not understand what had been said; but as he looked at him the dreamsickness came over him violently.

The man's companion, clad in a lieutenant's uniform of the mounted police, took the cigar from his lips and exclaimed, "By Jove, he's no —"

But just then a redheaded boy touched a lighted punk to a string which braided together hundreds of small red tubes. These he threw to the ground. At once there was a tremendous flashing and spluttering and banging, and the Indians, Ya-Koo leading, surged backward in terror.

Hoockla-Heen alone stood his ground. A sudden lightness came upon him, as when the fog rises from the earth and all things shine clear and bright in the sun. The fuzziness had left him. "*Firecrackers!*" he cried, dancing into the exploding mass. "*Firecrackers! The Fourth of July! Hurrah! Hurrah!*"

When the last cracker had gone off he came to himself, startled and blushing under his tanned skin. He looked timidly about him. His tribespeople had come back and were regarding him curiously. Kow-Whi, however, was looking straight before him, a sad expression on his face. But the lieutenant and the man who made notes had stepped up to him.

"What's your name?" the lieutenant demanded, seizing him by the arm.

"*Jimmy,*" he answered, as if it were the most natural thing in the world. Then the fuzzy sensation came back to him, and he fell to wondering why he had spoken that strange word. He did not know what the man had said. And what did *Jimmy* mean, anyway? Why had he spoken it?

"Jimmy what?" the lieutenant asked.

Hoockla-Heen shook his head. He did not understand the white man's speech. Besides, his tribespeople were pressing round him excitedly, and Ya-Koo was plucking at his sleeve for him to come away.

"How old are you?"

Again he shook his head, this time adding, "White River," as if it might help.

"Yes, um White River," Kootznaloo corroborated, glad of the chance to play interpreter. "Um White River, 'way up."

"White River, eh?" the lieutenant repeated, in sudden surprise. Then turning to his companion, "How old do you make him out, Dawes?"

Dawes considered. "Twelve or thirteen, I should judge."

The lieutenant pondered audibly: "Summer of '91 — winter of '92 — summer of '92 — four years and eight make twelve —" He broke off suddenly, then cried out, "Dawes! Dawes! It's the kid, sure! Hold him! As you love me, hold him tight!"

Before Hoockla-Heen could realize what was happening, the lieutenant had jerked open his squirrel-skin shirt, the soft leather tearing down under his grasp. Ya-Koo tried to come between, but the lieutenant thrust him roughly back. There was a murmuring and a snarl from the tribespeople, a flashing of knives from the sheaths and a clicking of rusty guns. But Kow-Whi quieted them with a sharp word of command.

"Look at that! White, eh?" The lieutenant pointed at Hoockla-Heen's naked chest.

Dawes looked carefully and shook his head. "Pretty black, I should judge."

"Oh, that's the sun!" the lieutenant exclaimed, impatiently, at the same time ripping and tearing away at the shirt. "Under the arms, man! Under the arms, where it's untouched!"

"It *is* white!" Dawes cried, with sudden conviction. "What shall we do?"

"Do! I'll show you!" The lieutenant beckoned to the redheaded boy, who was looking on with huge interest. "Hey, you, boy! Run and fetch Jim McDermott. He's right over there in that bunch of men. I saw him not five minutes ago."

The redheaded boy darted off, and Hoockla-Heen watched him go, wondering at it all, and yet aware, in a dim sort of way, that the thing which was to happen was happening.

Kootznaloo was jabbering excitedly to the lieutenant, who was nodding his head to every word and interjecting short, sharp questions.

"But I say, you know, I say, old man, what's up?" Dawes interrupted, pulling out his writing pad and poising his pencil.

"McDermott, Jim McDermott!" the lieutenant answered, hastily. "Old-timer in the country. A bonanza king, worth a couple of millions at least. Used to be an agent for the P. C. C. Company. In '94 came in with his kid and a party from the west coast of Alaska. The wife was to come in the following year by the regular way. Unknown country. First white people to come over it, and the last. Frightful time. Nearly starved to death. In fact, two did. They, being the weakest, were the very ones left in charge of McDermott's boy while McDermott and the others pushed out after game. I heard him tell the story once, how, after three days, when he had got a moose and returned, he found the two men stiff and cold and the boy missing."

"The boy missing?" Dawes's pencil was suspended in mid-air.

"Yes, missing; and never a sign. The camp was close by the river, and McDermott figured that the boy must have crawled to the bank and fallen in. Seems now, though, that some Indian must have landed from a canoe, found the two dead men, and carried the living boy away with him. Of course McDermott never dreamed of such an outcome — but here he is now."

Hoockla-Heen followed the lieutenant's eyes, and saw a tall, dark-bearded man. And wonder! Oh, wonder! Clothed in flesh and blood, it was one of the phantoms of his dreams! He felt suddenly very light again, and the fuzziness went from him.

"Da-da!" he cried. *"Oh da-da!"* and flung himself into the man's arms.

Then followed ten minutes of confusion, everybody explaining at once. Hoockla-Heen remembered nothing except that once or twice the man he had called "Da-da" stooped and kissed him, and that his clutch upon his hand kept growing tighter and tighter. Then the man said something to him and started to lead him away, still clutching his hand; but Hoockla-Heen did not understand, and stopped.

The man spoke to Kootznaloo, who said to Hoockla-Heen, "This man takes you to see a woman, white woman."

"Ask him if her hair be yellow," Hoockla-Heen commanded.

And when Kootznaloo had interpreted it, the man's face grew bright with gladness, and he stooped and kissed Hoockla-Heen again and yet again.

Kow-Whi was standing apart, silent, his eyes fixed steadily before him, as if he saw nothing of what was taking place. There was a dignity and nobleness about his demeanor, and withal a sadness which the dullest could read.

Hoockla-Heen turned his head and then ran back to him, his eyes filling with tears. There he hesitated, in doubt, looking first to one man and then the other.

"Tell him, and them, that they will see the boy again,"

McDermott ordered Kootznaloo to say. "And tell them that he shall always remember them, and that they are welcome ever to a place by my fire and his. And further, that due reward, and great reward, shall be given."

The thing had happened. It was all right to Hoockla-Heen that he should go up the hill holding this tall, dark-bearded man by the hand. For he knew he was going to see the woman, fair and soft, the woman whom he often remembered, whose hair was yellow.

Dutch Courage

"JUST OUR LUCK!"

Gus Lafee finished wiping his hands and sullenly threw the towel upon the rocks. His attitude was one of deep dejection. The light seemed gone out of the day and the glory from the golden sun. Even the keen mountain air was devoid of relish, and the early morning no longer yielded its customary zest.

"Just our luck!" Gus repeated, this time avowedly for the edification of another young fellow who was busily engaged in sousing his head in the water of the lake.

"What are you grumbling about, anyway?" Hazard Van Dorn lifted a soap-rimed face questioningly. His eyes were shut. "What's our luck?"

"Look there!" Gus threw a moody glance skyward. "Some duffer's got ahead of us. We've been scooped, that's all!"

Hazard opened his eyes, and caught a fleeting glimpse of a white flag waving arrogantly on the edge of a wall of rock nearly a mile above his head. Then his eyes closed even tighter; his face wrinkled spasmodically. Gus threw him the towel, and uncommiseratingly watched him wipe out the offending soap. He felt too blue himself to take stock in trivialities.

Hazard groaned.

"Does it hurt — much?" Gus queried, coldly, without interest, as if it were no more than his duty to ask after the welfare of his comrade.

"I guess it does," responded the suffering one.

"Soap's pretty strong, eh? Noticed it myself."

"'Tisn't the soap. It's — it's *that!*" He opened his reddened eyes and pointed toward the innocent little white flag. "That's what hurts."

Gus Lafee did not reply, but turned away to start the fire and begin cooking breakfast. His disappointment and grief were too deep for anything but silence, and Hazard, who felt likewise, never opened his mouth as he fed the horses, nor once laid his head against their arching necks or passed caressing fingers through their manes. The two boys were blind, also, to the manifold glories of Mirror Lake which reposed at their very feet. Nine times, had they chosen to move along its margin the short distance of a hundred yards, could they have seen the sunrise repeated; nine times, from behind as many successive peaks, could they have seen the great orb rear his blazing rim; and nine times, had they but looked into the waters of the lake, could they have seen the phenomena reflected faithfully and vividly. But all the Titanic grandeur of the scene was lost to them. They had been robbed of the chief pleasure of their trip to Yosemite Valley. They had been frustrated in their long-cherished design upon Half Dome, and hence were rendered disconsolate and blind to the beauties and the wonders of the place.

Half Dome rears its ice-scarred head fully five thousand feet above the level floor of Yosemite Valley. In the name itself of this great rock lies an accurate and complete description. Nothing more nor less is it than a cyclopean, rounded dome, split in half as cleanly as an apple that is divided by a knife. It is, perhaps, quite needless to state that but one-half remains, hence its name, the other half having been carried away by the great ice-river in the stormy time of the Glacial Period. In that dim day one of those frigid rivers gouged a mighty channel from out the solid rock. This channel to-day is Yosemite Valley. But to return to the Half Dome. On its northeastern side, by circuitous trails and stiff climbing, one may gain the Saddle. Against the slope of the Dome the Saddle leans like a gigantic slab, and from the top of this slab, one thousand feet in length, curves the great circle to the summit of the Dome. A few degrees too steep for unaided climbing, these one thousand feet defied for years the adventurous spirits who fixed yearning eyes upon the crest above.

One day, a couple of clear-headed mountaineers proceeded to insert iron eye-bolts into holes which they drilled into the rock every few feet apart. But when they found themselves three hundred feet above the Saddle, clinging like flies to the precarious wall with on either hand a yawning abyss, their nerves failed them and they abandoned the enterprise. So it remained for an indomitable Scotchman, one George Anderson, finally to achieve the feat. Beginning where they had left off, drilling and climbing for a week, he at last set foot upon that awful summit and gazed down into the depths where Mirror Lake reposed, nearly a mile beneath.

In the years which followed, many bold men took advantage of the huge rope ladder which he had put in place; but one winter, ladder, cables and all were carried away by the snow and ice. True, most of the eye-bolts, twisted and bent, remained. But few men essayed the hazardous undertaking, and of those few more than one gave up his life on the treacherous heights, and not one succeeded.

But Gus Lafee and Hazard Van Dorn had left the smiling valley land of California and journeyed into the high Sierras, intent on the great adventure. And thus it was that their disappointment was deep and grievous when they awoke on this morning to receive the forestalling message of the little white flag.

"Camped at the foot of the Saddle last night and went up at the first peep of day," Hazard ventured, long after the silent breakfast had been tucked away and the dishes washed.

Gus nodded. It was not in the nature of things that a youth's spirits should long remain at low ebb, and his tongue was beginning to loosen.

"Guess he's down by now, lying in camp and feeling as big as Alexander," the other went on. "And I don't blame him, either, only I wish it were we."

"You can be sure he's down," Gus spoke up at last. "It's mighty warm on that naked rock with the sun beating down on it at this time of year. That was our plan, you know, to go up early and come down early. And any man, sensible enough to get to the top, is bound to have sense enough to do it before the rock gets hot and his hands sweaty."

"And you can be sure he didn't take his shoes with him." Hazard rolled over on his back and lazily regarded the speck of flag fluttering briskly on the sheer edge of the precipice. "Say!" He sat up with a start. "What's that?"

A metallic ray of light flashed out from the summit of Half Dome, then a second and a third. The heads of both boys were craned backward on the instant, agog with excitement.

"What a duffer!" Gus cried. "Why didn't he come down when it was cool?"

Hazard shook his head slowly, as if the question were too deep for immediate answer and they had better defer judgment.

The flashes continued, and as the boys soon noted, at irregular intervals of duration and disappearance. Now they were long, now short; and again they came and went with great rapidity, or ceased altogether for several moments at a time.

"I have it!" Hazard's face lighted up with the coming of understanding. "I have it! That fellow up there is trying to talk to us. He's flashing the sunlight down to us on a pocket-mirror — dot, dash; dot, dash; don't you see?"

The light also began to break in Gus's face. "Ah, I know! It's what they do in wartime — signaling. They call it heliographing, don't they? Same thing as telegraphing, only it's done without wires. And they use the same dots and dashes, too."

"Yes, the Morse alphabet. Wish I knew it."

"Same here. He surely must have something to say to us, or he wouldn't be kicking up all that rumpus."

Still the flashes came and went persistently, till Gus exclaimed: "That chap's in trouble, that's what's the matter with him! Most likely he's hurt himself or something or other."

"Go on!" Hazard scouted.

Gus got out the shotgun and fired both barrels three times in rapid succession. A perfect flutter of flashes came back before the echoes had ceased their antics. So unmistakable was the message that even doubting Hazard was convinced that the man who had forestalled them stood in some grave danger.

"Quick, Gus," he cried, "and pack! I'll see to the horses. Our trip hasn't come to nothing, after all. We've got to go right up Half Dome and rescue him. Where's the map? How do we get to the Saddle?"

" 'Taking the horse trail below the Vernal Falls,' " Gus read from the guidebook, " 'one mile of brisk travelling brings the tourist to the world-famed Nevada Fall. Close by, rising up in all its pomp and glory, the Cap of Liberty stands guard —' "

"Skip all that!" Hazard impatiently interrupted. "The trail's what we want."

"Oh, here it is! 'Following the trail up the side of the fall will bring you to the forks. The left one leads to Little Yosemite Valley, Cloud's Rest, and other points.' "

"Hold on; that'll do! I've got it on the map now," again interrupted Hazard. "From the Cloud's Rest trail a dotted line leads off to Half Dome. That shows the trail's abandoned. We'll have to look sharp to find it. It's a day's journey."

"And to think of all that travelling, when right here we're at the bottom of the Dome!" Gus complained, staring up wistfully at the goal.

"That's because this is Yosemite, and all the more reason for us to hurry. Come on! Be lively, now!"

Well used as they were to trail life, but few minutes sufficed to see the camp equipage on the backs of the packhorses and the boys in the saddle. In the late twilight of that evening they hobbled their animals in a tiny mountain meadow, and cooked coffee and bacon for themselves at the very base of the Saddle. Here, also, before they turned into their blankets, they found the camp of the unlucky stranger who was destined to spend the night on the naked roof of the Dome.

Dawn was brightening into day when the panting lads threw themselves down at the summit of the Saddle and began taking off their shoes. Looking down from the great height, they seemed perched upon the ridgepole of the world, and even the snow-crowned Sierra peaks seemed beneath them. Directly below, on the one hand, lay Little Yosemite Valley, half a mile deep; on the other hand, Big Yosemite, a mile. Already the sun's rays wre striking about the adventurers, but the darkness of night still shrouded the two great gulfs into which they peered. And above them, bathed in the full day, rose only the majestic curve of the Dome.

"What's that for?" Gus asked, pointing to a leather-shielded flask which Hazard was securely fastening in his shirt pocket.

"Dutch courage, of course," was the reply. "We'll need all our nerve in this undertaking, and a little bit more, and," he tapped the flask significantly, "here's the little bit more."

"Good idea," Gus commented.

How they had ever come possessed of this erroneous idea, it would be hard to discover; but they were young yet, and there remained for them many uncut pages of life. Believers, also, in the efficacy of whisky as a remedy for snake-bite, they had brought with them a fair supply of medicine-chest liquor. As yet they had not touched it.

"Have some before we start?" Hazard asked.

Gus looked into the gulf and shook his head. "Better wait till we get up higher and the climbing is more ticklish."

Some seventy feet above them projected the first eye-bolt. The winter accumulations of ice had twisted and bent it down till it did not stand more than a bare inch and a half above the rock — a most difficult object to lasso at such a distance. Time and again Hazard coiled his lariat in true cowboy fashion and made the cast, and time and again was he baffled by the elusive peg. Nor could Gus do better. Taking advantage of inequalities in the surface, they scrambled twenty feet up the Dome and found they could rest in a shallow crevice. The cleft side of the Dome was so near that they could look over its edge from the crevice and gaze down the smooth, absolutely vertical wall for nearly two thousand feet. It was yet too dark down below for them to see farther.

The peg was now fifty feet away, but the path they must cover to get to it was quite smooth, and ran at an inclination of nearly fifty degrees. It seemed impossible, in that intervening space, to find a resting-place. Either the climber must keep going up, or he must slide down; he could not stop. But just here rose the danger. The Dome was sphere-shaped, and if he should begin to slide, his course would be, not to the point from which he had started and where the Saddle would catch him, but off to the south toward Little Yosemite. This meant a plunge of half a mile.

"I'll try it," Gus said, simply.

They knotted the two lariats together, so that they had over a hundred feet of rope between them; and then each boy tied an end to his waist.

"If I slide," Gus cautioned, "come in on the slack and brace yourself. If you don't, you'll follow me, that's all!"

"Ay, ay!" was the confident response. "Better take a nip before you start?"

Gus glanced at the proffered bottle. He knew himself and of what he was capable. "Wait till I make the peg and you join me. All ready?"

"Ay."

He struck out like a cat, on all fours, clawing energetically as he urged his upward progress, his comrade paying out the rope carefully. At first his speed was good, but gradually it dwindled. Now he was fifteen feet from the peg, now ten, now eight — but going, oh, so slowly! Hazard, looking up from his crevice, felt a contempt for him and disappointment in him. It did look easy. Now Gus was five feet away, and after a painful effort, four feet. But when only a yard intervened, he came to a standstill — not exactly a standstill, for, like a squirrel in a wheel, he maintained his position on the face of the Dome by the most desperate clawing.

He had failed, that was evident. The question now was, how to save himself. With a sudden, catlike movement he whirled over on his back, caught his heel in a tiny, saucer-shaped depression and sat up. Then his courage failed him. Day had at last penetrated to the floor of the valley, and he was appalled at the frightful distance.

"Go ahead and make it!" Hazard ordered; but Gus merely shook his head.

"Then come down!"

Again he shook his head. This was his ordeal, to sit, nerveless and insecure, on the brink of the precipice. But Hazard, lying safely in his crevice, now had to face his own ordeal, but one of a different nature. When Gus began to slide — as he soon must — would he, Hazard, be able to take in the slack and then meet the shock as the other tautened the rope and darted toward the plunge? It seemed doubtful. And there he lay, apparently safe, but in reality harnessed to death. Then rose the temptation. Why not cast off the rope about his waist? He would be safe at all events. It was a simple way out of the difficulty. There was no need that two should perish. But it was impossible for such temptation to overcome his pride of race, and his own pride in himself and in his honor. So the rope remained about him.

"Come down!" he ordered; but Gus seemed to have become petrified.

"Come down," he threatened, "or I'll drag you down!" He pulled on the rope to show he was in earnest.

"Don't you dare!" Gus articulated through his chattering teeth.

"Sure, I will, if you don't come!" Again he jerked the rope.

With a despairing gurgle Gus started, doing his best to work sideways from the plunge. Hazard, every sense on the alert, almost exulting in his perfect coolness, took in the slack with deft rapidity. Then, as the rope began to tighten, he braced himself. The shock drew him half out of the crevice; but he held firm and served as the center of the circle, while Gus, with the rope as a radius, described the circumference and ended up on the extreme southern edge of the Saddle. A few moments later Hazard was offering him the flask.

"Take some yourself," Gus said.

"No; you. I don't need it."

"And I'm past needing it." Evidently Gus was dubious of the bottle and its contents.

Hazard put it away in his pocket. "Are you game," he asked, "or are you going to give it up?"

"Never!" Gus protested. "I *am* game. No Lafee ever showed the white feather yet. And if I did lose my grit up there, it was only for the moment — sort of like seasickness. I'm all right now, and I'm going to the top."

"Good!" encouraged Hazard. "You lie in the crevice this time, and I'll show you how easy it is."

But Gus refused. He held that it was easier and safer for him to try again, arguing that it was less difficult for his one hundred and sixteen pounds to cling to the smooth rock than for Hazard's one hundred and sixty-five; also, that it was easier for one hundred and sixty-five pounds to bring a sliding one hundred and sixteen to a stop than *vice versa.* And further, that he had the benefit of his previous experience. Hazard saw the justice of this, although it was with great reluctance that he gave in.

Success vindicated Gus's contention. The second time, just as it seemed as if his slide would be repeated, he made a last supreme effort and gripped the coveted peg. By means of the rope, Hazard quickly joined him. The next peg was nearly sixty feet away; but for nearly half that distance the base of some glacier in the forgotten past had ground a shallow furrow. Taking advantage of this, it was easy for Gus to lasso the eye-bolt. And it seemed, as was really the case, that the hardest part of the task was over. True, the curve steepened to nearly sixty degrees above them, but a comparatively unbroken line of eye-bolts, six feet apart, awaited the lads. They no longer had even to use the lasso. Standing on one peg it was child's play to throw the bight of the rope over the next and to draw themselves up to it.

A bronzed and bearded man met them at the top and gripped their hands in hearty fellowship.

"Talk about your Mont Blancs!" he exclaimed, pausing in the midst of greeting them to survey the mighty panorama. "But there's nothing on all the earth, nor over it, nor under it, to compare with this!" Then he recollected himself and thanked them for coming to his aid. No, he was not hurt or injured in any way. Simply because of his own carelessness, just as he had arrived at the top the previous day, he had dropped his climbing rope. Of course it was impossible to descend without it. Did they understand heliographing? No? That was strange! How did they —

"Oh, we knew something was the matter," Gus interrupted, "from the way you flashed when we fired off the shotgun."

"Find it pretty cold last night without blankets?" Hazard queried.

"I should say so. I've hardly thawed out yet."

"Have some of this." Hazard shoved the flask over to him.

The stranger regarded him quite seriously for a moment, then said, "My dear fellow, do you see that row of pegs? Since it is my honest intention to climb down them very shortly, I am forced to decline. No, I don't think I'll have any, though I thank you just the same."

Hazard glanced at Gus and then put the flask back in his pocket. But when they pulled the doubled rope through the last eye-bolt and set foot on the Saddle, he again drew out the bottle.

"Now that we're down, we don't need it," he remarked, pithily. "And I've about come to the conclusion that there isn't very much in Dutch courage, after all." He gazed up the great curve of the Dome. "Look at what we've done without it!"

Several seconds thereafter a party of tourists, gathered at the margin of Mirror Lake, were astounded at the unwonted phenomenon of a whisky flask descending upon them like a comet out of a clear sky; and all the way back to the hotel they marveled greatly at the wonders of nature, especially meteorites.

The Lost Poacher

"BUT THEY WON'T TAKE excuses. You're across the line, and that's enough. They'll take you. In you go, Siberia and the salt mines. And as for Uncle Sam, why, what's he to know about it? Never a word will get back to the States. 'The *Mary Thomas*,' the papers will say, 'the *Mary Thomas* lost with all hands. Probably in a typhoon in the Japanese seas.' That's what the papers will say, and people, too. In you go, Siberia and the salt mines. Dead to the world and kith and kin, though you live fifty years."

In such manner John Lewis, commonly known as the "sea lawyer," settled the matter out of hand.

It was a serious moment in the forecastle of the *Mary Thomas*. No sooner had the watch below begun to talk the trouble over, than the watch on deck came down and joined them. As there was no wind, every hand could be spared with the exception of the man at the wheel, and he remained only for the sake of discipline. Even "Bub" Russell, the cabin boy, had crept forward to hear what was going on.

However, it was a serious moment, as the grave faces of the sailors bore witness. For the three preceding months the *Mary Thomas,* sealing schooner, had hunted the seal pack along the coast of Japan and north to Bering Sea. Here, on the Asiatic side of the sea, they were forced to give over the chase, or rather, to go no farther; for beyond, the Russian cruisers patrolled forbidden ground, where the seals might breed in peace. And here, on the very edge of the line, the *Mary Thomas* had hunted back and forth, picking up the laggards which had not gone on with the pack.

A week before she had fallen into a heavy fog accompanied by calm. Since then the fog bank had not lifted, and the only wind had been light airs and catspaws. This in itself was not so bad, for the sealing schooners are never in a hurry so long as they are in the midst of the seals; but the trouble lay in the fact that the current at this point bore heavily to the north. Thus the *Mary Thomas* had unwittingly drifted across the line, and every hour she was penetrating, unwillingly, farther and farther into the dangerous waters where the Russian bear kept guard.

How far she had drifted no man knew. The sun had not been visible for a week, nor the stars, and the captain had been unable to take observations in order to determine his position. At any moment a cruiser might swoop down and hale the crew away to Siberia. The fate of other poaching seal-hunters was too well known to the men of the *Mary Thomas,* and there was cause for grave faces.

"Mine friends," spoke up a German boat steerer, "it vas a pad piziness. Shust as ve make a big catch, und all honest, somedings go wrong, und der Russians nab us, dake our skins und our schooner, und send us mit der anarchists to Siberia. Ach! a pretty pad piziness!"

"Yes, that's where it hurts," the sea lawyer went on. "Fifteen hundred skins in the salt piles, and all honest, a big payday coming to every man Jack of us, and then to be captured and lose it all! It'd be different if we'd been poaching, but it's all honest work in open water."

"But if we haven't done anything wrong, they can't do anything to us, can they?" Bub queried.

"It strikes me as 'ow it ain't the proper thing for a boy o' your age shovin' in when 'is elders is talkin'," protested an English sailor, from over the edge of his bunk.

"Oh, that's all right, Jack," answered the sea lawyer. "He's a perfect right to. Ain't he just as liable to lose his wages as the rest of us?"

"Wouldn't give thruppence for them!" Jack sniffed back. He had been planning to go home and see his family in Chelsea when he was paid off, and he was now feeling rather blue over the highly possible loss, not only of his pay, but of his liberty.

"How are they to know?" the sea lawyer asked in answer to Bub's previous question. "Here we are in forbidden water. How do they know but what we came here of our own accord? Here we are, fifteen hundred skins in the hold. How do they know whether we got them in open water or in the closed sea? Don't you see, Bub, the evidence is all against us. If you caught a man with his pockets full of apples like those which grow on your tree, and if you caught him in your tree besides, what'd you think if he told you he couldn't help it, and had just been sort of blown there, and that anyway those apples came from some other tree — what'd you think, eh?"

Bub saw it clearly when put in that light, and shook his head despondently.

"You'd rather be dead than go to Siberia," one of the boat pullers said. "They put you into the salt mines and work you till you die. Never see daylight again. Why, I've heard tell of one fellow that was chained to his mate, and that mate died. And they were both chained together! And if they send you to the quicksilver mines you get salivated. I'd rather be hung than salivated."

"Wot's salivated?" Jack asked, suddenly sitting up in his bunk at the hint of fresh misfortunes.

"Why, the quicksilver gets into your blood; I think that's the way. And your gums all swell like you had the scurvy, only worse, and your teeth get loose in your jaws. And big ulcers form, and then you die horrible. The strongest man can't last long a-mining quicksilver."

"A pad piziness," the boat steerer reiterated, dolorously, in the silence which followed. "A pad piziness. I vish I vas in Yokohama. Eh? Vot vas dot?"

Every face lighted up. The *Mary Thomas* heeled over. The decks were aslant. A tin pannikin rolled down the inclined plane, rattling and banging. From above came the slapping of canvas and the quivering rat-tat-tat of the after-leech of the loosely stretched foresail. Then the mate's voice sang down the hatch. "All hands on deck and make sail!"

Never had such summons been answered with more enthusiasm. The calm had broken. The wind had come which was to carry them south into safety. With a wild cheer all sprang on deck. Working with mad haste, they flung out topsails, flying jibs and staysails. As they worked, the fog bank lifted and the black vault of heaven, bespangled with the old familiar stars, rushed into view. When all was shipshape, the *Mary Thomas* was lying gallantly over on her side to a beam wind and plunging ahead due south.

"Steamer's lights ahead on the port bow, sir!" cried the lookout from his station on the forecastle head. There was excitement in the man's voice.

The captain sent Bub below for his night glasses. Everybody crowded to the lee rail to gaze at the suspicious stranger, which already began to loom up vague and indistinct. In those unfrequented waters the chance was one in a thousand that it could be anything else than a Russian patrol. The captain was still anxiously gazing through the glasses, when a flash of flame left the stranger's side, followed by the loud report of a cannon. The worst fears were confirmed. It was a patrol, evidently firing across the bows of the *Mary Thomas* in order to make her heave to.

"Hard down with your helm!" the captain commanded the steersman, all the life gone out of his voice. Then to the crew, "Back over the jib and foresail! Run down the flying jib! Clew up the foretopsail! And aft here and swing on to the mainsheet!"

The *Mary Thomas* ran into the eye of the wind, lost headway, and fell to courtesying gravely to the long seas rolling up from the west.

The cruiser steamed a little nearer and lowered a boat. The sealers watched in heartbroken silence. They could see the white bulk of the boat as it was slacked away to the water, and its crew sliding aboard. They could hear the creaking of the davits and the commands of the officers. Then the boat sprang away under the impulse of the oars, and came toward them. The wind had been rising, and already the sea was too rough to permit the frail craft to lie alongside the tossing schooner; but watching their chance, and taking advantage of the boarding ropes thrown to them, an officer and a couple of men clambered aboard. The boat then sheered off into safety and lay to its oars, a young midshipman, sitting in the stern and holding the yoke lines, in charge.

The officer, whose uniform disclosed his rank as that of second lieutenant in the Russian navy, went below with the captain of the *Mary Thomas* to look at the ship's papers. A few minutes later he emerged, and upon his sailors removing the hatch covers, passed down into the hold with a lantern to inspect the salt piles. It was a goodly heap which confronted him — fifteen hundred fresh skins, the season's catch; and under the circumstances he could have had but one conclusion.

"I am very sorry," he said, in broken English to the sealing captain when he again came on deck, "but it is my duty, in the name of the tsar, to seize your vessel as a poacher caught with fresh skins in the closed sea. The penalty, as you may know, is confiscation and imprisonment."

The captain of the *Mary Thomas* shrugged his shoulders in seeming indifference, and turned away. Although they may restrain all outward show, strong men, under unmerited misfortune, are sometimes very close to tears. Just then the vision of his little California home, and of the wife and two yellow-haired boys, was strong upon him, and there was a strange choking sensation in his throat, which made him afraid that if he attempted to speak he would sob instead.

And also there was upon him the duty he owed his men. No weakness before them, for he must be a tower of strength to sustain them in misfortune. He had already explained to the second lieutenant, and knew the hopelessness of the situation. As the sea lawyer had said, the evidence was all against him. So he turned aft, and fell to pacing up and down the poop of the vessel over which he was no longer commander.

The Russian officer now took temporary charge. He ordered more of his men aboard, and had all the canvas clewed up and furled snugly away. While this was being done, the boat plied back and forth between the two vessels, passing a heavy hawser, which was made fast to the great towing bitts on the schooner's forecastle head. During all this work the sealers stood about in sullen groups. It was madness to think of resisting, with the guns of a man-of-war not a biscuit toss away; but they refused to lend a hand, preferring instead to maintain a gloomy silence.

Having accomplished his task, the lieutenant ordered all but four of his men back into the boat. Then the midshipman, a lad of sixteen, looking strangely mature and dignified in his uniform and sword, came aboard to take command of the captured sealer. Just as the lieutenant prepared to depart, his eyes chanced to alight upon Bub. Without a word of warning, he seized him by the arm and dropped him over the rail into the waiting boat;

and then, with a parting wave of his hand, he followed him.

It was only natural that Bub should be frightened at this unexpected happening. All the terrible stories he had heard of the Russians served to make him fear them, and now returned to his mind with double force. To be captured by them was bad enough, but to be carried off by them, away from his comrades, was a fate of which he had not dreamed.

"Be a good boy, Bub," the captain called to him, as the boat drew away from the *Mary Thomas's* side, "and tell the truth!"

"Aye, aye, sir!" he answered, bravely enough by all outward appearance. He felt a certain pride of race, and was ashamed to be a coward before these strange enemies, these wild Russian bears.

"Und be politeful!" the German boat steerer added, his rough voice lifting across the water like a foghorn.

Bub waved his hand in farewell, and his mates clustered along the rail as they answered with a cheering shout. He found room in the stern sheets, where he fell to regarding the lieutenant. He didn't look so wild or bearish, after all — very much like other men, Bub concluded, and the sailors were much the same as all other man-of-war's men he had even known. Nevertheless, as his feet struck the steel deck of the cruiser, he felt as if he had entered the portals of a prison.

For a few minutes he was left unheeded. The sailors hoisted the boat up, and swung it in on the davits. Then great clouds of black smoke poured out of the funnels, and they were under way — to Siberia, Bub could not help but think. He saw the *Mary Thomas* swing abruptly into line as she took the pressure from the hawser, and her sidelights, red and green, rose and fell as she was towed through the sea.

Bub's eyes dimmed at the melancholy sight, but — but just then the lieutenant came to take him down to the commander, and he straightened up and set his lips firmly, as if this were a very commonplace affair and he were used to being sent to Siberia every day in the week. The cabin in which the commander sat was like a palace compared to the humble fittings of the *Mary Thomas,* and the commander himself, in gold lace and dignity, was a most august personage, quite unlike the simple man who navigated his schooner on the trail of the seal pack.

Bub now quickly learned why he had been brought aboard, and in the prolonged questioning which followed, told nothing but the plain truth. The truth was harmless; only a lie could have injured his cause. He did not know much, except that they had been sealing far to the south in open water, and that when the calm and fog came down upon them, being close to the line, they had drifted across. Again and again he insisted that they had not lowered a boat or shot a seal in the week they had been drifting about in the forbidden sea; but the commander chose to consider all that he said to be a tissue of falsehoods, and adopted a bullying tone in an effort to frighten the boy. He threatened and cajoled by turns, but failed in the slightest to shake Bub's statements, and at last ordered him out of his presence.

By some oversight, Bub was not put in anybody's charge, and wandered up on deck unobserved. Sometimes the sailors, in passing, bent curious glances upon him, but otherwise he was left strictly alone. Nor could he have attracted much attention, for he was small, the night dark, and the watch on deck intent on its own business. Stumbling over the strange decks, he made his way aft where he could look upon the sidelights of the *Mary Thomas*, following steadily in the rear.

For a long while he watched, and then lay down in the darkness close to where the hawser passed over the stern to the captured schooner. Once an officer came up and examined the straining rope to see if it were chafing, but Bub cowered away in the shadow undiscovered. This, however, gave him an idea which concerned the lives and liberties of twenty-two men, and which was to avert crushing sorrow from more than one happy home many thousand miles away.

In the first place, he reasoned, the crew were all guiltless of any crime, and yet were being carried relentlessly away to imprisonment in Siberia — a living death, he had heard, and he believed it implicitly. In the second place, he was a prisoner, hard and fast, with no chance of escape. In the third, it was possible for the twenty-two men on the *Mary Thomas* to escape. The only thing which bound them was a four-inch hawser. They dared not cut it at their end, for a watch was sure to be maintained upon it by their Russian captors; but at his end, ah! at his end —

Bub did not stop to reason further. Wriggling close to the hawser, he opened his jack-knife and went to work. The blade was not very sharp, and he sawed away, rope-yarn by rope-yarn, the awful picture of the solitary Siberian exile he must endure growing clearer and more terrible at every stroke. Such a fate was bad enough to undergo with one's comrades, but to face it alone seemed frightful. And besides, the very act he was performing was sure to bring greater punishment upon him.

In the midst of such somber thoughts, he heard footsteps approaching. He wriggled away into the shadow. An officer stopped where he had been working, half-stooped to examine the hawser, then changed his mind and straightened up. For a few minutes he stood there, gazing at the lights of the captured schooner, and then went forward again.

Now was the time! Bub crept back and went on sawing. Now two parts were severed. Now three. But one remained. The tension upon this was so great that it readily yielded. Splash! The freed end went overboard. He lay quietly, his heart in his mouth, listening. No one on the cruiser but himself had heard.

He saw the red and green lights of the *Mary Thomas* grow dimmer and dimmer. Then a faint hallo came over the water from the Russian prize crew. Still nobody heard. The smoke continued to pour out of the cruiser's funnels, and her propellers throbbed as mightily as ever.

What was happening on the *Mary Thomas*? Bub could only surmise; but of one thing he was certain: his comrades would assert themselves and overpower the four sailors and the midshipman. A few minutes later he saw a small flash, and straining his ears heard the very faint report of a pistol. Then, oh joy! both the red and green lights suddenly disappeared. The crew had retaken the *Mary Thomas*!

Just as an officer came aft, Bub crept forward, and hid away in one of the boats. Not an instant too soon. The alarm was given. Loud voices rose in command. The cruiser altered her course. An electric searchlight began to throw its white rays across the sea, here, there, everywhere; but in its flashing path no tossing schooner was revealed.

Bub went to sleep soon after that, nor did he wake till the gray of dawn. The engines were pulsing monotonously, and the water, splashing noisily, told him the decks were being washed down. One sweeping glance, and he saw that they were alone on the expanse of ocean. The *Mary Thomas* had escaped. As he lifted his head, a roar of laughter went up from the sailors. Even the officer, who ordered him taken below and locked up, could not quite conceal the laughter in his eyes. Bub thought often in the days of confinement which followed, that they were not very angry with him for what he had done.

He was not far from right. There is a certain innate nobility deep down in the hearts of all men, which forces them to admire a brave act, even if it is performed by an enemy. The Russians were in nowise different from other men. True, a boy had outwitted them; but they could not blame him, and they were sore puzzled as to what to do with him. It would never do to take a little mite like him in to represent all that remained of the lost poacher.

So, two weeks later, a United States man-of-war, steaming out of the Russian port of Vladivostok, was signaled by a Russian cruiser. A boat passed between the two ships, and a small boy dropped over the rail upon the deck of the American vessel. A week later he was put ashore at Hakodate, and after some telegraphing, his fare was paid on the railroad to Yokohama.

From the depot he hurried through the quaint Japanese streets to the harbor, and hired a *sampan* boatman to put him aboard a certain vessel whose familiar rigging had quickly caught his eye. Her gaskets were off, her sails unfurled; she was just starting back to the United States. As he came closer, a crowd of sailors sprang upon the forecastle head, and the winlass bars rose and fell as the anchor was torn from its muddy bottom.

" 'Yankee ship come down the ribber!' " the sea lawyer's voice rolled out as he led the anchor song.

" 'Pull, my bully boys, pull!' " roared back the old familiar chorus, the men's bodies lifting and bending to the rhythm.

Bub Russell paid the boatman and stepped on deck. The anchor was forgotten. A mighty cheer went up from the men, and almost before he could catch his breath he was on the shoulders of the captain, surrounded by his mates, and endeavoring to answer twenty questions to the second.

The next day a schooner hove to off a Japanese fishing village, sent ashore four sailors and a little midshipman, and sailed away. These men did not talk English, but they had money and quickly made their way to Yokohama. From that day the Japanese village folk never heard anything more about them, and they are still a much-talked-of mystery. As the Russian government never said anything about the incident, the United States is still ignorant of the whereabouts of the lost poacher, nor has she ever heard, officially, of the way in which some of her citizens "shanghaied" five subjects of the tsar. Even nations have secrets sometimes.

An Adventure in the Upper Sea

I AM A RETIRED captain of the upper sea. That is to say, when I was a younger man (which is not so long ago) I was an aeronaut and navigated that aerial ocean which is all around about us and above us. Naturally it is a hazardous profession, and naturally I have had many thrilling experiences, the most thrilling, or at least the most nerve-racking, being the one I am about to relate.

It happened before I went in for hydrogen gas balloons, all of varnished silk, doubled and lined, and all that, and fit for voyages of days instead of mere hours. The *Little Nassau* (named after the *Great Nassau* of many years back) was the balloon I was making ascents in at the time. It was a fair-sized, hot air affair, of single thickness, good for an hour's flight or so and capable of attaining an altitude of a mile or more. It answered my purpose, for my act at the time was making half-mile parachute jumps at recreation parks and country fairs. I was in Oakland, a California town, filling a summer's engagement with a street railway company. The company owned a large park outside the city, and of course it was to its interest to provide attractions which would send the townspeople over its line when they went out to get a whiff of country air. My contract called for two ascensions weekly, and my act was an especially taking feature, for it was on my days that the largest crowds were drawn.

Before you can understand what happened, I must first explain a bit about the nature of the hot air balloon which is used for parachute jumping. If you have ever witnessed such a jump, you will remember that directly the parachute was cut loose the balloon turned upside down, emptied itself of its smoke and heated air, flattened out and fell straight down, beating the parachute to the ground. Thus there is no chasing a big deserted bag for miles and miles across the country, and much time, as well as trouble, is thereby saved. The maneuver is accomplished by attaching a weight, at the end of a long rope, to the top of the balloon. The aeronaut, with his parachute and trapeze, hangs to the bottom of the balloon, and, weighing more, keeps it right side down. But when he lets go, the weight attached to the top immediately drags the top down, and the bottom, which is the open mouth, goes up, the heated air pouring out. The weight used for this purpose on the *Little Nassau* was a bag of sand.

But to return. On the particular day I have in mind there was an unusually large crowd in attendance, and the police had their hands full keeping the people back. There was much pushing and shoving, and the ropes were bulging with the pressure of men, women, and children. As I came down from the dressing room I noticed two girls outside the ropes, of about fourteen and sixteen, and inside the rope a youngster of eight or nine. They were holding him by the hands, and he was struggling, excitedly and half in laughter, to get away from them. I thought nothing of it at the time — just a bit of childish play, no more; and it was only in the light of after events that the scene was impressed vividly upon me.

"Keep them cleared out, George!" I called to my assistant. "We don't want any accidents."

"Ay," he answered, "that I will, Charley."

George Guppy had helped me in no end of ascents, and because of his coolness, judgment and absolute reliability I had come to trust my life in his hands with the utmost confidence. His business it was to overlook the inflating of the balloon, and to see that everything about the parachute was in perfect working order.

The *Little Nassau* was already filled and straining at the guys. The parachute lay flat along the ground and beyond it the trapeze. I tossed aside my overcoat, took my position, and gave the signal to let go. As you know, the first rush upward from the earth is very sudden, and this time the balloon, when it first caught the wind, heeled violently over and was longer than usual in righting. I looked down at the old familiar sight of the world rushing away from me. And there were the thousands of people, every face silently upturned. And the silence startled me, for, as crowds went, this was the time for them to catch their first breath and send up a roar of applause. But there was no hand-clapping, whistling, cheering — only silence. And instead, clear as a bell and distinct, without the slightest shake or quaver, came George's voice through the megaphone:

"Ride her down, Charley! Ride the balloon down!"

What had happened? I waved my hand to show that I had heard, and began to think. Had something gone wrong with the parachute? Why should I ride the balloon down instead of making the jump which thousands were waiting to see? What was the matter? And as I puzzled, I received another start. The earth was a thousand feet beneath, and yet I heard a child crying softly, and seemingly very close to hand. And though the *Little Nassau* was shooting skyward like a rocket, the crying did not grow fainter and fainter and die away. I confess I was almost on the edge of a funk, when, unconsciously following up the noise with my eyes, I looked above me and saw a boy astride the sandbag which was to bring the *Little Nassau* to earth. And it was the same little boy I had seen struggling with the two girls — his sisters, as I afterward learned.

There he was, astride the sandbag and holding on to the rope for dear life. A puff of wind heeled the balloon slightly, and he swung out into space for ten or a dozen feet, and back again, fetching up against the tight canvas with a thud which even shook me, thirty feet or more beneath. I thought to see him dashed loose, but he clung on and whimpered. They told me afterward, how, at the moment they were casting off the ballon, the little fellow had torn away from his sisters, ducked under the rope, and deliberately jumped astride the sandbag. It has always been a wonder to me that he was not jerked off in the first rush.

Well, I felt sick all over as I looked at him there, and I understood why the balloon had taken longer to right itself, and why George had called after me to ride her down. Should I cut loose with the parachute, the bag would at once turn upside down, empty itself, and begin its swift descent. The only hope lay in my riding her down and in the boy holding on. There was no possible way for me to reach him. No man could climb the slim, closed parachute; and even if a man could, and made the mouth of the balloon, what could he do? Straight out, and fifteen feet away, trailed the boy on his ticklish perch, and those fifteen feet were empty space.

I thought far more quickly than it takes to tell all this, and realized on the instant that the boy's attention must be called away from his terrible danger. Exercising all the self-control I possessed, and striving to make myself seem very calm, I said cheerily:

"Hello, up there, who are you?"

He looked down at me, choking back his tears and brightening up, but just then the balloon ran into a cross-current, turned half around and lay over. This set him swinging back and forth, and he fetched the canvas another bump. Then he began to cry again.

"Isn't it great?" I asked heartily, as though it was the most enjoyable thing in the world; and, without waiting for him to answer, "What's your name?"

"Tommy Dermott," he answered.

"Glad to make your acquaintance, Tommy Dermott," I went on. "But I'd like to know who said you could ride up with me?"

He laughed and said he just thought he'd ride up for the fun of it. And so we went on, I sick with fear for him, and cudgeling my brains to keep up the conversation. I knew that it was all I could do, and that his life depended upon my ability to keep his mind off his danger. I pointed out to him the great panorama spreading away to the horizon and four thousand feet beneath us. There lay San Francisco Bay like a great placid lake, the haze of smoke over the city, the Golden Gate, the ocean fog rim beyond, and Mount Tamalpias over all, clearcut and sharp against the sky. Directly below us I could see a buggy, apparently crawling, but I knew from experience that the men in it were lashing the horses on our trail.

But he grew tired of looking around, and I could see he was beginning to get frightened.

"How would you like to go in for the business?" I asked.

He cheered up at once, and asked "Do you get good pay?"

But the *Little Nassau,* beginning to cool, had started on its long descent, and ran into counter currents which bobbed it roughly about. This swung the boy around pretty lively, smashing him into the bag once quite severely. His lip began to tremble at this, and he was crying again. I tried to joke and laugh, but it was no use. His pluck was oozing out, and at any moment I was prepared to see him go shooting past me.

I was in despair. Then, suddenly, I remembered how one fright could destroy another fright, and I frowned up at him and shouted sternly:

"You just hold on to that rope! If you don't I'll thrash you within an inch of your life when I get you down on the ground! Understand?"

"Ye-ye-yes, sir," he whimpered, and I saw that the thing had worked. I was nearer to him than the earth, and he was more afraid of me than of falling.

"Why, you've got a snap up there on that soft bag," I rattled on.

"Yes," I assured him, "this bar down here is hard and narrow, and it hurts to sit on it."

Then a thought struck him, and he forgot all about his aching fingers.

"When are you going to jump?" he asked. "That's what I came up to see."

I was sorry to disappoint him, but I wasn't going to make any jump.

But he objected to that. "It said so in the papers," he said.

"I don't care," I answered. "I'm feeling sort of lazy to-day, and I'm just going to ride down the balloon. It's my balloon and I guess I can do as I please about it. And, anyway, we're almost down now."

And we were, too, and sinking fast. And right there and then that youngster began to argue with me as to whether is was right for me to disappoint the people, and to urge their claims upon me. And it was with a happy heart that I held up my end of it, justifying myself in a thousand different ways, till we shot over a grove of eucalyptus trees and dipped to meet the earth.

"Hold on tight!" I shouted, swinging down from the trapeze by my hands in order to make a landing on my feet.

We skimmed past a barn, missed a mesh of clothesline, frightened the barnyard chickens into a panic, and rose up again clear over a haystack — all this almost quicker than it takes to tell. Then we came down in an orchard, and when my feet had touched the ground I fetched up the balloon by a couple of turns of the trapeze around an apple tree.

I have had my balloon catch fire in mid-air, I have hung on the cornice of a ten-story house, I have dropped like a bullet for six hundred feet when a parachute was slow in opening; but never have I felt so weak and faint and sick as when I staggered toward the unscratched boy and gripped him by the arm.

"Tommy Dermott," I said, when I had got my nerves back somewhat. "Tommy Dermott, I'm going to lay you across my knee and give you the greatest thrashing a boy ever got in the world's history."

"No, you don't," he answered, squirming around. "You said you wouldn't if I held on tight."

"That's all right," I said, "but I'm going to, just the same. The fellows who go up in balloons are bad, unprincipled men, and I'm going to give you a lesson right now to make you stay away from them, and from balloons, too."

And then I gave it to him, and if it wasn't the greatest thrashing in the world, it was the greatest he ever got.

But it took all the grit out of me, left me nerve-broken, that experience. I canceled the engagement with the street railway company, and later on went in for gas. Gas is much the safer, anyway.

Nam-Bok, the Liar

"A BIDARKA,* is it not so? Look! A bidarka, and one man who drives clumsily with a paddle!"

Old Bask-Wah-Wan rose to her knees, trembling with weakness and eagerness, and gazed out over the sea.

"Nam-Bok was ever clumsy at the paddle," she maundered, reminiscently, shading the sun from her eyes and staring across the silver-spilled water. "Nam-Bok was ever clumsy. I remember —"

But the women and children laughed loudly, and there was a gentle mockery in their laughter, and her voice dwindled till her lips moved without sound.

Koogah lifted his grizzled head from his bone-carving and followed the path of her eyes. Except when wild yaws took it off its course, a bidarka was heading in for the beach. Its occupant was paddling with more strength than dexterity, and made his approach along the zig-zag line of most resistance. Koogah's head dropped to his work again, and on the ivory tusk between his knees he scratched

*Skin boat of the Esquimo.

the dorsal fin of a fish the like of which never swam in the sea.

"It is doubtless the man from the next village," he said, finally, "come to consult with me about the making of things on bone. And the man is a clumsy man. He will never know how."

"It is Nam-Bok," old Bask-Wah-Wan repeated. "Should I not know my son?" she demanded, shrilly. "I say, and I say again, it is Nam-Bok."

"And so thou hast said these many summers," one of the women chided, softly. "Ever when the ice passed out of the sea hast thou sat and watched through the long day, saying at each chance canoe, 'This is Nam-Bok.' Nam-Bok is dead, O Bask-Wah-Wan, and the dead do not come back. It cannot be that the dead come back."

"Nam-Bok!" the old woman cried, so loud and clear that the whole village was startled and looked at her.

She struggled to her feet and tottered down the sand. She stumbled over a baby lying in the sun, and the mother hushed its crying and hurled harsh words after the old woman, who took no notice. The children ran down the beach in advance of her, and as the man in the bidarka drew closer, nearly capsizing with one of his ill-directed strokes, the women followed. Koogah dropped his walrus tusk and went also, leaning heavily upon his staff, and after him loitered the men in twos and threes.

The bidarka turned broadside and the ripple of surf threatened to swamp it, only a naked boy ran into the water and pulled the bow high up on the sand. The man stood up and sent a questioning glance along the line of villagers. A rainbow sweater, dirty and the worse for wear, clung loosely to his broad shoulders, and a red cotton handkerchief was knotted in sailor fashion about his throat. A fisherman's tam-o'-shanter on his close-clipped head, and dungaree trousers and heavy brogans, completed his outfit.

But he was, none the less, a striking personage to these simple fisher-folk of the great Yukon Delta, who all their lives had stared out on Bering Sea, and in that time had seen but two white men, the census enumerator and a lost Jesuit priest. They were a poor people, with neither gold in the ground nor valuable furs in hand, so the whites had passed them afar. Also, the Yukon, through the thousands of years, had shoaled that portion of the sea with the detritus of Alaska till vessels grounded out of sight of land. So the sodden coast, with its long inside reaches and huge mud-land archipelagoes, was avoided by the ships of men, and the fisher-folk knew not that such things were.

Koogah the Bone-Scratcher, retreated backward in sudden haste, tripping over his staff and falling to the ground. "Nam-Bok!" he cried, as he scrambled wildly for footing. "Nam-Bok, who was blown off to sea, come back!"

The men and women shrank away, and the children scuttled off between their legs. Only Opee-Kwan was brave, as befitted the head man of the village. He strode forward and gazed long and earnestly at the newcomer.

"It is Nam-Bok," he said, at last, and at the conviction in his voice the women wailed apprehensively and drew farther away.

The lips of the stranger moved indecisively, and his brown throat writhed and wrestled with unspoken words.

"La, la, it is Nam-Bok," Bask-Wah-Wan croaked, peering up into his face. "Ever did I say Nam-Bok would come back."

"Ah, it is Nam-Bok come back." This time it was Nam-Bok himself who spoke, putting a leg over the side of the bidarka and standing with one foot afloat and one ashore. Again his throat writhed and wrestled as he grappled after forgotten words. And when the words came forth they were strange of sound, and a spluttering of the lips accompanied the gutterals.

"Greeting, O brothers," he said, "brothers of old time before I went away with the offshore wind."

He stepped out with both feet on the sand, and Opee-Kwan waved him back.

"Thou art dead, Nam-Bok," he said.

Nam-Bok laughed. "I am fat."

"Dead men are not fat," Opee-Kwan confessed. "Thou hast fared well, but it is strange. No man may mate with the offshore wind and come back on the heels of the years."

"I have come back," Nam-Bok answered, simply.

"Mayhap thou art a shadow, then, a passing shadow of the Nam-Bok that was. Shadows come back."

"I am hungry. Shadows do not eat."

But Opee-Kwan doubted, and brushed his hand across his brow in sore puzzlement. Nam-Bok was likewise puzzled, and as he looked up and down the line found no welcome in the eyes of the fisher folk. The men and women whispered together. The children stole timidly back among their elders, and bristling dogs fawned up to him and sniffed suspiciously.

"I bore thee, Nam-Bok, and I gave thee suck when thou

wast little," Bask-Wah-Wan whimpered, drawing closer; "and shadow though thou be, or no shadow, I will give thee to eat now."

Nam-Bok made to come to her, but a growl of fear and menace warned him back. He said something in a strange tongue which sounded like "Goddam," and added, "No shadow am I, but a man."

"Who may know concerning the things of mystery?" Opee-Kwan demanded, half of himself and half of his tribespeople. "We are, and in a breath we are not. If the man may become shadow, may not the shadow become man? Nam-Bok was, but is not. This we know, but we do not know if this be Nam-Bok or the shadow of Nam-Bok."

Nam-Bok cleared his throat and made answer. "In the old time long ago, thy father's father, Opee-Kwan, went away and came back on the heels of the years. Nor was a place by the fire denied him. It is said"—he paused significantly, and they hung on his utterance—"it is said," he repeated, driving his point home with deliberation, "that Sipsip, his *klooch*,* bore him two sons after he came back."

"But he had no doings with the offshore wind," Opee-Kwan retorted. "He went away into the heart of the land, and it is in the nature of things that a man may go on and on into the land."

"And likewise the sea. But that is neither here nor there. It is said . . . that thy father's father told strange tales of the things he saw."

"Ay, strange tales he told."

"I, too, have strange tales to tell," Nam-Bok stated, insidiously. And, as they wavered, "and presents, likewise."

*Woman.

He pulled from the bidarka a shawl, marvelous of texture and color, and flung it about his mother's shoulders. The women voiced a collective sigh of admiration, and old Bask-Wah-Wan ruffled the gay material and patted it and crooned in childish joy.

"He has tales to tell," Koogah muttered. "And presents," a woman seconded.

And Opee-Kwan knew that his people were eager, and further, he was aware himself of an itching curiosity concerning those untold tales. "The fishing has been good," he said, judiciously, "and we have oil in plenty. So come, Nam-Bok; let us feast."

Two of the men hoisted the bidarka on their shoulders and carried it up to the fire. Nam-Bok walked by the side of Opee-Kwan, and the villagers followed after, save those of the women who lingered a moment to lay caressing fingers on the shawl.

There was little talk while the feast went on, though many and curious were the glances stolen at the son of Bask-Wah-Wan. This embarrassed him — not because he was modest of spirit, however, but for the fact that the stench of the seal-oil had robbed him of his appetite, and that he keenly desired to conceal his feelings on the subject.

"Eat; thou art hungry," Opee-Kwan commanded, and Nam-Bok shut both his eyes and shoved his fist into the big pot of putrid fish.

"La, la, be not ashamed. The seal were many this year, and strong men are ever hungry." And Bask-Wah-Wan sopped a particularly offensive chunk of salmon into the oil and passed it fondly and dripping to her son.

In despair, when premonitory symptoms warned him that his stomach was not so strong as of old, he filled his pipe and struck up a smoke. The people fed on noisily and watched. Few of them could boast of intimate acquaintance with the precious weed, though now and again small quantities and abominable qualities were obtained in trade from the Esquimos to the northward. Koogah, sitting next to him, indicated that he was not averse to taking a draw, and between two mouthfuls, with the oil thick on his lips, sucked away at the amber stem. And thereupon Nam-Bok held his stomach with a shaky hand and declined the proffered return. Koogah could keep the pipe, he said, for he had intended so to honor him from the first. And the people licked their fingers and approved of his liberality.

Opee-Kwan rose to his feet. "And now, O Nam-Bok, the feast is ended, and we would listen concerning the strange things you have seen."

The fisher folk applauded with their hands, and gathering about them their work, prepared to listen. The men were busy fashioning spears and carving on ivory, while the women scraped the fat from the hides of the hair seal and made them pliable or sewed muclucs with threads of sinew. Nam-Bok's eyes roved over the scene, but there was not the charm about it that his recollection had warranted him to expect. During the years of his wandering he had looked forward to just this scene, and now that it had come he was disappointed. It was a bare and meager life, he deemed, and not to be compared to the one he had become used to. Still, he would open their eyes a bit, and his own eyes sparkled at the thought.

"Brothers," he began, with the smug complacency of a man about to relate the big things he has done, "it was late summer of many summers back, with much such weather as this promises to be, when I went away. You all remember the day, when the gulls flew low, and the wind blew strong from the land, and I could not hold my bidarka against it. I tied the covering of the bidarka about me, so that no water could get in, and all of the night I fought with the storm. And in the morning there was no land, only the sea, and the offshore wind held me close in its arms and bore me along. Three such nights whitened into dawn and showed me no land, and the offshore wind would not let me go.

"And when the fourth day came I was as a madman. I could not dip my paddle for want of food, and my head went round and round, what of the thirst that was upon me. But the sea was no longer angry, and the soft south wind was blowing, and as I looked about me I saw a sight that made me think I was indeed mad."

Nam-Bok paused to pick a sliver of salmon lodged between his teeth, and the men and women, with idle hands and heads craned forward, waited.

"It was a canoe, a big canoe. If all the canoes I have ever seen were made into one canoe, it would not be so large."

There were exclamations of doubt, and Koogah, whose years were many, shook his head.

"If each bidarka were as a grain of sand," Nam-Bok defiantly continued, "and if there were as many bidarkas as there be grains of sand in this beach, still would they not make so big a canoe as this I saw on the morning of the fourth day. It was a very big canoe, and it was called a *schooner*. I saw this thing of wonder, this great schooner, coming after me, and on it I saw men —"

"Hold, O Nam-Bok!" Opee-Kwan broke in. "What manner of men were they — big men?"

"Nay, mere men like you and me."

"Did the big canoe come fast?"

"Ay."

"The sides were tall, the men short."

Opee-Kwan stated the premises with conviction. "And did these men dip with long paddles?"

Nam-Bok grinned. "There were no paddles," he said.

Mouths remained open, and a long silence ensued. Opee-Kwan reached for Koogah's pipe for a couple of contemplative sucks. One of the younger women giggled nervously, and drew upon herself angry eyes.

"There were no paddles?" Opee-Kwan asked, softly, returning the pipe.

"The south wind was behind," Nam-Bok explained.

"But the wind drift is slow."

"The schooner had wings — thus." He sketched a diagram of masts and sails in the sand, and the men crowded around and studied it. The wind was blowing briskly, and for more graphic elucidation he seized the corners of his mother's shawl and spread them out till it bellied like a sail. Bask-Wah-Wan scolded and struggled, but was blown down the beach for a score of feet and left breathless and stranded in a heap of driftwood. The men uttered sage grunts of comprehension, but Koogah suddenly tossed back his hoary head.

"Ho! ho!" he laughed. "A foolish thing, this big canoe!

A most foolish thing! The plaything of the wind! Wheresoever the wind goes, it goes, too. No man who journeys therein may name the landing beach, for always he goes with the wind, and the wind goes everywhere, but no man knows where."

"It is so," Opee-Kwan supplemented, gravely. "With the wind, the going is easy, but against the wind a man striveth hard, and for that they had no paddles these men on the big canoe did not strive at all."

"Small need to strive," Nam-Bok cried, angrily. "The schooner went likewise against the wind."

"And what said you made the sch-sch-schooner go?" Koogah asked, tripping craftily over the strange word.

"The wind," was the impatient response.

"Then the wind made the sch-sch-schooner go against the wind." Old Koogah dropped an open leer to Opee-Kwan, and, the laughter growing around him, continued: "The wind blows from the south and blows the schooner south. The wind blows against the wind. The wind blows one way and the other at the same time. It is very simple. We understand, Nam-Bok. We clearly understand."

"Thou art a fool!"

"Truth falls from thy lips," Koogah answered, meekly. "I was overlong in understanding, and the thing was simple."

But Nam-Bok's face was dark, and he said rapid words which they had never heard before. Bone-scratching and skin-scraping were resumed, but he shut his lips tightly on the tongue that could not be believed.

"This sch-sch-schooner," Koogah imperturbably asked, "it was made of a big tree?"

"It was made of many trees," Nam-Bok snapped, shortly. "It was very big."

He lapsed into sullen silence again, and Opee-Kwan nudged Koogah, who shook his head with slow amazement and murmured, "It is very strange."

Nam-Bok took the bait. "That is nothing," he said, airily, "you should see the *steamer*. As the grain of sand is to the bidarka, as the bidarka is to the schooner, so the schooner is to the steamer. Further, the steamer is made of iron. It is all iron."

"Nay, nay, Nam-Bok," cried the head man; "how can that be? Always iron goes to the bottom. For behold, I received an iron knife in trade from the head man of the next village, and yesterday the iron knife slipped from my fingers and went down, down, into the sea. To all things there be law. Never was there one thing outside the law. This we know. And, moreover, we know that things of a kind have the one law, and that all iron has the one law. So unsay thy words, Nam-Bok, that we may yet honor thee."

"It is so," Nam-Bok persisted. "The steamer is all iron and does not sink."

"Nay, nay; this cannot be."

"With my own eyes I saw it."

"It is not in the nature of things."

"But tell me, Nam-Bok," Koogah interrupted, for fear the tale would go no farther; "tell me the manner of these men in finding their way across the sea when there is no land by which to steer."

"The sun points out the path."

"But how?"

"At midday the head of the schooner takes a thing through which his eye looks at the sun, and then he makes the sun climb down out of the sky to the edge of the earth."

"Now, this be evil medicine!" cried Opee-Kwan, aghast at the sacrilege. The men held up their hands in horror and the women moaned. "This be evil medicine. It is not good to misdirect the great sun which drives away the night and gives us the seal, the salmon and warm weather."

"What if it be evil medicine?" Nam-Bok demanded, truculently. "I, too, have looked through the thing at the sun and made the sun climb down out of the sky."

Those who were nearest drew away from him hurriedly, and a woman covered the face of a child at her breast so that his eye might not fall upon it.

"But on the morning of the fourth day, O Nam-Bok," Koogah suggested; "on the morning of the fourth day when the sch-sch-schooner came after thee?"

"I had little strength left in me and could not run away. So I was taken on board, and water was poured down my throat and good food given me. Twice, my brothers, you have seen a white man. These men were all white and as many as have I fingers and toes. And when I saw they were full of kindness, I took heart, and I resolved to bring away with me report of all that I saw. And they taught me the work they did, and gave me good food and a place to sleep.

"And day after day we went over the sea, and each day the head man drew the sun down out of the sky and made it tell where we were. And when the waves were kind we hunted the fur seal, and I marveled much, for always did they fling the meat and the fat away and save only the skin."

Opee-Kwan's mouth was twitching violently, and he was about to make denunciation of such waste when Koogah kicked him to be still.

"After a weary time, when the summer was gone, and the bite of the frost come into the air, the head man pointed the nose of the schooner south. South and east we traveled for days upon days, with never the land in sight, and we were near to the village from which hailed the men —"

"How did they know they were near?" Opee-Kwan, unable to contain himself longer, demanded. "There was no land to see." Nam-Bok glowered on him wrathfully. "Did I not say the head man brought the sun down out of the sky?"

Koogah interposed, and Nam-Bok went on.

"As I say, when we were near to that village a great storm blew up, and in the night we were helpless, and knew not where we were —"

"Thou hast just said the head man knew —"

"O peace, Opee-Kwan! Thou art a fool and cannot understand. As I say, when we were helpless in the night, when I heard, above the roar of the storm, the sound of the sea on the beach. And next we struck with a mighty crash and I was in the water swimming. It was a rock-bound coast, with one patch of beach in many miles, and the law was that I should dig my hands into the sand and draw myself clear of the surf. The other men must have pounded against the rocks, for none of them came ashore but the head man, and him I knew only by the ring on his finger.

"When day came, there being nothing of the schooner, I turned my face to the land and journeyed into it that I might get food and look upon the faces of people. And when I came to a house I was taken in and given to eat, for I had learned their speech, and the white men are ever kindly. And it was a house bigger than all the houses built by us and our fathers before us."

"It was a mighty house," Koogah said, masking his unbelief with wonder.

"And many trees went into the making of such a house," Opee-Kwan added, taking the cue.

"That is nothing." Nam-Bok shrugged his shoulders in belittling fashion.

"As our houses are to that house, so that house was to the houses I was yet to see."

"And they are not big men?" Opee-Kwan queried.

"Nay; mere men like you and me," Nam-Bok answered. "I had cut a stick that I might walk in comfort, and remembering that I was to bring report to you, my brothers, I cut a notch in the stick for each person who lived in that house. And I stayed there many days, and worked, for which they gave me money, a thing of which you know nothing, but which is very good.

"And one day I departed from that place to go farther into the land. And as I walked I met many people, and I cut smaller notches in the stick that there might be room for all. Then I came upon a strange thing. On the ground before me was a bar of iron, as big in thickness as my arm, and a long step away was another bar of iron —"

"Then wert thou a rich man," Opee-Kwan asserted; "for iron be worth more than anything else in the world. It would have made many knives."

"Nay, it was not mine."

"It was a find, and a find be lawful."

"Not so; the white men had placed it there. And, further, these bars were so long that no man could carry them away — so long that as far as I could see, there was no end to them."

"Nam-Bok, that is very much iron," Opee-Kwan cautioned.

"Ay, it was hard to believe with my own eyes upon it; but I could not gainsay my eyes. And as I looked I heard —" He turned abruptly upon the head man. "Opee-Kwan, thou hast heard the sea lion bellow in his anger. Make it plain in thy mind of as many sea lions as there be waves to the sea, and make it plain that all these sea lions be made into one sea lion, and as that one sea lion would bellow so bellowed the thing I heard."

The fisher folk cried aloud in astonishment, and Opee-Kwan's jaw lowered and remained lowered.

"And in the distance I saw a monster like unto a thousand whales. It was one-eyed, and vomited smoke, and it snorted with exceeding loudness. I was afraid and ran with shaking legs along the path between the bars. But it came with the speed of the wind, this monster, and I leaped the iron bars, with its breath hot on my face —"

Opee-Kwan gained control of his jaw again. "And — and then, O Nam-Bok?"

"Then it came by on the bars, and harmed me not, and when my legs could hold me up again it was gone from sight. And it is a very common thing in that country. Even the women and children are not afraid. Men make them to do work, these monsters."

"As we make our dogs do work?" Koogah asked, with skeptic twinkle in his eye.

"Ay, as we make our dogs do work."

"And how do they breed, these — these things?" Opee-Kwan questioned.

"They breed not at all. Men fashion them cunningly of iron, and feed them with stone, and give them water to drink. The stone becomes fire, and the water becomes steam, and the steam of the water is the breath of their nostrils, and —"

"There, there, O Nam-Bok," Opee-Kwan interrupted. "Tell us of other wonders. We grow tired of this which we may not understand."

"You do not understand?" Nam-Bok asked, despairingly.

"Nay, we do not understand," the men and women wailed back. "We cannot understand."

Nam-Bok thought of a combined harvester, and of the machines wherein visions of living men were to be seen, and of the machines from which came the voices of men, and he knew his people could never understand.

"Dare I say I rode this iron monster through the land?" he asked, bitterly.

Opee-Kwan threw up his hands, palms outward, in open incredulity. "Say on; say anything. We listen."

"Then did I ride the iron monster, for which I gave money —"

"Thou saidst it was fed with stone."

"And likewise, thou fool, I said money was a thing of

which you know nothing. As I say, I rode the monster through the land, and through many villages, until I came to a big village on a salt arm of the sea. And the houses shoved their roofs among the stars in the sky, and the clouds drifted by them, and everywhere was much smoke. And the roar of that village was like the roar of the sea in storm, and the people were so many that I flung away my stick and no longer remembered the notches upon it."

"Hadst thou made small notches," Koogah reproved, "thou mightst have brought report."

Nam-Bok whirled upon him in anger. "Had I made small notches! Listen, Koogah, thou scratcher of bone! If I had made small notches, neither the stick, nor twenty sticks, could have bore them — nay, not all the driftwood of all the beaches between this village and the next. And if all of you, the women and children as well, were twenty times as many, and if you had twenty hands each, and in each hand a stick and a knife, still the notches could not be cut for the people I saw, so many were they and so fast did they come and go."

"There cannot be so many people in all the world," Opee-Kwan objected, for he was stunned and his mind could not grasp such magnitude of numbers.

"What dost thou know of all the world and how large it is?" Nam-Bok demanded.

"But there cannot be so many people in one place."

"Who art thou to say what can be and what cannot be?"

"It stands to reason there cannot be so many people in one place. Their canoes would clutter the sea till there was no room. And they could empty the sea each day of its fish and they would not all be fed."

"So it would seem," Nam-Bok made final answer; "yet it was so. With my own eyes I saw and flung my stick away." He yawned heavily and rose to his feet. "I have paddled far. The day has been long and I am tired. Now I will sleep, and tomorrow we will have further talk upon the things I have seen."

Bask-Wah-Wan, hobbling fearfully in advance, proud indeed, yet awed by her wonderful son, led him to her *igloo,* and stowed him away among the greasy, ill-smelling furs. But the men lingered by the fire, and a council was held wherein was there much whispering and low-voiced discussion.

An hour passed, and a second, and Nam-Bok slept and the talk went on. The evening sun dipped toward the northwest, and at eleven at night was nearly due north. Then it was that the head man and the bone-scratcher separated themselves from the council and aroused Nam-Bok. He blinked up into their faces and turned on his side to sleep again. Opee-Kwan gripped him by the arm and kindly but firmly shook his senses back into him.

"Come, Nam-Bok, arise!" he commanded. "It be time."

"Another feast?" Nam-Bok cried. "Nay, I am not hungry. Go on with the eating and let me sleep."

"Time to be gone!" Koogah thundered.

But Opee-Kwan spoke more softly. "Thou wast bidarka mate with me when we were boys," he said. "Together we first chased the seal and drew the salmon from the traps. And thou didst drag me back to life, Nam-Bok, when the sea closed over me, and I was sucked down to the black rocks. Together we hungered and bore the chill of the frost, and together we crawled beneath the one fur and lay close to each other. And because of these things, and the kindness in which I stood to thee, it grieves me sore that thou shouldst return such a remarkable liar. We cannot understand, and our heads be dizzy with the things thou hast spoken. It is not good, and there has been much talk in the council. Wherefore we send thee away, that our heads may remain clear and strong, and be not troubled by the unaccountable things."

"These things thou speakest of be shadows," Koogah took up the strain. "From the shadow world thou has brought them, and to the shadow world thou must return them. Thy bidarka be ready, and the tribespeople wait. They may not sleep until thou art gone."

Nam-Bok was perplexed, but hearkened to the voice of the head man.

"If thou art Nam-Bok," Opee-Kwan was saying, "thou art a fearful and most wonderful liar; if thou art the shadow of Nam-Bok, then thou speakest of shadows, concerning which it is not good that living men have knowledge. This great village thou has spoken of we deem the village of shadows. Therein flutter the souls of the dead; for the dead be many and the living few. The dead do not come back. Never have the dead come back — save thou with thy wonder tales. It is not meet that the dead come back, and should we permit it great trouble might be our portion."

Nam-Bok knew his people well and was aware that the voice of the council was supreme. So he allowed himself to be led down to the water's edge, where he was put aboard his bidarka and a paddle thrust into his hand. A stray wildfowl honked somewhere to seaward, and the surf broke limply and hollowly on the sand. A dim twilight brooded over land and water, and in the north the sun smoldered, vague and troubled, and draped about with blood-red mists. The gulls were flying low. The offshore wind blew keen and chill, and the black massed clouds behind it gave promise of bitter weather.

"Out of the sea thou camest," Opee-Kwan chanted, oracularly, "and back into the sea thou goest. Thus is balance achieved and all things brought to law."

Bask-Wah-Wan limped to the froth mark and cried, "I bless thee, Nam-Bok, for that thou hast remembered me."

But Koogah, shoving Nam-Bok clear of the beach, tore the shawl from her shoulders and flung it into the bidarka.

"It is cold in the long nights," she wailed, "and the frost is prone to nip old bones."

"The thing is a shadow," the bone-scratcher answered, "and shadows cannot keep thee warm."

Nam-Bok stood up that his voice might carry. "O Bask-Wah-Wan, mother that bore me!" he called. "Hear to the words of Nam-Bok. There be room in his bidarka for two, and he would that thou come with him. For his journey is to where there are fish and oil in plenty. There the frost comes not and life is easy, and the things of iron do the work of men. Wilt thou come, O Bask-Wah-Wan?"

She debated a moment, while the bidarka drifted swiftly from her, then raised her voice to a quavering treble. "I am old, Nam-Bok, and soon I shall pass down among the shadows. But I have no wish to go before my time. I am old, Nam-Bok, and I am afraid."

A shaft of light shot across the dim-lit sea and wrapped

boat and man in a splendor of red and gold. Then a hush fell upon the fisher folk, and the only sounds were the moan of the offshore wind and the cries of the gulls flying low in the air.

Jan, the Unrepentant

"For there's never a law of God or man
Runs north of Fifty-three."

JAN ROLLED OVER clawing and kicking. He was fighting hand and foot, now, and he fought grimly, silently. Two of the three men who hung upon him, shouted directions to each other, and strove to curb the short, hairy devil who would not curb. The third man howled. His finger was between Jan's teeth.

"Quit yer tantrums, Jan, an' ease up!" panted Red Bill, getting a strangle hold on Jan's neck. "Why on earth can't yeh hang decent and peaceable?"

But Jan kept his grip on the third man's finger, and squirmed over the floor of the tent, into the pots and pans.

"Youah no gentleman, suh," reproved Mr. Taylor, his body following his finger, and endeavoring to accommodate itself to every jerk of Jan's head. "You hev killed Mistah Gordon, as brave and honorable a gentleman as ever hit the trail aftah the dogs. Youah a murderah, suh, and without honah."

"An' yer no comrade," broke in Red Bill. "If you was,

you'd hang 'thout rampin' around an' roarin'. Come on, Jan, there's a good fellow. Don't give us no more trouble. Jes' quit, an' we'll hang yeh neat and handy, an' be done with it."

"Steady, all!" Lawson, the sailorman, bawled. "Jam his head into the bean pot and batten down."

"But my fingah, suh," Mr. Taylor protested.

"Leggo with y'r finger then! Always in the way!"

"But I can't, Mistah Lawson. It's in the critter's gullet, and nigh chewed off as 'tis."

"Stand by for stays!" As Lawson gave the warning, Jan half lifted himself, and the struggling quartet floundered across the tent into a muddle of furs and blankets. In its passage it cleared the body of a man, who lay motionless, bleeding from a bullet wound in the neck.

All this was because of the madness which had come upon Jan — the madness which comes upon a man who has stripped off the raw skin of earth and groveled long in primal nakedness, and before whose eyes rises the fat vales of the homeland, and into whose nostrils steals the whiff of hay, and grass, and flower, and new-turned soil. Through five frigid years Jan had sown the seed. Stuart River, Forty Mile, Circle City, Koyokuk, Kotzebue, had marked his bleak and strenuous agriculture, and now it was Nome that bore the harvest — not the Nome of golden beaches and ruby sands, but the Nome of '97, before Anvil City was located, or Eldorado District organized.

John Gordon was a Yankee, and should have known better. But he passed the sharp word at a time when Jan's bloodshot eyes blazed, and his teeth gritted in torment. And because of this, there was a smell of saltpeter in the tent, and one lay quietly, while the other fought like a cornered rat, and refused to hang in the decent and peaceable manner suggested by his comrades.

"If you will allow me, Mistah Lawson, befoah we go further in this rumpus, I would say it wah a good idea to pry this hyer varmint's teeth apart. Neither will he bite off, nor will he let go. He has the wisdom of the sarpint, suh, the wisdom of the sarpint."

"Lemme get the hatchet to him!" vociferated the sailor. "Lemme get the hatchet!" He shoved the steel edge close to Mr. Taylor's finger and used the man's teeth as a fulcrum. Jan held on and breathed through his nose, snorting like a grampus. "Steady, all! Now she takes it!"

"Thank you, suh; it is a powerful relief." And Mr. Taylor proceeded to gather into his arms the victim's wildly waving legs.

But Jan upreared in his berserker rage; bleeding, frothing, cursing; five frozen years thawing into sudden hell. They swayed backward and forward, panted, sweated, like some cyclopean, many-legged monster rising from the lower deeps. The slush lamp went over, drowned in its own fat, while the midday twilight scarce percolated through the dirty canvas of the tent.

"For the love of Gawd, Jan, get yer senses back!" pleaded Red Bill. "We ain't goin' to hurt yeh, 'r kill yeh, 'r anythin' of that sort. Jes' want to hang yeh, that's all, an' you a-messin' round an' rampagin' somethin' terrible. To think of travelin' trail together an' then bein' treated this-a way. Wouldn't 'bleeved it of yeh, Jan!"

"He's got too much steerageway. Grab holt his legs, Taylor, and heave'm over!"

"Yes, suh, Mistah Lawson. Do you press youah weight above, after I give the word." The Kentuckian groped about him in the murky darkness. "Now, suh, now is the accepted time!"

There was a great surge, and a quarter of a ton of human flesh tottered and crashed to its fall against the side wall. Pegs drew and guy ropes parted, and the tent, collapsing, wrapped the battle in its greasy folds.

"Yer only makin' it harder fer yerself." Red Bill continued, at the same time driving both his thumbs into a hairy throat, the possessor of which he had pinned down. "You've made nuisance enough a'ready, an' it'll take half the day to get things straightened when we've strung yeh up."

Red Bill grunted and loosed his grip, and the twain crawled out into the open. At the same instant Jan kicked clear of the sailor, and took to his heels across the snow.

"Hi! You lazy devils! Buck! Bright! Sic 'm! Pull 'm down!" sang out Lawson, lunging through the snow after the fleeing man. Buck and Bright, followed by the rest of the dogs, outstripped him and rapidly overhauled the murderer.

There was no reason that these men should do this; no reason for Jan to run away; no reason for them to attempt to prevent him. On the one hand stretched the barren snow land; on the other, the frozen sea. With neither food nor shelter, he could not run far. All they had to do was to wait till he wandered back to the tent, as he inevitably must, when the frost and hunger laid hold of him. But these men did not stop to think. There was a certain taint of madness running in the veins of all of them. Besides, blood had been spilled, and upon them was the blood lust, thick and hot. "Vengeance is mine," saith the Lord, and He saith it in temperate climes where the warm sun steals away the energies of men. But in the Northland they have discovered that prayer is only efficacious when backed by muscle, and they are accustomed to doing things for themselves. God is everywhere, they have heard, but He flings a shadow over the land for half the year that they may not find him; so they grope in darkness, and it is not to be wondered that they often doubt, and deem the Decalogue out of gear.

Jan ran blindly, reckoning not of the way of his feet, for he was mastered by the verb "to live." To live! To exist! The deepest instinct of all life, and the first. Likewise the last. Buck flashed gray through the air, but missed. The man struck madly at him, and stumbled. Then the white teeth of Bright closed on his mackinaw jacket, and he pitched into the snow. *To live! To exist!* He fought wildly as ever, the center of a tossing heap of men and dogs. His left hand gripped a wolf dog by the scruff of the back, while the arm was passed around the neck of Lawson. Every struggle of the dog helped to throttle the hapless sailor. Jan's right hand was buried deep in the curling tendrils of Red Bill's shaggy head, and beneath all, Mr. Taylor lay pinned and helpless. It was a deadlock, for the strength of his madness was prodigious; but suddenly, without apparent reason, Jan loosed his various grips and rolled over quietly on his back. His adversaries drew away a little, dubious and disconcerted by this strange manœuver. Jan grinned viciously.

"Mine friends," he said, still grinning, "you haf asked me to be politeful, und now I am politeful. Vot piziness vood you do mit me?"

"That's right, Jan. Be ca'm," soothed Red Bill. "I knowed you'd come to yer senses afore long. Jes' be ca'm, now, an' we'll do the trick with neatness and dispatch."

"Vot piziness? Vot trick?"

"The hangin' trick. An' yeh oughter thank yer lucky stars for havin' a man what knows his business. I've did it afore now, more'n once, down in the States, an' I can do it to a T."

"Hang who? Me?"

"Yep."

"Ha! ha! Shust hear der man speak foolishness! Gif me a hand, Bill, und I will get up und be hung." He crawled stiffly to his feet and looked about him. "Herr Gott! Listen to der man! He vood hang me! Ho! ho! ho! I tank not! Yes, I tank not!"

"And I tank yes, you swab," Lawson spoke up mockingly, at the same time cutting a sled lashing and coiling it up with ominous care. "Judge Lynch holds court this day."

"Von liddle while." Jan stepped back from the proffered noose. "I haf somedings to ask und to make der great proposition. Kentucky, you know about der Shudge Lynch?"

"Yes, suh. It is an institution of free men and of gentlemen, and it is an ole one and time-honored. Corruption may wear the robe of magistracy, suh, but Judge Lynch can always be relied upon to give justice without court fees. I repeat, suh, without court fees. Law may be bought and sold, but in this enlightened land justice is free as the air we breathe, strong as the licker we drink, prompt as —"

"Cut it short! Find out what the beggar wants," interrupted Lawson, spoiling the peroration.

"Vell, Kentucky, tell me dis: von man kill von odder man, Shudge Lynch hang dot man?"

"If the evidence is strong enough — yes, suh."

"An' the evidence in this here case is strong enough to hang a dozen men, Jan," broke in Red Bill.

"Nefer you mind, Bill. I talk mit you next. Now von anodder ding I ask Kentucky. If Shudge Lynch hang not der man, vot den?"

"If Judge Lynch does not hang the man, then the man goes free, and his hands are washed clean of blood. And further, suh, our great and glorious constitution has said, to wit: that no man may twice be placed in jeopardy of his life for one and the same crime, or words to that effect."

"Und dey can't shoot him, or hit him mit a club over der head alongside, or do nodings more mit him?"

"No, suh."

"Goot! You hear vot Kentucky speaks, all you noddleheads? Now I talk mit Bill. You know der piziness, Bill, und you hang me up brown, eh? Vot you say?"

" 'Betcher life, Jan, an' if yeh don't give no more trouble ye'll be almighty proud of the job. I'm a connesoor."

"You haf der great head, Bill, und know somedings or two. Und you know two und one makes tree — ain't it?"

Bill nodded.

"Und when you haf two dings, you haf not tree dings

— ain't it? Now you follow mit me close und I show you. It takes tree dings to hang. First ding, you haf to haf der man. Goot! I am der man. Second ding, you haf to haf der rope. Lawson haf der rope. Goot! Und third ding, you haf to haf someding to tie der rope to. Sling your eyes over der landscape und find der third ding to tie der rope to? Eh? Vot you say?"

Mechanically they swept the ice and snow with their eyes. It was a homogeneous scene, devoid of contrasts or bold contours, dreary, desolate, and monotonous — the ice-packed sea, the slow slope of the beach, the background of low-lying hills, and over all thrown the endless mantle of snow.

"No trees, no bluffs, no cabins, no telegraph poles, nothin'," moaned Red Bill; "nothin' respectable enough nor big enough to swing the toes of a five-foot man clear o' the ground. I give it up." He looked yearningly at that portion of Jan's anatomy which joins the head and shoulders. "Give it up," he repeated sadly to Lawson. "Throw the rope down. Gawd never intended this here country for livin' purposes, an' that's a cold frozen fact."

Jan grinned triumphantly. "I tank I go mit der tent und haf a smoke."

"Ostensiblee y'r correct, Bill, me son," spoke up Lawson; "but y'r a dummy, and you can lay to that for another cold frozen fact. Takes a sea farmer to learn you landsmen things. Ever hear of a pair of shears? Then clap y'r eyes to this."

The sailor worked rapidly. From the pile of dunnage where they had pulled up the boat the preceding fall, he unearthed a pair of long oars. These he lashed together, at nearly right angles, close to the ends of the blades. Where the handles rested he kicked holes through the snow to the sand. At the point of intersection he attached two guy ropes, making the end of one fast to a cake of beach ice. The other guy he passed over to Red Bill. "Here, me son, lay holt o' that and run it out."

And to his horror, Jan saw his gallows rise in the air. "No! no!" he cried, recoiling and putting up his fists. "It is not goot! I will not hang! Come, you noddleheads! I will lick you, all together, von after der odder! I will blay hell! I will do eferydings! Und I will die pefore I hang!"

The sailor permitted the two other men to clinch with the mad creature. They rolled and tossed about furiously, tearing up snow and tundra, their fierce struggle writing a tragedy of human passions on the white sheet spread by nature. And ever and anon a hand or foot of Jan emerged from the tangle, to be gripped by Lawson and lashed fast with rope yarns. Pawing, clawing, blaspheming, he was conquered and bound, inch by inch, and drawn to where the inexorable shears lay like a pair of gigantic dividers on the snow. Red Bill adjusted the noose, placing the hangman's knot properly under the left ear. Mr. Taylor and Lawson tailed onto the running guy, ready at the word to elevate the gallows. Bill lingered, contemplating his work with true artist love.

"Herr Gott! Vood you look at it!"

The horror in Jan's voice caused the rest to desist. The fallen tent had uprisen, and in the gathering twilight it flapped ghostly arms about and titubated toward them drunkenly. But the next instant John Gordon found the opening and crawled forth.

"What the flaming — !" For the moment his voice died away in his throat as his eyes took in the tableau. "Hold on! I'm not dead!" he cried out, coming up to the group with stormy countenance.

"Allow me, Mistah Gordon, to congratulate you upon youah escape," Mr. Taylor ventured. "A close shave, suh, a powerful close shave."

"Congratulate hell! I might have been dead and rotten and no thanks to you, you — !" And thereat John Gordon delivered himself of a vigorous flood of English, terse, intensive, denunciative, and composed solely of expletives and adjectives.

"Simply creased me," he went on when he had eased himself sufficiently. "Ever crease cattle, Taylor?"

"Yes, suh, many a time down in God's country."

"Just so. That's what happened to me. Bullet just grazed the base of my skull at the top of the neck. Stunned me but no harm done." He turned to the bound man. "Get up, Jan. I'm going to lick you to a standstill or you're going to apologize. The rest of you lads stand clear."

"I tank not. Shust tie me loose und you see," replied Jan, the Unrepentant, the devil within him still unconquered. "Und after as I lick you, I take der rest of der noddleheads, von after der odder, altogether!"

Diable, a Dog

THE DOG WAS A devil. This was recognized throughout the Northland. "Hell's Spawn" he was called by many men, but his master, Black Leclère, chose for him the shameful name, "Diable." Now Black Leclère was also a devil, and the twain were well matched. The first they met, Diable was a puppy, lean and hungry and with bitter eyes; and they met with snap and snarl and wicked looks, for Leclère's upper lip had a wolfish way of lifting and showing the cruel white teeth. And it lifted then and his eyes glinted viciously as he reached for Diable and dragged him out from the squirming litter. It was certain that they divined each other, for on the instant Diable had buried his puppy fangs in Leclère's hand and Leclère, with thumb and finger, was coolly choking his young life out of him.

"*Sacrédam!*" the Frenchman said softly, flirting the quick blood from his bitten hand and gazing down on the little puppy choking and gasping in the snow.

Leclère turned to John Hamlin, storekeeper of the Sixty Mile Post. "Dat fo' w'at Ah lak heem. 'Ow moch, eh, you, m'sieu'? 'Ow moch? Ah buy heem, now."

And because he hated him with an exceeding bitter hate, Leclère bought Diable. And for five years the twain adventured across the Northland, from St. Michael's and the Yukon Delta to the headreaches of the Pelly and even so far as the Peace River, Athabasca and the Great Slave. And they acquired a reputation for uncompromising wickedness the like of which never before had attached itself to man and dog.

Diable's father was a great gray timber wolf. But the mother of Diable, as he dimly remembered her, was a snarling, bickering husky, full-fronted and heavy-chested, with a malign eye, a catlike grip on life, and a genius for trickery and evil. There was neither faith nor trust in her. Much of evil and much of strength were there in these, Diable's progenitors, and, bone and flesh of their bone and flesh, he had inherited it all. And then came Black Leclère, to lay his heavy hand on the bit of pulsating puppy life, to press and prod and mold it till it became a big, bristling beast, acute in knavery, overspilling with hate, sinister, malignant, diabolical. With a proper master the puppy might have made a fairly ordinary, efficient sled dog. He never got the chance. Leclère but confirmed him in his congenital iniquity.

The history of Leclère and the dog is a history of war — of five cruel, relentless years, of which their first meeting is fit summary. To begin with, it was Leclère's fault, for he hated with understanding and intelligence, while the long-legged, ungainly puppy hated only blindly, instinctively, without reason or method. At first there were no refinements of cruelty (these were to come later), but simple beatings and crude brutalities. In one of these,

Diable had an ear injured. He never regained control of the riven muscles, and ever after the ear drooped limply down to keep keen the memory of his tormentor. And he never forgot.

His puppyhood was a period of foolish rebellion. He was always worsted, but he fought back because it was his nature to fight back. And he was unconquerable. Yelping shrilly from the pain of lash and club, he none the less always contrived to throw in the defiant snarl, the bitter, vindictive menace of his soul, which fetched without fail more blows and beatings. But his was his mother's tenacious grip on life. Nothing could kill him. He flourished under misfortune, grew fat with famine, and out of his terrible struggle for life developed a preternatural intelligence. His was the stealth and cunning of his mother, the fierceness and valor of his wolf sire.

Possibly it was because of his father that he never wailed. His puppy yelps passed with his lanky legs, so that he became grim and taciturn, quick to strike, slow to warn. He answered curse with snarl and blow with snap, grinning the while his implacable hatred; but never again, under the extremest agony, did Leclère bring from him the cry of fear or pain. This unconquerableness only fanned Leclère's wrath and stirred him to greater deviltries. Did Leclère give Diable half a fish and to his mates whole ones, Diable went forth to rob other dogs of their fish. Also he robbed caches and expressed himself in a thousand rogueries till he became a terror to all dogs and the masters of dogs. Did Leclère beat Diable and fondle Babette — Babette, who was not half the worker he was — why. Diable threw her down in the snow and broke her hind leg in his heavy jaws, so that Leclère was forced to shoot her. Likewise, in bloody battles Diable mastered all his teammates, set them the law of trail and forage, and made them live to the law he set.

In five years he heard but one kind word, received but one soft stroke of a hand, and then he did not know what manner of things they were. He leaped like the untamed thing he was, and his jaws were together in a flash. It was the missionary at Sunrise, a newcomer in the country, who spoke the kind word and gave the soft stroke of the hand. And for six months after, he wrote no letters home to the States, and the surgeon at McQuestion traveled two hundred miles on the ice to save him from blood poisoning.

Men and dogs looked askance at Diable when he drifted into their camps and posts, and they greeted him with feet threateningly lifted for the kick, or with bristling manes and bared fangs. Once a man did kick Diable, and Diable, with quick wolf snap, closed his jaws like a steel trap on the man's leg and crunched down to the bone. Whereat the man was determined to have his life, only Black Leclère, with ominous eyes and naked hunting knife, stepped in between. The killing of Diable — ah, *sacrédam! that* was a pleasure Leclère reserved for himself. Someday it would happen, or else — bah! who was to know? Anyway, the problem would be solved.

For they had become problems to each other, this man and beast, or rather, they had become a problem, the pair of them. The very breath each drew was a challenge and a menace to the other. Their hate bound them together as love could never bind. Leclère was bent on the coming of the day when Diable should wilt in spirit and cringe and whimper at his feet. And Diable — Leclère knew what was in Diable's mind, and more than once had read it in his eyes. And so clearly had he read that when the dog was at his back he made it a point to glance often over his shoulder.

Men marveled when Leclère refused large money for the dog. "Someday you'll kill him and be out his price," said John Hamlin, once, when Diable lay panting in the snow where Leclère had kicked him and no one knew whether his ribs were broken and no one dared look to see.

"Dat," said Leclère dryly, "dat is my biz'ness, m'sieu'."

And the men marveled that Diable did not run away. They did not understand. But Leclère understood. He was a man who had lived much in the open, beyond the sound of human tongue, and he had learned the voices of wind and storm, the sigh of night, the whisper of dawn, the clash of day. In a dim way he could hear the green things growing, the running of the sap, the bursting of the bud. And he knew the subtle speech of the things that moved, of the rabbit in the snare, the moody raven beating the air with hollow wing, the baldface shuffling under the moon, the wolf like a gray shadow gliding betwixt the twilight and the dark. And to him Diable spoke clear and direct. Full well he understood why Diable did not run away, and he looked more often over his shoulder.

When in anger, Diable was not nice to look upon, and more than once had he leaped for Leclère's throat, to be stretched quivering and senseless in the snow by the butt of the ever-ready dog whip. And so Diable learned to bide his time. When he reached his full strength and prime of youth, he thought the time had come. He was broad-chested, powerfully muscled, of far more than ordinary size, and his neck from head to shoulders was a mass of bristling hair — to all appearances a full-blooded wolf. Leclère was lying asleep in his furs when Diable deemed the time to be ripe. He crept upon him stealthily, head low to earth and lone ear laid back, with a feline softness of tread to which even Leclère's delicate tympanum could not responsively vibrate. The dog breathed gently, very gently, and not till he was close at hand did he raise his head. He paused for a moment and looked at the bronzed bull throat, naked and knotty and swelling to a deep and steady pulse. The slaver dripped down his fangs and slid off his tongue at the sight, and in that moment he remembered his drooping ear, his uncounted blows and wrongs, and without a sound sprang on the sleeping man.

Leclère awoke to the pang of the fangs in his throat, and, perfect animal that he was, he awoke clearheaded and with full comprehension. He closed on the hound's windpipe with both his hands and rolled out of his furs to get his weight uppermost. But the thousands of Diable's ancestors had clung at the throats of unnumbered moose and caribou and dragged them down, and the wisdom of those ancestors was his. When Leclère's weight came on top of him, he drove his hind legs upward and in and clawed down chest and abdomen, ripping and tearing through skin and muscle. And when he felt the man's body wince above him and lift, he worried and shook at the man's throat. His teammates closed around in a snarling, slavering circle, and Diable, with falling breath and fading sense, knew that their jaws were hungry for him. But that did not matter — it was the man, the man above him, and he ripped and clawed and shook and worried to the last ounce of his strength. But Leclère choked him with both his hands till Diable's chest heaved and writhed for the air denied, and his eyes glazed and his jaws slowly loosened and his tongue protruded black and swollen.

"Eh? *Bon,* you devil!" Leclère gurgled, mouth and throat clogged with his own blood, as he shoved the dizzy dog from him.

And then Leclère cursed the other dogs off as they fell upon Diable. They drew back into a wider circle, squatting alertly on their haunches and licking their chops, each individual hair on every neck bristling and erect.

Diable recovered quickly, and at sound of Leclère's voice, tottered to his feet and swayed weakly back and forth.

"A-h-ah! You beeg devil!" Leclère spluttered. "Ah fix you. Ah fix you plentee, by Gar!"

Diable, the air biting into his exhausted lungs like wine, flashed full into the man's face, his jaws missing and coming together with a metallic clip. They rolled over and over on the snow, Leclère striking madly with his fists. Then they separated, face to face, and circled back and forth before each other for an opening. Leclère could have drawn his knife. His rifle was at his feet. But the beast in him was up and raging. He would do the thing with his hands — and his teeth. The dog sprang in, but Leclère knocked him over with a blow of his fist, fell upon him, and buried his teeth to the bone in the dog's shoulder.

It was a primordial setting and a primordial scene, such as might have been in the savage youth of the world. An open space in a dark forest, a ring of grinning wolf dogs, and in the center two beasts, locked in combat, snapping and snarling, raging madly about, panting, sobbing, cursing, straining, wild with passion, blind with lust, in a fury of murder, ripping, tearing and clawing in elemental brutishness.

But Leclère caught the dog behind the ear with a blow from his fist, knocking him over and for an instant stunning him. Then Leclère leaped upon him with his feet, and sprang up and down, striving to grind him into the earth. Both Diable's hind legs were broken ere Leclère ceased that he might catch breath.

"A-a-ah! A-a-ah!" he screamed, incapable of articulate speech, shaking his fist through sheer impotence of throat and larynx.

But Diable was indomitable. He lay there in a hideous, helpless welter, his lip feebly lifting and writhing to the snarl he had not the strength to utter. Leclère kicked him, and the tired jaws closed on the ankle but could not break the skin.

Then Leclère picked up the whip and proceeded almost to cut him to pieces, at each stroke of the lash crying: "Dis taim Ah break you! Eh? By Gar, Ah break you!"

In the end, exhausted, fainting from loss of blood, he crumpled up and fell by his victim, and, when the wolf dogs closed in to take their vengeance, with his last consciousness dragged his body on top of Diable to shield him from their fangs.

This occurred not far from Sunrise, and the missionary, opening the door to Leclère a few hours later, was surprised to note the absence of Diable from the team. Nor did his surprise lessen when Leclère threw back the robes from the sled, gathered Diable into his arms, and staggered across the threshold. It happened that the surgeon of McQuestion was up on a gossip, and between them they proceeded to repair Leclère.

"*Merci, non,*" said he. "Do you fix firs' de dog. To die? *Non.* Eet is not good. Becos' heem Ah mus' yet break. Dat fo' w'at he mus' not die."

The surgeon called it a marvel, the missionary a miracle, that Leclère lived through at all; but so weakened was he that in the spring the fever got him and he went on his back again. The dog had been in even worse plight, but his grip on life prevailed, and the bones of his hind legs knitted and his internal organs righted themselves during the several weeks he lay strapped to the floor. And by the time Leclère, finally convalescent, sallow and shaky, took the sun by the cabin door, Diable had reasserted his supremacy and brought not only his own teammates but the missionary's dogs into subjection.

He moved never a muscle nor twitched a hair when for the first time Leclère tottered out on the missionary's arm and sank down slowly and with infinite caution on the three-legged stool.

"*Bon!*" he said. "*Bon!* De good sun!" And he stretched out his wasted hands and washed them in the warmth.

Then his gaze fell on the dog, and the old light blazed back in his eyes. He touched the missionary lightly on the arm. "*Mon père,* dat is one beeg devil, dat Diable. You will bring me one pistol, so dat Ah drink the sun in peace."

And thenceforth, for many days, he sat in the sun before the cabin door. He never dozed, and the pistol lay always across his knees. The dog had a way, the first thing each day, of looking for the weapon in its wonted place. At sight of it he would lift his lip faintly in token that he understood, and Leclère would lift his own lip in an answering grin. One day the missionary took note of the trick. "Bless me!" he said. "I really believe the brute comprehends."

Leclère laughed softly. "Look you, *mon père*. Dat w'at Ah now spik, to dat does he lissen."

As if in confirmation, Diable just perceptibly wriggled his lone ear up to catch the sound.

"Ah say 'keel'—"

Diable growled deep down in his throat, the hair bristled along his neck, and every muscle went tense and expectant.

"Ah lift de gun, so, like dat—" And suiting action to word, he sighted the pistol at the dog.

Diable, with a single leap sidewise, landed around the corner of the cabin out of sight.

"Bless me!" the missionary remarked. "Bless me!" he repeated at intervals, unconscious of his paucity of expression.

Leclère grinned proudly.

"But why does he not run away?"

The Frenchman's shoulders went up in a racial shrug which means all things from total ignorance to infinite understanding.

"Then why do you not kill him?"

Again the shoulders went up.

"*Mon père,*" he said, after a pause, "de taim is not yet. He is one beeg devil. Some taim Ah break heem, so, an' so, all to leetle bits. Heh? Some taim. *Bon!*" A day came when Leclère gathered his dogs together and floated down in a bateau to Forty Mile and on to the Porcupine, where he took a commission from the P. C. Company and went exploring for the better part of a year. After that he poled up the Koyokuk to deserted Arctic City, and later came drifting back, from camp to camp, along the Yukon. And during the long months Diable was well lessoned. He learned many tortures — the torture of hunger, the torture of thirst, the torture of fire, and, worst of all, the torture of music.

Like the rest of his kind, he did not enjoy music. It gave him exquisite anguish, racking him nerve by nerve and ripping apart every fiber of his being. It made him howl, long and wolflike, as when the wolves bay the stars on frosty nights. He could not help howling. It was his one weakness in the contest with Leclère, and it was his shame. Leclère, on the other hand, passionately loved music — as passionately as he loved strong drink. And when his soul clamored for expression, it usually uttered itself in one or both of the two ways. And when he had drunk, not too much but just enough for the perfect poise of exaltation, his brain alilt with unsung song and the devil in him aroused and rampant, his soul found its supreme utterance in the bearding of Diable.

"Now we will haf a leetle museek," he would say. "Eh? W'at you t'ink, Diable?"

It was only an old and battered harmonica, tenderly treasured and patiently repaired; but it was the best that money could buy, and out of its silver reeds he drew weird, vagrant airs which men had never heard before. Then the dog, dumb of throat, with teeth tight clenched, would back away, inch by inch, to the farthest cabin corner. And Leclère, playing, playing, a stout club tucked handily under his arm, followed the animal up, inch by inch, step by step, till there was no further retreat.

At first Diable would crowd himself into the smallest possible space, groveling close to the floor; but as the music came nearer and nearer he was forced to uprear, his back jammed into the logs, his fore legs fanning the air as though to beat off the rippling waves of sound. He still kept his teeth together, but severe muscular contractions attacked his body, strange twitchings and jerkings, till he was all aquiver and writhing in silent torment. As he lost control, his jaws spasmodically wrenched apart and deep, throaty vibrations issued forth, too low in the register of sound for human ear to catch. And then, as he stood reared with nostrils distended, eyes dilated, slaver dripping, hair bristling in helpless rage, arose the long wolf howl. It came with a slurring rush upward, swelling to a great heartbreaking burst of sound and dying away in sadly cadenced woe — then the next rush upward, octave upon octave; the bursting heart; and the infinite sorrow and misery, fainting, fading, falling, and dying slowly away.

It was fit for hell. And Leclère, with fiendish ken, seemed to divine each particular nerve and heartstring and, with long wails and tremblings and sobbing minors, to make it yield up its last least shred of grief. It was frightful, and for twenty-four hours after, the dog was nervous and unstrung, starting at common sounds, tripping over his own shadow, but withal, vicious and masterful with his teammates. Nor did he show signs of a breaking spirit. Rather did he grow more grim and taciturn, biding his time with an inscrutable patience which began to puzzle and weigh upon Leclère. The dog would lie in the firelight, motionless, for hours, gazing straight before him at Leclère and hating him with his bitter eyes.

Often the man felt that he had bucked up against the very essence of life — the unconquerable essence that swept the hawk down out of the sky like a feathered thunderbolt, that drove the great gray goose across the zones, that hurled the spawning salmon through two thousand miles of boiling Yukon flood. At such times he felt impelled to express his own unconquerable essence; and with strong drink, wild music, and Diable, he indulged in vast orgies, wherein he pitted his puny strength in the face of things and challenged all that was, and had been, and was yet to be. "Dere is somet'ing dere," he affirmed, when the rhythmed vagaries of his mind touched the secret chords of the dog's being and brought forth the long, lugubrious howl. "Ah pool eet out wid bot' my han's, so, an' so. Ha! Ha! Eet is fonee! Eet is ver' fonee! De mans swear, de leetle bird go peep-peep, Diable heem go yow-yow — an' eet is all de ver' same t'ing."

Father Gautier, a worthy priest, once reproved him with instances of concrete perdition. He never reproved him again.

"Eet may be so, *mon père,*" he made answer. "An' Ah t'ink Ah go troo hell a-snappin', lak de hemlock troo de fire. Eh, *mon père?*"

But all bad things come to an end as well as good, and so with Black Leclère. On the summer low water, in a poling boat, he left McDougall for Sunrise. He left Mc-

Dougall in company with Timothy Brown, and arrived at Sunrise by himself. Further, it was known that they had quarreled just previous to pulling out; for the *Lizzie*, a wheezy ten-ton sternwheeler, twenty-four hours behind, beat Leclère in by three days. And when he did get in, it was with a clean-drilled bullet hole through his shoulder muscle and a tale of ambush and murder.

A strike had been made at Sunrise, and things had changed considerably. With the infusion of several hundred gold seekers, a deal of whisky, and half a dozen equipped gamblers, the missionary had seen the page of his years of labor with the Indians wiped clean. When the squaws became preoccupied with cooking beans and keeping the fire going for the wifeless miners, and the bucks with swapping their warm furs for black bottles and broken timepieces, he took to his bed, said "Bless me!" several times, and departed to his final accounting in a rough-hewn oblong box. Whereupon the gamblers moved their roulette and faro tables into the mission house, and the click of chips and clink of glasses went up from dawn till dark and to dawn again.

Now Timothy Brown was well beloved among these adventurers of the north. The one thing against him was his quick temper and ready fist — a little thing, for which his kind heart and forgiving hand more than atoned. On the other hand, there was nothing to atone for Black Leclère. He was "black," as more than one remembered deed bore witness, while he was as well hated as the other was beloved. So the men of Sunrise put a dressing on his shoulder and haled him before Judge Lynch.

It was a simple affair. He had quarreled with Timothy Brown at McDougall. With Timothy Brown he had left McDougall. Without Timothy Brown he had arrived at Sunrise. Considered in the light of his evilness, the unanimous conclusion was that he had killed Timothy Brown. On the other hand, Leclère acknowledged their facts, but challenged their conclusion and gave his own explanation. Twenty miles out of Sunrise he and Timothy Brown were poling the boat along the rocky shore. From that shore two rifle shots rang out. Timothy Brown pitched out of the boat and went down bubbling red, and that was the last of Timothy Brown. He, Leclère, pitched into the bottom of the boat with a stinging shoulder. He lay very quietly, peeping at the shore. After a time two Indians stuck up their heads and came out to the water's edge, carrying between them a birch-bark canoe. As they launched it, Leclère let fly. He potted one, who went over the side after the manner of Timothy Brown. The other dropped into the bottom of the canoe, and then canoe and poling boat went down the stream in a drifting battle. Only they hung up on a split current, and the canoe passed on one side of an island, the poling boat on the other. That was the last of the canoe, and he came on into Sunrise. Yes, from the way the Indian in the canoe jumped, he was sure he had potted him. That was all.

This explanation was not deemed adequate. They gave him ten hours' grace while the *Lizzie* steamed down to investigate. Ten hours later she came wheezing back to Sunrise. There had been nothing to investigate. No evidence had been found to back up his statements. They told him to make his will, for he possessed a fifty-thousand-dollar Sunrise claim and they were a law-abiding as well as a law-giving breed.

Leclère shrugged his shoulders. "Bot one t'ing," he said; "a leetle, w'at you call, favor — a leetle favor, dat is eet. I gif my feefty t'ousan' dollair to de church. I gif my husky dog, Diable, to de devil. De leetle favor? Firs' you hang heem, an' den you hang me. Eet is good, eh?"

Good it was, they agreed, that Hell's Spawn should break trail for his master across the last divide, and the court was adjourned down to the riverbank, where a big spruce tree stood by itself. Slackwater Charley put a hangman's knot in the end of a hauling line, and the noose was slipped over Leclère's head and pulled tight around his neck. His hands were tied behind his back, and he was assisted to the top of a cracker box. Then the running end of the line was passed over an overhanging branch, drawn taut, and made fast. To kick the box out from under would leave him dancing on the air.

"Now for the dog," said Webster Shaw, sometime mining engineer. "You'll have to rope him, Slackwater."

Leclère grinned. Slackwater took a chew of tobacco, rove a running noose, and proceeded leisurely to coil a few turns in his hand. He paused once or twice to brush particularly offensive mosquitoes from off his face. Everybody was brushing mosquitoes, except Leclère, about whose head a small cloud was distinctly visible. Even Diable, lying full-stretched on the ground, with his fore paws rubbed the pests away from eyes and mouth.

But while Slackwater waited for Diable to lift his head, a faint call came down the quiet air and a man was seen waving his arm and running across the flat from Sunrise. It was the storekeeper.

"C — call 'er off, boys," he panted, as he came in among them. "Little Sandy and Bernadotte's jes' got in," he explained with returning breath. "Landed down below an' come up by the short cut. Got the Beaver with 'm. Picked 'm up in his canoe, stuck in a back channel, with a couple of bullet holes in 'm. Other buck was Klok-Kutz, the one that knocked spots out of his squaw and dusted."

"Eh? W'at Ah say? Eh?" Leclère cried exultantly. "Dat de one fo' sure! Ah know. Ah spik true."

"The thing to do is to teach these damned Siwashes a little manners," spoke Webster Shaw. "They're getting fat and sassy, and we'll have to bring them down a peg. Round in all the bucks and string up the Beaver for an object-lesson. That's the program. Come on and let's see what he's got to say for himself."

"Heh, m'sieu'!" Leclère called, as the crowd began to melt away through the twilight in the direction of Sunrise, "Ah lak ver' moch to see de fon."

"Oh, we'll turn you loose when we come back," Webster Shaw shouted over his shoulder. "In the mean time, meditate on your sins and the ways of Providence. It will do you good, so be grateful."

As is the way with men who are accustomed to great hazards, whose nerves are healthy and trained to patience, so Leclère settled himself down to the long wait—which is to say that he reconciled his mind to it. There was no settling for the body, for the taut rope forced him to stand rigidly erect. The least relaxation of the leg muscles pressed the rough-fibered noose into his neck, while the upright position caused him much pain in his wounded shoulder. He projected his under lip and expelled his breath upward along his face to blow the mosquitoes away from his eyes. But the situation had its compensation. To be snatched from the maw of death was well worth a little bodily suffering, only it was unfortunate that he should miss the hanging of the Beaver.

And so he mused, till his eyes chanced to fall upon Diable, head between fore paws and stretched on the ground asleep. And then Leclère ceased to muse. He studied the animal closely, striving to sense if the sleep were real or feigned. The dog's sides were heaving regularly, but Leclère felt that the breath came and went a shade too quickly; also he felt there was a vigilance or an alertness to every hair which belied unshackling sleep. He would have given his Sunrise claim to be assured that the dog was not awake, and once, when one of his joints cracked, he looked quickly and guiltily at Diable to see if he roused.

He did not rouse then, but a few minutes later he got up slowly and lazily, stretched, and looked carefully about him. "*Sacrédam!*" said Leclère under his breath.

Assured that no one was in sight or hearing, Diable sat down, curled his upper lip almost into a smile, looked up at Leclère, and licked his chops.

"Ah see my feenish," the man said, and laughed sardonically aloud.

Diable came nearer, the useless ear wobbling, the good ear cocked forward with devilish comprehension. He thrust his head on one side, quizzically, and advanced with mincing, playful steps. He rubbed his body gently against the box till it shook and shook again. Leclère teetered carefully to maintain his equilibrium.

"Diable," he said calmly, "look out. Ah keel you."

Diable snarled at the word and shook the box with greater force. Then he upreared and with his fore paws threw his weight against it higher up. Leclère kicked out with one foot, but the rope bit into his neck and checked so abruptly as nearly to overbalance him.

"Hi! Ya! Chook! Mush on!" he screamed.

Diable retreated for twenty feet or so, with a fiendish levity in his bearing which Leclère could not mistake. He remembered the dog's often breaking the scum of ice on the water hole by lifting up and throwing his weight upon it; and remembering, he understood what he now had in mind. Diable faced about and paused. He showed his white teeth in a grin, which Leclère answered; and then hurled his body through the air straight for the box.

Fifteen minutes later, Slackwater Charley and Webster Shaw, returning, caught a glimpse of a ghostly pendulum swinging back and forth in the dim light. As they hurriedly drew in closer, they made out the man's inert body, and a live thing that clung to it, and shook and worried, and gave to it the swaying motion.

"Hi! Ya! Chook! you Spawn of Hell!" yelled Webster Shaw.

Diable glared at him, and snarled threateningly, without loosing his jaws.

Slackwater Charley got out his revolver, but his hand was shaking as with a chill and he fumbled.

"Here, you take it," he said, passing the weapon over.

Webster Shaw laughed shortly, drew a sight between the gleaming eyes, and pressed the trigger. Diable's body twitched with the shock, thrashed the ground spasmodically a moment, and went suddenly limp. But his teeth still held fast locked.

The Law of Life

OLD KOSKOOSH LISTENED greedily. Though his sight had long since faded, his hearing was still acute, and the slightest sound penetrated to the glimmering intelligence which yet abode behind the withered forehead, but which no longer gazed forth upon the things of the world. Ah! that was Sit-cum-to-ha, shrilly anathematizing the dogs as she cuffed and beat them into the harnesses. Sit-cum-to-ha was his daughter's daughter, but she was too busy to waste a thought upon her broken grandfather, sitting alone there in the snow, forlorn and helpless. Camp must be broken. The long trail waited while the short day refused to linger. Life called her, and the duties of life, not death. And he was very close to death now.

The thought made the old man panicky for the moment, and he stretched forth a palsied hand which wandered tremblingly over the small heap of dry wood beside him. Reassured that it was indeed there, his hand returned to the shelter of his mangy furs, and he again fell to listening. The sulky crackling of half-frozen hides told him that the chief's moose-skin lodge had been struck, and even then was being rammed and jammed into portable compass. The chief was his son, stalwart and strong, head man of the tribesmen, and a mighty hunter. As the women toiled with the camp luggage, his voice rose, chiding them for their slowness. Old Koskoosh strained his ears. It was the last time he would hear that voice. There went Geehow's lodge! And Tusken's! Seven, eight, nine; only the Shaman's could be still standing. There! They were at work upon it now. He could hear the Shaman grunt as he piled it on the sled. A child whimpered, and a woman soothed it with soft, crooning gutterals. Little Koo-tee, the old man thought, a fretful child, and not over strong. It would die soon, perhaps, and they would burn a hole through the frozen tundra and pile rocks above to keep the wolverines away. Well, what did it matter? A few years at best, and as many an empty belly as a full one. And in the end, Death waited, ever-hungry and hungriest of them all.

What was that? Oh, the men lashing the sleds and drawing tight the thongs. He listened, who would listen no more. The whip lashes snarled and bit among the dogs. Hear them whine! How they hated the work and the trail! They were off! Sled after sled churned slowly away into the silence. They were gone. They had passed out of his life, and he faced the last bitter hour alone. No. The snow crunched beneath a moccasin; a man stood beside him; upon his head a hand rested gently. His son was good to do this thing. He remembered other old men whose sons had not waited after the tribe. But his son had. He wandered away into the past, till the young man's voice brought him back.

"Is it well with you?" he asked.

And the old man answered, "It is well."

"There be wood beside you," the younger man continued, "and the fire burns bright. The morning is gray, and the cold has broken. It will snow presently. Even now is it snowing."

"Ay, even now is it snowing."

"The tribesmen hurry. Their bales are heavy, and their bellies flat with lack of feasting. The trail is long and they travel fast. I go now. It is well?"

"It is well. I am as a last year's leaf, clinging lightly to the stem. The first breath that blows, and I fall. My voice is become like an old woman's. My eyes no longer show me the way of my feet, and my feet are heavy, and I am tired. It is well."

He bowed his head in content till the last noise of the complaining snow had died away, and he knew his son was beyond recall. Then his hand crept out in haste to the wood. It alone stood betwixt him and the eternity which yawned in upon him. At last the measure of his life was a handful of fagots. One by one they would go to feed the fire, and just so, step by step, death would creep upon him. When the last stick had surrendered up its heat, the frost would begin to gather strength. First his feet would yield, then his hands; and the numbness would travel, slowly, from the extremities to the body. His head would fall forward upon his knees, and he would rest. It was easy. All men must die.

He did not complain. It was the way of life, and it was just. He had been born close to the earth, close to the earth had he lived, and the law thereof was not new to him. It was the law of all flesh. Nature was not kindly to the flesh. She had no concern for that concrete thing called the individual. Her interest lay in the species, the race. This was the deepest abstraction old Koskoosh's barbaric mind was capable of, but he grasped it firmly. He saw it exemplified in all life. The rise of the sap, the bursting greenness of the willow bud, the fall of the yellow leaf—in this alone was told the whole history. But one task did nature set the individual. Did he not perform it, he died. Did he perform it, it was all the same, he died. Nature did not care; there were plenty who were obedient, and it was only the obedience in this matter, not the obedient, which lived and lived always. The tribe of Koskoosh was very old. The old men he had known when a boy, had known old men before them. Therefore it was true that the tribe lived, that it stood for the obedience of all its members, way down into the forgotten past, whose very resting places were unremembered. They did not count; they were episodes. They had passed away like clouds from a summer sky. He also was an episode, and would pass away. Nature did not care. To life she set one task, gave one law. To perpetuate was the task of life, its law was death. A maiden was a good creature to look upon, full-breasted and strong, with spring to her step and light in her eyes. But her task was yet before her. The light in her eyes brightened, her step quickened, she was now bold with the young men, now timid, and she gave them of her own unrest. And ever she grew fairer and yet fairer to look upon, till some hunter, able no longer to withhold himself, took her to his lodge to cook and toil for him and to become the mother of his children. And with the coming of her offspring her looks left her. Her limbs dragged and shuffled, her eyes dimmed and bleared, and only the little children found joy against the withered cheek of the old squaw by the fire. Her task was done. But a little while, on the first pinch of famine or the first long trail, and she would be left, even as he had been left, in the snow, with a little pile of wood. Such was the law.

He placed a stick carefully upon the fire and resumed his meditations. It was the same everywhere, with all things. The mosquitoes vanished with the first frost. The little tree squirrel crawled away to die. When age settled upon the rabbit it became slow and heavy, and could no longer outfoot its enemies. Even the big baldface grew clumsy and blind and quarrelsome, in the end to be dragged down by a handful of yelping huskies. He remembered how he had abandoned his own father on an upper reach of the Klondike one winter, the winter before the missionary came with his talk books and his box of medicines. Many a time had Koskoosh smacked his lips over the recollection of that box, though now his mouth refused to moisten. The "painkiller" had been especially good. But the missionary was a bother after all, for he brought no meat into the camp, and he ate heartily, and the hunters grumbled. But he chilled his lungs on the divide by the Mayo, and the dogs afterwards nosed the stones away and fought over his bones.

Koskoosh placed another stick on the fire and harked back deeper into the past. There was the time of the Great Famine, when the old men crouched empty-bellied to the fire, and from their lips fell dim traditions of the ancient day when the Yukon ran wide open for three winters, and then lay frozen for three summers. He had lost his mother in that famine. In the summer the salmon run had failed, and the tribe looked forward to the winter and the coming of the caribou. Then the winter came, but with it there were no caribou. Never had the like been known, not even in the lives of the old men. But the caribou did not come, and it was the seventh year, and the rabbits had not replenished, and the dogs were naught but bundles of bones. And through the long darkness the children wailed and died, and the women, and the old men; and not one in ten of the tribe lived to meet the sun when it came back in the spring. That *was* a famine!

But he had seen times of plenty, too, when the meat spoiled on their hands, and the dogs were fat and worthless with overeating—times when they let the game go unkilled, and the women were fertile, and the lodges were cluttered with sprawling men children and women children. Then it was the men became high-stomached, and revived ancient quarrels, and crossed the divides to the south to kill the Pellys, and to the west that they might sit by the dead fires of the Tananas. He remembered, when a boy, during a time of plenty, when he saw a moose pulled down by the wolves. Zing-ha lay with him in the snow and watched—Zing-ha, who later became the craftiest of hunters, and who, in the end, fell through an air hole on the Yukon. They found him, a month afterward, just as he had crawled halfway out and frozen stiff to the ice.

But the moose. Zing-ha and he had gone out that day to play at hunting after the manner of their fathers. On the bed of the creek they struck the fresh track of a moose, and with it the tracks of many wolves. "An old one," Zing-ha, who was quicker at reading the sign, said —"an old one who cannot keep up with the herd. The wolves have cut him out from his brothers, and they will never leave him." And it was so. It was their way. By day and by night, never resting, snarling on his heels, snapping at his nose, they would stay by him to the end. How Zing-ha and he felt the blood lust quicken! The finish would be a sight to see!

Eager-footed, they took the trail, and even he, Koskoosh, slow of sight and an unversed tracker, could have followed it blind, it was so wide. Hot were they on the heels of the chase, reading the grim tragedy, fresh written, at every step. Now they came to where the moose had made a stand. Thrice the length of a grown man's body, in every direction, had the snow been stamped about and uptossed. In the midst were the deep impressions of the splay-hoofed game, and all about, everywhere, were the lighter footmarks of the wolves. Some, while their brothers harried the kill, had lain to one side and rested. The full-stretched impress of their bodies in the snow was as perfect as though made the moment before. One wolf had been caught in a wild lunge of the maddened victim and trampled to death. A few bones, well picked, bore witness.

Again, they ceased the uplift of their snowshoes at a second stand. Here the great animal had fought desperately. Twice had he been dragged down, as the snow attested, and twice had he shaken his assailants clear and gained footing once more. He had done his task long since, but none the less was life dear to him. Zing-ha said it was a strange thing, a moose once down to get free again; but this one certainly had. The Shaman would see signs and wonders in this when they told him.

And yet again, they came to where the moose had made to mount the bank and gain the timber. But his foes had laid on from behind, till he reared and fell back upon them, crushing two deep into the snow. It was plain the kill was at hand, for their brothers had left them untouched. Two more stands were hurried past, brief in time length and very close together. The trail was red now, and the clean stride of the great beast had grown short and slovenly. Then they heard the first sounds of the battle—not the full-throated chorus of the chase, but the short, snappy bark which spoke of close quarters and teeth to flesh. Crawling up the wind, Zing-ha bellied it through the snow, and with him crept he, Koskoosh, who was to be chief of the tribesmen in the years to come. Together they shoved aside the under branches of a young spruce and peered forth. It was the end they saw.

The picture, like all of youth's impressions, was still strong with him, and his dim eyes watched the end played out as vividly as in that far-off time. Koskoosh marveled at this, for in the days which followed, when he was a leader of men and a head of councilors, he had done great deeds and made his name a curse in the mouths of the Pellys, to say naught of the strange white man he had killed, knife to knife, in open fight.

For long he pondered on the days of his youth, till the fire died down and the frost bit deeper. He replenished it with two sticks this time, and gauged his grip on life by what remained. If Sit-cum-to-ha had only remembered her grandfather, and gathered a larger armful, his hours would have been longer. It would have been easy. But she was ever a careless child, and honored not her ancestors from the time the Beaver, son of the son of Zing-ha, first cast eyes upon her. Well, what mattered it? Had he not done likewise in his own quick youth? For a while he listened to the silence. Perhaps the heart of his son might soften, and he would come back with the dogs to take his old father on with the tribe to where the caribou ran thick and the fat hung heavy upon them.

He strained his ears, his restless brain for the moment stilled. Not a stir, nothing. He alone took breath in the midst of the great silence. It was very lonely, Hark! What was that? A chill passed over his body. The familiar, long-drawn howl broke the void, and it was close at hand. Then on his darkened eyes was projected the vision of the moose — the old bull moose — the torn flanks and bloody sides, the riddled mane, and the great branching horns, down low and tossing to the last. He saw the flashing forms of gray, the gleaming eyes, the lolling tongues, the slavered fangs. And he saw the inexorable circle close in till it became a dark point in the midst of the stamped snow.

A cold muzzle thrust against his cheek, and at its touch his soul leaped back to the present. His hand shot into the fire and dragged out a burning fagot. Overcome for the nonce by his hereditary fear of man, the brute retreated, raising a prolonged call to his brothers; and greedily they answered, till a ring of crouching, jaw-slobbered gray was stretched round about. The old man listened to the drawing in of this circle. He waved his brand wildly, and sniffs turned to snarls; but the panting brutes refused to scatter. Now one wormed his chest forward, dragging his haunches after, now a second, now a third; but never a one drew back. Why should he cling to life? he asked, and dropped the blazing stick into the snow. It sizzled and went out. The circle grunted uneasily, but held its own. Again he saw the last stand of the old bull moose, and Koskoosh dropped his head wearily upon his knees. What did it matter after all? Was it not the law of life?

Siwash

"If I was a man——" Her words were in themselves indecisive, but the withering contempt which flashed from her black eyes was not lost upon the men-folk in the tent.

Tommy, the English sailor, squirmed, but chivalrous old Dick Humphries, Cornish fisherman and erstwhile American salmon capitalist, beamed upon her benevolently as ever. He bore women too large a portion of his rough heart to mind them, as he said, when they were in the doldrums, or when their limited vision would not permit them to see all around a thing. So they said nothing, these two men who had taken the half-frozen woman into their tent three days back, and who had warmed her, and fed her, and rescued her goods from the Indian packers. This latter had necessitated the payment of numerous dollars, to say nothing of a demonstration in force—Dick Humphries squinting along the sights of a Winchester while Tommy apportioned their wages among them at his own appraisement. It had been a little thing in itself, but it meant much to a woman playing a desperate single hand in the equally desperate Klondike rush of '97. Men were occupied with their own pressing needs, nor did they approve of women playing, singlehanded, the odds of the arctic winter.

"If I was a man, I know what I would do." Thus reiterated Molly, she of the flashing eyes, and therein spoke the cumulative grit of five American-born generations.

In the succeeding silence, Tommy thrust a pan of biscuits into the Yukon stove and piled on fresh fuel. A reddish flood pounded along under his sun-tanned skin, and as he stooped, the skin of his neck was scarlet. Dick palmed a three-cornered sail needle through a set of broken pack straps, his good nature in nowise disturbed by the feminine cataclysm which was threatening to burst in the storm-beaten tent.

"And if you was a man?" he asked, his voice vibrant with kindness. The three-cornered needle jammed in the damp leather, and he suspended work for the moment.

"I'd be a man. I'd put the straps on my back and light out. I wouldn't lay in camp here, with the Yukon like to freeze most any day, and the goods not half over the portage. And you—you are men, and you sit here, holding your hands, afraid of a little wind and wet. I tell you straight, Yankee men are made of different stuff. They'd be hitting the trail for Dawson if they had to wade through hell-fire. And you, you—— I wish I was a man."

"I'm very glad, my dear, that you're not." Dick Humphries threw the bight of the sail twine over the point of the needle and drew it clear with a couple of deft turns and a jerk.

A snort of the gale dealt the tent a broad-handed slap as it hurtled past, and the sleet rat-rat-tat-ted with snappy spite against the thin canvas. The smoke, smothered in its exit, drove back through the firebox door, carrying with it the pungent odor of green spruce.

"Good Gawd! Why can't a woman listen to reason?" Tommy lifted his head from the denser depths and turned upon her a pair of smoke-outraged eyes.

"And why can't a man show his manhood?"

Tommy sprang to his feet with an oath which would have shocked a woman of lesser heart, ripped loose the sturdy reef knots and flung back the flaps of the tent.

The trio peered out. It was not a threatening spectacle. A few water-soaked tents formed the miserable foreground, from which the streaming ground sloped to a foaming gorge. Down this ramped a mountain torrent. Here and there, dwarf spruce, rooting and groveling in the shallow alluvium, marked the proximity of the timber line. Beyond, on the opposing slope, the vague outlines of a glacier loomed dead white through the driving rain. Even as they looked, its massive front crumbled into the valley, on the breast of some subterranean vomit, and it lifted its hoarse thunder above the screeching voice of the storm. Involuntarily, Molly shrank back.

"Look, woman! Look with all your eyes! Three miles in the teeth of the gale to Crater Lake, across two glaciers, along the slippery rimrock, knee-deep in a howling river! Look, I say, you Yankee woman! Look! There's your Yankee men!" Tommy pointed a passionate hand in the direction of the struggling tents. "Yankees, the last mother's son of them. Are they on trail? Is there one of them with the straps to his back? And you would teach us men our work? Look, I say!"

Another tremendous section of the glacier rumbled earthward. The wind whipped in at the open doorway, bulging out the sides of the tent till it swayed like a huge bladder at its guy ropes. The smoke swirled about them, and the sleet drove sharply into their flesh. Tommy pulled the flaps together hastily, and returned to his tearful task at the firebox. Dick Humphries threw the mended pack straps into a corner and lighted his pipe. Even Molly was for the moment persuaded.

"There's my clothes," she half-whimpered, the feminine for the moment prevailing. "They're right at the top of the cache, and they'll be ruined, I tell you, ruined, I tell you, ruined!"

"There, there," Dick interposed, when the last quavering syllable had wailed itself out. "Don't let that worry you, little woman. I'm old enough to be your father's brother, and I've a daughter older than you, and I'll tog you out in fripperies when we get to Dawson if it takes my last dollar."

"When we get to Dawson!" The scorn had come back to her throat with a sudden surge. "You'll rot on the way, first. You'll drown in a mudhole. You—you—Britishers!"

The last word, explosive, intensive, had strained the limits of her vituperation. If that would not stir these men, what could? Tommy's neck ran red again, but he kept his tongue between his teeth. Dick's eyes mellowed. He had the advantage over Tommy, for he had once had a white woman for a wife.

The blood of five American-born generations is, under certain circumstances, an uncomfortable heritage; and among these circumstances might be enumerated that of being quartered with next of kin. These men were Britons. On sea and land her ancestry and the generations thereof had thrashed them and theirs. On sea and land they would continue to do so. The traditions of her race clamored for vindication. She was but a woman of the present, but in her bubbled the whole mighty past. It was not alone Molly Travis who pulled on gum boots, mackintosh, and straps; for the phantom hands of ten thousand forebears drew tight the buckles, just so as they squared her jaw and set her eyes with determination. She, Molly Travis, intended to shame these Britishers; they, the innumerable shades, were asserting the dominance of the common race.

The menfolk did not interfere. Once Dick suggested that she take his oilskins as her mackintosh was worth no more than paper in such a storm. But she sniffed her independence so sharply that he communed with his pipe till she tied the flaps on the outside and slushed away on the flooded trail.

"Think she'll make it?" Dick's face belied the indifference of his voice.

"Make it? If she stands the pressure till she gets to the cache, what of the cold and misery, she'll be stark, raving mad. Stand it? She'll be dumb crazed. You know it yourself, Dick. You've windjammed round the Horn. You know what it is to lay out on a topsail yard in the thick of it, bucking sleet and snow and frozen canvas till you're ready to just let go and cry like a baby. Clothes? She won't be able to tell a bundle of skirts from a gold pan or a teakettle."

"Kind of think we were wrong in letting her go, then?"

"Not a bit of it. So help me, Dick, she'd 'a made this tent a hell for the rest of the trip if we hadn't. Trouble with her she's got too much spirit. This'll tone it down a bit."

"Yes," Dick admitted, "she's too ambitious. But, then, Molly's all right. A cussed little fool to tackle a trip like this, but a plucky sight better than those pick-me-up-and-carry-me kind of women. She's the stock that carried you and me, Tommy, and you've got to make allowance for the spirit. Takes a woman to breed a man. Takes a she-cat, not a cow, to mother a tiger."

"And when they're unreasonable we've got to put up with it, eh?"

"The proposition. A sharp sheath-knife cuts deeper on a slip than a dull one; but that's no reason for to hack the edge off over a capstan bar."

"All right, if you say so, but when it comes to woman, I guess I'll take mine with a little less edge."

"What do you know about it?" Dick demanded.

"Some." Tommy reached over for a pair of Molly's wet stockings and stretched them across his knees to dry.

Dick, eyeing him querulously, went fishing in her hand satchel, then hitched up to the front of the stove with divers articles of damp clothing spread likewise to the heat.

"Thought you said you never were married?" he asked.

"Did I? No more was I — that is — yes, I was. And as

good a woman as ever cooked grub for a man."

"Slipped her moorings?" Dick symbolized infinity with a wave of his hand.

"Ay."

"Childbirth," he added, after a moment's pause.

The beans bubbled rowdily on the front lid, and he pushed the pot back to a cooler surface. After that he investigated the biscuits, tested them with a splinter of wood, and placed them aside under cover of a damp cloth. Dick, after the manner of his kind, stifled his interest and waited silently.

"A different woman to Molly. Siwash."

Dick nodded his understanding.

"Not so proud and wilful, but stick by a fellow through thick and thin. Sling a paddle with the next and starve as contentedly as Job. Go for'ard when the sloop's nose was more often under than not, and take in sail like a man. Went prospecting, once, up Teslin way, past Surprise Lake and the Little Yellow-Head. Grub gave out, and we ate the dogs. Dogs gave out, and we ate harnesses, moccasins and furs. Never a whimper; never a pick-me-up-and-carry-me. Before we went she said look out for grub, but when it happened, never a I-told-you-so. 'Never mind, Tommy,' she'd say, day after day, that weak she could bare lift a snowshoe and her feet raw with the work. 'Never mind. I'd sooner be flat-bellied of hunger and be your woman, Tommy, than have a potlatch every day and be Chief George's *klooch.*' George was chief of the Chilcoots, you know, and wanted her bad.

"Great days, those. Was a likely chap myself when I struck the coast. Jumped a whaler, the *Pole Star,* at Unalaska, and worked my way down to Sitka on an otter hunter. Picked up with Happy Jack there—know him?"

"Had charge of my traps for me," Dick answered, "down on the Columbia. Pretty wild, wasn't he, with a warm place in his heart for whiskey and women?"

"The very chap. Went trading with him for a couple of seasons—*hooch,* and blankets, and such stuff. Then got a sloop of my own, and not to cut him out, came down Juneau way. That's where I met Killisnoo; I called her Tilly for short. Met her at a squaw dance down on the beach. Chief George had finished the year's trade with the Sticks over the Passes, and was down from Dyea with half his tribe. No end of Siwashes at the dance, and I the only white. No one knew me, barring a few of the bucks I'd met over Sitka way, but I'd got most of their histories from Happy Jack.

"Everybody talking Chinook, not guessing that I could spit it better than most; and principally two girls who'd run away from Haine's Mission up the Lynn Canal. They were trim creatures, good to the eye, and I kind of thought of casting that way; but they were fresh as fresh-caught cod. Too much edge, you see. Being a newcomer, they started to twist me, not knowing I gathered in every word of Chinook they uttered.

"I never let on, but set to dancing with Tilly, and the more we danced the more our hearts warmed to each other. 'Looking for a woman,' one of the girls says, and the other tosses her head and answers, 'Small chance he'll get one when the women are looking for men.' And the bucks and squaws standing around began to grin and giggle and repeat what had been said. 'Quite a pretty boy,' says the first one. I'll not deny I was rather smooth-faced and youngish, but I'd been a man amongst men many's the day, and it rankled me. 'Dancing with Chief George's girl,' pipes the second. 'First thing George'll give him the flat of a paddle and send him about his business.' Chief George had been looking pretty black up to now, but at this he laughed and slapped his knees. He was a husky beggar and would have used the paddle on me, too.

"'Who's the girls?' I asked Tilly, as we went ripping down the center in a reel. And as soon as she told me their names I remembered all about them from Happy Jack. Had their pedigree down fine — several things he'd told me that not even their own tribe knew. But I held my hush, and went on courting Tilly, they a-casting sharp remarks and everybody roaring. 'Bide a wee, Tommy,' I says to myself, 'bide a wee.'

"And bide I did, till the dance was ripe to break up and Chief George had brought a paddle all ready for me. Everybody was on the lookout for mischief when we stopped; but I marched, easy as you please, slap into the thick of them. The Mission girls cut me up something clever, and for all I was angry I had to set my teeth to keep from laughing. I turned upon them suddenly.

"'Are you done?' I asked.

"You should have seen them when they heard me spitting Chinook. Then I broke loose. I told them all about themselves, and their people before them; their fathers, mother, sisters, brothers — everybody, everything. Each mean trick they'd played; every scrape they'd got into; every shame that'd falled them. And I burned them without fear or favor. All hands crowded round. Never had they heard a white man sling their lingo as I did. Everybody was laughing save the Mission girls. Even Chief George forgot the paddle, or at least he was swallowing too much respect to dare to use it.

"But the girls. 'Oh don't, Tommy,' they cried, the tears running down their cheeks. 'Please don't. We'll be good. Sure, Tommy, sure.' But I knew them well, and I scorched them on every tender spot. Nor did I slack away till they came down on their knees, begging and pleading with me to keep quiet. Then I shot a glance at Chief George; but he did not know whether to have at me or not, and passed it off by laughing hollowly.

"So be. When I passed the parting with Tilly that night I gave her the word that I was going to be around for a week or so, and that I wanted to see more of her. Not thick-skinned, her kind, when it came to showing like and dislike, and she looked her pleasure for the honest girl she was. Ay, a striking lass, and I didn't wonder that Chief George was taken with her.

"Everything my way. Took the wind from his sails on the first leg. I was for getting her aboard and sailing down Wrangel way till it blew over, leaving him to whistle; but I wasn't to get her that easy. Seems she was living with an uncle of hers — guardian, the way such things go — and seems he was nigh to shuffling off with consumption or some sort of lung trouble. He was good and bad by turns, and she wouldn't leave him till it was over with. Went up to the tepee just before I left, to speculate on how long it'd be; but the old beggar had promised her to

Chief George, and when he clapped eyes on me his anger brought on a hemorrhage.

"'Come and take me, Tommy,' she says when we bid good-by on the beach. 'Ay,' I answers; 'when you give the word.' And I kissed her, whiteman fashion and lover fashion, till she was all of a tremble like a quaking aspen, and I was so beside myself I'd half a mind to go up and give the uncle a lift over the divide.

"So I went down Wrangel way, past St. Mary's, and even to the Queen Charlottes, trading, running whiskey, turning the sloop to most anything. Winter was on, stiff and crisp, and I was back to Juneau, when the word came. 'Come,' the beggar says who brought the news. 'Killisnoo say, "Come now."' 'What's the row?' I asks. 'Chief George,' says he. 'Potlatch. Killisnoo makum *klooch.*'

"Ay, it was bitter — the Taku bowling down out of the north, the salt water freezing quick as it struck the deck, and the old sloop and I hammering into the teeth of it for a hundred miles to Dyea. Had a Douglass Islander for crew when I started, but midway up he was washed over from the bows. Jibed all over and crossed the course three times, but never a sign of him."

"Doubled up with the cold most likely," Dick suggested, putting a pause into the narrative while he hung one of Molly's skirts up to dry, "and went down like a pot of lead."

"My idea. So I finished the course alone, half-dead when I made Dyea in the dark of the evening. The tide favored, and I ran the sloop plump to the bank, in the shelter of the river. Couldn't go an inch farther, for the fresh water was frozen solid. Halyards and blocks were that iced up I didn't dare lower mainsail or jib. First I broached a pint of the cargo raw, and then, leaving all standing, ready for the start, and with a blanket around me, headed across the flat to the camp. No mistaking, it was a grand layout. The Chilcats had come in a body — dogs, babies and canoes — to say nothing of the Dog-Ears, the Little Salmons, and the Missions. Full half a thousand of them to celebrate Tilly's wedding, and never a white man in a score of miles.

"Nobody took note of me, the blanket over my head and hiding my face, and I waded knee deep through the dogs and youngsters till I was well up to the front. The show was being pulled off in a big open place among the trees, with great fires burning and the snow moccasin packed as hard as Portland cement. Next me was Tilly, beaded and scarlet-clothed galore, and against her Chief George and his head men. The shaman was being helped out by the big medicines from the other tribes, and it shivered my spine up and down, the deviltries they cut. I caught myself wondering if the folks in Liverpool could only see me now; and I thought of yellow-haired Gussie, whose brother I licked after my first voyage, just because he was not for having a sailorman courting his sister. And with Gussie in my eyes I looked at Tilly. A rum old world, thinks I, with man a-stepping in trails the mother little dreamed of.

"So be. When the noise was loudest, walrus hides booming and priests a-singing, I says, 'Are you ready?' Gawd! Not a start, not a shot of the eyes my way, not the twitch of a muscle. 'I knew,' she answers, slow and steady as a calm spring tide. 'Where?' 'The high bank at the edge of the ice,' I whispers back. 'Jump out when I give the word.'

"Did I say there was no end of huskies? Well, there was no end. Here, there, everywhere, they were scattered about — tame wolves and nothing less. When the strain runs thin they breed them in the bush with the wild, and they're bitter fighters. Right at the toe of my moccasin lay a big brute, and by the heel another. I doubled the first one's tail quick, till it snapped in my grip. As his jaws clipped together where my hand should have been, I threw the second one by the scruff straight into his mouth. 'Go!' I cried to Tilly.

"You know how they fight. In the wink of an eye there was a raging hundred of them, top and bottom, ripping and tearing each other, kids and squaws tumbling which way, and the camp gone wild. Tilly'd slipped away, so I followed. But when I looked over my shoulder at the skirt of the crowd, the devil laid me by the heart, and I dropped the blanket and went back.

"By then the dogs'd been knocked apart and the crowd was untangling itself. Nobody was in proper place, so they didn't note that Tilly'd gone. 'Hello,' I says, gripping Chief George by the hand. 'May your potlatch smoke rise often, and the Sticks bring many furs with the spring.'

"Lord love me, Dick, but he was joyed to see me — him with the upper hand and wedding Tilly. Chance to puff big over me. The tale that I was hot after her had spread through the camps, and my presence did him proud. All hands knew me, without my blanket, and set to grinning and giggling. It was rich, but I made it richer by playing unbeknowing.

" 'What's the row?' I asks. 'Who's getting married now?'

" 'Chief George,' the shaman says, ducking his reverence to him.

" 'Thought he had two *klooches*.'

" 'Him takum more — three,' with another duck.

" 'Oh!' And I turned away as though it didn't interest me.

"But this wouldn't do, and everybody begins singing out, 'Killisnoo! Killisnoo!'

" 'Killisnoo what?' I asked.

" 'Killisnoo, *klooch*, Chief George,' they blathered. 'Killisnoo, *klooch*.'

"I jumped and looked at Chief George. He nodded his head and threw out his chest.

" 'She'll be no *klooch* of yours,' I says, solemnly. 'No *klooch* of yours,' I repeats, while his face went black and his hand began dropping to his hunting knife.

" 'Look!' I cries, striking an attitude. 'Big medicine. You watch my smoke.'

"I pulled off my mittens, rolled back my sleeves, and made half a dozen passes in the air.

" 'Killisnoo!' I shouts. 'Killisnoo! Killisnoo!'

"I was making medicine, and they began to scare. Every eye was on me; no time to find out that Tilly wasn't there. Then I called Killisnoo three times again, and waited; and three times more. All for mystery and to make them nervous. Chief George couldn't guess what I was up to, and wanted to put a stop to the foolery; but the shamans said to wait, and that they'd see me and go me one better, or words to that effect. Besides, he was a superstitious cuss, and I fancy a bit afraid of the white man's magic.

"Then I called Killisnoo, long and soft like the howl of a wolf, till the women were all a-tremble and the bucks looking serious.

" 'Look!' I sprang for'ard, pointing my finger into a bunch of squaws — easier to deceive women than men, you know. 'Look!' And I raised it aloft as though following the flight of a bird. Up, up, straight overhead, making to follow it with my eyes till it disappeared in the sky.

" 'Killisnoo,' I said, looking at Chief George and pointing upward again. 'Killisnoo.'

"So help me, Dick, the gammon worked. Half of them, at least, saw Tilly disappear in the air. They'd drunk my whiskey at Juneau and seen stranger sights, I'll warrant. Why should I not do this thing, I, who sold bad spirits corked in bottles? Some of the women shrieked. Everybody fell to whispering in bunches. I folded my arms and held my head high, and they drew further away from me. The time was ripe to go. 'Grab him,' Chief George cries. Three or four of them came at me, but I whirled, quick, made a couple of passes like to send them after Tilly, and pointed up. Touch me? Not for the kingdoms of the earth. Chief George harangued them, but he couldn't get them to lift a leg. Then he made to take me himself; but I repeated the mummery and his grit went out through his fingers.

" 'Let your shamans work wonders the like of which I have done this night,' I says. 'Let them call Killisnoo down out of the sky whither I have sent her.' But the priests knew their limits. 'May your *klooches* bear you sons as the spawn of the salmon,' I says, turning to go, 'and may your totem pole stand long in the land, and the smoke of your camp rise always.'

"But if the beggars could have seen me hitting the high places for the sloop as soon as I was clear of them they'd thought my own medicine had got after me. Tilly'd kept warm by chopping the ice away, and was all ready to cast off. How we ran before it, the Taku howling after us and the freezing seas sweeping over at every clip. With everything battened down, me a-steering and Tilly chopping ice, we held on half the night, till I plumped the sloop ashore on Porcupine Island, and we shivered it out on the beach — blankets wet, and Tilly drying the matches on her breast.

"So I think I know something about it. Seven years, Dick, man and wife, in rough sailing and smooth. And then she died, in the heart of the winter, died in childbirth, up there on the Chilcat Station. She held my hand to the last, the ice creeping up inside the door and spreading thick on the gut of the window. Outside, the lone howl of the wolf and the Silence; inside, death and the Silence. You've never heard the Silence yet, Dick, and Gawd grant you don't ever have to hear it when you sit by the side of death. Hear it? Ay, till the breath whistles like a siren, and the heart booms, booms, booms, like the surf on the shore.

"Siwash, Dick, but a woman. White, Dick, white clear through. Towards the last she says, 'Keep my feather bed, Tommy, keep it always.' And I agreed. Then she opened her eyes, full with the pain. 'I've been a good woman to you, Tommy, and because of that I want you to promise

— to promise'— the words seemed to stick in her throat —'that when you marry, the woman be white. No more Siwash, Tommy. I know. Plenty white women down to Juneau now. I know. Your people call you squaw man, your women turn their heads to the one side on the street, and you do not go to their cabins like other men. Why? Your wife Siwash. Is it not so? And this is not good. Wherefore I die. Promise me. Kiss me in token of your promise.'

"I kissed her, and she dozed off, whispering, 'It is good.' At the end, that near gone my ear was at her lips, she roused for the last time. 'Remember, Tommy; remember my feather bed.' Then she died, in childbirth, up there on the Chilcat Station."

The tent heeled over and half flattened before the gale. Dick refilled his pipe, while Tommy drew the tea and set it aside against Molly's return.

And she of the flashing eyes and Yankee blood? Blinded, falling, crawling on hand and knee, the wind thrust back in her throat by the wind, she was heading for the tent. On her shoulders a bulky pack caught the full fury of the storm. She plucked feebly at the knotted flaps, but it was Tommy and Dick who cast them loose. Then she set her soul for the last effort, staggered in, and fell exhausted on the floor.

Tommy unbuckled the straps and took the pack from her. As he lifted it there was a clanging of pots and pans. Dick, pouring out a mug of whiskey, paused long enough to pass the wink across her body. Tommy winked back. His lips pursed the monosyllable, "clothes," but Dick shook his head reprovingly.

"Here, little woman," he said, after she had drunk the

whiskey and straightened up a bit. "Here's some dry togs. Climb into them. We're going out to extra peg the tent. After that, give us the call, and we'll come in and have dinner. Sing out when you're ready."

"So help me, Dick, that's knocked the edge off her for the rest of this trip," Tommy spluttered as they crouched to the lee of the tent.

"But it's the edge is her saving grace," Dick replied, ducking his head to a volley of sleet which drove around a corner of the canvas. "The edge that you and I've got, Tommy, and the edge of our mothers before us."

The Man With the Gash

JACOB KENT HAD suffered from cupidity all the days of his life. This, in turn, had engendered a chronic distrustfulness, and his mind and character had become so warped that he was a very disagreeable man to deal with. He was also a victim to somnambulic propensities, and very set in his ideas. He had been a weaver of cloth from the cradle, until the fever of Klondike had entered his blood and torn him away from his loom. His cabin stood midway between Sixty Mile Post and the Stuart River; and men who made it a custom to travel the trail to Dawson likened him to a robber baron, perched in his fortress and exacting toll from the caravans that used his ill-kept roads. Since a certain amount of history was required in the construction of this figure, the less cultured wayfarers from Stuart River were prone to describe him after a still more primordial fashion, in which a command of strong adjectives was to be chiefly noted.

This cabin was not his, by the way, having been built several years previously by a couple of miners who had got out a raft of logs at that point for a grubstake. They had been most hospitable lads, and, after they abandoned it, travelers who knew the route made it an object to arrive there at nightfall. It was very handy, saving them all the time and toil of pitching camp; and it was an unwritten rule that the last man left a neat pile of firewood for the next comer. Rarely a night passed but from half a dozen to a score of men crowded into its shelter. Jacob Kent noted these things, exercised squatter sovereignty, and moved in. Thenceforth, the weary travelers were mulcted a dollar per head for the privilege of sleeping on the floor, Jacob Kent weighing the dust and never failing to steal the downweight. Besides, he so contrived that his transient guests chopped his wood for him and carried his water. This was rank piracy, but his victims were an easygoing breed, and while they detested him, they yet permitted him to flourish in his sins.

One afternoon in April he sat by his door — for all the world like a predatory spider — marveling at the heat of the returning sun, and keeping an eye on the trail for prospective flies. The Yukon lay at his feet, a sea of ice, disappearing around two great bends to the north and south, and stretching an honest two miles from bank to bank. Over its rough breast ran the sled trail, a slender sunken line, eighteen inches wide and two thousand miles in length, with more curses distributed to the linear foot than any other road in or out of all Christendom.

Jacob Kent was feeling particularly good that afternoon. The record had been broken the previous night, and he had sold his hospitality to no less than twenty-eight visitors. True, it had been quite uncomfortable, and four had snored beneath his bunk all night; but then it had added appreciable weight to the sack in which he kept his gold dust. That sack, with its glittering yellow treasure, was at once the chief delight and the chief bane of his existence. Heaven and hell lay within its slender mouth. In the nature of things, there being no privacy to his one-roomed dwelling, he was tortured by a constant fear of theft. It would be very easy for these bearded, desperate-looking strangers to make away with it. Often he dreamed that such was the case, and awoke in the grip of nightmare. A select number of these robbers haunted him through his dreams, and he came to know them quite well, especially the bronzed leader with the gash on his right cheek. This fellow was the most persistent of the lot, and, because of him, he had, in his waking moments, constructed several score of hiding places in and about the cabin. After a concealment he would breathe freely again, perhaps for several nights, only to collar the Man with the Gash in the very act of unearthing the sack. Then, on awakening in the midst of the usual struggle, he would at once get up and transfer the bag to a new and more ingenious crypt. It was not that he was the direct victim of these phantasms; but he believed in omens and thought transference, and he deemed these dream-robbers to be the astral projection of real personages who happened at those particular moments, no matter where they were in the flesh, to be harboring designs, in the spirit, upon his wealth. So he continued to bleed the unfortunates who crossed his threshold, and at the same time to add to his trouble with every ounce that went into the sack.

As he sat sunning himself, a thought came to Jacob Kent that brought him to his feet with a jerk. The pleasures of life had culminated in the continual weighing and reweighing of his dust; but a shadow had been thrown upon this pleasant avocation, which he had hitherto failed to brush aside. His gold scales were quite small; in fact, their maximum was a pound and a half — eighteen ounces — while his hoard mounted up to something like three and a third times that. He had never been able to weigh it all at one operation, and hence considered himself to have been shut out from a new and most edifying coign of contemplation. Being denied this, half the pleasure of possession had been lost; nay, he felt that this miserable obstacle actually minimized the fact, as it did the strength, of possession. It was the solution of this problem flashing across his mind that had just brought him to his feet. He searched the trail carefully in either direction. There was nothing in sight, so he went inside.

In a few seconds he had the table cleared away and the scales set up. On one side he placed the stamped disks to the equivalent of fifteen ounces, and balanced it with dust on the other. Replacing the weights with dust, he then had thirty ounces precisely balanced. These, in turn, he placed together on one side and again balanced with more dust. By this time the gold was exhausted, and he was sweating liberally. He trembled with ecstasy, ravished beyond measure. Nevertheless he dusted the sack thoroughly, to the last least grain, till the balance was overcome and one side of the scales sank to the table. Equilibrium, however, was restored by the addition of a pennyweight and five grains to the opposite side. He stood, head thrown back, transfixed. The sack was empty, but the potentiality of the scales had become immeasurable. Upon them he could weigh any amount, from the tiniest grain to pounds upon pounds. Mammon laid hot fingers on his heart. The sun swung on its westering way till it flashed through the open doorway, full upon the yellow-burdened scales. The precious heaps flung back the light in a mellow glow. Time and space were not.

"Blime me! But you 'ave the makin' of several quid there, 'aven't you?"

Jacob Kent wheeled about, at the same time reaching for his double-barreled shotgun, which stood handy. But when his eyes lit on the intruder's face, he staggered back dizzily. *It was the face of the Man with the Gash!*

The man looked at him curiously.

"Oh, that's all right," he said, waving his hand deprecatingly. "You needn't think as I'll 'arm you or your blasted dust.

"You're a rum 'un, you are," he added reflectively, as he watched the sweat pouring from off Kent's face and the quavering of his knees.

"W'y don't you pipe up an' say somethin'?" he went on, as the other struggled for breath. "Wot's gone wrong o' your gaff? Anythink the matter?"

"W — w — where'd you get it?" Kent at last managed to articulate, raising a shaking forefinger to the ghastly scar which seamed the other's cheek.

"Shipmate stove me down with a marlinspike from the main royal. An' now as you 'ave your figger'ead in trim, wot I want to know is, wot's it to you? That's wot I want to know — wot's it to you? Gawd blime me! do it 'urt you? Ain't it smug enough for the likes o' you? That's wot I want to know!"

"No, no," Kent answered, sinking upon a stool with a sickly grin. "I was just wondering."

"Did you ever see the like?" the other went on truculently.

"No."

"Ain't it a beaut?"

"Yes." Kent nodded his head approvingly, intent on humoring this strange visitor, but wholly unprepared for the outburst which was to follow his effort to be agreeable.

"You blasted, bloomin', burgoo-eatin' son-of-a-sea-swab! Wot do you mean, a sayin' the most onsightly thing Gawd Almighty ever put on the face o' man is a beaut? Wot do you mean, you —"

And thereat this fiery son of the sea broke off into a string of Oriental profanity, mingling gods and devils, lineages and men, metaphors and monsters, with so savage a virility that Jacob Kent was paralyzed. He shrank back, his arms lifted as though to ward off physical violence. So utterly unnerved was he that the other paused in the midswing of a gorgeous peroration and burst into thunderous laughter.

"The sun's knocked the bottom out o' the trail," said the Man with the Gash between departing paroxysms of mirth. "An' I only 'ope as you'll appreciate the hoppertunity of consortin' with a man o' my mug. Get steam up in that firebox o' your'n. I'm goin' to unrig the dogs an' grub 'em. An' don't be shy o' the wood, my lad; there's plenty more where that come from, and it's you've got the time to sling an axe. An' tote up a bucket o' water while you're about it. Lively! or I'll run you down, so 'elp me!"

Such a thing was unheard of. Jacob Kent was making the fire, chopping wood, packing water — doing menial tasks for a guest! When Jim Cardegee left Dawson, it was with his head filled with the iniquities of this roadside Shylock; and all along the trail his numerous victims had added to the sum of his crimes. Now, Jim Cardegee, with the sailor's love for a sailor's joke, had determined, when he pulled into the cabin, to bring its inmate down a peg or so. That he had succeeded beyond expectation he could not help but remark, though he was in the dark as to the part the gash on his cheek had played in it. But while he could not understand, he saw the terror it created, and resolved to exploit it as remorselessly as would any modern trader a choice bit of merchandise.

"Strike me blind, but you're a 'ustler," he said admiringly, his head cocked to one side, as his host bustled about. "You never 'ort to 'ave gone Klondiking. It's the keeper of a pub' you was laid out for. An' it's often as I 'ave 'eard the lads up an' down the river speak o' you, but I 'adn't no idea you was so jolly nice."

Jacob Kent experienced a tremendous yearning to try his shotgun on him, but the fascination of the gash was too potent. This was the real Man with the Gash, the man who had so often robbed him in the spirit. This, then, was the embodied entity of the being whose astral form had been projected into his dreams, the man who had so frequently harbored designs against his hoard; hence — there could be no other conclusion — this Man with the Gash had now come in the flesh to dispossess him. And that gash! He could no more keep his eyes from it than stop the beating of his heart. Try as he would, they wandered back to that one point as inevitably as the needle to the pole.

"Do it 'urt you?" Jim Cardegee thundered suddenly, looking up from the spreading of his blankets and encountering the rapt gaze of the other. "It strikes me as 'ow it 'ud be the proper thing for you to draw your jib, douse the glim, an' turn in, seein' as 'ow it worrits you. Jes' lay to that, you swab, or so 'elp me I'll take a pull on your peak purchases!"

Kent was so nervous that it took three puffs to blow out the slush lamp, and he crawled into his blankets without even removing his moccasins. The sailor was soon snoring lustily from his hard bed on the floor, but Kent lay staring up into the blackness, one hand on the shotgun, resolved not to close his eyes the whole night. He had not had an opportunity to secrete his five pounds of gold, and it lay in the ammunition box at the head of his bunk. But, try as he would, he at last dozed off with the weight of his dust heavy on his soul. Had he not inadvertently fallen asleep with his mind in such condition, the somnambulic demon would not have been invoked, nor would Jim Cardegee have gone mining next day with a dishpan.

The fire fought a losing battle, and at last died away, while the frost penetrated the mossy chinks between the logs and chilled the inner atmosphere. The dogs outside ceased their howling, and, curled up in the snow, dreamed of salmon-stocked heavens where dog drivers and kindred taskmasters were not. Within, the sailor lay like a dog, while his host tossed restlessly about, the victim of strange fantasies. As midnight drew near he suddenly threw off the blankets and got up. It was remarkable that he could do what he then did without ever striking a light. Perhaps it was because of the darkness that he kept his eyes shut, and perhaps it was for fear he would see the terrible gash on the cheek of his visitor; but, be this as it may, it is a fact that, unseeing, he opened his ammunition box, put a heavy charge into the muzzle of the shotgun without spilling a particle, rammed it down with double wads, and then put everything away and got back into bed.

Just as daylight laid its steel-gray fingers on the parchment window, Jacob Kent awoke. Turning on his elbow, he raised the lid and peered into the ammunition box. Whatever he saw, or whatever he did not see, exercised a very peculiar effect upon him, considering his neurotic temperament. He glanced at the sleeping man on the floor, let the lid down gently, and rolled over on his back. It was an unwonted calm that rested on his face. Not a muscle quivered. There was not the least sign of excitement or perturbation. He lay there a long while, thinking, and when he got up and began to move about, it was in a cool, collected manner, without noise and without hurry.

It happened that a heavy wooden peg had been driven into the ridgepole just above Jim Cardegee's head. Jacob Kent, working softly, ran a piece of half-inch manila over it, bringing both ends to the ground. One end he tied about his waist, and in the other he rove a running noose. Then he cocked his shotgun and laid it within reach, by the side of numerous moose-hide thongs. By an effort of will he bore the sight of the scar, slipped the noose over the sleeper's head, and drew it taut by throwing back on his weight, at the same time seizing the gun and bringing it to bear.

Jim Cardegee awoke, choking, bewildered, staring down the twin wells of steel.

"Where is it?" Kent asked, at the same time slacking on the rope.

"You blasted — ugh —"

Kent merely threw back his weight, shutting off the other's wind.

"Bloomin'— Bur — ugh —"

"Where is it?" Kent repeated.

"Wot?" Cardegee asked, as soon as he had caught his breath.

"The gold dust."

"Wot gold dust?" the perplexed sailor demanded.

"You know well enough – mine."

"Ain't seen nothink of it. Wot do ye take me for? A safe deposit? Wot 'ave I got to do with it, any'ow?"

"Mebbe you know, and mebbe you don't know, but anyway, I'm going to stop your breath till you do know. And if you lift a hand, I'll blow your head off!"

"Vast heavin'!" Cardegee roared, as the rope tightened.

Kent eased away a moment, and the sailor, wriggling his neck as though from the pressure, managed to loosen the noose a bit and work it up so the point of contact was just under the chin.

"Well?" Kent questioned, expecting the disclosure.

But Cardegee grinned. "Go ahead with your 'angin', you bloomin' old pot-wolloper!"

Then, as the sailor had anticipated, the tragedy became

a farce. Cardegee being the heavier of the two, Kent, throwing his body backward and down, could not lift him clear of the ground. Strain and strive to the uttermost, the sailor's feet still stuck to the floor and sustained a part of his weight. The remaining portion was supported by the point of contact just under his chin. Failing to swing him clear, Kent clung on, resolved to slowly throttle him or force him to tell what he had done with the hoard. But the Man with the Gash would not throttle. Five, ten, fifteen minutes passed, and at the end of that time, in despair, Kent let his prisoner down.

"Well," he remarked, wiping away the sweat, "if you won't hang you'll shoot. Some men wasn't born to be hanged, anyway."

"An' it's a pretty mess as you'll make o' this 'ere cabin floor." Cardegee was fighting for time. "Now, look 'ere, I'll tell you wot we do; we'll lay our 'eads 'longside an' reason together. You've lost some dust. You say as 'ow I know, an' I say as 'ow I don't. Let's get a hobservation an' shape a course —"

"Vast heavin'!" Kent dashed in, maliciously imitating the other's enunciation. "I'm going to shape all the courses of this shebang, and you observe; and if you do anything more, I'll bore you as sure as Moses!"

"For the sake of my mother —"

"Whom God have mercy upon if she loves you. Ah! Would you?" He frustrated a hostile move on the part of the other by pressing the cold muzzle against his forehead. "Lay quiet, now! If you lift as much as a hair, you'll get it."

It was rather an awkward task, with the trigger of the gun always within pulling distance of the finger; but Kent was a weaver, and in a few minutes had the sailor tied hand and foot. Then he dragged him without and laid him by the side of the cabin, where he could overlook the river and watch the sun climb to the meridian.

"Now I'll give you till noon, and then —"

"Wot?"

"You'll be hitting the brimstone trail. But if you speak up, I'll keep you till the next bunch of mounted police come by."

"Well, blime me, if this ain't a go! 'Ere I be, innercent as a lamb, an' 'ere you be, lost all o' your top 'amper an' out o' your reckonin', run me foul an' goin' to rake me into 'ell-fire. You bloomin' old pirut! You —"

Jim Cardegee loosed the strings of his profanity and fairly outdid himself. Jacob Kent brought out a stool that he might enjoy it in comfort. Having exhausted all the possible combinations of his vocabulary, the sailor quieted down to hard thinking, his eyes constantly gauging the progress of the sun, which tore up the eastern slope of the heavens with unseemly haste. His dogs, surprised that they had not long since been put to harness, crowded around him. His helplessness appealed to the brutes. They felt that something was wrong, though they knew not what, and they crowded about, howling their mournful sympathy.

"Chook! Mush on! You Siwashes!" he cried, attempting, in a vermicular way, to kick at them, and discovering himself to be tottering on the edge of a declivity. As soon as the animals had scattered, he devoted himself to the significance of that declivity which he felt to be there but could not see. Nor was he long in arriving at a correct conclusion. In the nature of things, he figured, man is lazy. He does no more than he has to. When he builds a cabin he must put dirt on the roof. From these premises it was logical that he should carry that dirt no farther than was absolutely necessary. Therefore, he lay upon the edge of the hole from which the dirt had been taken to roof Jacob Kent's cabin. This knowledge, properly utilized, might prolong things, he thought; and he then turned his attention to the moose-hide thongs which bound him. His hands were tied behind him, and pressing against the snow, they were wet with the contact. This moistening of the rawhide he knew would tend to make it stretch, and, without apparent effort, he endeavored to stretch it more and more.

He watched the trail hungrily, and when in the direction of Sixty Mile a dark speck appeared for a moment against the white background of an ice jam, he cast an anxious eye at the sun. It had climbed nearly to the zenith. Now and again he caught the black speck clearing the hills of ice and sinking into the intervening hollows; but he dared not permit himself more than the most cursory glances for fear of rousing his enemy's suspicion. Once, when Jacob Kent rose to his feet and searched the trail with care, Cardegee was frightened, but the dog sled had struck a piece of trail running parallel with a jam, and remained out of sight till the danger was past.

"I'll see you 'ung for this," Cardegee threatened, attempting to draw the other's attention. "An' you'll rot in 'ell, jes' you see if you don't.

"I say," he cried, after another pause, "d'ye b'lieve in ghosts?" Kent's sudden start made him sure of his ground, and he went on: "Now a ghost 'as the right to 'aunt a man wot don't do wot he says; and you can't shuffle me off till eight bells — wot I mean is twelve o'clock — can you? 'Cos if you do, it'll 'appen as 'ow I'll 'aunt you. D'ye 'ear? A minute, a second too quick, an' I'll 'aunt you, so 'elp me, I will!"

Jacob Kent looked dubious, but declined to talk.

" 'Ow's your chronometer? Wot's your longitude? 'Ow do you know as your time's correct?" Cardegee persisted, vainly hoping to beat his executioner out of a few minutes. "Is it Barrack's time you 'ave, or is it the Company time? 'Cos if you do it before the stroke o' the bell, I'll not rest. I give you fair warnin'. I'll come back. An if you 'aven't the time, 'ow will you know? That's wot I want —'ow will you tell?"

"I'll send you off all right," Kent replied.

"Got a sundial here?"

"No good. Thirty-two degrees variation o' the needle."

"Stakes are all set."

" 'Ow did you set 'em? Compass?"

"No; lined them up with the North Star."

"Sure?"

"Sure."

Cardegee groaned, then stole a glance at the trail. The sled was just clearing a rise, barely a mile away, and the dogs were in full lope, running lightly.

" 'Ow close is the shadows to the line?"

Kent walked to the primitive timepiece and studied it. "Three inches," he announced, after a careful survey.

"Say, jes' sing out 'eight bells' afore you pull the gun, will you?"

Kent agreed, and they lapsed into silence. The thongs about Cardegee's wrists were slowly stretching, and he had begun to work them over his hands.

"Say, 'ow close is the shadows?"

"One inch."

The sailor wriggled slightly to assure himself that he would topple over at the right moment, and slipped the first turn over his hands.

" 'Ow close?"

"Half an inch." Just then Kent heard the jarring churn of the runners and turned his eyes to the trail. The driver was lying flat on the sled and the dogs swinging down the straight stretch to the cabin. Kent whirled back, bringing his rifle to shoulder.

"It ain't eight bells yet!" Cardegee expostulated. "I'll 'aunt you, sure!"

Jacob Kent faltered. He was standing by the sundial, perhaps ten paces from his victim. The man on the sled must have seen that something unusual was taking place, for he had risen to his knees, his whip singing viciously among the dogs.

The shadows swept into line. Kent looked along the sights.

"Make ready!" he commanded solemnly. "Eight b—"

But just a fraction of a second too soon, Cardegee rolled backward into the hole. Kent held his fire and ran to the edge. Bang! The gun exploded full in the sailor's face as he rose to his feet. But no smoke came from the muzzle; instead, a sheet of flame burst from the side of the barrel near its butt, and Jacob Kent went down. The dogs dashed up the bank, dragging the sled over his body, and the driver sprang off as Jim Cardegee freed his hands and drew himself from the hole.

"Jim!" The newcomer recognized him. "What's the matter?"

"Wot's the matter? Oh, nothink at all. It jest 'appens as I do little things like this for my 'ealth. Wot's the matter, you bloomin' idjit? Wot's the matter, eh? Cast me loose or I'll show you wot! 'Urry up, or I'll 'olystone the decks with you!"

"Huh!" he added, as the other went to work with his sheath knife. "Wot's the matter? I want to know. Jes' tell me that, will you, wot's the matter? Hey?"

Kent was quite dead when they rolled him over. The gun, an old-fashioned, heavy-weighted muzzle-loader, lay near him. Steel and wood had parted company. Near the butt of the right-hand barrel, with lips pressed outward, gaped a fissure several inches in length. The sailor picked it up, curiously. A glittering stream of yellow dust ran out through the crack. The facts of the case dawned upon Jim Cardegee.

"Strike me standin'!" he roared; " 'ere's a go! 'Ere's 'is bloomin' dust! Gawd blime me, an' you, too, Charley, if you don't run an' get the dishpan!"

Too Much Gold

THIS BEING A STORY — and a truer one than it may appear — of a mining country, it is quite to be expected that it will be a hard-luck story.

But that depends on the point of view. Hard luck is a mild way of terming it so far as Kink Mitchell and Hootchinoo Bill are concerned; and that they have a decided opinion on the subject is a matter of common knowledge in the Yukon country.

It was in the fall of 1896 that the two partners came down to the east bank of the Yukon, and drew a Peterborough canoe from a moss-covered cache. They were not particularly pleasant-looking objects. A summer's prospecting, filled to repletion with hardship and rather empty of grub, had left their clothes in tatters and themselves worn and cadaverous. A nimbus of mosquitoes buzzed about each man's head. Their faces were coated with blue clay. Each carried a lump of this damp clay, and whenever it dried and fell from their faces more was daubed on in its place. There was a querulous plaint in their voices, an irritability of movement and gesture, which told of broken sleep and a losing struggle with the little winged pests.

"Them skeeters'll be the death of me yet," Kink Mitchell whimpered, as the canoe felt the current on her nose and leaped out from the bank.

"Cheer up, cheer up! We're about done," Hootchinoo Bill answered, with an attempted heartiness in his funeral tones that was ghastly. "We'll be in Forty Mile in forty minutes, and then—Cursed little devil!"

One hand had left his paddle and landed on the back of his neck with a sharp slap. He put a fresh daub of clay on the injured part, swearing sulphurously the while. Kink Mitchell was not in the least amused. He merely improved the opportunity by putting a thicker coating of clay on his own neck.

They crossed the Yukon to its west bank, shot downstream with easy stroke, and at the end of forty minutes swung in close to the left around the tail of an island. Forty Mile spread itself suddenly before them. Both men straightened their backs, and gazed at the sight. They gazed long and carefully, drifting with the current, and in their faces slowly gathering an expression of mingled surprise and consternation.

Not a thread of smoke was rising from the hundreds of log cabins. There was no sound of axes biting sharply into wood, of hammering and sawing. Neither dogs nor men loitered before the big store. No steamboats lay at the bank, no canoes, or scows, or poling boats. The river was as bare of craft as the town was of life.

"Kind of looks like Gabriel's tooted his little horn, and you an' me has turned up missing," remarked Hootchinoo Bill.

His remark was casual, as though there were nothing

unusual about the occurrence. Kink Mitchell's reply was just as casual, as though he, too, were unaware of any strange perturbation of spirit.

"Looks as they was all Baptists, then, and took the boats to go by water," was his contribution.

"My ol' dad was a Baptist," Hootchinoo Bill supplemented. "An' he always did hold it was forty thousand miles nearer that way."

This was the end of their levity. They ran the canoe in and climbed the high earth bank. A feeling of awe descended upon them as they walked the deserted streets. The sunlight streamed placidly over the town. A gentle wind tapped the halyards against the flagpole before the closed doors of the Caledonia Dance Hall. Mosquitoes buzzed, robins sang, and moose birds tripped hungrily among the cabins; but there was no human life or sign of human life.

"I'm just dyin' for a drink," Hootchinoo Bill said, and unconsciously his voice sank to a hoarse whisper.

His partner nodded his head, loath to hear his own voice break the stillness. They trudged on in uneasy silence till surprised by an open door. Above this door, and stretching the width of the building, a rude sign announced the same as the Monte Carlo. But beside the door, hat over eyes, chair tilted back, a man sat sunning himself. He was an old man. Beard and hair were long and white and patriarchal.

"If it ain't ol' Jim Cummings, turned up like us, too late for resurrection," said Kink Mitchell.

"Most like he didn't hear Gabriel tootin'," was Hootchinoo Bill's suggestion.

"Hello, Jim! Wake up!" he shouted.

The old man unlimbered lamely, blinking his eyes and murmuring automatically: "What'll ye have, gents? What'll ye have?"

They followed him inside, and ranged up against the long bar where of yore half a dozen nimble barkeepers found little time to loaf. The great room, ordinarily a-roar with life, was gloomy and quiet as a tomb. There was no rattling of chips, no whirring of ivory balls. Roulette and faro tables were like gravestones under their canvas covers. No women's voices drifted merrily from the dance room behind. Ol' Jim Cummings wiped a glass with palsied hands, and Kink Mitchell scrawled his initials on the dust-covered bar.

"Where's the girls?" Hootchinoo Bill shouted, with affected geniality.

"Gone," was the ancient barkeeper's reply, in a voice thin and aged as himself, and as unsteady as his hand.

"Where's Bidwell and Barlow?"

"Gone."

"And Sweetwater Charley?"

"Gone."

"And his sister?"

"Gone, too."

"Your daughter, Sally, then, and her little kid?"

"Gone, all gone." The old man shook his head sadly, rummaging in an absent way among the dusty bottles.

"Great Sardanapalus! Where?" Kink Mitchell exploded, unable longer to restrain himself. "You don't say you've had the plague?"

"Why, ain't you heard?" The old man chuckled quietly. "They all's gone to Dawson."

"What like is that?" Bill demanded. "A creek? Or a bar? Or a place?"

"Ain't never heerd of Dawson, eh?" The old man chuckled exasperatingly. "Why Dawson's a town, a city; bigger'n Forty Mile! Yes, sir, bigger'n Forty Mile!"

"I've ben in this land seven year," Bill announced, emphatically, "an' I make free to say I never heard tell of the burg before. Hold on! Let's have some more of that whiskey. Your information's flabbergasted me, that it has. Now just whereabouts is this Dawson place you was a-mentionin'?"

"On the big flat jest below the mouth of Klondike," Ol' Jim answered. "But where has you all ben this summer?"

"Never you mind where we all's ben," was Kink Mitchell's testy reply. "We all's ben where the skeeters is that thick you've got to throw a stick into the air so as to see the sun and tell the time of day. Ain't I right, Bill?"

"Right you are," said Bill. "But speakin' of this Dawson place, how like did it happen to be, Jim?"

"Ounce to the pan on a creek called Bonanza, an' they ain't got to bed rock yet."

"Who struck it?"

"Carmack."

At mention of the discoverer's name the partners stared at each other disgustedly. Then they winked with great solemnity.

"Siwash George," sniffed Hootchinoo Bill.

"That squaw man," sneered Kink Mitchell.

"I wouldn't put on my moccasins to stampede after anything he'd ever find," said Bill.

"Same here," announced his partner. "A cuss that's too plumb lazy to fish his own salmon. That's why he took up with the Indians. S'pose that black brother-in-law of his — lemme see, Skookum Jim, eh? — s'pose he's in on it?"

The old barkeeper nodded. "Sure, an' what's more, all Forty Mile exceptin' me an' a few cripples."

"And drunks," added Kink Mitchell.

"No sir-ee!" the old man shouted, emphatically.

"I bet you the drinks Honkins ain't in on it!" Hootchinoo Bill cried, with certitude.

Ol' Jim's face lighted up. "I takes you, Bill, an' you loses."

"However did that ol' soak budge out of Forty Mile?" Mitchell demanded.

"They ties him down, an' throws him in the bottom of a polin' boat," Ol' Jim explained. "Come right in here, they did, an' takes him out of that there chair there in the corner, an' three more drunks they finds under the piany. I tell you alls the whole camp hits up the Yukon for Dawson jes' like Sam Scratch was after them — wimmen, children, babes in arms, the whole shebang. Bidwell comes to me, an' sez, sez he: 'Jim, I wants you to keep tab on the Monte Carlo. I'm goin'.' "

" 'Where's Barlow?' sez I. 'Gone,' sez he, 'an' I'm a-follerin' with a load of whiskey.' An' with that, never waitin' for me to decline, he makes a run for his boat, an' way he goes, polin' upriver like mad. So here I be, an' these is the first drinks I've passed out in three days."

The partners looked at each other.

"Gosh darn my buttons!" said Hootchinoo Bill. "Seems like you and me, Kink, is the kind of folks always caught out with forks when it rains soup."

"Wouldn't it take the saleratus out your dough, now?" said Kink Mitchell. "A stampede of tinhorns, drunks an' loafers."

"An' squaw men," added Bill. "Not a genooine miner in the whole caboodle."

"Genooine miners like you an' me, Kink," he went on, academically, "is all out an' sweatin' hard over Birch Creek way. Not a genooine miner in this whole crazy Dawson outfit, and I say right here, not a step do I budge for any Carmack strike. I've got to see the color of the dust first."

"Same here," Mitchell agreed. "Let's have another drink."

Having taken this resolution (and wetted it), they beached the canoe, transferred its contents to their cabin, and cooked dinner. But as the afternoon wore along they grew restive. They were men used to the silence of the great wilderness, but this gravelike silence of a town worried them. They caught themselves listening for familiar sounds—"waitin' for something to make a noise which ain't goin' to make a noise," as Bill put it. They strolled through the deserted streets to the Monte Carlo for more drinks, and wandered along the river bank to the steamer landing, where only water gurgled as the eddy filled and emptied, and an occasional salmon leaped flashing into the sun.

They sat down in the shade in front of the store, and

talked with the consumptive storekeeper whose liability to hemorrhage accounted for his presence. Bill and Kink told him how they intended loafing in their cabin, and resting up after the hard summer's work. They told him with a certain insistence, which was half appeal for belief, half challenge for contradiction, how much they were going to enjoy their idleness. But the storekeeper was uninterested. He switched the conversation back to the strike on Klondike, and they could not keep him away from it. He could think of nothing else, talk of nothing else, till Hootchinoo Bill rose up in anger and disgust.

"Gosh darn Dawson, say I !" he cried.

"Same here," said Kink Mitchell, with a brightening face. "One'd think something was doin' up there, 'stead of bein' a mere stampede of greenhorns an' tinhorns."

But a boat came into view from downstream. It was long and slim. It hugged the bank closely, and its three occupants, standing upright, propelled it against the swift current by means of long poles.

"Circle City outfit," said the storekeeper. "I was lookin' for 'em along by afternoon. Forty Mile had the start of them by a hundred and seventy miles. But gee! they ain't losin' any time!"

"We'll just sit here quietlike, and watch 'em string by," Bill said, complacently.

As he spoke, another boat appeared in sight, followed after a brief interval by two others. By this time the first boat was abreast of the men on the bank. Its occupants did not cease poling while greetings were exchanged, and, though its progress was slow, half an hour saw it out of sight upriver.

Still they came from below, boat after boat, in endless procession. The uneasiness of Bill and Kink increased. They stole speculative, tentative glances at each other, and when their eyes met looked away in embarrassment. Finally, however, their eyes met, and neither looked away.

Kink opened his mouth to speak, but words failed him, and his mouth remained open, while he continued to gaze at his partner.

"Just what I was thinkin', Kink," said Bill.

They grinned sheepishly at each other, and by tacit consent started to walk away. Their pace quickened, and by the time they arrived at their cabin they were on the run.

"Can't lose no time with all that multitude a-rushin' by," Kink spluttered, as he jabbed the sour dough can into the bean pot with one hand and with the other gathered in the frying pan and coffeepot.

"Should say not," gasped Bill, his head and shoulders buried in a clothes sack, wherein were stored winter socks and underwear.

"I say, Kink, don't forget the saleratus on the corner shelf back of the stove."

Half an hour later they were launching the canoe and loading up, while the storekeeper made jocular remarks about poor weak mortals and the contagiousness of "stampedin' fever." But when Bill and Kink thrust their long poles to bottom and started the canoe against the current, he called after them:

"Well, so long, and good luck! And don't forget to blaze a stake or two for me!"

They nodded their heads vigorously, and felt sorry for the poor wretch who remained perforce behind.

Kink and Bill were sweating hard. According to the revised northland scripture, the stampede is to the swift, the blazing of stakes to the strong, and the crown, in royalties, gathers to itself the fullness thereof. Kink and Bill were both swift and strong. They took the soggy trail at a long, swinging gait that broke the hearts of a couple of tenderfeet who tried to keep up with them. Behind, strung out between them and Dawson (where the boats were discarded, and land travel began), was the vanguard of the Circle City outfit. In the race from Forty Mile, the partners had passed every boat, winning from the leading boat by a length in the Dawson eddy, and leaving its occupants sadly behind the moment their feet struck the trail.

"Huh! couldn't see us for smoke," Hotchinoo Bill chuckled, flinging the stinging sweat from his brow, and glancing swiftly back along the way they had come.

Three men emerged from where the trail broke through the trees. Two followed close at their heels, and then a man and a woman shot into view.

"Come on, you Kink! Hit her up! Hit her up!"

Bill quickened his pace. Mitchell glanced back in more leisurely fashion.

"I declare, if they ain't lopin'!"

"And here's one that's loped himself out," said Bill, pointing to the side of the trail.

A man was lying on his back, panting, in the culminating stages of violent exhaustion. His face was ghastly, his eyes bloodshot and glazed, for all the world like a dying man.

"Chechaquo!" Kink Mitchell grunted, and it was the grunt of the old "sourdough" for the greenhorn, for the man who outfitted with "self-risin' " flour and used baking powder in his biscuits.

The partners, true to the old-timer custom, had intended to stake downstream from the strike, but when they saw claim "81 Below" blazed on a tree — which meant fully eight miles below Discovery — they changed their minds. The eight miles were covered in less than two hours. It was a killing pace over such rough trail, and they passed scores of exhausted men who had fallen by the wayside.

At Discovery little was to be learned of the upper creek. Carmack's Indian brother-in-law, Skookum Jim, had a hazy notion that the creek was staked as high as the thirties; but when Kink and Bill looked at the corner stakes of 79 Above, they threw their stampeding packs off their backs, and sat down to smoke. All their effort had been vain. Bonanza was staked from mouth to source —"Out of sight, and across the next divide," Bill complained that night as they fried their bacon and boiled their coffee over Carmack's fire at Discovery.

"Try that pup," Carmack suggested next morning.

"That pup" was a broad creek which flowed into Bonanza at 7 Above. The partners received his advice with the magnificent contempt of the sourdough for a squaw man, and, instead, spent the day on Adam's Creek, another and more likely looking tributary of Bonanza. But it was the old story over again — staked to the sky line.

For three days Carmack repeated his advice, and for

three days they received it contemptuously. But on the fourth day, there being nowhere else to go, they went up "that pup." They knew that it was practically unstaked, but they had no intention of staking. The trip was made more for the purpose of giving vent to their ill humor than for anything else. They had become quite cynical, skeptical. They jeered and scoffed at everything, and insulted every *chechaquo* they met along the way.

At number twenty-three the stakes ceased. The remainder of the creek was open to location.

"Moose pasture," sneered Kink Mitchell.

But Bill gravely paced off five hundred feet up the creek, and blazed the corner stakes. He had picked up the bottom of a candle box, and on the smooth side he wrote the notice for his center stake:

THIS MOOSE PASTURE IS RESERVED
FOR THE
SWEDES AND CHECHAQUOS.
BILL RADER.

Kink read it over with approval, saying:

"As them's my sentiments, I reckon I might as well subscribe."

So the name of Charles Mitchell was added to the notice; and many an old sour dough's face relaxed that day at sight of the handiwork of a kindred spirit.

"How's the pup?" Carmack inquired, when they strolled back into camp.

"To hell with pups!" was Hootchinoo Bill's reply. "Me and Kink's goin' a-lookin' for Too Much Gold when we get rested up."

Too Much Gold was the fabled creek of which all sour doughs dreamed, whereof it was said the gold was so thick, that, in order to wash it, gravel must first be shoveled into the sluice boxes. But the several days' rest preliminary to the quest for Too Much Gold brought a slight change in their plan, inasmuch as it brought one Ans Handerson, a Swede.

Ans Handerson had been working for wages all summer at Miller Creek, over on the Sixty Mile; and, the summer done, had strayed up Bonanza like many another waif helplessly adrift on the gold tides that swept willy-nilly across the land. He was tall and lanky. His arms were long, like prehistoric man's, and his hands were like soup plates, twisted, and gnarled, and big-knuckled from toil. He was slow of utterance and movement, and his eyes, pale blue as his hair was pale yellow, seemed filled with an immortal dreaming, the stuff of which no man knew, and himself least of all. Perhaps this appearance of immortal dreaming was due to a supreme and vacuous innocence. At any rate, this was the valuation men of ordinary clay put upon him, and there was nothing extraordinary about the composition of Hootchinoo Bill and Kink Mitchell.

The partners had spent a day of visiting and gossip, and in the evening met in the temporary quarters of the Monte Carlo — a large tent where stampeders rested their weary bones, and bad whiskey sold at a dollar a drink. Since the only money in circulation was dust, and since the house took the "downweight" on the scales, a drink cost something more than a dollar. Bill and Kink were not drinking, principally for the reason that their one and common sack was not strong enough to stand many excursions to the scales.

"Say, Bill, I've got a *chechaquo* on the string for a sack of flour," Mitchell announced, jubilantly.

Bill looked interested and pleased. Grub was scarce, and they were not over plentifully supplied for the quest after Too Much Gold.

"Flour's worth a dollar a pound," he answered. "How like do you calculate to get your finger on it?"

"Trade 'm a half interest in that there claim of our'n," Kink answered.

"What claim?" Bill was surprised. Then he remembered the reservation he had staked off for the Swedes, and said, "Oh!"

"I wouldn't be so close about it, though," he added. "Give 'm the whole thing while you're about it, in a right freehanded way."

Bill shook his head. "If I did he'd get clean scairt and prance off. I'm lettin' on as how the ground is believed to be valuable, an' that we're lettin' go half just because we're monstrous short on grub. After the dicker we can make him a present of the whole shebang."

"If somebody ain't disregarded our notice," Bill objected, though he was plainly pleased at prospect of exchanging the claim for a sack of flour.

"She ain't jumped," Kink assured him. "It's number twenty-four, and it stands. The *chechaquos* took it serious, and they begun stakin' where you left off. Staked clean over the divide, too. I was gassin' with one of them which has just got in with cramps in his legs."

It was then, and for the first time, that they heard the slow and groping utterance of Ans Handerson.

"Ay like the looks," he was saying to the barkeeper. "Ay tank ay gat a claim."

The partners winked at each other, and a few minutes later a surprised and grateful Swede was drinking bad whiskey with two hardhearted strangers. But he was as hardheaded as they were hardhearted. The sack made frequent journeys to the scales, followed solicitously each time by Kink Mitchell's eyes, and still Ans Handerson did not loosen up. In his pale blue eyes, as in summer seas, immortal dreams swam up and burned, but the swimming and the burning were due to the tales of gold and prospect pans he heard of, rather than to the whiskey he slid so easily down his throat.

The partners were in despair, though they appeared boisterous and jovial of speech and action.

"Don't mind me, my friend," Hootchinoo Bill hiccoughed, his hand upon Ans Handerson's shoulder. "Have another drink. We're just celebratin' Kink's birthday here. This is my pardner, Kink, Kink Mitchell. An' what might your name be?"

This learned, his hand descended resoundingly on Kink's back, and Kink simulated clumsy, self-consciousness in that he was for the time being the center of the rejoicing, while Ans Handerson looked pleased, and asked them to have a drink with him. It was the first and last time he treated, until the play changed, and his canny soul was aroused to unwonted prodigality. But he paid for the liquor from a fairly healthy looking sack.

"Not less'n eight hundred in it," calculated the lynx-eyed Kink; and on the strength of it he took the first opportunity of a privy conversation with Bidwell, proprietor of the bad whiskey and the tent.

"Here's my sack, Bidwell," Kink said, with the intimacy and surety of one old-timer to another. "Just weigh fifty dollars into it for a day or so, more or less, and we'll be yours truly, Bill an' me."

Thereafter the journeys of the sack to the scales were more frequent, and the celebration of Kink's natal day waxed hilarious. He even essayed to sing the old-timer's classic, "The Juice of the Forbidden Fruit," but broke down, and drowned his embarrassment in another round of drinks. Even Bidwell honored him with a round or two on the house; and he and Bill were decently drunk by the time Ans Handerson's eyelids began to droop and his tongue gave promise of loosening.

Bill grew affectionate, then confidential. He told his troubles and hard luck to the barkeeper and the world in general, and to Ans Handerson in particular. He required no histrionic powers to act the part. The bad whiskey attended to that. He worked himself into a great sorrow for himself and Bill, and his tears were sincere, when he told how he and his partner were thinking of selling a half interest in good ground just because they were short of grub. Even Kink listened and believed.

Ans Handerson's eyes were shining unholily, as he asked: "How much you tank you take?"

Bill and Kink did not hear him, and he was compelled to repeat his query. They appeared reluctant. He grew keener. And he swayed back and forward, holding on to the bar and listening with all his ears while they conferred together to one side, and wrangled as to whether they should or not, and disagreed in stage whispers over the price they should set.

"Two hundred and — hic! — fifty," Bill finally announced, "but we reckon as we won't sell."

"Which same is monstrous wise, if I might chip in my little say," seconded Bidwell.

"Yes, indeedy," added Kink. "We ain't in no charity business a-disgorgin' free an' generous to Swedes an' white men."

"Ay tank we haf another drink," hiccoughed Ans Handerson, craftily changing the subject against a more propitious time.

And thereafter, to bring about that propitious time, his own sack began a seesaw between his hip pocket and the scales. Bill and Kink were coy, but they finally yielded to his blandishments. Whereupon he grew shy, and drew Bidwell to one side. He staggered exceedingly, and held on to Bidwell for support, as he asked:

"They ban all right, them men, you tank so?"

"Sure," Bidwell answered, heartily. "Know 'em for years. Old sourdoughs. When they sell a claim they sell a claim. They ain't no air dealers."

"Ay tank ay buy," Ans Handerson announced, tottering back to the two men.

But by now he was dreaming deeply, and he proclaimed that he would have the whole claim or nothing. This was the cause of great pain to Hootchinoo Bill. He orated grandly against the "hawgishness" of *chechaquos* and Swedes, albeit he dozed between periods, his voice dying away to a gurgle and his head sinking forward on his breast. But whenever aroused by a nudge from Kink or Bidwell he never failed to explode another volley of abuse and insult.

Ans Handerson was calm under it all. Each insult added to the value of the claim. Such unamiable reluctance to sell advertised but one thing to him, and he was aware of a great relief when Hootchinoo Bill sank snoring to the floor, and he was free to turn his attention to his less intractable partner.

Kink Mitchell was persuadable, though a poor mathematician. He wept dolefully, but was willing to sell a half interest for two hundred and fifty dollars, or the whole claim for seven hundred and fifty. Ans Handerson and Bidwell labored to clear away his erroneous ideas concerning fractions, but their labor was vain. He spilled tears and regrets all over the bar and on their shoulders, which tears, however, did not wash away his opinion that if one-half was worth two hundred and fifty, two halves were worth three times as much.

In the end — and even Bidwell retained no more than hazy recollections of how the night terminated — a bill of sale was drawn up, wherein Bill Rader and Charles Mitchell yielded up all right and title to the claim known as 24 Eldorado, the same being the name the creek had received from some optimistic *chechaquo.*

When Kink had signed, it took the united efforts of the three to arouse Bill. Pen in hand, he swayed long over the document; and, each time he rocked back and forth, in Ans Handerson's eyes flashed and faded a wondrous golden vision. When the precious signature was at last appended and the dust paid over, he breathed a great sigh, and sank to sleep under a table, where he dreamed immortally until morning.

But the day was chill and gray. He felt badly. His first act, unconscious and automatic, was to feel for his sack. Its lightness startled him. Then, slowly, memories of the night thronged into his brain. Rough voices disturbed him. He opened his eyes, and peered out from under the table. A couple of early risers, or, rather, men who had been out on trail all night, were vociferating their opinions concerning the utter and loathable worthlessness of Eldorado Creek. He grew frightened, felt in his pocket, and found the deed to 24 Eldorado.

Ten minutes later Hootchinoo Bill and Kink Mitchell were aroused from their blankets by a wild-eyed Swede, who strove to force upon them an ink-scrawled and very blotty piece of paper.

"Ay tank ay take my money back," he gibbered. "Ay tank ay take my money back."

Tears were in his eyes and throat. They ran down his cheeks as he knelt before them, and pleaded and implored. But Bill and Kink did not laugh. They might have been harder hearted.

"First time I ever hear a man squeal over a minin' deal," Bill said. "An' I make free to say 'tis too onusual for me to savve."

"Same here," Kink Mitchell remarked. "Minin' deals is like horse tradin'."

They were honest in their wonderment. They could not conceive of themselves raising a wail over a business transaction, so they could not understand it in another man.

"The poor, ornery *chechaquo,*" murmured Hootchinoo Bill, as they watched the sorrowing Swede disappear up the trail.

"But this ain't Too Much Gold," Kink Mitchell said, cheerfully.

And ere the day was out they purchased flour and bacon at exorbitant prices with Ans Handerson's dust, and crossed over the divide in the direction of the creeks which lie between Klondike and Indian River.

Three months later they came back over the divide in the midst of a snowstorm, and dropped down the trail to 24 Eldorado. It merely chanced that the trail led them that way. They were not looking for the claim. Nor could they see much through the driving white till they set foot upon the claim itself. And then the air lightened, and they beheld a dump, capped by a windlass which a man was turning. They saw him draw a bucket of gravel from the hole, and tilt it on the edge of the dump. Likewise they saw another man, strangely familiar, filling a pan with the fresh gravel. His hands were large; his hair was pale yellow. But before they reached him, he turned with the pan and fled toward a cabin. He wore no hat, and the snow falling down his neck accounted for his haste. Bill and Kink ran after him, and came upon him in the cabin, kneeling by the stove, and washing the pan of gravel in a tub of water.

He was too deeply engaged to notice more than that somebody had entered the cabin. They stood at his shoulder and looked on. He imparted to the pan a deft circular motion, pausing once or twice to rake out the larger particles of gravel with his fingers. The water was muddy, and with the pan buried in it they could see nothing of its contents. Suddenly he lifted the pan clear, and sent the water out of it with a flirt. A mass of yellow, like butter in a churn, showed across the bottom.

Hootchinoo Bill swallowed. Never in his life had he dreamed of so rich a test pan.

"Kind of thick, my friend," he said, huskily. "How much might you reckon that all to be?"

Ans Handerson did not look up, as he replied:

"Ay tank fafty ounces."

"You must be scrumptious rich, then, eh?"

Still Ans Handerson kept his head down, absorbed in putting in the fine touches which wash out the last particles of dross, though he answered:

"Ay tank ay ban worth five hundred t'ousand dollar."

"Gosh!" said Hootchinoo Bill; and he said it reverently.

"Yes, Bill, gosh!" said Kink Mitchell; and they went out softly, and closed the door.

Keesh, the Son of Keesh

"THUS WILL I GIVE six blankets, warm and double; six files, large and hard; six Hudson Bay knives, keen-edged and long; two canoes, the work of Mogum, the Maker of Things; ten dogs, heavy-shouldered and strong in the harness, and three guns — the trigger of one be broken, but it is a good gun and can doubtless be fixed."

Keesh paused and swept his eyes over the circle of intent faces. It was the time of the Great Fishing, and he was bidding to Gnob for Su-Su, his daughter. The place was the St. George Mission by the Yukon, and the tribes had gathered for many a hundred miles. From north, south, east, and west they had come, even from Tozikakat and far Tana-naw.

"And, further, O Gnob, thou art chief of the Tana-naw, and I, Keesh, the son of Keesh, I am chief of the Thlunget. Wherefore, when my seed springs from the loins of thy daughter there shall be a friendship between the tribes, a great friendship and Tana-naw and Thlunget shall be brothers of the blood in the time to come. That which I have said I will do, that will I do. And how is it with you, O Gnob, in this matter?"

Gnob nodded his head gravely, his gnarled and age-twisted face inscrutably masking the soul that dwelt behind. His narrow eyes burned like twin coals through their narrow slits, as he piped in a high, cracked voice. "But that is not all."

"What more?" Keesh demanded. "Have I not offered full measure? Was there ever yet a Tana-naw maiden who fetched so great a price? Then name her!"

An open snicker passed round the circle, and Keesh knew that he stood in shame before these people.

"Nay, nay, good Keesh, thou dost not understand." Gnob made a soft, stroking gesture. "The price is fair. It is a good price. Nor do I question the broken trigger. But that is not all. What of the man?"

"Ah, what of the man?" the circle snarled.

"It is said," Gnob's shrill voice piped, "it is said that Keesh does not walk in the way of his fathers. It is said that he has wandered into the dark, after strange gods, and that he is become afraid."

The face of Keesh went dark. "It is a lie!" he thundered. "Keesh is afraid of no man!"

"It is said," old Gnob piped on, "that he has hearkened to the speech of the white man up at the Big House, and that he bends head to the white man's god, and, moreover, that blood is displeasing to the white man's god."

Keesh dropped his eyes, and his hands clenched passionately. The savage circle laughed derisively, and in the ear of Gnob whispered Madwan the Shaman, high priest of the tribe and maker of medicine.

The Shaman poked among the shadows on the rim of the firelight and roused up a slender young boy, whom he brought face to face with Keesh, and in the hand of Keesh he thrust a knife.

Gnob leaned forward. "Keesh! O Keesh! Darest thou to kill a man? Behold! This be Kitz-noo, a slave. Strike, O Keesh, strike with the strength of thy arm!"

The boy trembled and waited the stroke. Keesh looked at him and thoughts of Mr. Brown's higher morality floated through his mind, and strong upon him was a vision of the leaping flames of Mr. Brown's particular brand of hell-fire. The knife fell to the ground, and the boy sighed and went out beyond the firelight with shaking knees. At the feet of Gnob sprawled a wolf dog, which bared its gleaming teeth and prepared to spring after the boy. But the Shaman ground his foot into the brute's body, and so doing, gave Gnob an idea.

"And then, O Keesh, what wouldst thou do, should a man do this thing to you?" And as he spoke, Gnob held a ribbon of salmon to White Fang, and when the animal attempted to take it, smote him sharply on the nose with a stick. "And afterward, O Keesh, wouldst thou do thus?" White Fang was cringing back on his belly and fawning to the hand of Gnob.

"Listen!"—leaning on the arm of Madwan, Gnob had risen to his feet—"I am very old, and because I am very old I will tell thee things. Thy father, Keesh, was a mighty man. And he did love the song of the bowstring in battle, and these eyes have beheld him cast a spear till the head stood out beyond a man's body. But thou art unlike. Since thou left the Raven to worship the Wolf, thou art become afraid of blood, and thou makest thy people afraid. This is not good. For behold, when I was a boy, even as Kitz-noo there. There was no white man in all the land. But they came, one by one, these white men, till now they are many. And they are a restless breed, never content to rest by the fire with a full belly and let the morrow bring its own meat. A curse was laid upon them, it would seem, and they must work it out in toil and hardship."

Keesh was startled. A recollection of a hazy story told by Mr. Brown of one Adam, of old time, came to him, and it seemed that Mr. Brown had spoken true.

"So they lay hands upon all they behold, these white men, and they go everywhere and behold all things. And ever do more follow in their steps, so that if nothing be done they will come to possess all the land and there will be no room for the tribes of the Raven. Wherefore it is meet that we fight with them till none is left. Then will we hold the passes and the land, and perhaps our children and our children's children shall flourish and grow fat. There is a great struggle to come, when Wolf and Raven shall grapple; but Keesh will not fight, nor will he let his people fight. So it is not well that he should take to him my daughter. Thus have I spoken, I Gnob, chief of the Tana-naw."

"But the white men are good and great," Keesh made answer. "The white men have taught us many things. The white men have given us blankets and knives and guns, such as we have never made and never could make. I remember in what manner we lived before they came. I was unborn then, but I have it from my father. When we went on the hunt we must creep so close to the moose that a spear cast would cover the distance. Today we use the white man's rifle, and farther away than can a child's cry be heard. We ate fish and meat and berries — there was nothing else to eat — and we ate without salt. How many be there among you who care to go back to the fish and meat without salt?"

It would have sunk home had not Madwan leaped to his feet ere silence could come. "And first a question to thee, Keesh. The white man up at the Big House tells you that it is wrong to kill. Yet do we not know that the white men kill? Have we forgotten the great fight on the Koyokuk? Or the great fight at Nuklukyeto, where three white men killed twenty of the Tozikakats? Do you think we no longer remember the three men of the Tana-naw that the white man Macklewrath killed? Tell me, O Keesh, why does the Shaman Brown teach you that it is wrong to fight, when all his brothers fight?"

"Nay, nay, there is no need to answer," Gnob piped, while Keesh struggled with the paradox. "It is very simple. The Good Man Brown would hold the Raven tight whilst his brothers pluck the feathers." He raised his voice. "But so long as there is one Tana-naw to strike a blow, or one maiden to bear a man-child, the Raven shall not be plucked!"

Gnob turned to a husky young man across the fire. "And what sayest thou, Makamuk, who art brother to Su-Su?"

Makamuk came to his feet. A long face scar lifted his upper lip into a perpetual grin, which belied the glowering ferocity of his eyes. "This day," he began, with cunning irrelevance, "I came by the Trader Macklewrath's cabin. And in the door I saw a child laughing at the sun. And the child looked at me with the Trader Macklewrath's eyes, and it was frightened. But the mother ran to it and quieted it. The mother was Ziska, the Thlunget woman."

A snarl of rage rose up and drowned his voice, which he stilled by turning dramatically upon Keesh with outstretched arm and accusing finger.

"So? You give your women away, you Thlunget, and come to the Tana-naw for more? But we have need of our women, Keesh, for we must breed men, many men, against the day when the Raven grapples with the Wolf."

Through the storm of applause Gnob's voice shrilled clear: "And thou, Nossabok, who art her favorite brother?"

The young fellow was slender and graceful, with the strong aquiline nose and high brows of his type; but from some nervous affliction the lid of one eye drooped at odd times in a suggestive wink. Even as he arose it so drooped and rested a moment against his cheek. But it was not greeted with the accustomed laughter. Every face was grave. "I, too, passed by the Trader Macklewrath's cabin," he rippled in soft, girlish tones, wherein there was much of youth and much of his sister. "And I saw Indians, with the sweat running into their eyes and their knees shaking with weariness — I say, I saw Indians groaning under the logs for the store which the Trader Macklewrath is to build. And with my eyes I saw them chipping wood to keep the Shaman Brown's big house warm through the frost of the long nights. This be squaw work. Never shall the Tana-naw do the like. We shall be blood brothers to men, not squaws; and the Thlunget be squaws."

A deep silence fell, and all eyes centered on Keesh. He looked about him carefully, deliberately, full into the face of each grown man.

"So," he said, passionlessly. "And so," he repeated. Then

turned upon his heel without further word and passed out into the darkness.

Wading among sprawling babies and bristling wolf-dogs, he threaded the great camp, and on its outskirts came upon a woman at work by the light of a fire. With strings of bark stripped from the long roots of creeping vines, she was braiding rope for the fishing. For some time without speech, he watched her deft hands bringing law and order out of the unruly mass of curling fibers. She was good to look upon, swaying there to her task, strong-limbed, deep-chested, and with hips made for motherhood. And the bronze of her face was golden in the flickering light, her hair blue-black, her eyes jet.

"O Su-Su," he spoke finally, "thou hast looked upon me kindly in the days that have gone, and in the days yet young —"

"I looked kindly upon thee for that thou wert chief of the Thlunget," she answered quickly, "and because thou wert big and strong."

"Ay —"

"But that was in the old days of the fishing," she hastened to add, "before the Shaman Brown came and taught thee ill things and led thy feet."

"But I would tell the —"

She held one hand in a gesture which reminded him of her father. "Nay, I know already the speech that stirs in thy throat, O Keesh, and I make answer now. It so happens that the fish of the water and the beasts of the forest bring forth after their kind. And this is good. Likewise it happens to women. It is for them to bring forth their kind, and even the maiden, while she is yet a maiden, feels the pang of the birth, and the pain of the breast, and the small hands at the neck. And when such feeling is strong, then does each maiden look about her with secret eyes for the man — for the man who shall be fit to father her kind. So have I felt. So did I feel when I looked upon thee and found thee big and strong, a hunter and fighter of beasts and men, well able to win meat when I should eat for two, well able to keep danger afar off when my helplessness drew nigh. But that was before the day the Shaman Brown came into the land and taught thee —"

"But it is not right, Su-Su. I have it on good word —"

"It is not right to kill. I know what thou wouldst say Then breed thou after thy kind, the kind that does not kill; but come not on such quest among the Tana-naw. For it is said, in the time to come that the Raven shall grapple with the Wolf. I do not know, for this be the affair of men; but I do know that it is for me to bring forth men against that time."

"Su-Su," Keesh broke in; "thou must hear me —"

"A *man* would beat me with a stick and make me hear," she sneered. "But thou . . . here!" She thrust a bunch of bark into his hand. "I cannot give thee myself, but this, yes. It looks fittest in thy hands. It is squaw work, so braid away."

He flung it from him, the angry blood pounding a muddy path under his bronze.

"One thing more," she went on. "There be an old custom which thy father and mine were not strangers to. When a man fall in battle his scalp is carried away in token. Very good. But thou, who have foresworn the Raven, must do more. Thou must bring me, not scalps, but heads, two heads, and then will I give thee, not bark, but a brave-beaded belt, and sheath, and long Russian knife. Then will I look kindly upon thee once again and all will be well."

"So," the man pondered. "So." Then he turned and passed out through the light.

"Nay, O Keesh!" she called after him. "Not two heads, but three at least!"

But Keesh remained true to his conversion, lived uprightly and made his tribe people obey the gospel as propounded by the Reverend Jackson Brown. Through all the time of the fishing he gave no heed to the Tana-naw, nor took notice of the sly things which were said, or of the laughter of the women of the many tribes. After the fishing Gnob and his people, with great store of salmon, sun-dried and smoke-cured, departed for the hunting on the head reaches of the Tana-naw. Keesh watched them go, but did not fail in his attendance at mission service, where he prayed regularly and led the singing with his deep bass voice.

The Reverend Jackson Brown delighted in that deep bass voice, and because of his sterling qualities deemed him the most promising convert. Macklewrath doubted this. He did not believe in the efficacy of the conversion of the heathen, and he was not slow in speaking his mind. But Mr. Brown was a large man, in his way, and he argued it out with such convincingness, all of one long fall night, that the trader, driven from position after position, finally announced in desperation: "Knock out my brains with apples, Brown, if I don't become a convert myself — if Keesh holds fast, true blue, for two years!" Mr. Brown never lost an opportunity, so he clinched the matter on the spot with a virile hand grip, and thenceforth the conduct of Keesh was to determine the ultimate abiding place of Macklewrath's soul.

But there came news one day, after the winter's rime had settled down over the land sufficiently for travel. A Tana-naw man arrived at the St. George Mission in quest of ammunition and bringing information that Su-Su had set eyes on Nee-Koo, a nervy young hunter who had bid brilliantly for her by old Gnob's fire. It was at about this time that the Reverend Jackson Brown came upon Keesh by the wood trail which leads down to the river. Keesh had his best dogs in the harness, and shoved under the sled lashings was his largest and finest pair of snowshoes.

"Where goest thou, O Keesh? Hunting?" Mr. Brown asked, falling into the Indian manner.

Keesh looked him steadily in the eyes for a full minute, then started up his dogs. Then again, turning his deliberate gaze upon the missionary, he answered, "No, I go to hell."

In an open space, striving to burrow into the snow as though for shelter from the appalling desolateness, huddled three dreary lodges. Ringed all about a dozen paces away, was the somber forest. Overhead there was no keen blue sky of naked space, but a vague, misty curtain, pregnant with snow, which had drawn between. There was no wind, no sound, nothing but the snow and silence. Nor was there even the general stir of life about the camp; for the hunting party had run upon the flank of the caribou herd and the kill had been large. Thus, after the period of fasting had come the plenitude of feasting, and thus, in broad daylight, they slept heavily under their roost of moose hide.

By a fire, before one of the lodges, five pairs of snowshoes stood on end in their element, and by the fire sat Su-Su. The hood of her squirrelskin parka was about her hair and well drawn up around her throat; but her hands were unmittened and nimbly at work with needle and sinew, completing the last fantastic design on a belt of leather faced with bright, scarlet cloth. A dog, somewhere at the rear of one of the lodges, raised a short, sharp bark, then ceased as abruptly as it had begun. Once, her father, in the lodge at her back, gurgled and grunted in his sleep. "Bad dreams," she smiled to herself. "He grows old and that last joint was too much."

She placed the last bead, knotted the sinew, and replenished the fire. Then, after gazing long into the flames, she lifted her head to the harsh crunch-crunch of a moccasined foot against the flinty snow granules. Keesh was at her side, bending slightly forward to a load which he bore upon his back. This was wrapped loosely in a soft tanned moose hide, and he dropped it carelessly into the snow and sat down. They looked at each other long and without speech.

"It is a far fetch, O Keesh," she said at last; "a far fetch from St. George Mission by the Yukon."

"Ay," he made answer, absently, his eyes fixed keenly upon the belt and taking note of its girth. "But where is the knife?" he demanded.

"Here." She drew it from inside her parka and flashed its naked length in the firelight. "It is a good knife."

"Give it to me," he commanded.

"Nay, O Keesh," she laughed. "It may be that thou wast not born to wear it."

"Give it to me," he reiterated, without change of tone. "I was so born."

But her eyes, glancing coquettishly past him to the moose hide, saw the snow about it slowly reddening. "It is blood, Keesh?" she asked.

"Ay, it is blood. But give me the belt and the long Russian knife."

She felt suddenly afraid, but thrilled when he took the belt roughly from her, thrilled to the roughness. She looked at him softly, and was aware of a pain at the breast and of small hands clutching her throat.

"It was made for a smaller man," he remarked, grimly, drawing in his abdomen and clasping the buckle at the first hole.

Su-Su smiled, and her eyes were yet softer. Again she felt the soft hands at her throat. He was good to look upon, and the belt was indeed small, made for a smaller man; but what did it matter? She could make many belts.

"But the blood?" she asked, urged on by a hope new-born and growing. "The blood, Keesh? It is . . . are they . . . heads?"

"Ay."

"They must be very fresh, else would the blood be frozen."

"Ay: it is not cold, and they be fresh, quite fresh."

"Oh, Keesh!" Her face was warm and bright. "And for me?"

"Ay; for thee."

He took hold of a corner of the hide, flirted it open, and rolled the heads out before her.

"Three," he whispered, savagely, "nay, four at least."

But she sat transfixed. There they lay — the soft-featured Nee-Koo; the gnarled old face of Gnob; Makamuk, grinning at her with his lifted upper lip; and lastly, Nossabok, his eyelid, up to its old trick, drooped on his girlish cheek in a suggestive wink. There they lay, the firelight flashing upon and playing over them, and from each of them a widening circle dyed the snow to scarlet.

Once, in the forest, an overburdened pine dropped its load of snow, and the echoes reverberated hollowly down the gorge; but neither stirred. The short day had been waning fast, and darkness was wrapping round the camp when White Fang trotted up toward the fire. He paused to reconnoiter, but not being driven back, came closer. His nose shot swiftly to the side, nostrils a-tremble and bristles rising along the spine, and straight and true he followed the sudden scent to his master's head. He sniffed it gingerly at first, and licked the forehead. Then he sat abruptly down, pointed his nose up at the first faint star, and raised the long wolf howl.

This brought Su-Su to herself. She glanced across at Keesh, who had unsheathed the Russian knife and was watching her intently. His face was firm and set, and in it she read the law. Slipping back the hood of her parka, she bared her neck and rose to her feet. There she paused and took a long look about her, at the rimming forest, at the faint stars in the sky, at the camp, at the snowshoes in the snow — a last long, comprehensive look at life. A light breeze stirred her hair from the side, and for the space of one deep breath she turned her head and followed it around until she met it full-faced.

Then she walked over to Keesh and said: "I am ready."

In a Far Country

When a man journeys into a far country, he must be prepared to forget many of the things he has learned, and to acquire such customs as are inherent with existence in the new land; he must abandon the old ideals and the old gods, and oftentimes he must reverse the very codes by which his conduct has hitherto been shaped. To those who have the protean faculty of adaptability, the novelty of such change may even be a source of pleasure; but to those who happen to be hardened to the ruts in which they were created, the pressure of the altered environment is unbearable, and they chafe in body and in spirit under the new restrictions which they do not understand. This chafing is bound to act and react, producing divers evils and leading to various misfortunes. It were better for the man who cannot fit himself to the new groove, to return to his own country; if he delay too long, he will surely die.

The man who turns his back upon the comforts of an elder civilization, to face the savage youth, the primordial simplicity of the North, may estimate success at an inverse ratio to the quantity and quality of his hopelessly fixed habits. He will soon discover, if he be a fit candidate, that the material habits are the less important. The exchange of such things as a dainty menu for rough fare, of the stiff leather shoe for the soft, shapeless moccasin, of the feather bed for a couch in the snow, is after all a very easy matter. But his pinch will come in learning properly to shape his mind's attitude toward all things, and especially toward his fellow man. For the courtesies of ordinary life, he must substitute unselfishness, forbearance, and tolerance. Thus, and thus only, can he gain that pearl of great price — true comradeship. He must not say "Thank you"; he must mean it without opening his mouth, and prove it by responding in kind. In short, he must substitute the deed for the word, the spirit for the letter.

When the world rang with the tale of Arctic gold, and the lure of the North gripped the heartstrings of men, Carter Weatherbee threw up his snug clerkship, turned the half of his savings over to his wife, and with the remainder bought an outfit. There was no romance in his nature — the bondage of commerce had crushed all that; he was simply tired of the ceaseless grind, and wished to risk great hazards in view of corresponding returns. Like many another fool, disdaining the old trails used by the Northland pioneers for a score of years, he hurried to Edmonton in the spring of the year — and there, unluckily for his soul's welfare, he allied himself with a party of men.

There was nothing unusual about this party, except its plans. Even its goal, like that of all other parties, was the Klondike. But the route it had mapped out to attain that goal, took away the breath of the hardiest native, born and bred to the vicissitudes of the Northwest. Even Jacques Baptiste, born of a Chippewa woman and a renegade *voyageur* (having raised his first whimpers in a deerskin lodge north of the sixty-fifth parallel, and had the same hushed by blissful sucks of raw tallow), was surprised. Though he sold his services to them and agreed to travel even to the never-opening ice, he shook his head ominously whenever his advice was asked.

Percy Cuthfert's evil star must have been in the ascendant, for he too joined this company of argonauts. He was an ordinary man, with a bank account as deep as his culture, which is saying a good deal. He had no reason to embark on such a venture — no reason in the world, save that he suffered from an abnormal development of sentimentality. He mistook this for the true spirit of romance and adventure. Many another man has done the like, and made as fatal a mistake.

The first breakup of spring found the party following the ice run of Elk River. It was an imposing fleet, for the outfit was large and they were accompanied by a disreputable contingent of half-breed *voyageurs* with their women and children. Day in and day out, they labored with the batteaus and canoes, fought mosquitoes and other kindred pests, or sweated and swore at the portages. Severe toil like this lays a man naked to the very roots of his soul, and ere Lake Athabasca was lost in the south, each member of the party had hoisted his true colors.

The two shirks and chronic grumblers were Carter Weatherbee and Percy Cuthfert. The whole party complained less of its aches and pains than did either of them. Not once did they volunteer for the thousand and one petty duties of the camp. A bucket of water to be brought, an extra armful of wood to be chopped, the dishes to be washed and wiped, a search to be made through the outfit for some suddenly indispensable article — and these two effete scions of civilization discovered sprains or blisters requiring instant attention. They were the first to turn in at night, with a score of tasks yet undone; the last to turn out in the morning, when the start should be in readiness before the breakfast was begun. They were the first to fall to at mealtime, the last to have a hand in the cooking; the first to dive for a slim delicacy, the last to discover they had added to their own another man's share. If they toiled at the oars, they slyly cut the water at each stroke and allowed the boat's momentum to float up the blade. They thought nobody noticed; but their comrades swore under their breaths and grew to hate them, while Jacques Baptiste sneered openly and damned them from morning till night. But he was no gentleman.

At the Great Slave, Hudson Bay dogs were purchased, and the fleet sank to the guards with its added burden of dried fish and pemmican. Then canoe and batteau answered to the swift current of the Mackenzie, and they plunged into the Great Barren Ground. Every likely looking "feeder" was prospected, but the elusive "pay dirt" danced ever to the north. At the Great Bear, overcome by the common dread of the Unknown Lands, their *voyageurs* began to desert, and Fort of Good Hope saw the last and bravest bending to the towlines as they bucked the current down which they had so treacherously glided. Jacques Baptiste alone remained. Had he not sworn to travel even to the never-opening ice?

The lying charts, compiled in main from hearsay, were now constantly consulted. And they felt the need of hurry, for the sun had already passed its northern solstice and was leading the winter south again. Skirting the shores of the bay, where the Mackenzie disembogues into the Arctic Ocean, they entered the mouth of the Little Peel River. Then began the arduous upstream toil, and the two Incapables fared worse than ever. Towline and pole, paddle and tumpline, rapids and portages — such tortures served to give the one a deep disgust for great hazards, and printed for the other a fiery text on the true romance of adventure. One day they waxed mutinous, and being vilely cursed by Jacques Baptiste, turned, as worms sometimes will. But the half-breed thrashed the twain, and sent them, bruised and bleeding, about their work. It was the first time either had been manhandled.

Abandoning their river craft at the headwaters of the Little Peel, they consumed the rest of the summer in the great portage over the Mackenzie watershed to the West Rat. This little stream fed the Porcupine, which in turn joined the Yukon where that mighty highway of the North countermarches on the Arctic Circle. But they had lost in the race with winter, and one day they tied their rafts to the thick eddy ice and hurried their goods ashore. That night the river jammed and broke several times; the following morning it had fallen asleep for good.

"We can't be more'n four hundred miles from the

Yukon," concluded Sloper, multiplying his thumb nails by the scale of the map. The council, in which the two Incapables had whined to excellent disadvantage, was drawing to a close.

"Hudson Bay Post, long time ago. No use um now." Jacques Baptiste's father had made the trip for the Fur Company in the old days, incidentally marking the trail with a couple of frozen toes.

"Sufferin' cracky!" cried another of the party. "No whites?"

"Nary white," Sloper sententiously affirmed; "but it's only five hundred more up the Yukon to Dawson. Call it a rough thousand from here."

Weatherbee and Cuthfert groaned in chorus.

"How long'll that take, Baptiste?"

The half-breed figured for a moment. "Workum like hell, no man play out, ten—twenty—forty—fifty days. Um babies come," (designating the Incapables,) "no can tell. Mebbe when hell freeze over; mebbe not then."

The manufacture of snowshoes and moccasins ceased. Somebody called the name of an absent member, who came out of an ancient cabin at the edge of the campfire and joined them. The cabin was one of the many mysteries which lurk in the vast recesses of the North. Built when and by whom, no man could tell. Two graves in the open, piled high with stones, perhaps contained the secret of those early wanderers. But whose hand had piled the stones?

The moment had come. Jacques Baptiste paused in the fitting of a harness and pinned the struggling dog in the snow. The cook made mute protest for delay, threw a handful of bacon into a noisy pot of beans, then came to attention. Sloper rose to his feet. His body was a ludicrous contrast to the healthy physiques of the Incapables. Yellow and weak, fleeing from a South American fever hole, he had not broken his flight across the zones, and was still able to toil with men. His weight was probably ninety pounds, with the heavy hunting knife thrown in, and his grizzled hair told of a prime which had ceased to be. The fresh, young muscles of either Weatherbee or Cuthfert were equal to ten times the endeavor of his; yet he could walk them into the earth in a day's journey. And all this day he had whipped his stronger comrades into venturing a thousand miles of the stiffest hardship man can conceive. He was the incarnation of the unrest of his race, and the old Teutonic stubbornness, dashed with the quick grasp and action of the Yankee, held the flesh in the bondage of the spirit.

"All those in favor of going on with the dogs as soon as the ice sets, say aye."

"Aye!" rang out eight voices — voices destined to string a trail of oaths along many a hundred miles of pain.

"Contrary minded?"

"No!" For the first time the Incapables were united without some compromise of personal interests.

"And what are you going to do about it?" Weatherbee added belligerently.

"Majority rule! Majority rule!" clamored the rest of the party.

"I know the expedition is liable to fall through if you don't come," Sloper replied sweetly; "but I guess, if we try real hard, we can manage to do without you. What do you say, boys?"

The sentiment was cheered to the echo.

"But I say, you know," Cuthfert ventured apprehensively, "what's a chap like me to do?"

"Ain't you coming with us?"

"No—o."

"Then do as you please. We won't have nothing to say."

"Kind o' calkilate yuh might settle it with that canoodlin' pardner of yourn," suggested a heavy-going Westerner from the Dakotas, at the same time pointing out Weatherbee. "He'll be shore to ask yuh what yur a-goin' to do when it comes to cookin' an' gatherin' the wood."

"Then we'll consider it all arranged," concluded Sloper. "We'll pull out tomorrow, if we camp within five miles — just to get everything in running order and remember if we've forgotten anything."

The sleds groaned by on their steel-shod runners, and the dogs strained low in the harnesses in which they were born to die. Jacques Baptiste paused by the side of Sloper to get a last glimpse of the cabin. The smoke curled up pathetically from the Yukon stovepipe. The two Incapables were watching them from the doorway.

Sloper laid his hand on the other's shoulder. "Jacques Baptiste, did you ever hear of the Kilkenny cats?"

The half-breed shook his head.

"Well, my friend and good comrade, the Kilkenny cats fought till neither hide, nor hair, nor yowl, was left. You understand?—till nothing was left. Very good. Now, these two men, don't like work. They won't work. We know that. They'll be all alone in that cabin all winter — a mighty long, dark winter. Kilkenny cats — well?"

The Frenchman in Baptiste shrugged his shoulders, but the Indian in him was silent. Nevertheless, it was an eloquent shrug, pregnant with prophecy.

Things prospered in the little cabin at first. The rough badinage of their comrades had made Weatherbee and Cuthfert conscious of the mutual responsibility which had devolved upon them; besides, there was not so much work after all for two healthy men. And the removal of the cruel whip hand, or in other words, the bulldozing half-breed, had brought with it a joyous reaction. At first, each strove to outdo the other, and they performed petty tasks with an unction which would have opened the eyes of their comrades who were now wearing out bodies and souls on the Long Trail.

All care was banished. The forest, which shouldered in upon them from three sides, was an inexhaustible wood-yard. A few yards from their door slept the Porcupine, and a hole through its winter robe formed a bubbling spring of water, crystal clear and painfully cold. But they soon grew to find fault with even that. The hole would persist in freezing up, and thus gave them many a miserable hour of ice chopping. The unknown builders of the cabin had extended the side logs so as to support a cache at the rear. In this was stored the bulk of the party's provisions. Food there was, without stint, for three times the men who were fated to live upon it. But most of it was of the kind which built up brawn and sinew but did not tickle the palate. True, there was sugar in plenty for two ordinary men; but these two were little else than children. They early discovered the virtues of hot water judiciously saturated with sugar, and they prodigally swam their flapjacks and soaked their crusts in the rich, white syrup. Then coffee and tea, and especially the dried fruits, made disastrous inroads upon it. The first word they had was over the sugar question. And it is a really serious thing when two men, wholly dependent upon each other for company, begin to quarrel.

Weatherbee loved to discourse blatantly on politics, while Cuthfert, who had been prone to clip his coupons and let the commonwealth jog on as best it might, either ignored the subject or delivered himself of startling epigrams. But the clerk was too obtuse to appreciate the clever shaping of thought, and this waste of ammunition irritated Cuthfert. He had been used to blinding people by his brilliancy, and it worked him quite a hardship, this loss of an audience. He felt personally aggrieved and unconsciously held his muttonhead companion responsible for it.

Save existence, they had nothing in common — came in touch on no single point. Weatherbee was a clerk who had known naught but clerking all his life; Cuthfert was a master of arts, a dabbler in oils, and had written not a little. The one was a lower-class man who considered himself a gentleman, and the other was a gentleman who knew himself to be such. From this it may be remarked that a man can be a gentleman without possessing the first instinct of true comradeship. The clerk was as sensuous as the other was aesthetic, and his love adventures, told at great length and chiefly coined from his imagination, affected the supersensitive master of arts in the same way as so many whiffs of sewer gas. He deemed the clerk a filthy, uncultured brute, whose place was in the muck with the swine, and told him so, and he was reciprocally informed that he was a milk-and-water sissy and a cad. Weatherbee could not have defined "cad" for his life; but it satisfied its purpose, which after all seems the main point in life.

Weatherbee flatted every third note and sang such songs as "The Boston Burglar" and "The Handsome Cabin Boy," for hours at a time, while Cuthfert wept with rage, till he could stand it no longer and fled into the outer cold. But there was no escape. The intense frost could not be endured for long at a time, and the little cabin crowded them — beds, stove, table, and all — into a space of ten by twelve. The very presence of either became a personal affront to the other, and they lapsed into sullen silences which increased in length and strength as the days went by. Occasionally, the flash of an eye or the curl of a lip got the better of them, though they strove to wholly ignore each other during these mute periods. And a great wonder sprang up in the breast of each, as to how God had ever come to create the other.

With little to do, time became an intolerable burden to them. This naturally made them still lazier. They sank into a physical lethargy which there was no escaping, and which made them rebel at the performance of the smallest chore. One morning when it was his turn to cook the common breakfast, Weatherbee rolled out of his blankets, and to the snoring of his companion, lighted first the slush lamp and then the fire. The kettles were frozen hard, and there was no water in the cabin with which to wash. But he did not mind that. Waiting for it to thaw, he sliced the bacon and plunged into the hateful task of breadmaking. Cuthfert had been slyly watching through his half-closed lids. Consequently there was a scene, in which they fervently blessed each other, and agreed, henceforth, that each do his own cooking. A week later, Cuthfert neglected his morning ablutions, but none the less complacently ate the meal which he had cooked. Weatherbee grinned. After that the foolish custom of washing passed out of their lives.

As the sugar pile and other little luxuries dwindled, they began to be afraid they were not getting their proper shares, and in order that they might not be robbed, they fell to gorging themselves. The luxuries suffered in this gluttonous contest, as did also the men. In the absence of fresh vegetables and exercise, their blood became impoverished, and a loathsome, purplish rash crept over their bodies. Yet they refused to heed the warning. Next, their muscles and joints began to swell, the flesh turning black, while their mouths, gums, and lips, took on the color of rich cream. Instead of being drawn together by their misery, each gloated over the other's symptoms as the scurvy took its course.

They lost all regard for personal appearance, and for that matter, common decency. The cabin became a pigpen, and never once were the beds made or fresh pine boughs laid underneath. Yet they could not keep to their blankets, as they would have wished; for the frost was inexorable and the firebox consumed much fuel. The hair of their heads and faces grew long and shaggy, while their garments would have disgusted a ragpicker. But they did not care. They were sick, and there was no one to see; besides, it was very painful to move about.

To all this was added a new trouble — the Fear of the North. This Fear was the joint child of the Great Cold and the Great Silence, and was born in the darkness of December, when the sun dipped below the southern horizon for good. It affected them according to their natures. Weatherbee fell prey to the grosser superstitions, and did his best to resurrect the spirits which slept in the forgotten graves. It was a fascinating thing, and in his dreams they came to him from out of the cold, and snuggled into his blankets, and told him of their toils and troubles ere they died. He shrank away from the clammy contact as they drew closer and twined their frozen limbs about him, and when they whispered in his ear of things to come, the cabin rang with his frightened shrieks. Cuthfert did not understand – for they no longer spoke — and when thus awakened he invariably grabbed for his revolver. Then he would sit up in bed, shivering nervously, with the weapon trained on the unconscious dreamer. Cuthfert deemed the man going mad, and so came to fear for his life.

His own malady assumed a less concrete form. The mysterious artisan who had laid the cabin, log by log, had pegged a wind vane to the ridgepole. Cuthfert noticed it always pointed south, and one day, irritated by its steadfastness of purpose, he turned it toward the east. He watched eagerly, but never a breath came by to disturb it. Then he turned the vane to the north, swearing never again to touch it till the wind did blow. But the air frightened him with its unearthly calm, and he often rose in the middle of the night to see if the vane had veered — ten degrees would have satisfied him. But no, it poised above him as unchangeable as fate. His imagination ran riot, till it became to him a fetich, invested with all the attributes of a sphinx. Sometimes he followed the path it pointed across the dismal dominions, and allowed his soul to become saturated with the Fear. He dwelt upon the unseen and the unknown till the burden of eternity appeared to be crushing him. Everything in the Northland had that crushing effect — the absence of life and motion; the darkness; the infinite peace of the brooding land; the ghastly silence, which made the echo of each heart-beat a sacrilege; the solemn forest which seemed to guard an awful, inexpressible something, which neither word nor thought could compass.

The world he had so recently left, with its busy nations and great enterprises, seemed very far away. Recollections occasionally obtruded — recollections of marts and galleries and crowded thoroughfares, of evening dress and social functions, of good men and dear women he had known — but they were dim memories of a life he had lived long centuries agone, on some other planet. This phantasm was the Reality. Standing beneath the windvane, his eyes fixed on the polar skies, he could not bring himself to realize that the Southland really existed, that at that very moment it was a-roar with life and action. There was no Southland, no men being born of women, no giving and taking in marriage. Beyond his bleak sky line there stretched vast solitudes, and beyond these still vaster solitudes. There were no lands of sunshine, heavy with the perfume of flowers. Such things were only old dreams of paradise. The sunlands of the West and the spicelands of the East, the smiling Arcadias and blissful Islands of the Blest — ha! ha! His laughter split the void and shocked him with its unwonted sound. There was no sun. This was the Universe, dead and cold and dark, and he its only citizen. Weatherbee? At such moments Weatherbee did not count. He was a Caliban, a monstrous phantom, fettered to him for untold ages, the penalty of some forgotten crime.

He lived with Death among the dead, emasculated by the sense of his own insignificance, crushed by the passive mastery of the slumbering ages. The magnitude of all things appalled him. Everything partook of the superlative save himself — the perfect cessation of wind and motion, the immensity of the snow-covered wilderness, the height of the sky and the depth of the silence. That windvane — if it would only move. If a thunderbolt would fall, or the forest flare up in flame. The rolling up of the heavens as a scroll, the crash of Doom — anything, anything. But no, nothing moved; the silence crowded in, and the Fear of the North laid icy fingers on his heart.

Once, like another Crusoe, by the edge of the river he came upon a track — the faint tracery of a snowshoe rabbit on the delicate snow crust. It was a revelation. There was life in the Northland. He would follow it, look upon it, gloat over it. He forgot his swollen muscles, plunging through the deep snow in an ecstasy of anticipation. The forest swallowed him up, and the brief midday twilight vanished; but he pursued his quest till exhausted nature asserted itself and laid him helpless in the snow. There he groaned and cursed his folly, and knew the track to be the fancy of his brain; and late that night he dragged himself into the cabin on hands and knees, his cheeks frozen and a strange numbness about his feet. Weatherbee grinned malevolently, but made no offer to help him. He thrust needles into his toes and thawed them out by the stove. A week later mortification set in.

But the clerk had his own troubles. The dead men came out of their graves more frequently now, and rarely left him, waking or sleeping. He grew to wait and dread their coming, never passing the twin cairns without a shudder, One night they came to him in his sleep and led him forth to an appointed task. Frightened into inarticulate horror, he awoke between the heaps of stones and fled wildly to the cabin. But he had lain there for some time, for his feet and cheeks were also frozen.

Sometimes he became frantic at their insistent presence, and danced about the cabin, cutting the empty air with an ax and smashing everything within reach. During these ghostly encounters, Cuthfert huddled into his blankets and followed the madman about with a cocked revolver, ready to shoot him if he came too near. But, recovering from one of these spells, the clerk noticed the weapon trained upon him with deadly intent. His suspicions were aroused, and thenceforth he too lived in fear of his life. They watched each other closely after that, and faced about in startled fright whenever either passed behind the other's back. This apprehensiveness became a mania which controlled them even in their sleep. Through mutual fear they tacitly let the slush lamp burn all night, and saw to a plentiful supply of bacon grease before retiring. The slightest movement on the part of one was sufficient to arouse the other, and many a still watch their gazes countered as they shook beneath their blankets with fingers on the trigger guards.

What with the Fear of the North, the mental strain, and the ravages of the disease, they lost all semblance of humanity, taking on the appearance of wild beasts, hunted and desperate. Their cheeks and noses, as an aftermath of the freezing, had turned black. Their frozen toes had begun to drop away at the first and second joints. Every movement brought pain, but the firebox was insatiable, wringing a ransom of torture from their miserable bodies. Day in, day out, it demanded its food — a veritable pound of flesh — and they dragged themselves into the forest to chop wood on their knees. Once, crawling thus in search of dry sticks, unknown to each other they entered a thicket from opposite sides. Suddenly, with warning, two peering death's-heads confronted each other. Suffering had so transformed them that recognition was impossible. They sprang to their feet, shrieking with terror, and dashed away on their mangled stumps; and falling at the cabin door, they clawed and scratched like demons till they discovered their mistake.

Occasionally they lapsed normal, and during one of these sane intervals, the chief bone of contention, the sugar, had been divided equally between them. They guarded their separate sacks, stored up in the cache, with jealous eyes; for there were but a few cupfuls left, and they were totally devoid of faith in each other. But one day Cuthfert made a mistake. Hardly able to move, sick with pain, with his head swimming and eyes blinded, he crept into the cache, sugar canister in hand, and mistook Weatherbee's sack for his own.

January had been born but a few days when this occurred. The sun had some time since passed its lowest southern declination, and at meridian now threw flaunting streaks of yellow light upon the northern sky. On the day following his mistake with the sugar bag, Cuthfert found himself feeling better, both in body and in spirit. As noontime drew near and the day brightened, he dragged himself outside to feast on the evanescent glow, which was to him an earnest of the sun's future intentions. Weatherbee was also feeling somewhat better, and crawled out beside him. They propped themselves in the snow beneath the moveless wind vane and waited.

The stillness of death was about them. In others climes, when nature falls into such moods, there is a subdued air of expectancy, a waiting for some small voice to take up the broken strain. Not so in the North. The two men had lived seeming eons in this ghostly peace. They could remember no song of the past; they could conjure no song of the future. This unearthly calm had always been — the tranquil silence of eternity.

Their eyes were fixed upon the north. Unseen, behind their backs, behind the towering mountains to the south, the sun swept toward the zenith of another sky than theirs. Sole spectators of the mighty canvas, they watched the false dawn slowly grow. A faint flame began to glow and smolder. It deepened in intensity, ringing the changes of reddish-yellow, purple, and saffron. So bright did it become that Cuthfert thought the sun must surely be behind it — a miracle, the sun rising in the north. Suddenly, without warning and without fading, the canvas was swept clean. There was no color in the sky. The light had gone out of the day. They caught their breaths in half sobs. But lo! the air was a-glint with particles of scintillating frost, and there, to the north, the wind vane lay in vague outline on the snow. A shadow! A shadow! It was exactly midday. They jerked their heads hurriedly to the south. A golden rim peeped over the mountain's snowy shoulder, smiled upon them an instant, then dipped from sight again.

There were tears in their eyes as they sought each other. A strange softening came over them. They felt irresistibly drawn toward each other. The sun was coming back again. It would be with them tomorrow, and the next day, and the next. And it would stay longer every visit, and a time would come when it would ride their heaven day and night, never once dropping below the sky line. There would be no night. The ice-locked winter would be broken; the winds would blow and the forests answer; the land would bathe in the blessed sunshine and renew life. Hand in hand, they would quit this horrid dream and journey back to the Southland. They lurched blindly forward, and their hands met — their poor maimed hands, swollen and distorted beneath their mittens.

But the promise was destined to remain unfulfilled. The Northland is the Northland, and men work out their souls by strange rules, which other men, who have not journeyed into a far country, cannot come to understand

An hour later, Cuthfert put a pan of bread into the oven, and fell to speculating on what the surgeons could do with his feet when he got back. Home did not seem so very far away now. Weatherbee was rummaging in the cache. Of a sudden, he raised a whirlwind of blasphemy, which in turn ceased with startling abruptness. The other man had robbed his sugar sack. Still, things might have happened differently, had not the two dead men come out from under the stones and hushed the hot words in his throat. They led him quite gently from the cache, which he forgot to close. That consummation was reached; that something they had whispered to him in his dreams was about to happen. They guided him gently, very gently, to the woodpile, where they put the ax in his hands. Then they helped him shove open the cabin door, and he felt sure they shut it after him — at least he had heard it slam and the latch fall sharply into place. And he knew they were waiting just without, waiting for him to do his task.

"Carter! I say, Carter!"

Percy Cuthfert was frightened at the look on the clerk's face, and he made haste to put the table between them.

Carter Weatherbee followed, without haste and without enthusiasm. There was neither pity nor passion in his face, but rather the patient, stolid look of one who has certain work to do and goes about it methodically.

"I say, what's the matter?"

The clerk dodged back, cutting off his retreat to the door, but never opening his mouth.

"I say, Carter, I say; let's talk. There's a good chap."

The master of arts was thinking rapidly, now, shaping a skillful flank movement on the bed where his Smith & Wesson lay. Keeping his eyes on the madman, he rolled backward on the bunk, at the same time clutching the pistol.

"Carter!"

The powder flashed full in Weatherbee's face, but he swung his weapon and leaped forward. The ax bit deeply at the base of the spine, and Percy Cuthfert felt all consciousness of his lower limbs leave him. Then the clerk fell heavily upon him, clutching him by the throat with feeble fingers. The sharp bite of the ax had caused Cuthfert to drop the pistol, and as his lungs panted for release, he fumbled aimlessly for it among the blankets. Then he remembered. He slid a hand up the clerk's belt to the sheath knife; and they drew very close to each other in that last clinch.

Percy Cuthfert felt his strength leave him. The lower portion of his body was useless. The inert weight of Weatherbee crushed him — crushed him and pinned him there like a bear under a trap. The cabin became filled with a familiar odor, and he knew the bread to be burning. Yet what did it matter? He would never need it. And there were all of six cupfuls of sugar in the cache — if he had foreseen this he would not have been so saving the last several days. Would the wind vane ever move? It might even be veering now. Why not? Had he not seen the sun today? He would go and see. No; it was impossible to move. He had not thought the clerk so heavy a man.

How quickly the cabin cooled! The fire must be out. The cold was forcing in. It must be below zero already, and the ice creeping up the inside of the door. He could not see it, but his past experience enabled him to gauge its progress by the cabin's temperature. The lower hinge must be white ere now. Would the tale of this ever reach the world? How would his friends take it? They would read it over their coffee, most likely, and talk it over at the clubs. He could see them very clearly. "Poor Old Cuthfert," they murmured; "not such a bad sort of a chap, after all." He smiled at their eulogies, and passed on in search of a Turkish bath. It was the same old crowd upon the streets. Strange, they did not notice his moose-hide moccasins and tattered German socks! He would take a cab. And after the bath a shave would not be bad. No; he would eat first. Steak, and potatoes, and green things — how fresh it all was! And what was that? Squares of honey, streaming liquid amber! But why did they bring so much? Ha! ha! He could never eat it all. Shine! Why certainly. He put his foot on the box. The bootblack looked curiously up at him, and he remembered his moose-hide moccasins and went away hastily.

Hark! The wind vane must be surely spinning. No; a mere singing in his ears. That was all — a mere singing. The ice must have passed the latch by now. More likely the upper hinge was covered. Between the moss-chinked roof poles, little points of frost began to appear. How slowly they grew! No; not so slowly. There was a new one, and there another. Two — three — four; they were coming too fast to count. There were two growing together. And there, a third had joined them. Why, there were no more spots. They had run together and formed a sheet.

Well, he would have company. If Gabriel ever broke the silence of the North, they would stand together, hand in hand, before the great White Throne. And God would judge them, God would judge them!

Then Percy Cuthfert closed his eyes and dropped off to sleep.

The Men of Forty Mile

When Big Jim Belden ventured the apparently innocuous proposition that mush ice was "rather pecooliar," he little dreamed of what it would lead to. Neither did Lon McFane, when he affirmed that anchor ice was even more so; nor did Bettles, as he instantly disagreed, declaring the very existence of such a form to be a bugaboo.

"An' ye'd be tellin' me this," cried Lon, "after the years ye've spint in the land! An' we atin' out the same pot this many's the day!"

"But the thing's agin reason," insisted Bettles. "Look you, water's warmer than ice——"

"An' little the difference, once ye break through."

"Still it's warmer, because it ain't froze. An' you say it freezes on the bottom?"

"Only the anchor ice, David, only the anchor ice. An' have ye niver drifted along, the water clear as glass, whin suddin, belike a cloud over the sun, the mushy ice comes bubblin' up an' up, till from bank to bank an' bind to bind it's drapin' the river like a first snowfall?"

"Unh hunh! more'n once when I took a doze at the

steering oar. But it allus come out the nighest side channel, an' not bubblin' up an' up."

"But with niver a wink at the helm?"

"No; nor you. It's agin reason. I'll leave it to any man!"

Bettles appealed to the circle about the stove; but the fight was on between himself and Lon McFane.

"Reason or no reason, it's the truth I'm tellin' ye. Last fall, a year gone, 'twas Sitka Charley and meself saw the sight, droppin' down the riffle ye'll remember below Fort Reliance. An' regular fall weather it was – the glint o' the sun on the golden larch an' the quakin' aspens; an' the glister of light on ivery ripple; an' beyand, the winter an' the blue haze of the north comin' down hand in hand. It's well ye know the same, with a fringe to the river an' the ice formin' thick in the eddies — an' a snap an' sparkle to the air, an' ye a-feelin' it through all ye'r blood, a-takin' new lease of life with ivery suck of it. 'T is then, me boy, the world grows small an' the wandtherlust lays ye by the heels.

"But it's meself as wandthers. As I was sayin', we a paddlin', with niver a sign of ice, barrin' that by the eddies, when the Injin lifts his paddle an' sings out, 'Lon McFane! Look ye below! So have I heard, but niver thought to see!' As ye know, Sitka Charley, like meself, niver drew first breath in the land; so the sight was new. Then we drifted, with a head over ayther side, peerin' down through the sparkly water. For the world like the days I spint with the pearlers, watchin' the coral banks a-growin' the same as so many gardens under the sea. There it was, the anchor ice, clingin' an' clusterin' to ivery rock, after the manner of the white coral.

"But the best of the sight was to come. Just after clearin' the tail of the riffle, the water turns quick the color of milk, an' the top of it in wee circles, as when the graylin' rise in the spring or there's a splatter of wet from the sky. 'Twas the anchor ice comin' up. To the right, to the lift, as far as iver a man cud see, the water was covered with the same. An' like so much porridge it was, slickin' along the bark of the canoe, sticken' like glue to the paddles. It's many's the time I shot the selfsame riffle before, and it's many's the time after, but niver a wink of the same have I seen. 'Twas the sight of a lifetime."

"Do tell!" dryly commented Bettles. "D' ye think I'd b'lieve such a yarn? I'd ruther say the glister of light'd gone to your eyes, and the snap of the air to your tongue."

" 'Twas me own eyes that beheld it, an' if Sitka Charley was here, he'd be the lad to back me."

"But facts is facts, an' they ain't no gittin' round 'em. It ain't in the nature of things for the water fartherest away from the air to freeze first."

"But me own eyes——"

"Don't git het up over it." admonished Bettles, as the quick Celtic anger began to mount.

"Then ye'r not after belavin' me?'

"Sence you're so blamed forehanded about it, no; I'd b'lieve nature first, and facts."

"Is it the lie ye'd be givin' me?" threatened Lon. "Ye'd better be askin' that Siwash wife of yours. I'll lave it to her, for the truth I spake."

Bettles flared up in sudden wrath. The Irishman had unwittingly wounded him; for his wife was the half-breed daughter of a Russian fur trader, married to him in the

Greek Mission of Nulato, a thousand miles or so down the Yukon, thus being of much higher caste than the common Siwash, or native, wife. It was a mere Northland nuance, which none but the Northland adventurer may understand.

"I reckon you kin take it that way," was his deliberate affirmation.

The next instant Lon McFane had stretched him on the floor, the circle was broken up, and half a dozen men had stepped between.

Bettles came to his feet, wiping the blood from his mouth. "It hain't new, this takin' and payin' of blows, and don't you never think but that this will be squared."

"An' niver in me life did I take the lie from mortal man," was the retort courteous. "An' it's an avil day I'll not be to hand, waitin' an' willin' to help ye lift yer debts, barrin' no manner of way."

"Still got that 38–55?"

Lon nodded.

"But you'd better git a more likely caliber. Mine'll rip holes through you the size of walnuts."

"Niver fear; it's me own slugs smell their way with soft noses, an' they'll spread like flapjacks against the coming out beyand. An' when'll I have the pleasure of waitin' on ye? The water hole's a strikin' locality."

" 'T ain't bad. Jest be there in an hour, and you won't set long on my coming."

Both men mittened and left the Post, their ears closed to the remonstrances of their comrades. It was such a little thing; yet with such men, little things, nourished by quick tempers and stubborn natures, soon blossomed into big things. Besides, the art of burning to bedrock still lay in the womb of the future, and the men of Forty Mile, shut in by the long Arctic winter, grew high-stomached with overeating and enforced idleness, and became as irritable as do the bees in the fall of the year when the hives are overstocked with honey.

There was no law in the land. The Mounted Police was also a thing of the future. Each man measured an offense and meted out the punishment in as much as it affected himself. Rarely had combined action been necessary, and never, in all the dreary history of the camp, had the eighth article of the Decalogue been violated.

Big Jim Belden called an impromptu meeting. "Scruff" Mackenzie was placed as temporary chairman, and a messenger dispatched to solicit Father Roubeau's good offices. Their position was paradoxical, and they knew it. By the right of might could they interfere to prevent the duel; yet such action, while in direct line with their wishes, went counter to their opinions. While their rough-hewn, obsolete ethics recognized the individual prerogative of wiping out blow with blow, they could not bear to think of two good comrades, such as Bettles and McFane, meeting in deadly battle. Deeming the man who would not fight on provocation, a dastard, when brought to the test, it seemed wrong that he should fight.

But a scurry of moccasins and loud cries, rounded off with a pistol shot, interrupted the discussion. Then the storm doors opened and Malemute Kid entered, a smoking Colt's in his hand and a merry light in his eye.

"I got him." He replaced the empty shell, and added, "Your dog, Scruff."

"Yellow Fang?" Mackenzie asked.

"No; the lop-eared one."

"The devil! Nothing the matter with him."

"Come out and take a look."

"That's all right, after all. Guess he's got 'em, too. Yellow Fang came back this morning and took a chunk out of him, and came near to making a widower of me. Made a rush for Zarinska, but she whisked her skirts in his face and escaped with the loss of the same and a good roll in the snow. Then he took to the woods again. Hope he don't come back. Lost any yourself?"

"One — the best one of the pack — Shookum. Started amuck this morning, but didn't get very far. Ran foul of Sitka Charley's team, and they scattered him all over the street. And now two of them are loose and raging mad; so you see he got his work in. The dog census will be small in the spring if we don't do something."

"And the man census, too."

"How's that? Who's in trouble now?"

"O, Bettles and Lon McFane had an argument, and they'll be down by the water hole in a few minutes to settle it."

The incident was repeated for his benefit, and Malemute Kid, accustomed to an obedience which his fellow men never failed to render, took charge of the affair. His quickly formulated plan was explained, and they promised to follow his lead implicitly.

"So you see," he concluded, "we do not actually take away their privilege of fighting; and yet I don't believe they'll fight when they see the beauty of the scheme. Life's a game, and men the gamblers. They'll stake their whole pile on the one chance in a thousand. Take away that one chance, and — they won't play."

He turned to the man in charge of the Post. "Storekeeper, weigh out three fathoms of your best half-inch manila."

"We'll establish a precedent which will last the men of Forty Mile to the end of time," he prophesied. Then he coiled the rope about his arm and led his followers out of doors, just in time to meet the principals.

"What danged right'd he to fetch my wife in?" thundered Bettles to the soothing overtures of a friend. " 'Twa' n't called for," he concluded decisively. " 'Twa' n't called for," he reiterated again and again, pacing up and down and waiting for Lon McFane.

And Lon McFane — his face was hot and tongue rapid, as he flaunted insurrection in the face of the Church. "Then, father," he cried, "it's with an aisy heart I'll roll in me flamy blankets, the broad of me back on a bed of coals. Niver shall it be said Lon McFane took a lie 'twixt the teeth without iver liftin' a hand! An' I'll not ask a blessin'. The years have been wild, but it's the heart was in the right place."

"But it's not the heart, Lon," interposed Father Roubeau, "it's pride that bids you forth to slay your fellow man."

"Ye'r Frinch," Lon replied. And then, turning to leave him, "An' will ye say a mass if the luck is against me?"

But the priest smiled, thrust his moccasined feet to the fore, and went out upon the white breast of the silent river. A packed trail, the width of a sixteen-inch sled, led out to the water hole. On either side lay the deep, soft snow. The men trod in single file, without conversation; and the black-stoled priest in their midst gave to the function the solemn aspect of a funeral. It was a warm winter's day for Forty Mile — a day in which the sky, filled with heaviness, drew closer to the earth, and the mercury sought the unwonted level of twenty below. But there was no cheer in the warmth. There was little air in the upper strata, and the clouds hung motionless, giving sullen promise of an early snowfall. And the earth, unresponsive, made no preparation, content in its hibernation.

When the water hole was reached, Bettles, having evidently reviewed the quarrel during the silent walk, burst out in a final " 'Twa' n't called for," while Lon McFane kept grim silence. Indignation so choked him that he could not speak.

Yet deep down, whenever their own wrongs were not uppermost, both men wondered at their comrades. They had expected opposition, and this tacit acquiescence hurt them. It seemed more was due them from the men they had been so close with, and they felt a vague sense of wrong, rebelling at the thought of so many of their brothers coming out, as on a gala occasion, without one word of protest, to see them shoot each other down. It appeared their worth had diminished in the eyes of the community. The proceedings puzzled them.

"Back to back, David. An' will it be fifty paces to the man, or double the quantity?"

"Fifty," was the sanguinary reply, grunted out, yet sharply cut.

But the new manila, not prominently displayed but

casually coiled about Malemute Kid's arm, caught the quick eye of the Irishman and thrilled him with a suspicious fear.

"An' what are ye doin' with the rope?"

"Hurry up!" Malemute Kid glanced at his watch. "I've a batch of bread in the cabin, and I don't want it to fall. Besides, my feet are getting cold."

The rest of the men manifested their impatience in various suggestive ways.

"But the rope, Kid? It's bran' new, an' sure ye'r bread's not that heavy it needs raisin' with the like of that?"

Bettles by this time had faced around. Father Roubeau, the humor of the situation just dawning on him, had a smile behind his mittened hand.

"No, Lon; this rope was made for a man." Malemute Kid could be very impressive on occasion.

"What man?" Bettles was becoming aware of a personal interest.

"The other man."

"An' which is the one ye'd mane by that?"

"Listen, Lon — and you, too, Bettles! We've been talking this little trouble of yours over, and we've come to one conclusion. We know we have no right to stop your fighting —"

"True for ye, me lad!"

"And we're not going to. But this much we can do, and shall do — make this the only duel in the history of Forty Mile, set an example for every *chechaqua* that comes up or down the Yukon. The man who escapes killing shall be hanged to the nearest tree. Now, go ahead!"

Lon smiled dubiously, then his face lighted up. "Pace her off, David — fifty paces, wheel, an' niver a cease firin' till a lad's down for good. 'Tis their hearts 'll niver let them do the deed, an' it's well ye should know it for a true Yankee bluff."

He started off with a pleased grin on his face, but Malemute Kid halted him.

"Lon! It's a long while since you first knew me?"

"Many's the day."

"And you, Bettles?"

"Five year next June high water."

"And have you once, in all that time, known me to break my word? Or heard of me breaking it?"

Both men shook their heads, striving to fathom what lay beyond.

"Well, then, what do you think of a promise made by me?"

"As good as your bond," from Bettles.

"The thing to safely sling yer hopes of heaven by," promptly indorsed Lon McFane.

"Listen! I, Malemute Kid, give you my word — and you know what that means — that the man who is not shot, stretches rope within ten minutes after the shooting." He stepped back as Pilate might have done after washing his hands.

A pause and a silence came over the men of Forty-Mile. The sky drew still closer, sending down a crystal flight of frost — little geometric designs, perfect, evanescent as a breath, yet destined to exist till the returning sun had covered half its northern journey. Both men had led forlorn hopes in their time — led, with a curse or a jest on their tongues, and in their souls an unswerving faith in the God of Chance. But that merciful deity had been shut out from the present deal. They studied the face of Malemute Kid, but they studied as one might the Sphinx. As the quiet minutes passed, a feeling that speech was incumbent on them, began to grow. At last, the howl of a wolf-dog cracked the silence from the direction of Forty Mile. The weird sound swelled with all the pathos of a breaking heart, then died away in a long-drawn sob.

"Well I be danged!" Bettles turned up the collar of his mackinaw jacket and stared about him helplessly.

"It's a gloryus game ye'r runnin', Kid," cried Lon McFane. "All the percentage to the house an' niver a bit to the man that's buckin'. The Devil himself'd niver tackle such a cinch."

There were chuckles, throttled in the conception, and winks brushed away with the frost which rimed the eyelashes, as the men climbed the ice-notched bank and started across the street to the Post. But the long howl had drawn nearer, invested with a new note of menace. A woman screamed round the corner. There was a cry of, "Here he comes!" Then an Indian boy, at the head of half a dozen frightened dogs, racing with death, dashed into the crowd. And behind came Yellow Fang, a bristle of hair and a flash of gray. Everybody but the Yankee fled. The Indian boy had tripped and fallen. Bettles stopped long enough to grip him by the slack of his furs, then headed for a pile of cordwood already occupied by a number of his comrades. Yellow Fang, doubling after one of the dogs, came leaping back. The fleeing animal, free of the rabies but crazed with fright, whipped Bettles off his feet and flashed on up the street. Malemute Kid took a flying shot at Yellow Fang. The mad dog whirled a half air spring, came down on his back, then, with a single leap, covered half the distance between himself and Bettles.

But the fatal spring was intercepted. Lon McFane leaped from the woodpile, encountering him in midair. Over they rolled, Lon holding him by the throat at arm's length, blinking under the fetid slaver which sprayed his face. Then Bettles, revolver in hand and coolly waiting a chance, settled the combat.

" 'Twas a square game, Kid," Lon remarkerd, rising to his feet and shaking the snow from out his sleeves, "with a fair percentage to meself that bucked 'it."

That night, while Lon McFane sought the forgiving arms of the Church in the direction of Father Roubeau's cabin, Malemute Kid and Scruff Mackenzie talked long to little purpose.

"But would you," persisted Mackenzie, "supposing they had fought?"

"Have I ever broken my word?"

"No; but that isn't the point. Answer the question. Would you?"

Malemute Kid straightened up. "Scruff, I've been asking myself that question ever since, and——"

"Well?"

"Well, as yet, I haven't been able to answer."

The Marriage of Lit-lit

When John Fox came into a country where whiskey freezes solid and may be used as a paperweight for a large part of the year, he came without the ideals and illusions which usually hamper the progress of more delicately nurtured adventurers. Born and reared on the frontier fringe of the United States, he took with him into Canada a primitive cast of mind, an elemental simplicity and grip on things, as it were, which insured him immediate success in his new career. From a mere servant of the Hudson's Bay Company, driving a paddle with the *voyageurs* and carrying goods on his back across the portages he swiftly rose to a Factorship and took charge of a trading post at Fort Angelus.

Here, because of his elemental simplicity, he took to himself a native wife, and by reason of the connubial bliss which followed he escaped the unrest and vain longings which curse the days of more fastidious men, spoil their work, and conquer them in the end. He lived contentedly, was at single purposes with the business he was set there to do, and achieved a brilliant record in the service of the Company. About this time his wife died, was claimed by her people, and buried with savage circumstance in a tin trunk in the top of a tree.

Two sons she had borne him, and when the Company promoted him he journeyed with them still deeper into the vastness of the Northwest Territory to a place called Sin Rock, where he took charge of a new post in a more important fur field. Here he spent several lonely and depressing months, eminently disgusted with the unprepossessing appearance of the Indian maidens, and greatly worried by his growing sons who stood in need of a mother's care. Then his eyes chanced upon Lit-lit.

"Lit-lit—well, she is Lit-lit," was the fashion in which he despairingly described her to his chief clerk, Alexander McLean.

McLean was too fresh from his Scottish upbringing—"not dry behind the ears yet," John Fox put it—to take to the marriage customs of the country. Nevertheless he was not averse to the Factor imperiling his own immortal soul, and, especially, feeling an ominous attraction himself for Lit-lit, he was somberly content to clinch his own soul's safety by seeing her married to the Factor.

Nor is it to be wondered at that McLean's austere Scots soul stood in danger of being thawed in the sunshine of Lit-lit's eyes. She was pretty, and slender, and willowy, without the massive face and temperamental stolidity of the average squaw. "Lit-lit," so called from her fashion, even as a child, of being fluttery, or darting about from place to place like a butterfly, of being inconsequent and merry, and of laughing as lightly as she darted and danced about.

Lit-lit was the daughter of Snettishane, a prominent

chief in the tribe, by a half-breed mother, and to him the Factor fared casually one summer day to open negotiations of marriage. He sat with the chief in the smoke of a mosquito smudge before his lodge, and together they talked about everything under the sun, or, at least, everything which in the Northland is under the sun, with the sole exception of marriage. John Fox had come particularly to talk of marriage; Snettishane knew it, and John Fox knew he knew it, wherefore the subject was religiously avoided. This is alleged to be Indian subtlety. In reality it is transparent simplicity.

Two hours slipped by, and Fox and Snettishane smoked interminable pipes, looking each other in the eyes with a guilelessness superbly histrionic. In the midafternoon McLean and his brother clerk, McTavish, strolled past, innocently uninterested, on their way to the river. When they strolled back again, an hour later, Fox and Snettishane had attained to a ceremonious discussion of the condition and quality of the gunpowder and bacon which the Company was offering in trade. Meanwhile Lit-lit, divining the Factor's errand, had crept in under the rear wall of the lodge and through the front flap was peeping out at the two logomachists by the mosquito smudge. She was flushed and happy-eyed, proud that no less a man than the Factor (who stood next to God in the Northland hierarchy) had singled her out, femininely curious to see at close range what manner of man he was. Sun glare on the ice, camp smoke, and weather beat had burned his face to a copper brown, so that her father was as fair as he while she was fairer. She was remotely glad of this, and more immediately glad that he was large and strong, though his great black beard half-frightened her, it was so strange.

Being very young, she was unversed in the ways of men. Seventeen times she had seen the sun travel south and lose itself beyond the sky line, and seventeen times she had seen it travel back again and ride the sky day and night till there was no night at all. And through these years she had been cherished jealously by Snettishane, who stood between her and all suitors, listening disdainfully to the young hunters as they bid for her hand, and turning them away as though she were beyond price. Snettishane was mercenary. Lit-lit was to him an investment. She represented so much capital, from which he expected to receive, not a certain definite interest, but an incalculable interest.

And having thus been reared in a manner as near to a nunnery as tribal conditions would permit, it was with a great and maidenly anxiety that she peeped out at the man who had surely come for her, at the husband who was to teach her all that was yet unlearned of life, at the masterful being whose word was to her law and who was to mete and bound her actions and comportment for the rest of her days.

But, peeping through the front flap of the lodge, flushed and thrilling at the strange destiny reaching out for her, she grew disappointed as the day wore along and the Factor and her father still talked pompously of things concerning other things and not connected with marriage things at all. As the sun sank lower and lower toward the north and midnight approached, the Factor began making unmistakable preparations of departure. As he turned to stride away Lit-lit's heart sank; but it rose again as he halted, half-turning on one heel.

"Oh, by the way, Snettishane," he said, "I want a squaw to wash for me and mend my clothes."

Snettishane grunted and suggested Wanidani, who was an old woman and toothless.

"No, no," interposed the Factor. "What I want is a wife. I've been kind of thinking about it, and the thought just struck me that you might know of someone that would suit."

Snettishane looked interested, whereupon the Factor retraced his steps, casually and carelessly to linger and discuss this new and incidental topic.

"Kattou?" suggested Snettishane.

"She has but one eye," objected the Factor.

"Laska?"

"Her knees be wide apart when she stands upright. Kips, your biggest dog, can leap between her knees when she stands upright."

"Senatee?" went on the imperturbable Snettishane.

But John Fox feigned anger, crying, "What foolishness be this? Am I old, that thou shouldst mate me with old women? Am I toothless? lame of leg? blind of eye? Or am I poor that no bright-eyed maiden may look with favor upon me? Behold! I am the Factor, both rich and great, a power in the land, whose speech makes men tremble and is obeyed!"

Snettishane was inwardly pleased, though his sphinx-like visage never relaxed. He was drawing the Factor, and making him break ground. Being a creature so elemental as to have room for but one idea at a time, Snettishane could pursue that one idea a greater distance than could John Fox. For John Fox, elemental as he was, was still complex enough to entertain several glimmering ideas at a time, which debarred him from pursuing the one as singleheartedly or as far as did the chief.

Snettishane calmly continued calling the roster of eligible maidens, which, name by name, as fast as uttered, were stamped ineligible by John Fox, with specified objections appended. Again he gave it up and started to return to the Fort. Snettishane watched him go, making no effort to stop him, but seeing him, in the end, stop himself.

"Come to think of it," the Factor remarked, "we both of us forgot Lit-lit. Now I wonder if she'll suit me?"

Snettishane met the suggestion with a mirthless face, behind the mask of which his soul grinned wide. It was a distinct victory. Had the Factor gone but one step farther, perforce Snettishane would himself have mentioned the name of Lit-lit, but—the Factor had not gone that one step farther.

The chief was noncommittal concerning Lit-lit's suitability, till he drove the white man into taking the next step in the order of procedure.

"Well," the Factor meditated aloud, "the only way to find out is to make a try of it." He raised his voice. "So I will give for Lit-lit ten blankets and three pounds of tobacco which is good tobacco."

Snettishane replied with a gesture which seemed to say that all the blankets and tobacco in all the world could not compensate him for the loss of Lit-lit and her manifold virtues. When pressed by the Factor to set a price, he coolly placed it at five hundred blankets, ten guns, fifty pounds of tobacco, twenty scarlet cloths, ten bottles of rum, a music box, and lastly, the good will and best offices of the Factor with a place by his fire.

The Factor apparently suffered a stroke of apoplexy, which stroke was successful in reducing the blankets to two hundred and in cutting out the place by the fire—an unheard of condition in the marriages of white men with the daughters of the soil. In the end, after three hours more of chaffering, they came to an agreement. For Lit-lit Snettishane was to receive one hundred blankets, five pounds of tobacco, three guns, and a bottle of rum, good will and best offices included, which, according to John Fox, was ten blankets and a gun more than she was worth. And as he went home through the "wee sma'" hours, the three o'clock sun blazing in the due northeast, he was unpleasantly aware that Snettishane had bested him over the bargain.

Snettishane, tired and victorious, sought his bed, and discovered Lit-lit before she could escape from the lodge.

He grunted knowingly, "Thou hast seen. Thou hast heard. Wherefore it be plain to thee thy father's very great wisdom and understanding. I have made for thee a great match. Heed my words and walk in the way of my words, go when I say go, come when I bid thee come, and we shall grow fat with the wealth of this big white man who is a fool according to his bigness."

The next day no trading was done at the store. The Factor opened whiskey before breakfast to the delight of McLean and McTavish, gave his dogs double rations, and wore his best moccasins. Outside the Fort preparations were under way for a *potlatch.* Potlatch means "a giving," and John Fox's intention was to signalize his marriage with Lit-lit by a potlatch as generous as she was good-looking. In the afternoon the whole tribe gathered to the feast. Men, women, children and dogs gorged to repletion, nor was there one person, even among the chance visitors and stray hunters from other tribes, who failed to receive some token of the bridegroom's largess.

Lit-lit, tearfully shy and frightened, was bedecked by her bearded husband with a new calico dress, splendidly beaded moccasins, a gorgeous silk handkerchief over her raven hair, a purple scarf about her throat, brass earrings and finger rings, and a whole pint of pinchbeck jewelry, including a Waterbury watch. Snettishane could scarce contain himself at the spectacle, but watching his chance drew her aside from the feast.

"Not this night, nor the next night," he began ponderously, "but in the nights to come when I shall call like a raven by the riverbank, it is for thee to rise up from thy big husband who is a fool and come to me.

"Nay, nay," he went on hastily, at sight of the dismay in her face at turning her back upon her wonderful new life. "For no sooner shall this happen, than thy big husband who is a fool will come wailing to my lodge. Then it is for thee to wail likewise, claiming that this thing is not well, and that the other thing thou dost not like, and that to be the wife of the Factor is more than thou didst bargain for, only wilt thou be content with more blankets, and more tobacco, and more wealth of various sorts for thy poor old father Snettishane. Remember well, when I call in the night, like a raven, from the riverbank."

Lit-lit nodded; for to disobey her father was a peril she knew of well; and furthermore, it was a little thing he asked, a short separation from the Factor, who would know only greater gladness at having her back. She returned to the feast, and, midnight being well at hand, the Factor sought her out and led her away to the Fort amid joking and outcry in which the squaws were especially conspicuous.

Lit-lit quickly found that married life with the head man of a fort was even better than she had dreamed. No longer did she have to fetch wood and water and wait hand and foot upon cantankerous menfolk. For the first time in her life she could lie abed till breakfast was on the table. And what a bed!—clean and soft, and comfortable as no bed she had ever known. And such food! Flour, cooked into biscuits, hot cakes, and bread, three times a day and every day and all one wanted! Such prodigality was hardly believable.

To add to her contentment, the Factor was cunningly kind. He had buried one wife, and he knew how to drive with a slack rein which went firm only on occasion, and then went very firm. "Lit-lit is boss of this ranch," he announced significantly at the table the morning after the wedding. "What she says, goes. Understand?" And McLean and McTavish understood. Also, they knew that the Factor had a heavy hand.

But Lit-lit did not take advantage. Taking a leaf from the book of her husband, she at once assumed charge of his two growing sons, giving them added comforts and a measure of freedom like to that which he gave her. The two sons were loud in the praise of their new mother; McLean and McTavish lifted their voices, and the Factor bragged of the joys of matrimony, till the story of her good behavior and her husband's satisfaction became the property of all the dwellers in the Sin Rock district.

Whereupon Snettishane, with visions of his incalculable interest keeping him awake of nights, thought it time to bestir himself. On the tenth night of her wedded life Lit-lit was awakened by the croaking of a raven, and she knew that Snettishane was waiting for her by the river bank. In her great happiness she had forgotten her pact, and now it came back to her with behind it all the childish terror of her father. For a time she lay in fear and trembling, loth to go, afraid to stay. But in the end the Factor won the silent victory, and his kindness, plus his great muscles and square jaw, nerved her to disregard Snettishane's call.

But in the morning she arose very much afraid, and went about her duties in momentary fear of her father's coming. As the day wore along, however, she began to recover her spirits. John Fox, soundly berating McLean and McTavish for some petty dereliction of duty, helped her to pluck up courage. She tried not to let him go out of her sight, and when she followed him into the huge cache and saw him twirling and tossing great bales around as though they were feather pillows, she felt strengthened in her disobedience to her father. Also (it was her first visit to the warehouse, and Sin Rock was the chief distributing point to several chains of lesser posts), she was astounded at the endlessness of the wealth there stored away.

This sight, and the picture in her mind's eye of the bare lodge of Snettishane, put all doubts at rest. Yet she capped her conviction by a brief word with one of her stepsons. "White daddy good?" was what she asked, and the boy answered that his father was the best man he had ever known. That night the raven croaked again. On the night following, the croaking was more persistent. It awoke the Factor, who tossed restlessly for a while. Then he said aloud, "Damn that raven," and Lit-lit laughed quietly under the blankets.

In the morning, bright and early, Snettishane put in an ominous appearance, and was set to breakfast in the kitchen with Wanidani. He refused "squaw food," and a little later bearded his son-in-law in the store where the trading was done. Having learned, he said, that his daughter was such a jewel, he had come for more blankets, more tobacco and more guns, especially more guns. He had certainly been cheated in her price, he held, and he had come for justice. But the Factor had neither blankets nor justice to spare. Whereupon he was informed that Snettishane had seen the missionary at Three Forks, who had notified him that such marriages were not made in heaven and that it was his father's duty to demand his daughter back.

"I am good Christian man now," Snettishane concluded. "I want my Lit-lit to go to heaven."

The Factor's reply was short and to the point; for he

directed his father-in-law to go to the heavenly antipodes, and by the scruff of the neck and the slack of the blanket propelled him on that trail as far as the door.

But Snettishane sneaked around and in by the kitchen, cornering Lit-lit in the great living room of the Fort.

"Mayhap thou didst sleep oversound last night when I called by the riverbank," he began glowering darkly.

"Nay, I was awake and heard." Her heart was beating as though it would choke her, but she went on steadily: "And the night before I was awake and heard, and yet again the night before."

And thereat, out of her great happiness and out of the fear that it might be taken from her, she launched into an original and glowing address upon the status and rights of women—the first new-woman lecture delivered north of Fifty-three.

But it fell on unheeding ears. Snettishane was still in the dark ages. As she paused for breath he said threateningly: "Tonight I shall call again like the raven."

At this moment the Factor entered the room and again helped Snettishane on his way to the heavenly antipodes.

That night the raven croaked more persistently than ever. Lit-lit, who was a light sleeper, heard and smiled. John Fox tossed restlessly. Then he awoke and tossed about with greater restlessness. He grumbled and snorted, swore under his breath and over his breath, and finally flung out of bed. He groped his way to the great living room and from the rack took down a loaded shotgun—loaded with birdshot, left therein by the careless McTavish.

The Factor crept carefully out of the Fort and down

to the river. The croaking had ceased, but he stretched out in the long grass and waited. The air seemed a chilly balm and the earth, after the heat of the day, now and again breathed soothfully against him. The Factor, gathered into the rhythm of it all, dozed off with his head upon his arm and slept.

Fifty yards away, head resting on knees and with his back to John Fox, Snettishane likewise slept, gently conquered by the quietude of the night. An hour slipped by and then he awoke and, without lifting his head, set the night vibrating with the hoarse gutterals of the raven call.

The Factor roused, not with the abrupt start of civilized man, but with the swift and comprehensive glide from sleep to waking of the savage. In the night light he made out a dark object in the midst of the grass and brought his gun to bear upon it. A second croak began to rise and he pulled the trigger. The crickets ceased from their sing-song chant, the wild fowl from their squabbling, and the raven croak broke midmost and died away in gasping silence.

John Fox ran to the spot and reached for the thing he had killed, but his fingers closed on a coarse mop of hair and he turned Snettishane's face upward to the starlight. He knew how a shotgun scattered at fifty yards, and he knew that he had peppered Snettishane across the shoulders and in the small of the back. And Snettishane knew that he knew, but neither referred to it.

"What dost thou here?" the Factor demanded. "It were time old bones should be in bed."

But Snettishane was stately in spite of the birdshot tingling under his skin.

"Old bones will not sleep," he said solemnly. "I weep for my daughter, for my daughter Lit-lit, who liveth and who yet is dead, and who goeth without doubt to the white man's hell."

"Weep henceforth on the far bank, beyond earshot of the Fort," said John Fox turning on his heel, "for the noise of thy weeping is exceeding great and will not let one sleep of nights."

"My heart is sore," Snettishane answered, "and my days and nights be black with sorrow."

"As the raven is black," said John Fox.

"As the raven is black," Snettishane said.

Never again was the voice of the raven heard by the river bank. Lit-lit grows matronly day by day and is very happy. Also, there are sisters to the sons of John Fox's first wife who lies buried in a tree. Old Snettishane is no longer a visitor at the Fort, and spends long hours raising a thin, aged voice against the filial ingratitude of children in general and of his daughter Lit-lit in particular. His declining years are embittered by the knowledge that he was cheated, and even John Fox has withdrawn the assertion that the price for Lit-lit was too much by ten blankets and a gun.

The Leopard Man's Story

He had a dreamy, faraway look in his eyes, and his sad, insistent voice, gentle spoken as a maid's, seemed the placid embodiment of some deep-seated melancholy. He was the Leopard Man, but he did not look it. His business in life, whereby he lived, was to appear in a cage of performing leopards before vast audiences, and to thrill those audiences by certain exhibitions of nerve for which his employers rewarded him on a scale commensurate with the thrills he produced.

As I say, he did not look it. He was narrow-hipped, narrow-shouldered and anaemic, while he seemed not so much oppressed by gloom as by a sweet and gentle sadness, the weight of which was as sweetly and gently borne. For an hour I had been trying to get a story out of him, but he appeared to lack imagination. To him there was no romance in his gorgeous career, no deeds of daring, no thrills—nothing but a gray sameness and infinite boredom.

Lions? Oh, yes! he had fought with them. It was nothing. All you had to do was to stay sober. Anybody could whip a lion to a standstill with an ordinary stick. He had fought one for half an hour once. Just hit him on the nose every time he rushed, and when he got artful and rushed with his head down, why, the thing to do was to stick out your leg. When he grabbed at the leg you drew it back and hit him on the nose again. That was all.

With the faraway look in his eyes and his soft flow of words he showed me his scars. There were many of them, and one recent one where a tigress had reached for his shoulder and gone down to the bone. I could see the neatly mended rents in the coat he had on. His right arm, from the elbow down, looked as though it had gone through a threshing machine, what of the ravage wrought by claws and fangs. But it was nothing, he said, only the old wounds bothered him somewhat when rainy weather came on.

Suddenly his face brightened with a recollection, for he was really as anxious to give me a story as I was to get it.

"I suppose you've heard of the lion tamer who was hated by another man?" he asked.

He paused and looked pensively at a sick lion in the cage opposite.

"Got the toothache," he explained. "Well, the lion tamer's big play to the audience was putting his head in a lion's mouth. The man who hated him attended every performance in the hope sometime of seeing that lion crunch down. He followed the show about all over the country. The years went by and he grew old, and the lion tamer grew old, and the lion grew old. And at last one day, sitting in a front seat, he saw what he had waited for. The lion crunched down, and there wasn't any need to call a doctor."

The Leopard Man glanced casually over his fingernails in a manner which would have been critical had it not been so sad.

"Now that's what I call patience," he continued, "and it's my style. But it was not the style of a fellow I knew. He was a little, thin, sawed-off, sword-swallowing and juggling Frenchman. De Ville he called himself, and he had a nice wife. She did trapeze work and used to dive from under the roof into a net, turning over once on the way as nice as you please.

"De Ville had a quick temper, as quick as his hand, and his hand was as quick as the paw of a tiger. One day, because the ringmaster called him a frogeater, or something like that and maybe a little worse, he shoved him against the soft pine background he used in his knife-throwing act so quick the ringmaster didn't have time to think, and there, before the audience, De Ville kept the air on fire with his knives, sinking them into the wood all around the ringmaster so close that they passed through his clothes and most of them bit into his skin.

"The clowns had to pull the knives out to get him loose, for he was pinned fast. So the word went around to watch out for De Ville, and no one dared be more than barely civil to his wife. And she was a sly bit of baggage, too, only all hands were afraid of De Ville.

"But there was one man, Wallace, who was afraid of nothing. He was the lion tamer, and he had the self-same trick of putting his head into the lion's mouth. He'd put it into the mouths of any of them, though he preferred

Augustus, a big good-natured beast who could always be depended upon.

"As I was saying, Wallace—'King' Wallace we called him—was afraid of nothing alive or dead. He was a king and no mistake. I've seen him drunk, and on a wager go into the cage of a lion that'd turned nasty and without a stick beat him to a finish. Just did it with his fist on the nose.

"Madame De Ville—"

At an uproar behind us the Leopard Man turned quietly around. It was a divided cage, and a monkey, poking through the bars and around the partition, had had its paw seized by a big gray wolf who was trying to pull it off by main strength. The arm seemed stretching out longer and longer like a thick elastic, and the unfortunate monkey's mates were raising a terrible din. No keeper was at hand, so the Leopard Man stepped over a couple of paces, dealt the wolf a sharp blow on the nose with the light cane he carried, and returned with a sadly apologetic smile to take up his unfinished sentence as though there had been no interruption.

"—looked at King Wallace and King Wallace looked at her, while De Ville looked black. We warned Wallace, but it was no use. He laughed as us, as he laughed at De Ville one day when he shoved De Ville's head into a bucket of paste because he wanted to fight.

"De Ville was in a pretty mess—I helped to scrape him off; but he was cool as a cucumber and made no threats at all. But I saw a glitter in his eyes which I had seen often in the eyes of wild beasts, and I went out of my way to give Wallace a final warning. He laughed, but he did not look so much in Madame De Ville's direction after that.

"Several months passed by. Nothing had happened and I was beginning to think it all a scare over nothing. We were West by that time, showing in 'Frisco. It was during the afternoon performance, and the big tent was filled with women and children, when I went looking for Red Denny, the head canvasman, who had walked off with my pocketknife.

"Passing by one of the dressing tents I glanced in through a hole in the canvas to see if I could locate him. He wasn't there, but directly in front of me was King Wallace, in tights, waiting for his turn to go on with his cage of performing lions. He was watching with much amusement a quarrel between a couple of trapeze artists. All the rest of the people in the dressing tent were watching the same thing, with the exception of De Ville, whom I noticed staring at Wallace with undisguised hatred. Wallace and the rest were all too busy following the quarrel to notice this or what followed.

"But I saw it through the hole in the canvas. De Ville drew his handkerchief from his pocket, made as though to mop the sweat from his face with it (it was a hot day), and at the same time walked past Wallace's back. He never stopped, but kept right on to the doorway, where he turned his head, while passing out, and shot a swift look back at the unconscious man. The look troubled me at the time, for not only did I see hatred in it, but I saw triumph as well.

" 'De Ville will bear watching,' I said to myself, and I really breathed easier when I saw him go out the entrance to the circus grounds and board an electric car for downtown. A few minutes later I was in the big tent, where I had overhauled Red Denny. King Wallace was doing his turn and holding the audience spellbound. He was in a particularly vicious mood, and he kept the lions stirred up till they were all snarling and growling around him, that is, all of them except Augustus, and he was just too fat and lazy and old to get stirred up over anything.

"Finally Wallace cracked the old lion's knees with his whip and got him into position. Old Augustus, blinking good-naturedly, opened his mouth and in popped Wallace's head. Then the jaws came together, *crunch,* just like that."

The Leopard Man smiled in a sweetly wistful fashion, and the faraway look came into his eyes.

"And that was the end of King Wallace," he went on in his sad, low voice. "After the excitement cooled down I watched my chance and bent over and smelled Wallace's head. Then I sneezed."

"It . . . it was . . . ?" I queried with halting eagerness.

"Snuff—that De Ville dropped on his hair in the dressing tent. Old Augustus never meant to do it. He only sneezed."

AN IMPRESSION:

Gold Hunters of the North

THE AUTHOR'S SPECIAL REPORT ON ALASKA AND THE GOLD STRIKE

About Jack London

Gold Hunters of the North

"Where the Northern Lights come down o'
nights to dance on the houseless snow."

"Ivan, I forbid you to go farther in this undertaking. Not a word about this, or we are all undone. Let the Americans and the English know that we have gold in these mountains, then we are ruined. They will rush in on us by thousands, and crowd us to the wall—to the death."

So spoke the old Russian governor, Baranov, at Sitka, in 1804, to one of his Slavonian hunters, who had just drawn from his pocket a handful of golden nuggets. Full well Baranov, fur trader and autocrat, understood and feared the coming of the sturdy, indomitable gold hunters of Anglo-Saxon stock. And thus he suppressed the news, as did the governors that followed him, so that when the United States bought Alaska in 1867, she bought it for its furs and fisheries, without a thought of its treasures underground.

No sooner, however, had Alaska become American soil

than thousands of our adventurers were afoot and afloat for the North. They were the men of "the days of gold," the men of California, Fraser, Cassiar, and Cariboo. With the mysterious, infinite faith of the prospector, they believed that the gold streak, which ran through the Americas from Cape Horn to California, did not "peter out" in British Columbia. That it extended farther north, was their creed, and "Farther North!" became their cry. No time was lost, and in the early seventies, leaving the Treadwell and the Silver Bow Basin to be discovered by those who came after, they went plunging on into the white unknown. North, farther north, till their picks rang in the frozen beaches of the Arctic Ocean, and they shivered by driftwood fires on the ruby sands of Nome.

But first, in order that this colossal adventure may be fully grasped, the recentness and the remoteness of Alaska must be emphasized. The interior of Alaska and the contiguous Canadian territory was a vast wilderness. Its hundreds of thousands of square miles were as dark and chartless as Darkest Africa. In 1847, when the first Hudson's Bay Company agents crossed over the Rockies from the Mackenzie to poach on the preserves of the Russian Bear, they thought that the Yukon flowed north and emptied into the Arctic Ocean. Hundreds of miles below, however, were the outposts of the Russian traders. They, in turn, did not know where the Yukon had its source, and it was not till later that Russ and Saxon learned that it was the same mighty stream they were occupying. In 1850, Lieutenant Barnard, of the English navy, in search of Sir John Franklin, was killed in a massacre of Russians at Nulato, on the Lower Yukon. And a little over ten years later, Frederick

Whymper voyaged up the Great Bend to Fort Yukon under the Arctic Circle.

From fort to fort, from York Factory on Hudson's Bay to Fort Yukon in Alaska, the English traders transported their goods — a round trip requiring from a year to a year and a half. It was one of their deserters, in 1867, escaping down the Yukon to Bering Sea, who was the first white man to make the Northwest Passage by land from the Atlantic to the Pacific. It was at this time that the first accurate description of a fair portion of the Yukon was given by Dr. W. H. Ball, of the Smithsonian Institution. But even he had never seen its source, and it was not given him to appreciate the marvel of that great natural highway.

No more remarkable river in this one particular is there in the world — taking its rise in Crater Lake, thirty miles from the ocean, the Yukon flows for twenty-five-hundred miles, through the heart of the continent, ere it empties into the sea. A portage of thirty miles, and then a highway for traffic one tenth the girth of the earth!

As late as 1869, Frederick Whymper, fellow of the Royal Geographical Society, stated on hearsay, that the Chilcat Indians were believed occasionally to make a short portage across the Coast Range from salt water to the headreaches of the Yukon. But it remained for a gold hunter, questing north, ever north, to be first of all white men to cross the terrible Chilcoot Pass, and tap the Yukon at its head. This happened only the other day, but the man has become a dim legendary hero. Holt was his name, and already the mists of antiquity have wrapped about the time of his passage. 1872, 1874, and 1878 are the dates variously given — a confusion which time will never clear.

Holt penetrated as far as the Hootalinqua, and on his return to the coast reported coarse gold. The next recorded adventurer is one Edward Bean, who in 1880 headed a party of twenty-five miners from Sitka into the uncharted land. And in the same year, other parties (now forgotten, for who remembers or ever hears the wanderings of the gold hunters?) crossed the Pass, built boats out of the standing timber, and drifted down the Yukon and farther north.

And then, for a quarter of a century, the unknown and unsung heroes grappled with the frost, and groped for the gold they were sure lay somewhere among the shadows of the Pole. In the struggle with the terrifying and pitiless natural forces, they returned to the primitive, garmenting themselves in the skins of wild beasts, and covering their feet with the walrus *mucluc* and the moose-hide moccasin. They forgot the world and its ways, as the world had forgotten them; killed their meat as they found it; feasted in plenty and starved in famine, and searched unceasingly for the yellow lure. They crisscrossed the land in every direction, threaded countless unmapped rivers in precarious birch-bark canoes, and with snowshoes and dogs broke trail through thousands of miles of silent white, where man had never been. They struggled on, under the aurora borealis or the midnight sun, through temperatures that ranged from one hundred degrees above zero to eighty degrees below, living in the grim humor of the land, on "rabbit tracks and salmon bellies."

Today, a man may wander away from the trail for a hundred days, and just as he is congratulating himself that at last he is treading virgin soil, he will come upon some ancient and dilapidated cabin, and forget his disappointment in wonder at the man who reared the logs. Still, if one wanders from the trail far enough and deviously enough, he may chance upon a few thousand square miles which he may have all to himself. On the other hand, no matter how far and how deviously he may wander, the possibility always remains that he may stumble, not alone upon a deserted cabin, but upon an occupied one.

As an instance of this, and of the vastness of the land, no better case need be cited than that of Harry Maxwell. An able seaman, hailing from New Bedford, Massachusetts, his ship, the brig *Fannie E. Lee*, was pinched in the Arctic ice. Passing from whaleship to whaleship, he eventually turned up at Point Barrow in the summer of 1880. He was *north* of the Northland, and from this point of vantage he determined to pull south into the interior in search of gold. Across the mountains from Fort Macpherson, and a couple of hundred miles eastward from the Mackenzie, he built a cabin and established his headquarters. And here, for nineteen continuous years, he hunted his living and prospected. He ranged from the never-opening ice to the north as far south as the Great Slave Lake. Here he met Warburton Pike, the author and explorer — an incident he now looks back upon as chief among the few incidents of his solitary life.

When this sailor-miner had accumulated $20,000 worth of dust he concluded that civilization was good enough for him, and proceeded "to pull for the outside." From the Mackenzie he went up the Little Peel to its headwaters, found a pass through the mountains, nearly starved to death on his way across to the Porcupine Hills, and eventually came out on the Yukon River, where he learned for the first time of the Yukon gold hunters and their discoveries. Yet for twenty years they had been working there, his next-door neighbors, virtually, in a land of such great spaces. At Victoria, British Columbia, just previous to going east over the Canadian Pacific (the existence of which he had just learned), he pregnantly remarked that he had faith in the Mackenzie watershed, and that he was going back after he had taken in the World's Fair, and got a whiff or two of civilization.

Faith! It may or may not remove mountains, but it has certainly made the Northland. No Christian martyr ever possessed greater faith than did the pioneers of Alaska. They never doubted the bleak and barren land. Those who came remained, and more ever came. They could not leave. They "knew" the gold was there, and they persisted. Somehow, the romance of the land and the quest entered into their blood, the spell of it gripped hold of them and would not let them go. Man after man of them, after the most terrible privation and suffering, shook the muck of the country from his moccasins and departed for good. But the following spring always found him drifting down the Yukon on the tail of the ice jams.

Jack McQuestion aptly vindicates the grip of the North. After a residence of thirty years he insists that the climate is delightful, and declares that whenever he makes a trip to the States he is afflicted with homesickness. Needless to say, the North still has him and will keep tight hold of him until he dies. In fact, for him to die elsewhere would be inartistic and insincere. Of three of the "pioneer" pioneers, Jack McQuestion alone survives. In 1871, from one to seven years before Holt went over Chilcoot, in the company of Al Mayo and Arthur Harper, McQuestion came into the Yukon from the Northwest over the Hudson's Bay Company route from the Mackenzie to Fort Yukon. The names of these three men, as their lives, are bound up in the history of the country, and so long as there be histories and charts, that long will the Mayo and McQuestion rivers and the Harper and Ladue town site of Dawson be remembered. As an agent of the Alaska Commercial Company, in 1873, McQuestion built Fort Reliance, six miles below the Klondike River. In 1898 the writer met Jack McQuestion at Minook, on the Lower Yukon. The old pioneer, though grizzled, was hale and hearty, and as optimistic as when he first journeyed into the land along the path of the Circle. And no man more beloved is there in all the North. There will be great sadness there when his soul goes questing over the Last Divide —"farther north," perhaps — who can tell?

Frank Dinsmore is a fair sample of the men who made the Yukon Country. A Yankee, born in Auburn, Maine, the wanderlust early laid him by the heels, and at sixteen he was heading west on the trail that led "farther north." He prospected in the Black Hills, Montana, and in the Coeur d'Alene, then heard the whisper of the North, and went up to Juneau on the Alaskan Panhandle. But the North still whispered, and more insistently, and he could not rest till he went over Chilcoot, and down into the mysterious Silent Land. This was in 1882, and he went down the chain of lakes, down the Yukon, up the Pelly, and tried his luck on the bars of McMillan River. In the fall, a perambulating skeleton, he came back over the Pass in a blizzard, with a rag of a shirt, tattered overalls, and a handful of raw flour.

But he was unafraid. That winter he worked for a grubstake in Juneau, and the next spring found the heels of his moccasins turned toward salt water and his face toward Chilcoot. This was repeated the next spring, and the following spring, and the spring after that, until, in 1885, he went over the Pass for good. There was to be no return for him until he found the gold he sought.

The years came and went, but he remained true to his resolve. For eleven long years, with snowshoe and canoe, pickax and gold pan, he wrote out his life on the face of the land. Upper Yukon, Middle Yukon, Lower Yukon — he prospected faithfully and well. His bed was anywhere. The sky was his coverlet. Winter or summer he carried neither tent nor stove, and his six-pound sleeping robe of arctic hare was the warmest thing he was ever known to possess. Rabbit tracks and salmon bellies were his diet with a vengeance, for he depended largely on his rifle and fishing tackle. His endurance equaled his courage. On a wager he lifted thirteen fifty-pound sacks of flour and walked off with them. Winding up a seven-hundred-mile trip on the ice with a forty-mile run, he came into camp at six o'clock in the evening and found a "squaw dance" under way. He should have been exhausted. Anyway, his *muclucs* were frozen stiff. But he kicked them off and danced all night in stocking feet.

At the last fortune came to him. The quest was ended, and he gathered up his gold and pulled for the outside.

And his own end was as fitting as that of his quest. Illness came upon him down in San Francisco, and his splendid life ebbed slowly out as he sat in his big easy chair, in the Commercial Hotel, the "Yukoner's home." The doctors came, discussed, consulted, the while he matured more plans of Northland adventure; for the North still gripped him and would not let him go. He grew weaker day by day, but each day he said, "Tomorrow I'll be all right." Other old-timers, "out on furlough," came to see him. They wiped their eyes and swore under their breaths, then entered and talked largely and jovially about going in with him over the trail when spring came. But there in the big easy chair it was that his Long Trail ended, and the life passed out of him still fixed on "farther north."

From the time of the first white man, famine loomed black and gloomy over the land. It was chronic with the Indians and Eskimos; it became chronic with the gold hunters. It was ever present, and so it came about that life was commonly expressed in terms of "grub"—was measured by cups of flour. Each winter, eight months long, the heroes of the frost faced starvation. It became the custom, as fall drew on, for partners to cut the cards or draw straws to determine which should hit the hazardous trail for salt water, and which should remain and endure the hazardous darkness of the arctic night.

There was never food enough to winter the whole population. The A. C. Company worked hard to freight up the grub, but the gold hunters came faster and dared more audaciously. When the A. C. Company added a new sternwheeler to its fleet, men said, "Now we shall have plenty." But more gold hunters poured in over the passes to the

South, more *voyageurs* and fur traders forced a way through the Rockies from the East, more seal hunters and coast adventurers poled up from Bering Sea on the West, more sailors deserted from the whaleships to the North, and they all starved together in right brotherly fashion. More steamers were added, but the tide of prospectors welled always in advance. Then the N. A. T. & T. Company came up the scene, and both companies added steadily to their fleets. But it was the same old story; famine would not depart. In fact, famine grew with the population, till, in the winter of 1897-98, the United States government was forced to equip a reindeer relief expedition. As of old, the winter partners cut the cards and drew straws, and remained or pulled for salt water as chance decided. They were wise of old time, and had learned never to figure on relief expeditions. They had heard of such things, but no mortal man of them had ever laid eyes on one.

The hard luck of other mining countries pales into insignificance before the hard luck of the North. And as for the hardship, it cannot be conveyed by printed page or word of mouth. No man may know who has not undergone. And those who have undergone, out of their knowledge claim that in the making of the world God grew tired, and when he came to the last barrowload, "just dumped it anyhow," and that was how Alaska happened to be. While no adequate conception of the life can be given to the stay-at-home, yet the men themselves sometimes give a clue to its rigors. One old Minook miner testified thus: "Haven't you noticed the expression on the faces of us fellows? You can tell a newcomer the minute you see him; he looks alive, enthusiastic, perhaps jolly. We old miners are always grave, unless we're drinking."

Another old-timer, out of the bitterness of a "home mood," imagined himself a Martian astronomer explaining to a friend, with the aid of a powerful telescope, the institutions of the earth. "There are the continents," he indicated, "and up there near the polar cap is a country, frigid and burning and lonely and apart, called Alaska. Now in other countries and states there are great insane asylums, but, though crowded, they are insufficient; so there is Alaska given over to the worst cases. Now and then some poor insane creature comes to his senses in those awful solitudes, and, in wondering joy, escapes from the land and hastens back to his home. But most cases are incurable. They just suffer along, poor devils, forgetting their former life quite, or recalling it like a dream."—Again the grip of the North, which will not let one go—for "*most cases are incurable.*"

For a quarter of a century the battle with frost and famine went on. The very severity of the struggle with Nature seemed to make the gold hunters kindly toward one another. The latchstring was always out, and the open hand was the order of the day. Distrust was unknown, and it was no hyperbole for a man to take the last shirt off his back for a comrade. Most significant of all, perhaps, in this connection, was the custom of the old days, that when August the first came around, the prospectors who had failed to locate "pay dirt" were permitted to go upon the ground of their more fortunate comrades and take out enough for the next year's grubstake.

In 1885 rich bar washing was done on the Stewart

River, and in 1886 Cassiar Bar was struck just below the mouth of the Hootalinqua. It was at this time that the first moderate strike was made on Forty-Mile Creek, so called because it was judged to be that distance below Fort Reliance of Jack McQuestion fame. A prospector named Williams started for the outside with dogs and Indians to carry the news, but suffered such hardship on the summit of Chilcoot that he was carried dying into the store of Captain John Healy at Dyea. But he had brought the news through—*coarse gold!* Inside three months more than two hundred miners had passed in over Chilcoot, stampeding for Forty Mile. Find followed find — Sixty Mile, Miller, Glacier, Birch, Franklin, and the Koyokuk. But they were all moderate discoveries, and the miners still dreamed and searched for the fabled stream, "Too Much Gold," where gold was so plentiful that gravel had to be shoveled into the sluice boxes in order to wash it.

And all the time the Northland was preparing to play its own huge joke. It was a great joke, albeit an exceeding bitter one, and it has led the old-timers to believe that the land is left in darkness the better part of the year because God goes away and leaves it to itself. After all the risk and toil and faithful endeavor, it was destined that few of the heroes should be in at the finish when Too Much Gold turned its yellow belly to the stars.

First, there was Robert Henderson — and this is true history. Henderson had faith in the Indian River district. For three years, by himself, depending mainly on his rifle, living on straight meat a large portion of the time, he prospected many of the Indian River tributaries, just missed finding the rich creeks, Sulphur and Dominion, and managed to make grub (poor grub) out of Quartz Creek and Australia Creek. Then he crossed the divide between Indian River and the Klondike, and on one of the "feeders" of the latter found eight cents to the pan. This was considered excellent in those simple days. Naming the creek "Gold Bottom," he recrossed the divide and got three men, Munson, Dalton, and Swanson, to return with him. The four took out $750. And be it emphasized, and emphasized again, *that this was the first Klondike gold ever shoveled in and washed out.* And be it also emphasized, *that Robert Henderson was the discoverer of Klondike, all lies and hearsay tales to the contrary.*

Running out of grub, Henderson again recrossed the divide, and went down the Indian River and up the Yukon to Sixty Mile. Here Joe Ladue ran the trading post, and here Joe Ladue had originally grubstaked Henderson. Henderson told his tale, and a dozen men (all it contained) deserted the Post for the scene of his find. Also, Henderson persuaded a party of prospectors, bound for Stewart River, to forego their trip and go down and locate with him. He loaded his boat with supplies, drifted down the Yukon to the mouth of the Klondike, and towed and poled up the Klondike to Gold Bottom. But at the mouth of the Klondike he met George Carmack, and thereby hangs the tale.

Carmack was a squaw man. He was familiarly known as "Siwash" George — a derogatory term which had arisen out of his affinity for the Indians. At the time Henderson encountered him he was catching salmon with his Indian wife and relatives on the site of what was to become Dawson, the Golden City of the Snows. Henderson, bubbling over with good will and prone to the open hand, told Carmack of his discovery. But Carmack was satisfied where he was. He was possessed by no overweening desire for the strenuous life. Salmon were good enough for him. But Henderson urged him to come on and locate, until, when he yielded, he wanted to take the whole tribe along. Henderson refused to stand for this, said that he must give the preference over Siwashes to his old Sixty Mile friends, and it is rumored, said some things about Siwashes that were not nice.

The next morning Henderson went on alone up the Klondike to Gold Bottom. Carmack, by this time aroused, took a short cut afoot for the same place. Accompanied by his two Indian brothers-in-law, Skookum Jim and Tagish Charley, he went up Rabbit Creek (now Bonanza), crossed into Gold Bottom, and staked near Henderson's discovery. On the way up he had panned a few shovels on Rabbit Creek, and he showed Henderson "colors" he had obtained. Henderson made him promise, if he found anything on the way back, that he would send up one of the Indians with the news. Henderson also agreed to pay for this service, for he seemed to feel that they were on the verge of something big, and he wanted to make sure.

Carmack returned down Rabbit Creek. While he was taking a sleep on the bank about half a mile below the mouth of what was to be known as Eldorado, Skookum Jim tried his luck, and from surface prospects got from ten cents to a dollar to the pan. Carmack and his brothers-in-law staked and "hit the high places" for Forty Mile, where they filed on the claims before Captain Constantine, and renamed the creek Bonanza. And Henderson was forgotten. No word of it reached him. Carmack broke his promise.

Weeks afterward, when Bonanza and Eldorado were staked from end to end and there was no more room, a party of later comers pushed over the divide and down to Gold Bottom, where they found Henderson still at work. When they told him they were from Bonanza, he was nonplused. He had never heard of such a place. But when they described it, he recognized it as Rabbit Creek. Then they told him of its marvelous richness, and, as Tappan Adney relates, when Henderson realized what he had lost through Carmack's treachery, "he threw down his shovel and went and sat on the bank, so sick at heart that it was some time before he could speak."

Then there were the rest of the old-timers, the men of Forty Mile and Circle City. At the time of the discovery, nearly all of them were over to the West at work in the old diggings or prospecting for new ones. As they said of themselves, they were the kind of men who are always caught out with forks when it rains soup. In the stampede that followed the news of Carmack's strike very few old miners took part. They were not there to take part. But the men who did go on the stampede were mainly the worthless ones, the newcomers, and the camp hangers-on. And while Bob Henderson plugged away to the East, and the heroes plugged away to the West, the greenhorns and rounders went up and staked Bonanza.

But the Northland was not yet done with its joke. When fall came on and the heroes returned to Forty Mile and to Circle City, they listened calmly to the up-river tales of Siwash discoveries and loafers' prospects, and shook their heads. They judged by the caliber of the men interested, and branded it a bunco game. But glowing reports continued to trickle down the Yukon, and a few of the old-timers went up to see. They looked over the ground — the unlikeliest place for gold in all their experience — and they went down the river again, "leaving it to the Swedes."

Again the Northland turned the tables. The Alaskan gold hunter is proverbial, not so much for his unveracity, as for his inability to tell the precise truth. In a country of exaggerations, he likewise is prone to hyperbolic description of things actual. But when it came to Klondike, he could not stretch the truth as fast as the truth itself stretched. Carmack first got a dollar pan. He lied when he said it was two dollars and a half. And when those who doubted him did get two-and-a-half pans, they said they were getting an ounce, and lo! ere the lie had fairly started on its way, they were getting, not one ounce but five ounces. This they claimed was six ounces; but when they filled a pan of dirt to prove the lie, they washed out twelve ounces. And so it went. They continued valiantly to lie, but the truth continued to outrun them.

But the Northland's hyperborean laugh was not yet ended. When Bonanza was staked from mouth to source, those who had failed "to get in," disgruntled and sore, went up the "pups" and feeders. Eldorado was one of these feeders, and many men, after locating on it, turned their backs upon their claims and never gave them a second thought. One man sold a half-interest in five hundred feet of it for a sack of flour. Other owners wandered around trying to bunco men into buying them out for a song.

And then Eldorado "showed up." It was far, far richer than Bonanza, with an average value of a thousand dollars a foot to every foot of it.

A Swede named Charley Anderson had been at work on Miller Creek the year of the strike, and arrived in Dawson with a few hundred dollars. Two miners who had staked No. 29 Eldorado, decided that he was the proper man upon whom to "unload." He was too canny to approach sober, so at considerable expense they got him drunk. Even then it was hard work, but they kept him befuddled for several days, and finally inveigled him into buying No. 29 for $750. When Anderson sobered up, he wept at his folly, and pleaded to have his money back. But the men who had duped him were hardhearted. They laughed at him, and kicked at themselves for not having tapped him for a couple of hundred more. Nothing remained for Anderson but to work the worthless ground. This he did, and out of it he took over three quarters of a million of dollars.

It was not till Frank Dinsmore, who already had big holdings on Birch Creek, took a hand, that the old-timers developed faith in the new diggings. Dinsmore received a letter from a man on the spot, calling it "the biggest thing in the world," and harnessed his dogs and went up to investigate. And when he sent a letter back saying that he had "never seen anything like it," Circle City for the first time believed, and at once was precipitated one of the wildest stampedes the country had ever seen or ever will see. Every dog was taken, many went without dogs, and even the women and children and weaklings hit the three hundred miles of ice through the long arctic night for the biggest thing in the world. It is related that twenty people, mostly cripples and unable to travel, were left in Circle City when the smoke of the last sled disappeared up the Yukon.

Since that time gold has been discovered in all manner of places, under the grass-roots of the hillside benches, in the bottom of Monte Cristo Island, and in the sands of the sea at Nome. And now the gold hunter who knows his business shuns the "favorable looking" spots, confident in his hard-won knowledge that he will find the most gold in the least likely place. This is sometimes adduced to support the theory that the gold hunters, rather than the explorers, are the men who will ultimately win the Pole. Who knows? It is in their blood, and they are capable of it.

About Jack London

Jack London crammed into his forty years all the color and excitement that he put into his stories. He joined the gold rush to Alaska; he went to sea on a sealing schooner; he bummed his way around the country; and he traveled all over the world. Sheer love of life is in all his work, a life that was filled with action and stirring adventure.

London's life of excitement started, interestingly enough, as a result of his own reading.

He was born in San Francisco and spent his childhood in poverty. By the time he was ten, he had found his way to the public library—where he escaped the harshness of his early years by reading tales of adventure, exploration, and travel. This early reading did much to guide his own writing later.

Even as a boy he took on all kinds of odd jobs to keep alive. At sixteen he was a longshoreman on the water front. He managed to get through high school, but dropped out of the University of California in his freshman year to help support his family.

At twenty he joined the gold rush to Alaska, but never reached the Klondike. On his way home, he decided to turn his adventure into money by writing about it. Magazines bought his work and he was on his way. London's greatest book, *The Call of the Wild,* which is Part One of this volume, grew out of his experience in Alaska.

Both as writer and as adventurer, London continued to read at every opportunity. His favorite authors were Rudyard Kipling and Robert Louis Stevenson. The Macmillan Company and S.S. McClure, editor of *McClure's Magazine,* gave him monthly allowances so he could write without financial worries. London made a million dollars from his books and spent it all.

London died when he was forty and is buried near his California home.